HUMMINGBIRD
GOD

HUMMINGBIRD
GOD

Ron Braithwaite

AUGUSTA, GEORGIA

Hummingbird God
By Ron Braithwaite
A Harbor House Book/2008

Copyright 2008 by Ron Braithwaite

For information address:
HARBOR HOUSE
111 TENTH STREET
AUGUSTA, GA 30901

Jacket and book design by Nathan Elliott
ISBN: 978-1-891799-24-2

Library of Congress Cataloging-in-Publication Data is available on the Library of Congress Web site.

Printed in the United States of America
10 9 8 7 6 5 4 3 2 1

DEDICATION

Erich, Mark, Larry and Ron:
From the thornbush of Africa to the Siberian tundra...

Warrior, girded and plumed
Maiden, plaited and groomed
Flower, budded and bloomed
Doomed

Merchant laden with wealth
Athlete glowing with health
Jaguar, power and stealth
Doomed

City, temples and towers
Empire, terrible power
Victims tremble and cower
Doomed

In ten thousand years, know
We will be ten thousand years ago
And the grass will continue to grow
And the wind...the icy wind...will blow

—Nezahualcoyotl

Enrique Mendoza, Jesuit Prelate and Inquisitor of Alcalá, trembled in front of the seated Obispo Rodrigo de la Peña, Inquisitor-General of the *Suprema*, one of the most powerful men in España, and one of the most dangerous men in the world.

"You may take your seat."

Without taking his eyes off his enemy, Mendoza seated himself cautiously.

The Bishop almost smiled. "I must say, Padre, that I've seen you in better fettle. Those bruises and scrapes don't become you at all and your clothing is disgraceful. Not only are you filthy but your garb is that of a common peasant." The ancient man smoothed his robes "Why are you not clad in the vestments of your order? Disgraceful."

Mendoza said nothing. His otherwise handsome face was a mass of swollen bruises. The tissues around his eyes were in the process of turning purple. There was a large abrasion on his left cheekbone and lesser scrapes on his throat and the backs of his hands. He was wearing filthy green pantalones and a torn brown tunic. One foot was shod in a torn and dangling leather sandal and the other foot was bare and bleeding.

The old man went on, "I've taken the liberty of bringing your notes from your apartment. I would like to hear your summary of our progress, thus far."

Mendoza had indeed planned to give a summary of events but not to this sadistic Jew. If his escape had succeeded as planned, he would have delivered his report directly to the Vatican. There, he would seek an audience with the Holy Father—*Papa Gregoria*—and tell him of all of the criminal dealings of the old Bishop.

He would have reported that, not only was the Inquisitor-General *not* an ordained Priest of the Dominican Order, but he had purchased his Bishopric from corrupt Church and State officials. He would go on to inform the Holy Father that de la Peña was an admitted heretic and atheist who systematically persecuted the loyal officers of the

Holy Office. He especially welcomed the moment when he would tell the Pope how de la Peña had falsely imprisoned him and had forced him to alter his own Catholic account of the Divine Conquest of Nueva España.

What Padre Mendoza couldn't know, of course, was that both the Holy Father, Gregory XIII, and the King of Spain, Phillip II, were not only aware of the background and motives of their Inquisitor-General, they had deliberately elevated him to his post and quietly approved of his actions—his interests, if not identical to theirs, complemented their own. De la Peña served as a useful counterweight to *La Inquisición Sagrada*, a secret and subversive organization that, although politically useful, had to be held in check for the good of Mother Church and the safety of the State. These realities, of course, the Jesuit Priest couldn't know—for weeks he had plotted and dreamed of the day he would meet the Pope and reveal the truth.

Now, however, Mendoza's plans for revenge had turned to dust. Months of careful planning and bribery had gone to nothing and, as he was forced to admit to himself, the ancient Bishop had not lied. The guards were loyal to de la Peña, *not* Mother Church or the Holy Office. To be certain, Mendoza had tested the validity of the Bishop's claims. Over the months he had tried to make friends with the six men who alternately guarded him. All of these men greeted his efforts with scowls and threats.

However, all things come to he who waits. Two short fortnights ago everything changed. A seventh and younger man, Ruben Villalobos, was added to the guard detail. He was less than twenty-five years of age, seemed to be intelligent and was infinitely vulnerable. To Mendoza's relief, the man was also cunning and greedy. When no one was listening, Villalobos was perfectly willing to plot with Mendoza.

The young man was attractive and, judging by the young man's friendliness, seduction was a foregone conclusion. On the other hand, intimacy might bring complications...Mendoza was forced to choke down his mounting desire. All efforts must be directed towards freedom. Pleasure could follow.

After their friendship seemed well-established, Mendoza raised the possibility of escape.

"Ruben, have you considered the fact that by serving the Bishop, you are not only risking your soul but your life?"

"What do you mean?"

"The Episcopus is a confirmed heretic and his discovery is but a matter of time. Those who serve him will burn."

Young Villalobos was threatened. "I know nothing of heresy. I'm in the employ of the *Suprema*."

"But you know it now, Ruben, and you are in danger. If you were to help me...*escape*...you'd have nothing to fear."

He replied cautiously, "Not from you, Padre, but the Tribunal would destroy me."

"Not if they didn't know you were involved."

"*Gracias no, Padre*, it isn't worth it."

"Perhaps with the inducement of a little gold."

Ruben shook his head. "Do you take me for a fool, Padre? You don't have any money. *Santo Oficio* has sequestered all that you have. Every day you have even less because your wealth is tapped to pay for your imprisonment and interrogation."

"No," Mendoza whispered, "that's not true. I have property and accounts in other names and I have extensive holdings in Portugal, in France and in Italy."

The young man had an engaging smile. "The Holy Office has been good to you, Padre."

"And it will be good to you, Ruben."

"Not likely. Even if you *are* still wealthy, what good does that do me? You're locked in this dungeon and your wealth is far away."

"There is a way. I can write legal notes transferring money and property into your name."

"How do I know that your notes will be honored?"

"Check with my bankers—I'll give you their names. You will find that the transfers will occur as I say—once, that is, you have effected my release."

Ruben was nervous but interested. He and Mendoza spent hours negotiating the expense of the escape. The young man drove a hard bargain and, before the negotiations were complete, had secured Mendoza's promise to transfer much of his money and property into the names of members of Ruben's family. Mendoza bargained only for the show of it—once free, he would secure his own property and arrange for the arrest and humiliation of the young fool. His groin warmed at the thought of it.

"The plan is this, Padre. Tomorrow night—at 1:00 in the morning—Frederico Encanto will be on duty. I've arranged to lace Encanto's ale with a fast-acting poison. By 1:30 he will be dead or very close to it—your cell won't be locked. Put on these clothes for the journey." Ruben tossed him a bundle of filthy rags. "Go down the corridor to the right. You'll find a stairwell. Go down three flights, which will take you to ground level. The door to the outside will be open. A carriage will be waiting for you outside. The French frontier is a three-day journey."

Mendoza was relieved but fearful. "How many nights on the road?"

"Two in España. I've arranged for safe houses and a carriage driver."

"Can he be trusted, Ruben?"

"He's my cousin and best friend, Padre," Ruben leaned forward. "I'm trusting him with *both* of our lives.

●●●

The first part of the escape went smoothly. As planned, the cell was not locked. Mendoza cracked open the heavy door and peered down the ill-lit corridor. With infinite relief, he saw Encanto's body sprawled awkwardly, a spilled flagon of ale on the floor. Abandoning his comfortable cell, he bade a silent farewell to his cats. He stepped over the Encanto's corpse and, as quietly as possible, he stole along the musty corridor and then down the dripping stairwell.

As expected, there was a great door to the outside and freedom. Mendoza tried to lift the rusty bolt. It wouldn't move and there was a moment of terror. Mendoza applied more force but the bolt wouldn't give. Desperate, he slammed the bolt with the palm of his hand and the handle gave with a heart-stopping grate. He pushed on the door—it wouldn't open. He put his shoulder to it and gave it all of his strength but still it wouldn't budge. Panicked, he couldn't think. Forcing himself to breathe more slowly, he recognized his mistake—the door opened to the *inside*. He jerked on the handle. *Nothing.* He braced his feet on the floor, leaned backward and pulled with every fiber of his power. Nothing! He considered retracing his steps but heard footsteps on the stairwell behind him. He redoubled his efforts on the door and felt something give in his back. It barely registered. He put one foot against the doorjamb and pushed and with all his might.

"I changed my mind, Padre."

Mendoza jerked around to find the grinning Ruben Villalobos accompanied by Alejandro Miraflores and a very lively Frederico Encanto. The beating followed. Using their fists, elbows, knees and feet, the guards beat Padre Mendoza to a state of semi-consciousness. They revived him with water and beat him again. They dragged him to the room where he always met with the Bishop. The Inquisitor-General was calmly waiting with a sheath of papers in his hands.

●●●

"These are the financial and property notes that you wrote to my man, Ruben—we have checked them out and they are good. The *Suprema* has seen fit to add these monies and properties to those already sequestered. Also, we have arrested your bankers and put them to the test. They have revealed other unreported wealth. We have seized all that belongs to you along with everything that belongs to your bankers and notarios. I must say that the members of the Council are delighted."

Mendoza mumbled through his battered lips, "Excelencia, I can explain..."

"You can?"

"I will admit, Excelencia, that my actions—at first glance—may appear to be disloyal...but I was only trying to uncover traitors in your camp."

The ancient Bishop's eyes were frozen ice. "You are nothing if not nimble, Padre. I admire your spirit but not your judgment."

"Excelencia, you promised that my property would not be..."

"Correct, as usual, Padre. I said it would not be confiscated and your life would be spared if you worked diligently on our mutual project. It seems that you have failed in your part of the bargain."

Mendoza, who had tried to maintain his courage, broke down completely.

The Bishop licked his scarred lips. "As a man of God, I'm sure that your tears are for your unfortunate business partners and not for yourself. Still, my Jesuit friend..." He mouthed the word 'Jesuit' as if it were an obscenity. "I am open to compromise."

"...Compromise?" Mendoza snuffled.

"I can no longer protect your property but, should you renew your efforts, I will guarantee your life."

"Anything...Your Grace."

"Good. Let's not waste time. Let's review your work," The ancient man leaned forward and placed a pile of papers on the table. "I have recovered your papers from your apartment."

Mendoza tried to pull himself together as he clumsily thumbed through his notes. "I have extensive notes on your early life and your experiences in the Italian Wars."

The old Bishop was impatient. "All of it."

"Do you wish to hear a detailed narration or my summary?"

"Summary."

"As you will, Excelencia. I'll start at the beginning. Although your parents were aristocrats, they were condemned by the *La Inquisición* for being Jews."

The old Bishop stopped him with an upraised hand and stared at him for long moments. "Your wording—especially considering that your life is hanging by a thread—is most unfortunate. My parents were *not* Jews. They were loyal Christians with the misfortune of having Jewish ancestors and the misfortune of having accumulated a little property. They were condemned because of the greed of *Santo Oficio*."

"A technicality, Your Grace."

"Incineration is no technicality, Padre."

Mendoza quickly read on, "You were orphaned but survived as a farm laborer. You decided to become a soldier in Italy..."

"You are skipping a few things, Padre."

"I'm trying to summarize."

"A detailed summary."

Mendoza scanned through his notes. "Your injury by the leopard...?"

"Correct, Padre."

"But it's of no relevance to the conquest..."

"It's relevant to *me*—besides—I want to see if you've included *everything.*"

Mendoza, still confused by his reversal of fortunes, looked up from his notes and froze. Across the table from him sat *El Diablo*—Satan, Lucifer, Beelzebub, the Anti-Christ—buried in the pristine white robes of a Dominican Bishop. His lifeless face was death itself—skeletal, ancient, timeless—with eyes of frozen ice. Three linear scars ran from his right chin and disappeared into his colorless hair. One of the scars ran across his right eye but the eye was intact...*or was it?*

"Proceed, Padre. You are wasting my precious time."

Mendoza looked down at his notes. "To make money, you snared animals for their pelts. Once, however, you had the misfortune to snare a leopard, an animal unknown to Castilla."

"Perhaps it wasn't a leopard, Padre."

"What do you mean?"

"*Nada.* Go on."

"The beast—whatever it was—escaped from the snare but you managed to strangle it."

"Correct, Padre, but it was a near thing." The old man's high-pitched laugh was infernal. "By ripping my face the cat not only spoiled my good looks but also ruined my sweet nature."

"I've noticed, Obispo."

"But—in those far-off days—my hair was dark—and my scars gave me a distinctive appearance. Where the claws raked my chin and scalp the hair grew out pale, producing white slashes from my chin to the back of my scalp."

"Yes, yes, yes, Obispo, I have it here...then you decided to go for a soldier in Italy..."

"You are leaving things out, Padre. Tell me about Señor Tamayo."

Mendoza leafed back through his notes. "Tamayo—a Moor and false convert to Catholicism—befriended you because he sensed that your Jewishness trumped your Christianity."

"I have no idea what he *sensed* but it is correct that he took me under his wing."

"...And you became a convert to Moorish Paganism."

"Padre, you are deliberately testing my patience. You know full well that I am a convert to *nothing.*"

"But you *did* learn their gutter language and you *did* study their filthy texts?"

"I have a way with languages—Arabic is a complex and expressive tongue and their religious texts are powerful with dire promises to unbelievers like you."

"Tamayo taught you to kill."

"No, Padre. He taught me the use of the Moorish bow and he encouraged me to hunt the beasts of the field, nothing more."

"Then, Excellency, you decided to join our mercenary fighters in Italy but, before leaving Castile, your patrón—Don Pedro Ortega—gave you armor and a remarkable sword."

"Indeed, Padre, a weapon of most curious workmanship—a weapon, which by tradition was forged by the gods and tempered with blood. For this reason, I named the sword *Bebidor*—Blood Drinker—*Bebidor de Sangre*."

"*Si, Excelencia, un espada magica.*"

"No, Padre. *No magico pero una espada mui superior.*"

"I'll note that, Your Grace." Mendoza scribbled rapidly. "'*Simply a well made weapon.*' Then, armed and armored, you walked to the coast and enlisted. You sailed to Italy where, for the next several years, you were a common soldier with our Spanish heroes fighting primarily against the French. You took a mistress, a whore following the army."

"Angela was no whore, Padre. She was simply an unfortunate girl caught up in terrible circumstances."

Mendoza although battered was not out. "Then why, Excelencia, did you abruptly abandon the woman after impregnating her?"

"A very good question, Padre, and one I have asked myself a thousand—a hundred thousand—times. Angela was a thoroughly good woman but *my* actions were dishonorable and wrong—*indecent*—even evil. Does that answer your question?"

"Ah then, Your Grace, does your personal...*evil*...explain why—after your abandonment of the girl—you sailed back to España and butchered multiple innocent people?"

"The cabrónes were *guilty*, Padre—guilty of participating with the Holy Office in the slaughter of my family. If I had my life to live over, I would do it again except the next time...I would kill them more *slowly*."

"Let me get that down, Excelencia... '*More slowly*.'"

"Please do, Padre."

"To escape the wrath of the law you sailed to the Indies where, in

1519 you enlisted in Santiago de Cuba, under Hernán Cortés. Along with 500 men on thirteen ships you sailed to Cozumel and then to Tabasco, where you fought a great battle against the Maya at a place called Cintla. In Tabasco you forced the indígenos to accept Christianity and the suzerainty of the Crown. After this, you sailed to the coast of Nueva España and made contact with the Mexica and their Totonac subjects. Cortés accepted huge gifts of gold and other precious things from the Mexican governor."

"You've missed something important, Padre."

"I'm trying to summarize things."

"A little more detail."

"The Mexican woman?"

"Yes—*Malinali, Malinitzin, Malinche*—Doña Marina."

Mendoza looked down at his notes, "She was a Mexican slave of the Tabascans given to the army as part of the loot from the Battle of Cintla."

"Her importance, Padre?"

"She knew both the Maya and Mexican tongues and—already having a Castellano who could speak Mayan—it became possible to translate from Castilian to Mexican."

"Correct, Padre, and Cortés—recognizing her value—secured her loyalty by making her his mistress. Without the extremely fortuitous acquisition of this young woman the conquest of Mexico would have been *impossible*."

"A gift from God, Obispo."

"A gift from Satan, Padre. Go on."

Mendoza tried to ignore the old man's sacrilege but it was difficult. He gritted his teeth, leafed through his notes and read on.

"Cortés established the pueblo of La Villa Rica de la Vera Cruz and broke his ties with his sponsor in Cuba, the Governor Diego de Velásquez. Then, because many of the men where fearful and wished to return home, Cortés burned his ships."

"You are mistaken, Padre. Cortés did not burn the ships. He demolished them and removed their useful parts."

"Sorry, Excelencia, a clerical error. 'Then Cortés took all of the treasure collected and, using one of his remaining ships, had it returned to España, where much of it was given to the King.'"

"Good. At the same time a sizeable portion of the treasure—as we suspected at the time and confirmed after the conquest—was placed in the hands of Martín Cortés, Hernán's father. Go on."

Mendoza squinted at his notes before continuing, "Leaving a garrison, in Villa Rica, and against the expressed wishes of the Mexicans, Cortés marches inland with three hundred and fifty men. The Tlaxcalteca make war against Cortés. These Indios, after a series of battles, are defeated and submit to Spanish authority. They enlist in Cortés' efforts to defeat the Mexica."

"Padre, to state that we defeated the Tlaxcalteca is an overstatement. More correct, is that we Castellanos staved off our own defeat. These people had a change of heart and enlisted in our cause—most enthusiastically, I might add. Without these allies, we could have never accomplished the destruction of *Anahuac*."

Mendoza looked up from his notes. "Isn't it true that you struck up this relationship with an adventuress on the expedition—one Doña Francesa de la Barca—an aristocrat in name but, in fact, just another soldiers' whore?"

"You seem to be fixated on harlotry, Padre. Why is that?"

"Your Grace, I have no particular interest in female sin. I've just recorded your tale as you told it."

"Then, if you know what's good for you, my good Padre, you had better be more accurate. Francesca, although an adventuress, was also an aristocrat in both fact and deed. At the time we are speaking of, I was not even particularly close to her."

"But you will admit, Obispo, that you pleasured yourself with a slave girl given to you by the Indios of *Tlaxcala*?"

"Doña Amelia? She was no slave but a highborn woman scheduled to be the victim to one of their filthy gods. I saved her life."

"But you also..."

"Yes, Padre, I '*also*'... I am human."

"From the way you treat *me*, Your Excellency, your humanity is suspect."

The old man shook his head in disbelief. "Let's say then, Padre, that I am just human enough to appreciate grace and beauty. Doña Amelia's beauty was that of a delicate spring blossom. Francesca...glorious Francesca...was *more* beautiful than Helen, the most beautiful woman who ever was."

"Yes, yes, I have it all here, Your Grace. From *Tlaxcala*, you marched to *Cholula* and, although the Cholulans admitted the Castilians peacefully, Cortés suspected a plot. Cortés turned the tables and called all of the nobles and chieftains of the city into the central square. The army attacked these *paganos* and slaughtered them all. *Cholula* was sacked."

"A very pretty victory, Padre," the old man commented.

"The army then marched toward Méxíco, through the high pass between the volcanoes of *Popacatapetl* and *Ixtaccihuatl*. We left off with the army in sight of *Lago de Texcoco* and the cities of *Anahuac*, including *Tenochtitlan*, itself."

"You have it, Padre. If you hadn't," the ancient Inquisitor leered at the broken Mendoza, "I would have found myself another assistant."

Mendoza shuddered again.

"Now we will continue."

PART 1

Chapter 1

Below, laid out as in a portrait, was the land we had come to conquer. The Valley was filled with a lake around which were studded numerous pueblos and cities. Smoke swirled into the sky from a thousand fires and hung over the valley in a thin brown haze. Far to the north and west was a great shining city located on an island and connected to the mainland by multiple long bridges.

An order echoed up and down the line. "*Adelante!* You've gawked long enough."

Like an armored beast the army lurched forward. The men's voices, however, were a murmur of fear.

"*Quiet in the ranks!* Don't let our Tlaxcalteca know you're worried."

I was making a strong point and the men knew it. Our allies were essential to victory. If they sensed that we were weak, they would melt away like snow on a warm spring day. The sounds of complaint diminished.

With scouts and skirmishers to the front, we descended down a rocky pass towards the southern shores of the lake. We were greeted by a Mexican delegation including several black-robed priests—*teopixquia* in their primitive language—and a great chieftain— *pilli*—borne in a litter. The man was every inch a great leader. He was tall and erect with a narrow face and delicate features. He was richly adorned in jewelry and had more feathers than a bird. Disdainfully, he scanned our gathered captains before his imperious black eyes locked on the grinning, golden-haired Pedro de Alvarado.

"Oh great *Tonatiuh*—Child of the Sun—I am the Moctecuzoma whom you have traveled far to meet. I bring gifts and I welcome you."

Slaves placed rich gifts before Alvarado. There were sheathes of green feathers, beautiful golden necklaces and streamers of gold that fluttered in the wind. Pedro was delighted and roared with laughter. He picked up one of these streamers and played with it as if he were a child.

Cortés, realizing that the man had mistaken Alvarado for himself, smiled patronizingly. "I—the Ambassador of Emperor Carlos I—thank you for your gifts."

The bejeweled man was suddenly uncertain of himself. "I honor your Emperor and will give him an annual tribute of gold, silver and sacred emerald and jade—*chalchihuitl*. You are denied entrance to my country, however. My chieftains are angry and I cannot guarantee your safety."

"Doña Marina, stop your translation." Cortés referred to his Captains directly, "What do you think of our glittering Moctecuzoma, Cristóbal?"

Cristóbal de Olid replied, "He certainly knows how to dress."

Cortés waved for me to come up and join his bemused Captains. "What do you think of our *Emperador*, Señor de la Peña?"

I was surprised that he would ask my opinion. I looked the nobleman up and down before answering, "The great Lord Moctecuzoma here is an imposter—and a pathetic imposter at that. I can hardly believe how transparent these *ignorantes* are. An emperor, even a cowardly one, would never abase himself to meet us here miles from *Tenochtitlan*. Besides, we have been told that the Emperor is a man of fifty. This fool is barely thirty. I almost feel sorry for the real Prince Moctecuzoma. He must be so confused that he doesn't know up from down.

Burgos, Castilla-León

Mendoza, recovering slightly from the shock of his failed escape and beating, felt it wise to tender a question. "How is it possible that Moctecuzoma thought he could trick you with a man so many years younger than himself?"

The old Bishop, recognizing that the priest was trying to placate him, answered as if the escape had never happened. "He was a very vain man. Later, after studying the features of the real Moctecuzoma, I realized that our imposter, although taller and twenty years younger, was indeed an excellent copy. I believe that he saw this taller and younger man as a near perfect replica of himself."

"It doesn't make sense."

"No? Examine yourself. When you look at your reflection do you not see yourself as you are now or as you used to be?"

Having barely escaped the Bishop's noose, Mendoza knew it was best to play along with the old man. "My *attitude* is youthful and, yes—in my mind's eye—I may even subtract a year or two."

"Certainly, Padre," the Bishop nodded. "Most of us do. It is only natural. In the case of an absolute ruler, foibles become reality. After all, did not the great Augustus commission sculptures of himself as a young God, even when he was in his dotage?"

"Yes," Mendoza agreed, "but there were political considerations, too."

"Politics and vanity, religion and self-deception"—the old man shrugged—"Moctecuzoma, from the point of view of Mexico, was the wrong man, in the wrong place, at the wrong time. From the point of view of Cortés and our noble Carlos, he was precisely the *right* man."

"Cynical, Excelencia."

"Accurate, Padre."

"Very good, Don Rodrigo." Cortés grinned in agreement, "You are as perceptive as I thought you to be."

Cortés turned back to the counterfeit Moctecuzoma. "I do not know who you are and I do not care. You must tell the real Lord Moctecuzoma, however, that we are men who can never be tricked. Return to your Lord, and tell him that we teules can divine his every thought. Tell him that we would prefer to come to *Tenochtitlan* with his blessings, but if we do not have them, we are coming whether he likes it or not."

The false Moctecuzoma wilted like a dying flower. He turned back without another word.

Burgos, Castilla-León

Later, Padre Mendoza, we learned that one of the *teopixquia* accompanying the false Moctecuzoma, was the chief sorcerer of *Tenochtitlan*. He used magic potions and amulets that had no effect against us. As we learned later, on the return trip to their city, the party beheld a strange apparition. They encountered a man drunken on octli, which is the same brew we now call pulque. This borracho confronted the sorcerer who made ominous signs and gestures and then, in a strange hollow voice, predicted the end of the world. Before the eyes of the entire party, the man disappeared into thin air. It was then that the priest realized that the man had been none other than *Tezcatlipoca*, the God of Hell.

"Do you believe that there is any truth to this story, Excelencia?"

"*Homines quod volunt*," the old man quoted, "The Mexican Emperor was tied in the knot of his own superstition. A mystic himself, he refused to listen to more practical chieftains who recommended resistance to our insignificant force. Bewildered, he relied on his priests to guide him. The priests themselves relied on the inspiration of octli and visions produced by plants that grew in the marsh. The information that these teopixquia gave was therefore inconstant and contradictory. No doubt, some did predict disaster based on their strange dreams, but then priests from Delphi in ancient Greece to Revelations in our Testaments have always predicted disaster. Moctecuzoma, not knowing what else to do, drew his own blood and sacrificed dozens of men and women—including, by the way, the failed impersonater—and prayed that his gods would protect him," The Bishop turned the palms of his hands upward. "Hopeless."

Mendoza considered the old man's words. "Perhaps the dreams of the priests were *real* but were placed in their minds by God in order to ease the Conquest. After all the prediction *did* come true."

"Yes but, if our expedition had failed, there would have been other reports that our doom had also been prophesied. Predictions go both ways. One should never base his actions on a heavenly prediction, but only on as many facts as can be accumulated."

We continued our descent, picking our way through dense forests of pine and oak. Most of these forests are long gone now, Padre. After the Conquest of Mexico, Cortés and others, lonesome for the plains of Extremadura, saw to it that most of the trees were cut down. Our journey led us through small hillside towns.

A crowd of bejeweled dignitaries met us in the foothills.

"Our Lord Moctecuzoma loves you, Malinche, but he begs you—for your own good—to return to the coast. There is no food in our City and our Prince fears that you will all starve."

Cortés scowled at the uneasy pipiltin. "Do you not know, My Lords, that the men of Castile eat only for pleasure? We do not require food for life. Tell your prince that we sorrow that his people are in such a pitiful state and will come their aid just as quickly as possible."

●●●

We came to the garden city of *Chalco*, on the edge of the lake. Most of the buildings and temples were ancient and obscured by avenues of trees and flowers. The people there, who were vassals of the Mexica, greeted us with wonder and joy. Despite the welcome, we kept moving forward and spent the next night in the unimpressive and odiferous pueblo of *Ayotzingo*. We were again preparing to push forward when we were greeted by another Mexican delegation, including four great chiefs. An even greater pilli soon arrived borne on a magnificent litter.

His litter was richly worked in green feathers with much silver decoration and precious stones. The stones were set in tree designs, worked in filigrees of the finest gold. The litter was borne by the chieftains of four subject cities—sickly looking slaves whisked dust from its path. Chieftains helped the great lord from his litter as priests wafted copal smoke over him while still other chieftains dusted him with feathered whisks. The nobleman greeted Cortés with deep bows. He had now way of knowing, of course, that the Caudillo was fated to torture and murder him.

"I am Cacama, the nephew of Moctecuzoma and ruler of the city of *Texcoco*." Cacama, who appeared to be genuine, knew exactly who our leader was. "Malinche, we have come to place ourselves at your service and to give everything needed for you and for your companions, and to arrange for you to settle in your home, which is our City. This, the great Moctecuzoma, our Lord, has decreed. He begs your pardon for not coming himself. This is because of ill-health not because of ill-will."

Cacama, unlike the imposter, was not impressive. He was a small brown man of middle years with a peasant's face. Despite this, he radiated power.

Cortés recognized the man's importance and—before even speaking—he produced three pearls—*margaritas*, as we called them then—from the Darien Sea.

"A Prince as great as Moctecuzoma does not need to apologize." He said, "I offer these precious gems in his honor."

To the rest of the chieftains he gave the usual blue glass.

"The Great Moctecuzoma loves you teoteoh,"—Cacama continued as if reading from a script—"and prays that you and your warriors will reside in peace and happiness at his house in sacred *Tenochtitlan*. He prays that all the gods will smile on you and shower you and Great Carlos with their bounty."

Cortés, without changing expression, elbowed me in the ribs. "Divine permission to loot their heathen treasury, how much more could we ask for?"

Cacama, whose face was immobile, clearly expected a reply. Cortés didn't disappoint him. He pointed to the Sky, the Lake and the Land as if they already belonged to him. "Tell your Lord Moctecuzoma that we will soon—*very soon*—visit him in his house."

●●●

We set out again, accompanied by throngs of curious Indios who crowded around and in front of us. They were so numerous that, at times, that the army had to force a passage through them.

"A *la Chingada!* What are we doing?" Hector Herrera was marching at my side. "We're drowning in a sea of our enemies."

I was equally uneasy. "Most are women and children and all of them seem friendly enough."

"They're curious, Rodrigo, not friendly. If things should change they will be decidedly *unfriendly*. What does our brilliant Caudillo think he's doing? He might as well march us up to one of their mosques and let their priests take care of all of us once and for all. It would save everybody a lot of trouble."

I was sweating but tried to sound optimistic. "He's gotten us in a little deep but he has a plan."

"*Locura, estupidez...*" Herrera mumbled to himself.

I looked around, trying to appear confident. Throngs of amazed Mexicans jostled our troops and some of them even picked at our clothing and armor as we marched by, hoping for some kind of a souvenir. I shouted at our women, "Francesca, Amelia, stay close! Stay here in the middle of the men!"

Francesca had the terrified Amelia by the hand. Without questioning, they quickly moved to the center of the troop.

I turned to Herrera. "The Caudillo thinks that if he can get into their City he can intimidate Moctecuzoma and achieve a bloodless victory," I licked my lips. "I hope he hasn't miscalculated but...by all of the Saints in Heaven, we can't go back now."

Herrera clinched his jaw and continued to march on, his fingers white around the pommel of his sword.

●●●

We came to the shores of the lake and to the great southern causeway that the Mexicans called *Cuitlahuac*. This great road was well made, a lance-length in width and a lance-length above the turbid waters below. Cortés ordered a halt to the army and eyed the causeway. It butted against land far to the northwest.

Cortés had a smile on his face but his voice was taut, "Perhaps we should stick to the mainland."

He hadn't asked my opinion but I gave it anyway. "The Mexica will see that as weakness—retreat, Jefe, would now seem to be out of the question."

He nodded and seemed to speak to himself, "I have no choice." He turned to me. "Your people are in the van and must set the pace. As long as we are on the causeway we are at risk. I want you to set a brisk pace until we are back on the mainland."

"Double-time, Caudillo?"

"No, but,"—he looked around apprehensively—"don't waste time."

"*Adelante, Compadres!*" Cortés shouted towards our strung out army and then stepped out on the causeway.

We marched rapidly along the causeway to the peninsula of *Culhua-can* ahead. Narrow Indio boats, some carrying many noisy passengers, crowded against the causeway. Sometimes an excited Indio would leap onto the stones, clamor up to the roadway and attempt to touch a passing soldier or, more often—stand in open-mouthed awe—immobile as a statue. Some of the boat passengers carried fishing spears but no one showed the least sign of aggression. Still, our situation was perilous and we pushed forward.

The vista was enough to take one's breath away. Both near and in the distance there were gleaming white cities lining the shores of the lake. We were astounded and terrified in equal measure. Benumbed soldiers asked if the whole thing were not all but a dream.

Francesca de la Barca left Amelia in the middle of the troop and found me marching in front of my company—she was completely caught up in the drama of our undertaking. "Isn't it exciting, Rodrigo? Who could have imagined it? Who would have thought that mere Indios could have achieved such things?"

I remembered burning the hovels of naked savages in Cuba. "We were told but, without seeing it myself, I would have never believed."

Francesca wasn't listening. "Look at that great castle over there and, on the other side, see the templo. That pyramid, yonder, looks like the Tower of Babel and look, over there, that one looks Egyptian."

I knew nothing of Babylonian or Egyptian architecture. "It does, indeed, Señora."

"Francesca." She corrected me.

"It's all wonderful, Francesca, but such wonders require organization and manpower. I just hope that the Caudillo has calculated this correctly because we are mice nibbling the cheese."

A worried Juan de Alva had marched to our side and was listening to our conversation. "I wonder if seeing these things," he gestured toward the far-off *Tenochtitlan*. "Is worth the price of our lives?"

●●●

That afternoon we arrived at the small city of *Iztapalapa*. The Lord of *Culuacan*—a dissipated appearing man dressed in robes more appropriate to a woman—came out to greet us and presented Cortés with treasure worth two thousand pesos. He saw that we were quartered comfortably stone buildings—palaces beyond description. They were as spacious and well-built as any cathedral in Christendom and constructed of magnificent stone and the wood of sweet-smelling trees. There were great rooms and courts, the walls of which were finished with flawless lime and decorated with mosaics and colorful paintings. The floors of the courts were of tile—polished marble and fired red brick—and were divided by awnings of fine cotton.

There were orchards and gardens covered by trees and the paths through these gardens were choked with roses and other flowers. There were ponds filled with water lilies and, most remarkably, channels to the ponds had been cut in from the Lake so that it was possible for large canoes to enter the ponds without their occupants ever disembarking.

The trees, flowers and fruit attracted noisy flocks of colorful birds. Boys, and even grown men, stalked the birds through the foliage. They killed them with their blowpipes with which they were great experts. They used pellets of hardened clay or rounded stone and could blow them with enough force and accuracy to kill a bird as large as a duck. The more I saw of the many gardens both here and later in their Capital, the more I came to realize that one of their major purposes was to provide sport for the city-dwellers. For, you see, the urge to hunt is universal and powerful.

Burgos, Castilla-León

"I've never heard this before, Your Grace. The beautiful gardens of

the Mexica were created only to provide their men with target practice?"

"Women, too, Padre. Many were excellent shots."

"But still, Excelencia, these gardens were but artificial forests to provide the Mexicans with meat?"

"Not entirely. The Indios love color and beauty but they also love
the hunt. All of these things made a seamless whole. To the Mexica
there is no contradiction."

"And you actually believe that there is a universal urge to hunt?
Once again you seem to see only the darkness in the human soul."

"Darkness? Hardly. Men enjoy the chase almost as much as does a
cat or a hawk. I have traveled the world and nowhere is such an urge
lacking. Here in España as well as in the rest of Europe, the Great
Lords and Prelates reserve this right for themselves. The result is the
common man—whose desire is every bit as great as that of a noble—
will, at the risk of his life, sneak onto the great estates in order to snare
a hare or a partridge."

"Merely to feed his family."

"Ridiculous. He does it because he must. It is much like a man's
desire for a woman. It can be *stifled* but it will, in some way, be expressed." The old man pointed a bony finger at Mendoza. "Take yourself, for example."

Mendoza stiffened at the insult but the Bishop continued as if he
didn't notice, "The Mexica recognized that the stifling of normal impulses was dangerous and, in order to avoid frustration and revolt,
they permitted the common Indio their simple pleasures."

"I hope, Your Grace, that you are not implying that priestly celibacy
is anything other than Holy?"

The old Bishop fixed Mendoza with his unblinking eyes. "I imply
nothing but I will tell you what I know and what I think—the Priesthood has an excessive number of abnormal men. I think that removing young men from the normal company of women invites perver-
sion."

Mendoza sneered, "Has it occurred to you, Excelencia, that there
are forms of love more pure than that between a man and woman?"

The old man fixed Mendoza with his blue stare. "I think we were
talking about the Mexica. They, at least, recognized that the stifling

of normal impulses was dangerous and, in order to avoid frustration and possible revolt, they permitted their citizens to hunt small birds in their gardens. It's really very simple."

"By an extension of your logic, Excelencia, the structure of our Spanish society—*Ordained by God*—is threatened by the frustrations of its peasantry."

Amazingly—the old man thought—the captive was trying to trap his captor. The ancient Bishop leaned forward, baring his yellowed teeth. "Give that unto Caesar that which is Caesar's."

Mendoza, not understanding the Bishop's meaning, continued, "Under what circumstances do *you* believe that the ignorant peasantry might threaten their King?"

The old man leaned back, licked his dry lips and quoted an ancient maxim, "*Donde no hay harina, todo es mohina.*"

"No wheat no peace?" questioned the younger priest. "What is *that* supposed to mean?"

"It means, Padre, that your head is attached to your body by a thin shred of skin."

The next morning we set out again and started out along the main causeway. We now left the peninsula of *Culhuacan* and marched on the causeway to *Tenochtitlan*. We arranged ourselves as if on parade. We must have presented almost as much of a spectacle to the Mexica as they presented to us. We were all clanking armor and clopping hooves with swords and spear-points shining in the sun. Our fighting-dogs ranged out in front with Alvarado, Olid, Sandoval and Velázquez de León riding directly behind them. Then came our standard-bearer, our álfarez, Cristóbal del Corral, twirling his standard and throwing it high in the air. Then, on foot, came Diego de Ordaz, followed by four others and myself. For effect, we marched with drawn swords.

Then came the rest of the horsemen followed by crossbowmen with gleaming helmets surmounted by multi-colored plumes. Finally there were the mosqueteros and Hernán Cortés, followed by our Indio allies, colorful in their red and white tunics. They were painted for war and pounded drums and blew on their pipes and whistles. Their war cries became more and more triumphant as we approached the City. Their excitement was almost beyond containment.

Cortés ordered me to control our unruly allies. "I want you to take several of our men and watch these Tlaxcalteca—I don't want them getting out of hand. If any one of them shows signs of going berserk, kill him immediately. Now is *not* the time for trouble."

I obeyed the order without protest. The Caudillo was right. If our paganos got out of control, we were as good as dead. We kept our swords at the ready as the disorderly Tlaxcalteca marched past. These Indios, seeing the looks on our faces, understood our meaning and calmed down. One painted savage, however, had worked himself into a mindless rage. He seized a passing woman and dropped her with a blow from his war club.

My scream stilled the shouts of the Tlaxcalteca. I forced my way through the excited mob and seized the guilty cabrón by his long hair, lifted him bodily and threw him from the causeway into the water. To enforce the lesson, I caused his fellow warriors to spear him as he floundered in the water below. Subdued, our Indios trudged on, dragging our cannons.

The causeway doubled in width, which gave us plenty of marching room. Unfortunately, however, the causeway could be easily breached. I saw that the earthen causeway was periodically interrupted and connected by wooden bridges—this could only be for defense. If the bridges were removed or burned, we'd be trapped. Once again, I pondered the wisdom of Hernán Cortés. He had destroyed our ships and now, we were fulfilling his dream by volunteering for our own destruction. Death or Victory? I suspect for him and, now for the rest of us, there was never a choice.

Chapter 2

Awestruck Indios, coming and going from *Tenochtitlan*, passed on either side of our army. The lake was crowded with unarmed spectators in their canoes. Some of the canoes were huge, holding as many as sixty men. How easy it would be, I thought, for the Mexica to load these canoes with fighting men?

Still, live or die, I was witness to things that few Europeans have seen. Their heathen capital stood before us in all its heathen glory. There were castellated fortresses, royal palaces and sacred shrines. Great mosques surmounted by multi-colored temples, gleamed everywhere. I had seen Napoles, which was almost as big but not nearly so grand. Francesca, who had traveled to Turkish Constantinople, said it was both large and beautiful but not nearly so much as this Mexican capital. I wondered if the Caudillo would have dared to attack either Napoles or Constantinople with fewer than 400 men? I wouldn't put it past him.

The causeway cleared of common people as chieftains arrived. Some were clad in brilliantly embroidered linens and others in the spotted skins of tigres mexicanos, the heads of which fit them like caps. Other chieftains wore cotton garments that looked like the skeletons of men—their heads fitting in the artificial skulls and their faces showing from the open mouths. Still others were dressed in similar garb resembling various animals and monsters. Some wore the skins of wolves and deer. Many wore green feathers on their heads. Still others had—attached to their backs—devices that towered well over their heads. These devices were made of fur and feathers and—as I came to find out—each style of device was awarded to those chieftains who had taken a certain number of enemy captives. To a very real extent, a chieftain's device revealed his rank and his rank was determined by the number of captives he had given to the gods. The finery and rank of these pipiltin increased as we neared the city. It was clear that we were now to be honored with the great Moctecuzoma, himself.

First came slaves—better nourished than those who served Cacama—who swept the ground and laid cotton cloaks on the ground. Then followed another great chief who bore a stick carved in the form of a misshapen demon. Then Moctecuzoma—for it was truly the Emperor—approached in a magnificent litter covered by a canopy and fringe of the shiny green feathers. The litter itself was borne by great nobles and decorated with gold work, silver, pearls and blue and green chilchihuitl. Moctecuzoma was beautifully clad in a tunic decorated in tiny iridescent feathers and precious gems. His head was covered with a glory of long green feathers from the sacred quetzal bird and he wore the sandals that the Mexica call *cactli*. The soles were of gold and the tops sparkled red, green and blue with precious stones. Yet for all his fine trappings, the man was still a miserable barbarian. His face, which might have been handsome, was marred by the presence of green chalchihuitl lip, ear and nose plugs.

Moctecuzoma descended from his litter, careful to step on the cloaks. I noticed that all of his pipiltin kept their heads downcast, never looking their Lord in the eye.

"Are you not he? Are you not the great Prince Moctecuzoma?" asked Cortés, looking the great man straight in the eye.

"Yes, I am He."

Our Caudillo took a necklace of glass diamonds from his neck and placed it around the Emperor's neck. Immobile, the Emperor tolerated this indignity but, when Cortés tried to embrace him, two Mexica nobles roughly pulled him back. Sandoval, de la Concha and Olid grabbed the hilts of their swords and—for a brief moment—Cortés seemed to be uncertain as to what he should do. Deciding, he motioned for his captains to sheathe their weapons. He seized the Emperor's limp hand and shook it vigorously.

Moctecuzoma, shaken by the insult, paused but then—considering his own options, slowly—ceremoniously—placed two necklaces around Cortes' neck. The necklaces were made of brilliant red snails—*caracoles*—and beautifully wrought golden shrimp—*camerones*.

"I am glad to see you, Malinche. I invite you to your home." Moctecuzoma looked anything but glad. Even though his face was impassive, he crinkled up his nose as if the odor of this chief of teules offended him.

"I am glad to see you, friend Moctecuzoma," said Cortés. "I have come a great distance to teach you and your people of our God, the great Jesus Christ and his mother, Mary, the Blessed Virgin."

"I have heard of these from my messengers," Moctecuzoma replied, "but, for now, it is best that you rest from your journey."

"*We Teules never need res...*" Cortés argued but Moctecuzoma had had enough for one day. Averting his eyes from the protesting Caudillo, he held out his hands to his nobles who helped back onto his litter. The Emperor's party reversed direction and marched back toward fabled *Tenochtitlan*. Cortés stood flatfooted, starring at the disappearing Emperor.

"What are we supposed to do?" He asked of the equally perplexed Pedro de Alvarado.

Alvarado shrugged. "We can't stand out here on this sun-baked levee all day. Probably,"—he pointed toward the nearby City—"we're supposed to follow your Compadre."

Cortés agreed, "That's why we're here."

Our army followed the Emperor and his entourage all the way into the city. The tops of the houses and templos as well as the canals and the waterways were crowded with spectators. As I have said earlier, the City is built on a lake and, much like Venecia, has more canals than roads. The road that was the causeway became a great highway that, on either side, was intersected by narrow roads and canals. The highway led to a great plaza, which was in the center of the city. Both within and bordering the plaza were numerous templos and teocallis, the greatest of which was nearly as tall as that of *Cholula* and is the one that we Castilians called *El Templo Mayor*. We were led to a sprawling residence close to the west gate of this plaza.

Burgos, Castilla-León

Mendoza was puzzled. "From the description of Cortés himself, I know something of the basic layout of the city still it is difficult to understand. The original city was a small island and it seems likely that, at the time of the conquest, *Tenochtitlan* must have been larger than this. Also, a natural island does not have canals."

The Bishop agreed, "The original Mexica were like the Venetians in more ways than one. Like the early Venetians they were a weak people and were prevented by stronger tribes from settling on the shores of the lake. With little alternative they made their camp on two tiny islands covered by little more than nopal cactus. They fished and they hunted birds but—when their population expanded—they needed much more. Being an observant people they had noticed how the people of *Xochimilco*, to the south, cultivated their crops. These people made great rafts—*tinampas*—of wood and reeds and filled them with earth and rubble. The Mexica, copying them, did the same and, on these rafts they were able to plant their crops and build their huts. The lake was shallow so, as the Mexica continued to dredge the bottom and put the sediment onto their tinampas, they not only weighted their tinampas until they contacted the bottom, but they also deepened the adjacent canals."

The ancient priest interrupted his lecture to readjust himself in his chair and scratch at his crotch. He continued, "As time went on the tinampas extended out into the lake, increasing the size of the island, the size of their new pueblo, and the productivity of the land. They always left room between the tinampas so that canoes could go back and forth, helping with sowing and reaping. Later, as the city became large, the canals also became the arteries of trade. Many canals therefore, penetrated the city and the many bridges joined the canals. Later, the city itself was connected to the mainland by causeways. These were the secrets of Mexican power—they lived on water and never had to fear drought. Also, their situation was superbly defensible. Defensible, that is, if they had used their heads."

"But many of the temples and cues were made of stone and must have been frightfully heavy. It is difficult to believe that the sodden tinampas could have supported their weight."

"True. Their greatest and heaviest structures were built on the island. Any buildings out on the tinampas had to be made of lighter materials or had to be supported by posts driven into the bottom. Still, buildings sinking and cracking was and, to my understanding, is still is a problem."

We were led to our quarters—the great palace of Axayacatl, the father of Moctecuzoma and a previous Emperor. We entered a large court around which were many large rooms, whose walls were painted white, yellow and red and decorated with frightful obscenities. The Mexica had carefully counted our number and they had—for each individual soldier—prepared sleeping mats overhung with canopies of cotton cloth. These canopies were a very good thing because biting flies and mosquitoes were a misery.

The palace itself was a wonderful building with innumerable

rooms, antechambers, splendid halls, mattresses of large cloaks, pillows of leather and tree fiber, feather quilts, beautiful fur blankets and well-made wooden tables and stools. The palace was so large that our horses, mastiffs—and even our Tlaxcaltec allies—were easily quartered. Fodder for the horses was no problem...at least during this early time of good feelings. Transport vessels carried maize and rolled hay from the mainland. The mastiffs were fed with fish captured in the Lake and—as special treats—meat from their heathen mosques.

Moctecuzoma descended from his litter and personally led the Caudillo to the room that had been set-aside for him. It was by far the largest and the most richly furnished of all and—over time—the Caudillo needed the space because he collected a great menagerie of women.

The Great Prince spoke, "Malinche, you and your brothers are in your own house. Rest awhile."

Before Cortés or anyone else could reply, he turned, remounted his litter and, along with his entourage of beplumed noblemen and priests, left for his own palace.

As soon as Moctecuzoma was out of sight, the Caudillo started to laugh. He laughed to the point that he turned red in the face and couldn't catch his breath.

"*We've gone and done it!* What do you say, Compadres?" Cortes' grin was that of a mad man. "Shall we fire off a salute in thanksgiving? It should give the old cabrón something to think about."

I was appalled as were Herrera, Ordaz and several others. "Have you completely lost your mind? *Now* is exactly the wrong time to give Moctecuzoma and his chieftains *anything* extra to think about."

"Rodrigo, you are an old woman. Light them up, muchachos. Let's give them a volley."

The soldiers appeared uncertain but, even so, most obeyed the Caudillo's order.

Arquebuses and cannons were aimed out over the city and went off like the crack of doom. Spectators on the steps of teocallis and the roofs of templos screamed and disappeared as if by magic.

"That should show them." A strange light burned in Cortés' eyes. "Our next shots will be at those shrines on top of that big tower over there."

Now even Gonzalo de Sandoval and Velásquez de León stood forward. "No you won't, Caudillo. You've pushed our luck too far already."

The look of madness subsided. "You're as bad as Rodrigo, Gonzalo. You never learned to have fun. As a baby, you probably never even played with the worm between your legs." He made a great show of giving in. "Well, muchachos, I'm as hungry as a three-legged hog and if we can't do any more celebrating I vote that we get right to our dinners."

Despite the earlier Mexica warnings of starvation, food was there in abundance as were women to prepare and serve it. I would have not wanted to be one of these women—they had to run the gauntlet of our soldiers' groping hands. The women responded with frantic squeals and acrobatic dodges. Half of the food ended up on the floor.

"If you wish to eat," laughed our Caudillo, "leave the damas alone. After we have all had our fill, you gentlemen can have your fill of *them*."

Most of the men laughed at the joke, but Padre Olmedo was not amused. "We have come to this pagan land to spread the truth of Christ, *not* indulge in carnal pleasures."

Alvarado picked up a great slice of meat—ciervo, I think—but it could have come from one of their pagan mosques. "*Ay, Padre, Mira!*" He stuffed the steak into his mouth and—grease running down his beard—spit it out again. "*I* came to this pagan land to indulge in all *carne* pleasures."

"That goes for me, too," said Juan Maldinado as he hacked at a piece of fowl. "With all the *pinches Indios* I've killed, my salvation is guaranteed. A couple of these *brujas* under me will make no difference."

I was too hungry to comment and wolfed down the food. We had the usual guajalote, tortillas and frijoles but now pescado, pato, hongos and tomates were added. We also had things I'd not tasted before. There was the boiled and fried scum from the Lake that—as the Mexica told me later—was composed of the innumerable eggs of tiny water things. The translation is uncertain, though, and it is possible that this scum made up tiny caracoles or even nearly invisible water worms—*lombrices*. It doesn't matter. In any event, once fried in grease—I know not where the grease came from—it was edible. This strange dish was drenched in a salsa just as unusual as was the scum, itself. It was—as I learned later—prepared by mixing chiles with ground maguey beetles and cacao beans. It was all quite delicious and we gorged ourselves.

"How do we know this stuff hasn't been poisoned?" asked Bernal Díaz with a mouthful of fish.

Several of the men spit their food out of their mouths. I had previously considered this possibility and rejected it. "It doesn't matter. Poison or not they can kill us anytime they want. Besides, these paganos prefer *live* people for sacrifice. Eat up, gentlemen, we have nothing to lose."

Despite my reassurance I noticed that many of our soldiers refused to take another bite.

●●●

After dinner Moctecuzoma and his pipiltin rejoined us. I was able to get closer to the man than I had earlier and could better make out his features. He was fifty years or older and he was of he was of medium complexion for a Mexica. He was not tall but he was taller than I am. His hair was cut just over his ears and he had a short and scraggly beard. His face was long and his eyes were serious, even sorrowful. Amazingly, as I was to discover, he bathed daily and he changed his clothing three or four times a day. He never wore the same garment twice, giving them instead to his servants. He had many mistresses, all of whom were the daughters of his most important pipiltin. As we came to observe, he had an impressive sexual appetite, sometimes servicing four or more women—one after another—in a single evening. In his case—an erect cock was the *opposite* of manhood for he was a fool and a coward in equal measure.

Sometimes when he tired of a woman or if he favored a chieftain or a warrior, he gave them one of his women. During our stay in the City, Moctecuzoma, in an effort to ingratiate himself with his captors, gave some of his mistresses to our soldiers. He even gave Cortés several of his many daughters and a few of his nieces.

Burgos, Castilla-León

"Wait a moment, Excelencia, I have caught you in another untruth."

"*Qué?*" The old man was amazed by his victim's impertinence. The bruises from his recent beating were still livid on Mendoza's skin.

"Earlier you told me that your Caudillo would accept no woman of higher rank than Doña Marina."

The Bishop stifled an impulse to murder the younger priest. "That's true but you must always remember something about our Caudillo—he was always looking for an advantage. Clearly he felt that adding the Emperor's daughters to his string of concubines was a political necessity."

"Necessity?"

"Of course. He hoped to control Mexico from the inside out. What better way than to bed the daughters of the Uei Tlatloani, himself."

"It makes sense—but Doña Marina?"

"She knew that her lover was playing for high stakes and she was as devious as Cortés himself. In fact, she *insisted* that he take the women. Once Moctecuzoma was dead, however, these women lost value other than as objects of pleasure. It should be noted that not one of these women survived La Noche Triste—fascinating don't you think?"

Chapter 3

Moctecuzoma was moved to speak to our Captains. "Our Lords, you must be tired; you have experienced fatigue, but now you have arrived at your City." Moctecuzoma hesitated but clearly had more to say. "You teotoh are those sent by your great Emperor Carlos who is undoubtedly the Great God. Two years ago I was *amazed* to hear that strange beings were seen riding on great white houses over the Eastern Sea. I was even more amazed when these same teotoh fought a great battle in Champoton against the barbarians. Last year I had another report of more teotoh floating on four white houses. They landed and spoke with the people of the coast before disappearing in the direction of the morning sun. Now, you teotoh also come from the east, having prevailed in great battles in *Tabasco, Tlaxcala* and *Cholula*. We know from these things that you are the ones who have been prophesied to return and reclaim your kingdom. I—as have all of those kings who have come before me—have been but your stewards. It grieves me to tell you that your governors have long since gone but I will do all in my power to see that your will is done. With your arrival, all things are now fulfilled."

All of us were perplexed, including Cortés. He replied carefully, "Yes, we are the same but, even for us, it has been a very long time and we wish to hear the prophecy again."

Moctecuzoma recited from memory, "We Mexica came from *Aztlan*, far to the north. Our god—the one wearing the same hat that I filled with gold—led our ancestors here. Once we reached the shores of Lake Texcoco, our people—against the advice of our god—refused to go on. Alas, he became angry—as he departed from us, he warned that he would one day return from the east and lead his people again."

Cortés now caught the meaning. "Yes—and now he comes to bring you the word of the Lord, Jesus Christ, and of our Emperor, Carlos I. Enough of this now, for I can see that you, my Prince, are very tired. Later I shall teach you all of the principles of the gospel. Tomorrow we can talk more of these things."

● ● ●

Cortés was always thinking of the future battles, whether it with lance and sword or in a court of law. I can still see him, standing there and rubbing his hands together. "Señores, you have all heard Moctecuzoma. He is superstitious, to be certain, but there can be no question that he admits his subservience to Carlos I. With this admission all things become legally possible."

The Mercedian friar, Olmedo, was unconvinced. "You have heard what you wish to hear, Hernán—the man is clearly confused—to take his confusion as submission to Castile, would be an injustice. Worse than an injustice, it would be a mistake."

Cortés went on as if Padre Olmedo had not spoken: "His superstitions present us with both opportunities and problems. The fact that he has confused us with one or more of his gods is clearly why he has failed to take significant action thus far. It gives us the opportunity to manipulate events to our own advantage. On the other hand, our opportunity is not unlimited. The longer we stay under his roof, the more doubts he will have about our divinity. Once he believes we are fully human, we'll be in danger."

Alonso de Grado was disgusted. "Real danger, Caudillo? Any fool could see, weeks ago, that marching into the center of their Capital was suicidal."

Cortés raised his eyebrows. "Not suicidal, Alonso—smart. It is only from here that we have any chance of achieving our conquest. If any of you have doubts, remember the miracles that we have accomplished already. We humiliated the Tabascans and we have freed the Totonacs. We have defeated the Tlaxcalteca and turned them into allies. We have decimated *Cholula* and we are in the process of bending Moctecuzoma to our will. God, my reluctant conquistadores, marches beside us."

"If that is true, Caudillo," joked Velásquez de León, "why not leave it all to God? I'm comfortable here in his great hacienda. I'm tired of long marches and bad food."

Padre Olmedo didn't appreciate de León's humor. "God will not be mocked, Don Velásquez. He only helps those who have the faith and the strength to carry his banner."

"I agree that we must do something," I said, "but we are limited by our ignorance. All we have seen of this city are some of its buildings, canals and bridges. We need to spy out this place to see exactly what we are up against."

"Thank you, Rodrigo," the Caudillo said, "your thoughts are my own. Given Moctecuzoma's present state of mind, he will eagerly show us *Tenochtitlan* and, in so showing us, we should be able to observe if there is evidence of military preparations against us."

Diego de Ordaz looked doubtful. "We are in a tight place, amigos, and, if things go wrong, we'll have to fight our way out of here. We are not only separated from the mainland by causeways but there are canals and bridges. If we could get up on top of that big mosque, we could get a better look. We need to know how things are laid out and plan for a retreat."

"Retreat?" Cortés said, "I think you are being dramatic but, I agree that we should make reasonable plans. As soon as possible, we shall take a sightseeing tour of our new city. I expect all of you to participate and remember what you see."

●●●

Cannons were mounted on the watchtowers; guards were carefully posted, and no one was permitted to leave the palace under pain of death. There were no alarms, however, and the next morning Cortés, dressed out in his finest clothing, visited Moctecuzoma's palace that was but a short distance away. I accompanied him along with Alvarado, Sandoval, Concha, Velásquez, Ordaz, Grado and several others.

The palace was even more sumptuous than the one that we were quartered in. It was huge with rooms that were large and numerous and walls covered with the skins of animals and colorful paintings. Still others were covered with drapes of beautiful feather-work. The ceilings were of rich wood carved in many designs and the courts had fountains of clear water that fed crystalline pools filled with exotic fish of all kinds.

Slaves scurried to-and-fro, even as richly dressed pipiltin sauntered about the halls. When such a noble was granted audience with Moctecuzoma, he was forced to put off his fine clothes and put on a cloak of *nequen*, which is coarse maguey fiber. The noble was thus clothed as if he were but a slave—he was obliged to approach his monarch barefooted and to prostrate himself on the ground. He could not—under penalty of death—look the mighty Moctecuzoma directly in the face. We Castellanos never imitated this craven behavior.

Moctecuzoma, who was surrounded by his advisors, greeted us warmly enough. Cortés, believing that our safety lay in immediate conversion of Moctecuzoma to Christianity, wasted no time in making his preachment.

"We have come here to spread the good news of our God—Jesus Christ—who is the also the Son of God."

Confusion spread over Moctecuzoma's face. "This god, Jesus, is the son of himself?"

"He is also the Father." Our Caudillo explained.

Most of our Captains were disinterested but, I was hearing things I'd never heard before and *knew* the Caudillo was toying with heresy; I followed word-for-word just in case I could use it later. With great solemnity, Moctecuzoma scratched his head, his beard and then his testicles.

"God, Jesus, is both his own father and son?"

Our Caudillo hesitated, but he was in too deep, now. "He is also one with the Holy Spirit which is the Principle of the Trinity."

"Trinity?" Moctecuzoma tried to pronounce the Castilian word. Evidently this word was not in Doña Marina's vocabulary.

The Caudillo tried to explain, "Trinity—three. Three aspects of the absolute perfection that is God."

Much of the Emperor's life had been spent following the infinite complexities of an intricate religion. To him Christianity was child's play. His eyes ignited with understanding. "Yes, I see it now. God-Father God-Son God-Sacred Spirit."

"Precisely correct, My Prince."

His face clouded again. "But—God-Carlos—makes four?"

The Caudillo, when he wanted to, could be delicate. "Emperor Carlos I is Lord of all the earth but Jesus is God of the firmament—he was sacrificed on a cross to atone for our sins. The Mass and the Holy Sacrament is the way we worship our God. In the sacrament, we taste of the bread and wine, which, by the Grace of God, is transmuted to the flesh and blood of Christ in our bodies. In this way we are cleansed of our sins."

Moctecuzoma nodded in acceptance. "This Jesus is a good and powerful God. We shall worship this Jesus along with *Tlaloc* and *Huitzilopotchli.*"

Cortés frowned in frustration. "Our God is a jealous God and will tolerate no others. These idols that you worship are but Satan in his various guises. If you should fail to destroy these monsters and give up the sacrifice of innocent men and women, you will be condemned to the Fiery Pit of Hell where you must suffer for all of eternity."

Moctezumoma, impassive, considered this possibility. "Malinche, I know that your god is good but so are ours. They save our people from disaster. They bring the rain that waters the land and they protect us from our enemies. We would be foolish to give them up and we will not do so."

"Do you not recognize, Moctecuzoma, that the sacrificing and eating of human beings is evil?"

"Evil? Have you not just told me that God-Jesus, was sacrificed and that you now eat his flesh and drink his blood? I *will* honor Him and sacrifice to Him. Enough of this now, for I have gifts for you."

The Caudillo, who always looked forward to the accumulation of treasure, didn't continue his preachment.

Moctecuzoma proceeded to distribute gifts of gold and silver. Our disinterested Captains became interested, again. Even the common soldiers who accompanied us received at least two collars of gold. Still something was wrong. Moctecuzoma recoiled when Cortés drew near.

"What is his problem, Doña Marina?"

She spoke rapid sounds to the obviously unhappy Prince and he, with hesitation, spoke back to her.

"He says that he does not wish to be impolite, My Lord." The woman translated.

"Tell him that he is a King and can speak openly to us." Cortes said.

Moctecuzoma glanced uneasily in my direction. "He says that some of you have eyes like *búhos*—owls that fly by night."

"Indeed." Cortés replied.

"And he says that you do not have skin, only naked flesh."

"Tell him, My Dear, that we do have sk... *No, don't!* Perhaps it is better that he believes us to be as unusual as possible."

"As you will, My Lord." Doña Marina agreed.

"What else is there, My Lady?"

"He also says that you and your teules have an offensive odor."

Several days were spent in idleness as we wandered through our palace, marveling at the beauty of its gardens and fountains. Cortés, growing increasingly restless and anxious about the layout of the city, sent a message to Moctecuzoma asking permission to visit the Great Mosque as well as other places in the city. Moctecuzoma, the fool, not only agreed that we—all of us—could visit the city but he volunteered to welcome us at the top of the great teocalli. He first proposed, though, that we visit the market place, in the district known as *Tlatelolco*, in the western part of the city.

Burgos, Castilla-León

"Speaking of permission, Episcopus de la Peña, would you mind if I smoke? This is one habit that I *did* acquire from the travelers to the

Indies."

The old man leaned forward on the table. "Where did you get tobacco?"

"I managed to buy some from one of the guards but now I'm out. I was hoping that..."

"It's a filthy habit, Padre."

"Actually not. It's quite therapeutic. It bathes one's air passages with its beneficial fumes. One never need worry about congestion of the pulmones."

"Still, it is bad for the spleen. I'm afraid I cannot give you more tobacco and, I must forewarn you, I will give orders that the guards are not to sell you any."

"But, Excelencia, I'm asking for very little. It gives me something to do as I wile away the hours in my cell."

"Masturbation doesn't entertain you sufficiently?"

"I...uh...never...uh..." Mendoza stammered.

"That's not what the guards report, Padre. They claim you have refined the act to an art." The old man pointed to the fire crackling in the hearth. "Those who engage in self-humiliation will *burn*—in the next world if not in this."

"Then *I* have nothing to worry about."

"You constantly surprise me, Padre. Although caught in the act—many times I might add—you deny the reality of it. Come now, Padre, despite the preachments of the Church, masturbation is but a natural act especially for a man denied access to an orifice."

Mendoza's eyes switched back and forth, looking for an escape. "The guards lie. It is they who..."

"Come now, my friend, even I—back in the days of my heedless youth—have been known to stroke my..."

Mendoza was filled with relief. "Of course, I'm not perfect."

"Do you use your right or your left hand, Padre?"

"With little else to do, I have learned to use both."

The old man's smile was benign. "Is not confession a cleansing act?"

"Indeed, Episcopus, I feel better already."

With the smile still on his lips, the old man banged the table. Mendoza jumped. "*You* are going to *Hell*, Padre."

"But you said *you...*"

"Correct, Padre, but, then again, I'm going to Hell for acts far more significant than the triviality of solitary sex."

Mendoza, realizing that the Bishop was baiting him, changed the subject. "My tobacco?"

"I'm sorry, Padre, I can't help you. My responsibility to you, as a fellow Inquisitor, is to see that you get the best of all possible medical care. Besides, I can't stand the smell of the stinking stuff."

Chapter 4

Most of our men—arrayed as if for battle—set out for a sightseeing visit. Mexican men and women gawked at us. Most of the men wore a loincloth but their primary covering was a cloak known as *tlamatli* that was thrown over their heads. In this way their fronts and backs were covered down to their knees but their arms were free. Many of these garments were richly done and tasseled. The women wore several skirts of different lengths with ornamented borders. Over this they wore loose flowing robes, which reached to the ankles.

There was another category of women—especially interesting to some of our soldiers—for these fallen flowers were professional whores. These women, like putas all over the earth, were identifiable by their appearance and behavior. They reddened their cheeks and lips with the red pigment known as cochineal and arranged their hair into peaks that looked like horns. They were brazen and would gesture to passing men—it was all we officers could do to keep the soldiers together.

As we traveled I was careful to observe the roads and bridges. The greater highways which, I found out a short time later, connected to the causeways and terminated at the central plaza were broad and, except where spanned by bridges, were covered by a kind of cement. Unfortunately, from our military point of view, there were *many* wooden bridges permitting boats to travel from one area to another without hindrance. These bridges made the place superbly defensible.

The smaller roads were even worse. Many would accommodate

scarcely two men abreast and were also broken by bridges. Houses of the common folk, made of wood, reeds and brick, lined these roads. Walls, open to the road by single gates, encompassed these homes. Small rooms were attached to the interior walls and these rooms, in turn fronted a small open patio. In some way, I could see that the layout of the large public plazas was but an enlargement of this simple house plan.

Most of the houses were single-storied and, being flat-roofed, made rooftop defense easy, indeed. Wooden ladders were in place. I wondered if stones and other missiles had already been secreted on the roofs in preparation for our annihilation—and—I considered exploring the rooftops. Seeing armed warriors hovering in the shadows, I reconsidered this option and continued marching.

In all areas there were trees and flower bearing plants, for the Tenochca, despite or perhaps because of their barbarous practices, had a keen eye for beauty. The streets, unlike those of Castilla and Italia, were impeccably clean and, as I was told later, one thousand sweepers were constantly busy cleaning dust and debris. I was also told that there were severe penalties for those foolish enough to litter the city.

Nevertheless, soldiers—as soldiers will—broke ranks to attend to their bodily functions. Most looked for the privacy of a stone fence or garden corner. Others passed water or defecated right in the street. Indios, seeing this, averted their eyes or glared at our men with contempt. One Tenochca man, recognizing our ignorance, pointed out thatched huts along the boulevard. These huts were elevated on stilts an arm's breadth in length although dried grass thatching protected the undersides of these huts from the eyes of passersby. They were, however, surrounded by clouds of moscas, and the odor was fearful.

Suspicious as to the nature of these structures, I climbed the short steps and entered one. The purpose was obvious. There was a wooden seat with a hole of the usual diameter. Next to the seat, on the wooden floor, was a wide-mouthed jar filled with dirty water and in the water was a wooden rod with a filthy amatl sponge tied to its end.

Such structures are common in España and Italia and are, of course, for the purpose of relieving one's self. The purpose of the amatl stick was not so clear but then—scratching my memory—I remembered accounts of ancient Roman public houses. The amatl sponge was to wipe one's ass. Unlike the Romans, however, waste did not drop into water but accumulated on the ground beneath the hole. As I learned later, miserable slaves—fortunate only in that workers in such filth were *never* used for holy sacrifice—removed the dung that collected under them each day. In *Tenochtitlan*, as well as other cities of the Empire, human excrement was used for the tanning of hides and to fertilize the tinampa gardens. None of this precious commodity was allowed to go to waste.

●●●

"*Whew!*" José Maldinado was making the rounds. "This smells as bad as back home in Badajoz."

"But, you must admit, José, that *Tenochtitlan* is more interesting." Francesca said. Disobeying orders that women were to stay in the palace, she had clad herself in a man's armor and was marching happily beside us. "Did *you* see some of those women, José—those ridiculous looking harlots with their hair done up like horns?"

"I am blind in your presence, señora."

"Ha!" she laughed, "if Rodrigo hadn't held you back you'd now be absent without leave."

"What did you think of them, Rodrigo?" She was heady with the exotic wonder of the place.

"I recognized a couple of them from Italy."

She shook her head, her ill-fitting helmet glinting in the sun. "This is what happens, José, when those of us with good breeding fraternize with low men. They turn around and insult your country."

"No, señora," Maldinado offered, "That will never do. A woman with your breeding and standards needs a man of quality. I'm at your service, My Lady, any time day or *night*."

She actually giggled, "I thank you for your consideration, but," she glanced in my direction, "I'm saving myself for a nunnery."

●●●

We had to slow down as we approached the marketplace because of the thickening crowds—we were astounded by the size of the place—it was three times the size of the great Plaza de Salamanca and was absolutely packed with people. At first glance, the scene was chaotic but, as we grew more used to the bustle, we could see that everything was conducted with the greatest order. The plaza was flanked by canals from which there was a constant going-and-coming of canoes, most of which were piled high with goods of various sorts. Business was arranged into quarters and arcades.

We were in wide-eyed astonishment at the things we were seeing. Francesca's good mood got even better.

"This is *so* wonderful! It's just like traveling to ancient Roma. Look! There is the slave market."

Indeed, in one quarter of the market, dejected men, women and children were being traded. Most of these were bound at the necks by long poles but some women with their children were allowed to move without these restraints. As we watched, a naked woman stepped onto a pedestal where potential buyers—including several highborn women—examined and prodded her.

I spotted something of more immediate interest. "Let's visit the next stall."

The trader showed us his wares. There were copper spear points, hatchets, hammers and harpoon heads. There were even plates meant to protect the chest and the legs. I tested a spear point against an axe.

"Look at this, *Paco*." I pointed out the place I had etched on the axe. "This stuff is harder than copper. Have you noticed those little snips of metal they use for money?"

"Yes," Migues said, "I got a pocketful of them for a couple of beads."

"It might be tin. If I'm right, the hardness of this copper will be because it has been alloyed with tin—this might be bronze."

"Is that important, Rodrigo?" Francesca asked.

"I'm afraid so. Judging by what they have right here they must have quite a bit of this stuff. It's not nearly as good as our steel but it is better than flint and itzli."

●●●

There were also piles of weaponry of all kinds and, nearby, was a stall where itzli and stone was not only bartered but the buyer could actually have it chipped to his specifications. I watched as the craftsman heated stones in an oven, broke them apart with a stone hammer, and then chipped the fragments with the tip of an antler.

Using a glass bead as payment and by using signs, I ordered the worker to produce a knife from a large orange stone with gray whorls—

it was quite astounding to see how fast the work proceeded. First, he fashioned the hilt in the form of a fat woman with large sagging breasts, then he flaked the blade to razor-like perfection. I handed the finished piece to Francesca, who held it up to the sunlight and examined it carefully.

"Is this how you think I look, Rodrigo?"

"Of course not, My Lady." I bowed. "Can I help it if these stupid Tenochca have no eye for real beauty."

Not to be outdone, Maldinado gave her a fist-sized stone demonio—it was beautifully done. It was squatting and, by the pained expression on its face, it seemed to be constipated.

"Better yet" she laughed. "It will remind me that I must never have a baby."

We continued our tour.

There were stalls that sold nequen fiber in the form of string and rope wound in coils. In other arcades raw cotton, cotton mantles, and feather work were being sold. Others dealt in baskets and pottery peculiar to their districts. Here one could obtain the various fruits of the field as well as meat from game animals. The flesh of fish, rabbit, hare, deer and dog was all sold here. Living eels, fish, ducks and turkeys—*guajalotes*—were also available. The fish and eels were kept in great stone basins and some of the fish were the result of the mating between *trucha*—trout—and *cocodrilos*. They were longer than my outstretched arms and, although they had a fish's fins, they were covered with great scales and had long heads and mouths filled with sharp teeth, exactly like a cocodrilo. I wondered if they were fed with the sacrificial meat from human victims.

"Would you like to see how one of these things tastes, My Lady?"

"You must be mad, Rodrigo. Those things look like they would eat *me*."

"I'm serious, Francesca. I've eaten meat from the tails of cocodrilos in Cuba—quite edible. It would be interesting to test the flesh of these crossbreeds."

Migues was interested. "I want that big ugly one."

"Francesca?" I intended to buy one, anyway, but wanted to know how adventurous the lady *really* was.

Our Caudillo, who had been studying Mexica weapons in an adjacent stall, walked over. He tried to control his interest in the crocodile-fish but he did a poor job. "It is always good to show these savages that *we* are afraid of nothing," he said. "There are six of those things. Buy them all, Señor de la Peña, and have them cut up for dinner tonight. *All* of us—no exceptions—will sample these monstrosities."

Some of our nearby Castellanos made faces but when Cortés glared at them, they stopped.

He continued his inspection and I continued with the fish. Using sign language and a clear glass bead, I indicated to the fishmonger—a tiny filthy man—that I wished to purchase these reptilian fish. He was delighted and immediately started heading and gutting the squirming eels. I tried to stop him but it was too late. Then, despite my protests, he went to work on the other fish until only the monster fish were left alive. He didn't stop.

The little man was powerful and, despite their slashing teeth and flopping around, he managed the huge fish without any help. With Francesca looking on, I was embarrassed to be doing so little so—without the fishmonger asking assistance—I waded in. The fish he was manhandling recognized me as a novice. It lashed out with its croco-dile head and slashed my hand. Fortunately the wound wasn't deep but my hand was left running with blood and the episode—especially because Francesca laughed at me—bruised my pride.

The fishmonger never noticed. He picked up a stone axe and, with a blow that would have stunned an ox, rendered the fish senseless. Then, using the same axe and—with a great outpouring of blood—he chopped the fish open from stem to stern, then scooped out the writh-ing guts and went to work on the pale meat. There were numerous bones and the tiny man—whom I now had much respect for—chopped the meat away from both the horny skin and the bone—exactly as I had cleaned cocodrilos back in Cuba.

"Now why didn't you think of *that?*" Francesca asked sweetly.

Disgusted, I didn't reply, but watched the little Indio place the flesh of the fish in amatl sacs and, when those were used up, he ran to near-by booths and obtained more. Finally, the blood-soaked, fish-slimed work was over, and I had more fish than ten men could carry and all for the price of one glass bead!

I wasn't defeated. I commandeered nearby Mexica and, using unmistakable sign language, ordered them to return the fish to our quarters. That night we had enough fish for all of our Castilian men and women but, to this day, I don't know what meat came from our monster fish although, to be certain, some of the toothsome flesh tasted a lot like Castilian pollo.

●●●

We continued our tour. There was a quarter set aside for the gold-smiths. As a matter of fact, although much of the trading was done by barter, the Mexica did have forms of money other than tin. Gold dust, in transparent goose quills, was the most valuable but, curiously, cacao beans was also used as money. On the other hand, they had no weights and measures. Trades were conducted by other means.

"What is that?" Francesca held her nose.

Pyramids of salt were piled up nearby but further on, there were even greater mountains of dried and drying human dung.

"My dear," Maldinado explained, "did I not tell you that I was reminded of my home town."

"But piles of..."

"They don't have animals to produce fertilizer." I said. "They put their body waste back into the soil—efficient."

Francesca rolled her eyes. "The pigs didn't have to pile it right next to places where they are selling food..."

She was right. Immediately next to the mountains of dung, there were stalls selling tamales, tortillas, molé de chocolotl y chiles, and a dish prepared with maíz and the tripas de ciervos—deer guts.

In other places were piles of skins and hides including those of birds. I searched through one of these piles and was able to identify the skins of the Mexican tiger, the deer, wolf, and rabbit. I wasn't able to identify most of the skins, however. Neither was I able to identify most of the herbs that were in an area set aside for medicines. Nevertheless, using sign language, some of the soldiers tried to communicate with the vendors—most of us suffered from various ailments and hoped for a cure. When our Caudillo saw what we were doing, he ordered an immediate halt to the sales. He did not wish the Mexica to see that Castilians suffered from illnesses. Before he intervened, however, some of us obtained herbs.

Embarrassed, I slipped away from Francesca and José as they bartered for new cotton clothing. I, as well as many other soldiers, was suffering from a burning irritation that affected the insides of my thighs. This made marching painful and—in my case at least—the irritation had become so inflamed as to produce running sores. The vendor produced fresh green leaves that he indicated we must rub on the affected areas. With a small chalchihuitl I purchased some of these leaves.

Burgos, Castilla-León

"Did it work, Your Grace?" Mendoza was delighted by the Bishop's long ago misery.

"It did, indeed, Padre, but, as they say, '*El remedio puede ser peor que la enfermedad*'—the cure can be worse than the disease. Later, in the privacy of our own quarters and away from the curious Amelia, I examined my purchase. The leaves were heavy and wet and exuded pungent oil. Cautiously—for I was in much pain—I rubbed the leaf over the most heavily inflamed skin. The sensation was soothing so, now with more courage, I applied it to the delicate skin of my genitals and halfway down the inside of my legs.

To my considerable alarm, there was a tingling of discomfort that quickly grew into a pain so severe as to compare—unfavorably—with a fiery torch held to one's cojónes. If it would have helped, I would have screamed. If it would have helped, I would have *killed*. Instead, I danced around clutching at my scorched parts. After many minutes, the pain subsided but, fearful of the consequences of this Mexican trick, I had not the courage to look. That evening, to Amelia's disquiet, I slept alone. During the night, I reached down to scratch myself, and could feel—nothing—*absolutely nothing*. In my terror, I thought that I my *huevos* had rotted off. Fortunately, however, it was but a dream. Over a period of days, however, all of the skin peeled from the area in perfect whole sheets—like the shed skin of a serpent—it did this three times."

"But were you cured?"

"Yes—when the skin grew back it was fresh and perfect and I had no more problems with the rash. Some of the others were not so lucky and despite the fact that their agonies resembled my own, they continued to suffer with this dread illness. Later some of these men died, not directly because of the disease, but because of their incapacity—it slowed them down and they were unable to avoid capture."

At one end of the great market there was a place in which sat twelve judges who were the final arbitrators of disputed trades. Their officers patrolled the marketplace, quick to put down signs of unrest or to detect evidence of unfair dealings. Because of this there was absolute order. The judges were empowered to issue the penalty of death for any and all infractions.

The marketplace was a remarkable place for traders assembled from all of Mexico and here it was possible to obtain goods unique to the various regions. Here was also the reason why it would have been best to leave the City as intact as possible. It was a thing that ran very nicely by itself, and could have been manipulated to serve Castile.

Burgos, Castilla-León

"Yes, Your Grace, but such a state would have never served God."

"In the short term that is true but, given a major Spanish presence, conversion would have been inevitable. A Catholic *Tenochtitlan* with all of its tentacles of commerce would have been a worthy thing, indeed, to set before Emperor Carlos."

"Could this have been achieved, however?"

"Certainly not by Hernán Cortés—it would have required patience and time, neither of which he had—not, however, that it didn't occur to him. At first, probably before we personally witnessed the size and power of the enemy's Empire, he had a dream of using Moctecuzoma as his puppet and bleeding him *slowly* for our benefit. Our force was too small and weak to achieve this, however. Paradoxically, because of our weakness, total destruction became the only alternative. A more potent military force, led by a Captain of wisdom, might have taken all of Mexico intact."

"Ah, Obispo, you are forgetting—we could have never left the Indios their pagan monuments and idols. We would have had to destroy them and, when we did, the Indios would have resisted."

The old man looked at his scarred hands for a long time. "You are right, Padre."

Chapter 5

After viewing the Great Market we marched to the *Plaza Mayor*, where Moctecuzoma and multiple teopixquia were waiting for us on top of the great teocalli, *El Templo Mayor*. It has been a long time but some things one never forgets. This enormous mosque was built like a layer-cake with two great staircases, side-by-side, leading to its flattened top. On the sides were the raised likenesses of huge and encircling serpents—serpents we now call *cascabels*, for they have castanets—*castañuelas*—for tails.

In their language, this teocalli was called *Coatepec*—the Mountain of Serpents. On its top were two templos. At the bottom of the staircase was a great disc engraved with the dismembered body parts of the female god, *Coyoloxauqui*. This goddess was she who was slain and dismembered by her sacred brother—*Huitzilopotchli*—the one to whom the mosque was dedicated. The disc, as well as the stairway, was slippery with blood. During their evil rites, men and women were hurled down the steep steps and—if all went well according to their heathen religion—came to rest on this disc. Just as the goddess was dismembered, so were the bodies of the dead victims. Thus the unfortunate victims themselves came to be sacred and godlike.

A chieftain took the Caudillo by the elbow to help him up the steep stairs but he pushed the man off roughly and I could hear him shouting, '*Castilians never need help!*' I tried to make a good show of it but, suffering as I was from the blisters on my groin, the climb was painful and, indeed, and I *could* have used some help. Once I had achieved the summit, I had something of a shock. The ascent had been steep but now, looking down, I was on the precipice of a cliff.

Francesca, who had climbed in front of me, had a similar revelation. "I'm *not* climbing down off this thing!"

If I hadn't been hurting so much, I would have laughed. "The Caudillo won't send food up here for you and I'm not going to carry you down so, unless you wish to descend head first—like one of their victims—I suggest that you back-up and *crawl* down."

Juan de Alva was a short distance from us and had little interest in Mexica marvels. Instead he was performing a death-defying stunt. He was standing at the top of the blood-slippery, cliff-like steps, his arms outstretched. He was facing the city and his toes were suspended in space.

"Careful there, muchacho," Maldinado warned him. "The Caudillo wants us to display our bravery to these Mexicans, not our guts."

De Alva looked over his shoulder at José and grinned.

Not to be outdone, the very young Gonzalo de Sandoval walked over, placed his toes over the precipice, balancing on his heels. Then, in an equal display of machismo and stupidity, he lifted one leg and teetered on the other

One of their blood-caked, black-robed teopixqui noticed the two conquistadores balancing over the precipice. I don't know whether the priest thought this a religious ritual, a display of bravado or simple fun. Stepping next to de Alva, he shuffled his feet until he too was balanced only on his heels and then, without expression, he stared out over the city, raised his arms and stood on only one leg. Awkward as this position was, he knelt—*held it*—and leaped into the air. He somersaulted backward, coming to rest, one-legged, in the same position as before his jump. Still expressionless, he walked away from the precipice as if nothing had happened.

"Want to give that one a try, too?" Old Herrera joked.

Chastened, both de Alva and Sandoval backed away and we turned our attention to Great Mosque's evil spectacle.

The top was flat—a platform—on which there was a large green stone they call *Techcatl*—curved in such a way as when a victim was laid upon it, his chest was pushed upward. This stone—like everything around it—was covered with fresh, gelatinous blood.

"Behold, Malinche, the beauty of *Anahuac*," intoned the nearby Moctecuzoma.

From the top of *Coatepec* we could see many leagues. The city, beneath, was laid out like spokes on a wheel with the large avenues meeting at the main plaza that was in the middle of the city. The avenues divided the city into quadrants, each of which had its own major plazas and templos. The city itself—I was told—was made up of sixty thousand dwellings. In the distance there were tributary cities and pueblos that swelled that number of inhabitants.

"See, Malinche." Moctecuzoma pointed west to a hill on the mainland a league away. "There is the place we call *Chapultepec*. There is my favorite palace and there you can see my form and that of my predecessor, the mighty Ahuizotl, carved in the stone of the hill. There, look Malinche, you can see two cities, the great *Texcoco* and the smaller *Tlacopan*, our great comrades in our Triple Alliance."

"*Alliance?*" Cortés tried to control the alarm in his voice.

"Yes, we have long since agreed to support one another in our various wars. *Tlacopan* gets one-fifth of the spoil. *Texcoco* and *Tenochtitlan* share the rest." Moctecuzoma went on, not noticing the Caudillo's discomfort, "There is the causeway of *Ixtapalapan* by which you teotoh entered. To the north is the causeway of *Tepeyac* and to the west is the causeway of *Tlacopan*, also called *Tacuba*. On another dike from *Chapultepec* is our great aqueduct. It is as wide as a very fat man and supplies the city with sweet water. Behold, My Lords—you will see that the pipe is double—should repairs be necessary on one, we can use the other. You will also see canoes pulled up to the aqueduct. At these places there are outlets from which water flows. The canoes collect water that is used in those houses where water is not piped."

"Yes, Moctecuzoma," Cortés lied, "your cities are large but not so beautiful or powerful as those of the Emperor Carlos."

Moctecuzoma ignored him. "Also, know that this lake is not all one body of water. When the season is dry the water dries back and then five lakes can be seen. *Tenochtitlan* is on Lake Texcoco, which is not only the largest but also the lowest and has the most salt. To the north there are the Lakes Xaltocan and Zumpango, which have the best water, and to the south, there are Lakes Xochimilco and Chalco."

"Very interesting, my Prince"—Cortés pretended boredom—"but would you mind showing us your infernal shrines?"

Moctecuzoma consulted an elderly especially filthy teopixqui, before answering. "Because you are a teotl, yourself, you may enter our holy places."

●●●

There were two large templos, the fronts of which were embossed in unearthly creatures. A flame in a large brazier burned in front of each shrine. The fires were to honor the gods and were never permitted to fail.

Some of us entered the first temple—I was revolted—it smelled worse than the worst slaughterhouse in Castile and I've seen and smelled some bad ones. The floors and walls were black with blood. In a recess of this temple was a shrine that contained the great bejeweled devil—*Huitzilopotchli*—their god of war. The idol's face was broad and hideous and, in his right claw-hand, were a golden bow and a sheath of arrows. A huge serpent, made of gems and pearls, twisted around his waist and feathers of the tiny hummingbird—*Huitzilin*—for which the god was named, were glued to his left foot. Around his neck hung a necklace of gold and silver—alternating graven hearts and human heads. In front of the god was an altar containing smoking copal and three fresh human hearts.

In a second recess was the god *Tezcatlipoca*, also known as *Smoking Mirror*. He was the brother of *Huitzilopotchli* and was the god of Hell. His image was that of a young man with a scarred face—severe and arrogant—and was entirely made up of shiny itzli and glittering quartz. The thing was decorated with plates of gold and held a shield of itzli that was burnished and mirror-like. On his head was a helmet, resembling our own and, on his back, was a large mirror—identical to the one the Mexica had tried to place on my back in San Juan de Ulua. Small wonder, I thought, that the Mexica had been confused as to my nature. Smoking copal and five hearts lay in a golden platter to the honor of the god.

In the second templo was the image of a god even more terrible than the others. It was black and stinking and had the misshapen body of a thing that was half-man and half-toad. Like the others, it was encrusted with precious stones. The monster's skin was grainy because, as Moctecuzoma informed us, the idol was molded from all of the seeds that existed in the world. The monster was black, not because of paint, but because these seeds had been glued together with the blood of innumerable infants and children.

Mendoza stopped his transcription. "I hadn't heard this before. Why would even the Mexica create such an unholy thing?"

"Mexican religion followed a brutal logic. In some way the Mexicans themselves recognized that their gods were devils. They were dangerous and if not propitiated properly, the consequences could be beyond imagination. This terrible black god was he who controlled clouds and storms, and the tears of terrified children were like drops of rain. These tears reminded the god to do his duty by pouring his abundance on the land. So there you see it. Sacrifice of weeping children promoted the growth of all of the world's seeds. Of course, the blood that made up the idol's body was not adequate in-and-of itself—the god needed constant reminders. Infants and children were routinely slain at the foot of this monster. Children were kept in a building within the *Plaza Mayor* for this purpose. Sometimes, to insure rainfall, the children, during their sacrifice, had their fingernails pulled out with copper instruments. These tortures produced torrents of tears and, as the Mexica told it, abundant rainfall."

Mendoza screwed up his face. "To think that they would have committed such atrocities on innocent children..."

"Yes," the old man smiled mirthlessly, "those who harm children will pave the Halls of Hell."

Mendoza ignored the implication. "Why would the Mexicans use a tiny bird as a symbol of their most terrible god, *Huitzilopotchli?*"

The old Bishop leaned back in his chair and stared at a stain on the wall. "Do you remember Padre, that as children, we had a fear—a superstition—about dragonflies?"

"I know they must be avoided."

"Yes, and what other name are these creatures known by?"

Mendoza had no idea why the conversation had suddenly shifted to bugs. Perhaps it was evidence of the Bishop's senility.

Mendoza replied, "Children refer to them as *Las Agujas de Diablo*—the Devil's darning needles."

The old man snapped his fingers, "It was the same with the Mexica. They had a similar legend about the hummingbird. Although tiny, the bird has a long needlelike beak. The Indios believed—against all evidence and despite the frequent observation that they suck nectar from flowers—that the birds were capable of sucking blood. Their word for hummingbird—*huitzilin*—is almost identical with their word for thorn—*huitztli*. Priests used the huitztli thorn of the maguey cactus to draw their blood in honor of *Huitzilopotchli*. The connections, I think, are obvious."

Cortés, whose face had remained expressionless, had now assumed the look of a fanatic or maybe a madman. "Compadres, I think that we should ask Moctecuzoma if we could cleanse these criminal places and sanctify them with a Cross and a Christian shrine."

I paled at Cortés' suggestion and, I wasn't diplomatic. "I warn you, Caudillo! You may be our leader but *now* is the time to hold your tongue."

Cristóbal de Velásquez seized his arm as if he could hold him back.

Cortés—beyond control—laughed and turned to Moctecuzoma, "I don't understand how a great and wise Prince, can put faith in filthy devils. If you will but permit us to erect here the True Cross, and place the images of the blessed Virgin and her Son in your sanctuaries, you will soon see how your false gods shrink before them!"

"What is he trying to do? Kill us all?" whispered Francesca in my ear.

Moctecuzoma reacted with cold dignity but the teopixqui beside him, who had also heard Doña Marina's translation, was outraged. Moctecuzoma, who had been conciliatory, now spoke with the anger of absolute authority. "These are the gods who have led the Mexica on to victory since we became a nation, and these are the gods who send the seed-time and harvest in their seasons. They give us health and wisdom, so we are bound to worship them and sacrifice to them. Had I thought you would insult them, I would have *not* admitted you into their presence—you *must* speak no more ill of our gods!"

Cortés, dropping his pretense of religious indignation, responded cheerfully, as if he had not noticed Moctecuzoma's outrage. "It is time for your Majesty and us to depart."

"Would that I could do so, Malinche," Moctecuzoma replied, "but to atone for your sacrilege I must remain and give more victims to my gods."

Somewhat sobered, Cortés did something he never did—he apologized, "If that is so, my Lord. I ask your pardon but would still like permission to visit your other shrines. We will speak no ill of your gods."

Moctecuzoma considered the issue and—true to his craven nature—backed down, "That being the case, you may enter as many templos as you like. Remember, however, that the consequences of impiety"—he raised his face to the sky—"will be terrible."

●●●

We descended the stairs accompanied by several priests and chieftains. Alvarado knelt down, running his hand over the white stones of the plaza. "They've been polished, Caudillo—poor footing for horses—worse than *Cholula*."

Cortés didn't seem to notice. He kept smiling and acted as if we were on nothing more than a sightseeing trip.

There were several other mosques, all smaller than the *Templo Mayor* and all dedicated to their special devils. From the top of each burned perpetual flames, which at night, along with those fires on the numerous templos in other quarters of the Capital, shed a flickering illumination over its streets.

One of the templos was dedicated to the great god *Quetzalcoatl*. Its entrance was an imitation of a serpent's mouth with great fangs dripping with blood. The name *Quetzalcoatl* means quetzal bird-snake for the word *coatl* is the Mexican word for serpent and also explains the serpent-headed entrance. Next to this door were idols in the form of grotesque serpents of the kind with castanets on their tails.

Several of our softer men gagged and vomited. Cortés, who never changed expression, spit out an order. "If you cannot control yourselves, hombres, look the other way. It is poor form to show these Mexicans that we have weak stomachs."

Francesca had come up behind me and was clutching my arm with both hands and buried her face in my shoulder. "Oh, Rodrigo! Now I wish I'd never come."

I had no words for her because I was staring into our future and the future was hideous.

There were large blood-covered chopping blocks of stone and wood along with itzli knives of various shapes and sizes. Sacrificed corpses were being chopped into pieces and, a short distance away, there were great piles of firewood along with pots and cauldrons of water. Soot-covered teopixquia scurried to-and-fro, butchering newly slain victims and grilling their sliced meat on braziers. I'm ashamed to admit, perhaps because I was hungry, that the smell was not altogether unpleasant.

"*Este lugar*," Francesca whispered. "*Esta El Infierno.*"

Burgos, Castilla-León

"I don't understand, Your Grace. My records show that *Quetzalcoatl* was a gentle god. They show that one of the reasons for Cortés' triumph was that this was the god with which he was confused."

"You must consider, Padre Mendoza, that Moctecuzoma was above all other things, *completely* bewildered. He didn't really know who or what we were. *Quetzalcoatl* was one of the gods that he must have considered but, from his words and those of his chieftains, he also worried that we might be the representatives of *Tezcatlipoca* or *Huitzilopotchli*. The fact that we always claimed to be the ambassadors of an even higher authority—Emperor Carlos I—was a puzzle that he never solved. And the fact that we Castilians worshiped a god far loftier than ourselves must have completely addled him. You are right, though, about *Quetzalcoatl*. By Mexican legend he was an ancient ruler who may actually have taught against human sacrifice, preferring instead, the blood of animals—codornices, liebres, perros—as well as other beasts. Because of this, he offended other gods who drove him out of *Anahuac*—according to the legend, he got on a boat and departed over the Eastern Sea, promising to return one day and reclaim his throne. It's easy to see how the superstitious Mexica might see our arrival as the reappearance of such a god."

"But the legend doesn't explain his bloody temple."

"No. I think that the legend was a contrivance that helped the Mexica justify their defeat. *Quetzalcoatl*, from the very beginning, may have been a sanguinary god just like all of the others. On the other hand, the Mexican religion had clearly involved itself in an unsustainable cycle of murder. It is possible this homicidal drive of the Mexican Priesthood overwhelmed their worship of more benevolent gods."

There were still other templos and mosques decorated with twisted things and horrible paintings. Surprisingly, one of these terrible places was dedicated to weddings and marriages. Also present were buildings that housed teopixquia and others that—disturbingly—housed a military garrison. Another building was a kind of a convent where the eligible girls lived before marriage. Paradoxically, from our Christian point of view, there were two great idols—horrific, malformed but obviously female—to whom victims were sacrificed in order to assure that the girls would get good husbands. Associated with this were storehouses for maíz, frijoles and other dried foodstuffs, as well as academies—*calcemeca*, in their language—for the instruction of youths. There were also stone houses, painted in bright colors, for the accommodation of visiting dignitaries.

Close to these was another templo on which there were great racks of skulls and putrid heads—*tzompantlin*—strung along parallel poles. The number of these trophies was astounding. Because of the order in which they were arranged it was possible to do an approximate count—one hundred and thirty-six thousand skulls."

Burgos, Castilla-León

"Do you mind if I ask another question, Your Grace?"

"Ask."

"I have read of the enormous figure before—but—as I and other scholars calculate, the figure—if for no other reason than the enormous space necessary for displaying these heads—is *impossible*."

The old man ran his index finger over his teeth. "Your talents are remarkable, Padre. Not only are you a man of God, but a talented mathematician."

"Not at all, Excelencia—simple arithmetic."

"Well, you're wrong, Padre. Not only are you wrong but—as I personally observed—many more skulls were added to the racks before the collapse..."

"Ridiculous!"

A smile played at the corners of the old man's mouth. "You test my patience—*and*—you test my good nature."

"Simple arithmetic shows..."

The old man shrugged and shook his head. "That I should be plagued by simpletons is my fate." He put his two hands up, palms facing each other. "This, Padre, is the width of a human skull." He placed his hands slightly farther apart. "This is the length of an average skull less its mandible and this" Changing the position of his hands, slightly—"is the front to back dimension."

"But..." Mendoza protested.

"Now, Mendoza, I will *teach* you mathematics: Given a multi-tiered rack, half as long as a half city block in—let's say—Grenada, with skulls touching one another—*and*—given multiple racks with the front of each skull close to the back of a skull on the forward rack... Then, as I hope you can see, a simple multiplication of racks produces 136,000 and more."

"But the racks would have to reach to the sky."

"Not quite, Padre. In the privacy of your own apartment—*if* you can take time off from self-abuse—*do* the calculations."

Close to these skull racks was a huge pool of clear water that came from the *Chapultepec* aqueduct. In the front of the plaza was a great court where the Mexica played *tlachtli*, a magical ball game. Tiers of seats flanked the court for the Tenochca enjoyed the performance of this sport.

In still another place was a large building that served as a storage area for all of the weapons of Mexico. Despite and maybe because of the fact that all boys were trained to be soldiers, weapons were only distributed prior to battle.

"What do you make of this place, Caudillo?" I had come to an immediate opinion and wondered if he was of the same mind.

"Military storehouse."

"Yes, Caudillo, but the indígenos also say that the Mexica place stations along their roads and their warriors search all passers-by for weapons. They even enter homes searching for hidden weapon caches."

"A sensible precaution."

"Precaution, indeed." I observed. "The rulers of *Tenochtitlan* are worried about the possibility of revolution. They don't trust their own population to keep weapons in their homes."

He rubbed his hands together and spoke to me as if we were friends, "If you're right, we may yet devise a strategy which causes the Mexica to turn upon one another."

"True, Caudillo, but it also has negative implications. If we should actually manage to convince Moctecuzoma to do our bidding, his subjects may revolt against both him and *us*."

"Defeatist, as usual, Rodrigo." He put his hand up and clinched his fist. "Our small force cannot prevail against such an empire—but—it won't be necessary. I have the measure of Moctecuzoma. Did you notice the way I got him to back down about our visiting these templos? When the time is right, I'll have them obeying my every order."

"I hope you're right, Caudillo, because we are a very long way from home."

Burgos, Castilla-León

"If I had not mentioned it already, Padre, the Great Plaza was made even more remarkable by the extensive gardens of trees and beautiful flowers. It was alive with activity of thousands of people who lived and worshipped there. Of teopixquia alone, there were four thousand. Added to this were pipiltin, warriors, common peasants and children. Nevertheless, except for the bloodstained altars, everything was kept spotless and everything was orderly—certainly not what you might expect of untutored savages. Here was the Mexican paradox, the grandeur of their architecture softened by the beauty of growing things and flowers. At the same time the entire place was dedicated to death and the perfume of the flowers mingled with the foul odor of rotting flesh. Perhaps it was all deliberate—the beauty of life tempered by the reality of death and dissolution."

The old man took a deep breath through his nose. "After all these years I can still smell it—somehow the stink stays in your nostrils. Have you ever noticed, Padre, how the odor of putrefying corpses gets into your hair and does not leave it even after washing it thoroughly?"

Mendoza felt a wave of nausea. "No, Your Grace. Like most reasonable people, I have made a practice to avoid such unpleasantness."

The ancient priest went on, "There's no odor quite like it, not even that of a dead beast. I think about these things sometimes. Not only is the odor foul—especially at close range—but it is penetrating, clinging to one's clothing, skin and hair. Of course, like anything else, it's possible to get used to it. Clearly the Mexican priests lived in this putrid atmosphere without any ill effects. The adaptability of man is one of our strongest and most terrible attributes."

Chapter 6

We returned to our quarters, all of us disturbed by what we had seen. The cannibal rites were terrible, indeed, but more shocking was our ever-increasing knowledge of the power and very size of Mexico. Although we always had daily Mass, many felt that God would hear our prayers more clearly if we had a Church. Cortés applied to Moctecuzoma for permission to set up a chapel in our palace. The emperor agreed.

We did it right and took a full three days to complete our chapel. We erected a cross and set out a portrait of Our Lady holding the infant Jesus. Frailes Díaz and Olmedo conducted daily services and took many confessions. Our simple soldiers were relieved that Our Savior could now better hear our prayers. In addition Cortés hoped that Moctecuzoma, seeing our soldiers on our knees in front of the altar, would help to convince him to give up his superstition—here is where he placed much of his effort. A Christianized Moctecuzoma would be easier to deal with. Unfortunately, the Prince showed no evidence of a change in faith.

●●●

During the construction of our chapel, one of our soldiers made an interesting observation. Alonso Yáñez, who had been a carpenter back in Old Castile, noticed an irregularity in one of the walls. Yáñez, who trusted me, called me to take a look.

"What do you make of this, Señor de la Peña?"

A depressed line ran down the wall to the floor. I ran my hand along it and then along the top and down to the bottom again. "There's a door here, Alonso. Interesting—it seems to have been painted over."

Yáñez, like the rest of us, had heard idle rumors of a treasure hidden in the palace. "Let's open it and see what's inside."

"No, Alonso. Whatever's there belongs to the Mexica and, given our delicate situation, we don't want to start a war."

"Then let's tell the Caudillo."

I wasn't sure if this was an intelligent alternative but, then again, there was no chance that Yáñez would keep silent.

I acceded, "He is our Jefe."

Yáñez informed Cortés who, in turn, told him to keep silent. Cortés then called his leaders together to witness the unsealing of the room. Yáñez, basking in his newfound fame, rapidly chipped the paint and plaster away revealing the underlying door. The door wasn't bolted—held in place only by plaster—Yáñez put his shoulder to it and the door squeaked open. The room beyond was black but a torch revealed wonders. Everywhere was the glint of gold. Cortés, probably regretting his decision to have witnesses, fairly salivated with greed.

The rest of us salivated, too.

"Now that we have had a look," the Caudillo said, "we will seal the door, again."

Our treasurer, Gonzalo de Mexía, stepped forward. "Not until I tabulate the contents."

Cortés exploded, "*You* don't trust *me*, Gonzalo?"

"I wouldn't trust my dead grandmother with such a treasure." Mexía spat back.

Cortés looked to his loyal Captains for support. He found none. Like starving wolves at a carcass, each one would fight for his share.

He seemed to collapse in on himself. "Then get to it, Gonzalo, so that we can seal the door as soon as possible. I don't want Moctecuzoma—or any of his Mexican cabrónes—to learn of our discovery."

We all stood at the door's entrance and watched Mexía, plume in hand, tally the room's contents on a wood tablet. He pulled each item from the hoard and meticulously marked it down.

The room wasn't small and was filled with the imperial treasure of generations—gold and silver plate as well as animals and frightful beasts made of wrought gold. There were silver and gold ingots and colorful vases filled with gold dust. Along with this were other beautiful things of gold along with pots full of chalchihuitl, great sheathes of precious feathers, huge stacks of feathered mats and tlamatlis, and finely wrought jewelry—necklaces, earrings, lip and nose plugs—studded with precious stones, pearls and iridescent sea shells. Indeed, it seemed as if all of the riches of the world had been gathered into this place.

The tabulation went on for hours and, when completed to Mexía's satisfaction, he ordered the door to be resealed. By the time Yáñez finished with it, the entrance was more skillfully hidden than it had been originally. It was all for naught. News of this discovery spread to every soldier and, in all probability, to all of our Tlaxcalteca and to the entire Mexican nation. Now, every man knew that the promise of unlimited wealth was very close, indeed. The only problem was how to get it out of the city.

Burgos, Castilla-León

The Bishop stopped his dictation. "Now here I must make another observation, Padre Mendoza, or should I phrase it as a question? Why do you think that the Mexicans would leave their imperial treasure in the same palace that they housed their potential enemies?"

"Perhaps they didn't have time to move it to a secure location."

"Ridiculous. We were on the march for months. It wouldn't have taken more than a few hours to move the treasure."

"Stupidity?"

"It *was* stupidity, Padre, but of a very particular type—it was the stupidity of indecision. There would seem to be no other explanation for it. Up until the last moment, Moctecuzoma must have believed that we could be deflected from his capital. Every priest and sorcerer in all of Mexico must have been beseeching their gods to that end."

Mendoza considered the point. "Yes, but still...by the time you were on the causeways, they must have considered the real possibility that you were going to march into their City. Is it possible that Moctecuzoma believed that subterfuge was useless? Did he believe that, with your supposedly supernatural powers, you would locate his wealth no matter where he put it?"

The old man enjoyed a good discussion, even if it were with a creature like the Jesuit Mendoza. "You may have hit the nail on the head. It's also just possible that he *wanted* us to find it. Certainly, this is what he said after the discovery became public. If he wanted us to find it, however, it is difficult to explain the amateurish attempts to cover the door with a little plaster and paint."

"Maybe the room had been covered up for a long time."

"No, Padre, it wasn't. Even Moctecuzoma admitted that the treasure was reduced by the amount that he had already given us. Up until one or two days of our entering the City the Mexica had been removing treasure—maybe more treasure than we ever saw. This leads us to the last possibility and the one that Cortés certainly believed."

"What might that be?"

"That the treasure room was a decoy—as evidenced by its easy discovery. He believed that its treasure was but a fraction of the Empire's wealth. After the fall of *Tenochtitlan*, Cortés searched furiously for the hidden treasure. He tore up the countryside and tortured hundreds of nobles including Moctecuzoma's successor, Cuahtemoc himself."

"But where did it go?"

"I wouldn't know. Maybe it never existed—maybe it is still hidden away—maybe Cortés found it."

The Caudillo called another meeting of his leaders.

"Señores, we have now had a chance to see the City and to see the imperial treasure. It is now time to assess our tactical situation. I'd like to hear your ideas."

The grinning Pedro de Alvarado promptly leapt to his feet. "I'm for taking it to them—*now!* Seize the plaza, the mosques and Moctecu-

zoma's palace—kill everything in sight. We'll paralyze the Tenochca."
He slammed his fist into his hand. "They'll fold like a wet hide. We'll
sack *Tenochtitlan* and all of their cities."

Cortés spoke softly because Alvarado was his friend. "A bold plan.
Pedro, maybe a little too bold."

Diego de Ordaz spoke, "What I have seen confirms what I already
thought. This city is too powerful for us and we are caught like a bird
in a cage. It will be dangerous, but I recommend that we gather up
the treasure and, in the dead of night, creep from the city and make a
forced march back to the coast."

Gonzalo de Sandoval proposed a modification of Ordaz' plan, "To
sneak out is too big of a risk. No doubt, the savages are observing us
day and night and, any move on our part will be countered by an immediate attack—bottled up by these canals we will all be slaughtered.
Right now we're on good terms with Moctecuzoma. It's best that we
thank him for his hospitality and march out openly in broad daylight.
Maybe he'll let us go peacefully. If he doesn't, at least we have daylight
to fight by."

"Well spoken, Señores." Cortés scratched the scar on his lip—the
scar he had received in a fight over a puta in Española. "But even if
we should get back to the coast safely, we're in almost as much danger.
Remember we have no ships and, by the time we construct new ones.
Moctecuzoma is bound to rethink the whole situation, especially when
he finds that we have lifted his treasure. Our best course is to continue
to flatter Moctecuzoma and to manipulate him. It may take time, but
judging by his weakness, he'll be doing our bidding soon enough."

"Too risky," I retorted, "If we follow your plan, Caudillo, it will
take weeks, probably months. There are bound to be problems with
the Mexica and there are already real problems with our Tlaxcalteca.
Right now Moctecuzoma still thinks of us as teules—that *will* change.
We all know how the Mexicans deal with their enemies. There is only
one path and even that one will probably fail—seize Moctecuzoma and
make him our prisoner. Trust in his cowardice and we'll hold him as
a hostage until we can build ships and leave this land."

"And if he won't permit himself to be taken prisoner?" Cortés asked
mildly. "He is, after all, surrounded by hundreds of guards."

I raised my voice so that everyone could hear me, "Then we must kill him and try to fight our way out! We won't make it but at least we'll die on our feet."

"Quite a plan, Rodrigo. Bold, but not too bold." Cortés' eyes were odd. "Perhaps Velásquez should have made *you* Commandante? The only problem with your plan is that it is tinged with a little too much... discretion. If we *should* take Moctecuzoma hostage, we will *not* turn tail and head for the coast. We will use him as we would a woman. Through him we will rule his Empire."

I instantly bristled, my voice low, "Do you wish to define *discretion*, Caudillo?"

Cortés never took his eyes from mine—a smile spread slowly over his face. "There was no insult intended, Rodrigo. I simply meant that you are...careful. I certainly understand why all of us need to be cautious. I think we will follow my plan and, for now, continue to flatter Moctecuzoma."

●●●

The next day, however, we learned that our plans to mollify Moctecuzoma had already failed. A Tlaxcaltec messenger—disguised as a woman to avoid Mexican spies—arrived with fateful news. There had been a battle with the Mexicans near Villa Rica and the Totonacs were in revolt. It seems that a Mexican officer named Quauhpopoca—Governor of the district to the north of Villa Rica—requested that Commandante Escalante send him several Spaniards to whom he would personally swear his allegiance. Escalante—hoping for the best and hoping for our Caudillo's acclaim—did so, but the treacherous Mexican murdered two of his Castilian envoys. Two others escaped to Villa Rica with the news.

Escalante retaliated. He marched out with his under-strength force and engaged the enemy at a place called Almería. The battle was hard fought but, in the end, our men were forced to retreat. Unfortunately, many Totonacs and seven Christians were slain. Escalante later died of his wounds back in Villa Rica. The Totonac Indios—fearful of the triumphant Mexica—rose against the Castilians and laid siege to Villa Rica. Cortés called a hasty meeting,

"We now have no choice, compadres. We will attempt to take Moctecuzoma hostage and, should that prove impossible, we will kill him. Tomorrow, I invite all of you here to join me as we visit Moctecuzoma in his palace. We'll take several mosqueteros with us and have the rest of the army prepared for instant action. We will try to convince the Emperor to come peacefully but, if he does not, we'll chop him down on the spot. Our musketeers will then fire warning shots so that our main force knows to move. We, ourselves, will fight our way out and join the others. We'll then fight our way out along the same causeway that we entered the city—it's the longest but I've learned that its bridges are still intact. By using this causeway, we'll reduce the chance of interception and we'll be closer to our own ally of *Tlaxcala*."

●●●

The next morning Padre Olmedo held mass for our undertaking that was nothing short of desperate. Cortés asked for and—so very fortunately—received permission for an audience with Moctecuzoma. During the audience, some of us in twos and threes, as if by accident, were to also arrive at the palace. As usual, we were armed, but now we were prepared for a last-ditch fight.

I spoke both to Amelia and Dona Francesca, "If you hear gunfire, move out with the rest of the troops—don't wait for me. I have already spoken with Paco Migues and Juan de Alva. They'll protect you."

Amelia didn't seem to understand but Francesca's eyes were wide. "You won't be with us?"

"I'm coming with the rear guard but you must go in the van." I thought a moment and removed Bebidor and strapped it to Francesca's waist.

"What are you doing, Rodrigo?"

"I'll get another weapon but this sword is an especially good one. It may give you a margin of extra protection."

"I can't..." She put her hand on hilt and saw the surprise on her face. I had given Bebidor to the right person.

"Yes, you can. Just use it the way I have trained you. God knows I hope you don't have to use it at all."

Amelia, who didn't know exactly what was happening, placed both of her arms around my waist and had to be pried away. I tried to console her with a kiss. "Now, now Amelia. Go with Francesca and do what she tells you."

I left Amelia sobbing but Francesca's willpower was astounding. If it were not for a single tear running down her cheek, I would have thought that she had not a care in the world.

●●●

Most of our men were stationed in plaza but our stronger men and our Captains were posted in the palace at its various entrances. I, along with Cortés and several other Captains, were at the actual audience. Cortés, at first, engaged the Emperor in friendly banter but Moctecuzoma seemed uneasy.

"I was expecting you, Malinche, and have prepared gifts." His attendants passed out bracelets and armbands of silver and gold. "More importantly, my friend, I give you one of my daughters." At this—clearly in preparation for this moment—a girl stepped out from behind a screen. She was twelve or thirteen and, judging by her weight, had never missed a meal.

"Thank you, Great Prince but—and I hesitate to bring up the subject... *Why* have your warriors attacked my men on the coast?"

Moctecuzoma visibly started. "I know nothing of this."

Cortés placed his face very close to that of Moctecuzoma. "You forget that I can divine your thoughts. You have *ordered* this atrocity and you have *insulted* your sovereign."

"It was not I." Moctecuzoma was a poor liar. "It was the fault of my Governor—he has been in rebellion against me. I will order his arrest and punishment." Without waiting for Cortés' to respond, the Prince spoke rapidly to his attendants and ordered the unsuspecting Quaupoepoca's arrest.

"Thank you, Great Lord." Cortés feigned relief. "I was worried that you might have ordered this attack but I can see by your actions that you are innocent. I am afraid, though, that our sovereign, Carlos, will be less convinced. In order to allay any fears he might have, I suggest that you accompany us back to our residence where you shall be our honored guest."

He was dumbstruck. "I could never do such a thing. My subjects would never..."

"I'm afraid you have no choice," whispered Hernán Cortés.

"*I will not go!*"

Velásquez de León, recognizing the danger of Emperor's resistance, stepped forward, jerking his sword from its scabbard. "I'll kill him now and be done with it!"

Moctecuzoma didn't understand the words but, nevertheless, he understood perfectly. He wilted.

"Take my son and two daughters as hostages. Save me this disgrace."

"I'm sorry, my Prince." Cortés purred. "You *must* come with us. I promise you that you will be treated with all respect and that you may conduct the affairs of your Empire without interference."

The Emperor slumped on his throne. "I do not understand what is happening but I do not want violence in my palace. I will tell my pipiltin that it is the will of *Huitzilopotchli* and that I am going of my free will."

Moctecuzoma spoke to his chief advisors, who glanced suspiciously towards us but obeyed his command. Soon, his litter arrived. Borne by his noble attendants and flanked by armed Castilians, he was brought back to our quarters. The Emperor was now our prisoner without the shedding of a single drop of blood.

Chapter 7

Burgos, Castilla-León
March 2, 1581 8:30 A.M.

"You're improved, Padre."

Two weeks had passed and Mendoza's wounds had healed and his bruises were fading. The blows to Mendoza's pride and security had not healed, however. He hated and feared the ancient man more than he would a venomous reptile.

"I'm recovering, Excelencia. I am, however, continuing to lose weight."

"But your gout? I haven't heard any complaints."

"My toe is better. I don't wish to be impertinent but perhaps we could add a few items to my diet. I have had problems with constipation."

The old man raised his eyebrows. "Do you have any suggestions?"

"Wine, even white wine, would be appreciated. I would like to have at least one goodly portion of meat on a daily basis and a nice fish or lobster."

"I'd like to help you, Padre, but all of these items you mentioned are, for you, slow poison. I'll arrange to let the chef add a portion of carrots and turnips."

"Your Grace, I don't like turnips."

"As you will, Padre. Rather than turnips I'll give you two extra portions of very nice sauerkraut and, instead of wine, one cup of *suero de leche*—good buttermilk."

"Obispo, I'm sure that an extra portion of fish wouldn't hurt."

"No. I'd rather not take the chance, Padre. You are much too important to me but—as a special treat—I will ask my housekeeper to prepare breakfast for the two of us. Would you like some carne asada con chile serraños y habañero? I'm sure you will find it quite tasty."

"Meat?"

"Yes, meat with a very nice chile pepper sauce—I have personally attended to its preparation. Not only should it be delicious but it is also therapeutic. It should really clean you out."

"Perhaps your cook could hold back a little on the pepper?"

"The meal has already been prepared, Padre. Of course, I don't insist that you share my breakfast."

"*No, no, no, Excelencia!* I very much wish to have breakfast with you. I'll eat anything you put before me. Wine?"

"For you, Padre, anything. I've procured a good but fresh white wine from the south." The ancient Bishop eyed the expectant Mendoza, watching his every reaction. "You may have your own bottle but—I'm warning you—we have work to do and you mustn't get drunk."

Mendoza could barely believe his good fortune. "I thank you from the bottom of my heart."

Dishes, overflowing with slabs of meat and other good things, were brought in by two members of the Bishop's household staff. The one carrying the Bishop's dishes was a young man stylishly attired in a white ruffled shirt and red coat and trousers. The servant carrying Mendoza's dishes was entirely more disreputable. He was a sallow, cachectic man of indeterminate age wearing a filthy red vest and a faded black coat with too-long sleeves. His head was a disturbing patchwork of dull, cracked skin and fuzzy hair—running sores covered the corners of his mouth as well as the backs of his hands. The man placed two dishes in front of Mendoza. He then produced silverware from a coat pocket, held them up to the light and studied them carefully. He wiped them on his moth-eaten vest and placed them down in front of the shocked priest.

"Who was *that*?" Mendoza asked after the servants had gone.

"Which one, Padre?" The Bishop very well knew which one.

"The miserable creature who bore my food."

"An Englishman—a sailor—arrested in the port of Palos for being a heretic—a follower of Calvin. I managed to get him acquitted."

"An English Calvinist as your slave—a fitting punishment."

"He's not my slave, Padre. I employ him out of pity."

"Pity, Your Grace?"

"He's suffering from the French Disease. I don't imagine he has that much longer to live."

Mendoza, who had been chewing a piece of overly spiced meat, gagged.

"Just as I feared, Padre. The meal is too rich for you. I'll have it taken away."

Mendoza seized his plate with both hands. "Just give me time to catch my breath."

"Of course, Padre. Have some wine." The old man poured the clear liquid from a pot-bellied flask into a delicate goblet and then pushed it over to his victim. Mendoza sucked up the liquid as if he could clean out his mouth.

"A *syphilitic*, Excelencia? I thought you wished to *preserve* my health."

The ancient man licked his thin lips. "In that you didn't have the opportunity to fuck him, I think you are safe. But, then again, you never know."

We soldiers respectfully greeted Moctecuzoma. Cortés permitted the Emperor to select his own apartments and to have them decorated according to his tastes. His women, advisors, priests and chieftains all came and the Prince continued to receive the elaborate meals to which he was accustomed. He was provided rooms in which he could receive dignitaries and make decisions of state. From all outward appearances, the only aspect of the Emperor's rule that had changed was the location. Of course, the veneer of normality was thin, as Moctecuzoma and all of Mexico soon came to realize.

●●●

Under Castilian escort, Quauhpopoca, his son and fifteen Mexican chiefs arrived from the coast. Moctecuzoma, at the insistence of our Caudillo, called a summary court martial within Moctecuzoma's apartment. The Prince sat on his throne and the Caudillo sat beside him in a plain wooden chair. Cortes' chair had very long legs so that the top of Cortes' head was higher than that of Moctecuzoma. On the other hand, the chair legs were so long that Cortés' short legs didn't touch the floor. He looked ridiculous.

We soldiers and several Mexican noblemen stood to the sides while the prisoner—proud as a peacock—stood facing his Emperor. The chieftain was, for an Indio, an exceptionally handsome man. He was tall and proud with chiseled features. He was also attired in a patterned maxtlatl lion cloth and a tlamatli mantle of black and red feathers.

Cortés thundered, "Under whose authority did you act?"

"Under the authority of my Lord, the Great Moctecuzoma."

"Then Moctecuzoma ordered you to attack my teules on the coast?"

No matter how he answered, Quauhpopoca was a dead man.

"No, Malinche," he lied, "I ordered it myself."

Moctecuzoma leaned closer to Cortés. "It is as I told you, Malinche—I knew nothing of it. This dog must die at the alter of *Huitzilopotchli.*"

"No!" Cortés had Moctecuzoma by the cojónes and intended to squeeze them hard. "He and his treacherous officers shall die as heretics against Mother Church—they shall *burn* in your Great Plaza. It will be good that your subjects see a *civilized* punishment." Cortés fixed Moctecuzoma with his leopard's eyes and spoke in a voice barely above a whisper. "Don't *you* agree, Great Lord?"

Quauhpopoca, although a dark-skinned Indio, actually blanched. "If I must die so ingloriously, I will tell all of the truth. The Great

Prince *did* order me to sacrifice the teotoh."

Moctecuzoma shrilled, "He lies! Burn him alive and do it soon!"

●●●

Cortés ordered the armories in the Great Plaza emptied of their contents. The weapons were then placed in seventeen piles to serve as fuel for the executions. In this way, we not only punished the guilty but we eliminated much of the Mexican capacity for war. The Tenochca nobles never considered the possibility that their keeping weapons from the hands of their citizens could work to their disadvantage.

Quauhpopoca and his officers were bound to wooden posts in preparation for their incineration. Each one—expressionless—faced eternity. I couldn't help but thinking of my father dying in the fires of the Inquisition but there was nothing I could do.

Thousands of agitated Indios gathered on the rooftops to watch a spectacle that, even to their eyes, was bizarre. With a seeming unity of purpose, Cortés and Moctecuzoma entered the Plaza. Cortés, however—before the eyes of all of the Tenochca—proved where the real power of Mexico lay. He shouted at the Prince so that all might hear. Doña Marina, proud and elegant in a feathered dress, translated simultaneously.

"Lord Moctecuzoma, you have rebelled against your Emperor, Carlos I, and you,"—Cortés gestured toward the condemned men—"deserve the same death as your followers."

Moctecuzoma's mouth dropped.

Without warning Olid and de la Concha struck him with their fists and shoulders, knocking him to the tiles. Andrés de Tapía produced manacles and, despite squeals of protest, bound the Prince in ankle braces. Grasping him by the scruff of his neck, Olid jerked him to his feet. De la Concha wrapped a chain around his waist and locked it to the ankle braces. The spectators gasped as one person when they saw the swelling on his cheek, the blood pouring from his nostrils and the filth ground into his garments. His attendants stood speechless with sheer disbelief—one of the teopixquia lifted his hands in supplication.

Cortés, however was filled with power. "Look on, Great Moctecuzoma, and behold the death that you will certainly suffer should you ever again challenge your Emperor."

Moctecuzoma, completely unmanned, began to weep. As he blubbered, soldiers ignited the great pyres. I stood close to the one in which the youngest victim was staked. As the flames started to mount, I picked my way to the top of the pile—I had my knife in my hand.

"What are you doing, fool?" one of our Captains shouted. I placed the point of my knife at the base of the man's skull and, using the butt of my other hand as a hammer, drove it to its hilt. He died without a whimper. I jumped off, scorching one foot.

Flames licked at the other sixteen. Pain replaced their courage—they screamed like trapped beasts. As their skins fried, they writhed like snakes. The arrows, lances and maquahuitls used for fuel were good dry wood and burned explosively. The screams diminished to gurgling sobs and then there were no sounds except for the popping of resin and the sizzling of flesh.

Cortés strode up to me, alive with anger. "You insubordinate swine!"

"Caudillo," I said, "The boy accepted the Holy Faith before the flames reached him. I acted according to Church law."

"He knew nothing of the Church. He couldn't even speak our language!"

"The Holy Spirit spoke to me."

The Caudillo was literally frothing at the mouth. "This is a matter for our frailes."

"No, Señor. The answer belongs to God."

I think that was the moment when I realized that the teachings of the Church could be useful, indeed. Cortés was powerless.

●●●

His rage subsided along with the flames. When the pyres were reduced to little more than coals, he bent down and freed Moctecuzoma from his chains.

"I'm sorry that you forced me to humiliate you but even teules are bound by our Emperor's law." Cortés' face, which minutes before had been livid with anger, was now suffused with compassion. His words, which had been harsh, were now soft and soothing.

"In truth, our Emperor ordered your death but I love you so much I would rather die myself. I only did the least that I could do to allay our Emperor's wrath and prevent him from punishing you more severely.

I want you to know that I think of you as more than a brother—I am your servant. In the fullness of time, we teules will conquer lands that will be added to your Empire. *Santiago!* Then your glory will be even greater than now. Until then, I beg your pardon. I hope that you will continue to want to live with us but, if you do not, you may return to your own palace." Cortés had Moctecuzoma's full measure.

The Emperor's sorrow was mixed with relief and confusion. "Malinche, I hear your words and they are good but I know that they are only words—I am concerned for the welfare of my Tenochca—I do not want rebellion. Even should you permit me to return back to my palace, my chieftains will force me to make war against you. My love for you is strong and I will not permit anyone to hurt you. It is better that I remain a hostage."

Burgos, Castilla-León

Mendoza, as usual, didn't understand. "How can you explain this, Your Grace? After all the risk that Cortés had gone through to seize Moctecuzoma, why would he consider releasing him?"

The Bishop ran his hand over the table. "He would have never released him. It amused him to see if he had as much control over his soul as he had over his body."

"I still don't quite understand, Excelencia. Within the space of a few days, he became utterly servile. Here again is proof that your Santa Compañía was touched by God."

"Or by Satan?" the ancient man said. "For a moment let's take the issue out of the supernatural and consider the facts. Moctecuzoma admitted that his submission to the Castilians was resented by many of his Lords. He *knew* that some of these would take action against him once he was free of Castilian control. On the other hand, Moctecuzoma may have been responding from the heart. You must remember that, like most monarchs, he lived a life of privilege and was surrounded by sycophants. Even though, in his youth, he had lived the life of a soldier—that was long ago. He lived in unbelievable luxury and the loftiest pilli did his every bidding. As much as was humanly possible, he was totally protected from reality. Any toughness of character that he once may have had softened like butter on a warm day. Cortés made certain that any small strengths that the man may have had were totally erased. He knew men and he broke Moctecuzoma as skillfully as a horse-handler breaks a colt. Once broken, Cortés trained him to do his bidding. It was easy."

Chapter 8

After the executions things returned to normal in Axayacatl's palace. Under Cortés' eye, the Emperor continued to hold court and be served by his pipiltin. We received word that the Totonacs, learning of our imprisonment of Moctecuzoma and the execution of his officers, had once more become friends. Cortés ordered Alonso de Grado to Villa Rica, to replace the killed Escalante. De Grado, to be certain, was a grumbler and not much of a fighter, but he claimed that he knew how to run a pueblo. Later, however, we learned that de Grado—in a way totally Castilian—set himself up as a great lord, treating his men badly and taking the best for himself. Despite the distance, word reached him that the Caudillo was preparing a well-deserved punishment so he began to repair a brigantine for an escape to Cuba. Reports from the coast were that de Grado was loading the ship with loot extorted from both his men and the local Indios.

●●●

"Gonzalo," ordered the Caudillo, "take a force and make for the coast in the morning. Arrest de Grado and any men who may have joined him and put them in chains."

"*Si, Caudillo.*"

"I'm making you responsible for Villa Rica. Defend it from Indio raids—keep your eye out for ships from Cuba. If I've calculated correctly, we should soon receive an unfriendly visit from the Governor. When it happens, send word by fast couriers and delay our enemies as long as you can."

"*Claro, Caudillo.*"

"I also want for you to send up sails, nails, rigging and everything else necessary for us to build brigantines here on the lake. As things stand now, we have no retreat except for over the causeways—it's best we have an alternative."

"*Excelente, Caudillo.*"

● ● ●

Cortés asked the Emperor's permission to build small brigs to sail on the Lake's waters. He lied in telling him that the ships were to be used as pleasure craft. In truth, they were to be used to effect a retreat should it become necessary to flee from the city. To be certain, Cortés would have built the brigantines even had Moctecuzoma refused. He thought it easier, however, to manipulate the Mexican empire by permitting the Emperor the semblance of power. In this, and many other cases, his strategy worked. Moctecuzoma not only gave his permission but he ordered his subjects to provide us with planed timber.

Martín López was an argumentative young man of low background but he had experience in the building of boats in both España and Cuba. We would have preferred someone older and with more experience—but—for good or bad, he was all we had. To him went the responsibility of building our boats. Our several carpenters directed parties of Mexican laborers and it wasn't long before we had two brigantines capable of holding our entire Castilian force. Our Tlaxcaltec allies would provide the needed distraction should we have to retreat in the brigs. They would die—and horribly, too—which was unfortunate but of little consequence.

The new ships sailed beautifully and scudded over the surface of the Lake like water birds. Moctecuzoma himself, having never seen such craft before, was as delighted as a child.

"Malinche," he said, "you are my friend and protector and have done me many favors but I must ask for one more."

"If I have the power to grant it, My Prince, I will certainly do so."

"It has been a very long time since I have hunted the sacred animals on the islands of my gods. Now that you have built your great acallin, would it be possible to transport me and my chieftains to these places?"

This was a request that Malinche could readily grant. Besides we Castilians were bored by our forced inactivity. "Of course, My Prince, and, in that my Captains and I also enjoy the chase, we will be glad to accompany you."

Moctecuzoma was pleased. "To think that I may float on the craft of the teotoh—even my ancestors never had such an honor."

● ● ●

The day of the hunt was appointed. The vessels were filled with pipiltin and two hundred of us soldiers. Several of our Captains as well as our remaining soldiers—all of whom wished to go hunting—were obliged to stay in our fortress to react to any possible Mexican trickery. Our leaders met to make defensive plans.

The Caudillo spoke first. "I've been watching our Prince and he doesn't have the balls or the sense to plan an attack during the hunt. Still, it would be foolish not to provide for contingencies."

Padre Olmedo said, "I personally think it foolish to divide our force while we are in the enemy's belly."

"On the other hand, Padre," Cortés replied, "the men are restless and this diversion will bolster morale. Besides, most of us will be safe in the brigs and can respond promptly should trouble arise back here in *Tenochtitlan*."

I was bored to death and wanted to go hunting—still—there were risks. I came to my own conclusions and spoke bluntly. "Most of us will indeed be on the brigs *but* we will also be carrying more than a hundred chieftains and *fully* armed Tenochca hunters. How do we know that—by prearranged plan—these chieftains won't fall upon those of us in the brigs while—simultaneously—the rest of their warriors mount an attack on our garrison here in the palace? Is this not what you would do, Caudillo, if you were the enemy?"

Without lifting his head, Cortes peered at me through half-closed eyes. "Yes, Rodrigo, it is *precisely* what I would do. But, then again, I'm not a filthy savage. If I know anything about Moctecuzoma there will be no attack. At the same time, however, I want everyone prepared. Those of us on the brigs must—without being obvious—watch our Mexica chieftains. At the first sign of trouble, we will butcher them to the man and toss them over the sides."

Cortés continued to speak: "Moctecuzoma made me a map of Lake Texcoco so that I might know where this island of his gods—the island of the hunt—is located. It is a distance from the City, much too far away for us to hear the clang of arms or even musket shots. Our cannons here will be loaded with twice the usual amount of powder to serve as alarm signals. Should the alarm sound, we will kill our Mexica, dump them and sail back to the city. Any questions?"

De la Concha had a question. "Why wait for an attack? Look at this as a Heaven-sent opportunity. Once we get Moctecuzoma and all of his chieftains on the brigs—kill them all—and then attack the city from the palace and water,"—he slammed his fists together—"it will be just like *Cholula*, only better. What better way to deal with a little boredom?"

Cortés stood silently. He was actually considering de la Concha's incredible idea.

I directed my comment at our Caudillo, "The sparrows have the cat surrounded?"

Cortés made his decision. "No, Javier. Militarily, we are in no position to mount a full-scale attack on the Mexican Empire—far better that we coddle and mollify the cabrónes and plan for all possibilities. There will be no preemptive attack. We are going *hunting*, compadres and, Javier, my old friend, you are staying *here!*"

●●●

The Caudillo, dressed in his finest vest and pantalones, and Moctecuzoma, arrayed in a magnificence of feathers, traveled in the same launch. Colorful awnings were attached to the rigging to protect all of us from the full glare of the sun. Hundreds of noisy Mexica followed in canoes but were left behind by the fast-sailing brigantines.

The island was several leagues distant and was small and covered with naked rock, brush, nopal and stunted trees—it took some time to bring the brigantines close enough to the shore so that Moctecuzoma could disembark with suitable dignity—not only did he keep his feet dry but one noble lay down in the mud so that his Lord's feet never had to touch the filth. This, I thought, is a most unusual hunt.

In the meantime, the men in the canoes arrived at the opposite side of the island and, by prearrangement and with military precision, the canoe men positioned themselves. The designated hunters—of which I was one—found hiding places and then waited. The other Castilian hunters used only spears but I—thanks to Señor Tamayo—knew how to hunt with a bow. Besides, I wished to test the effectiveness of this Mexica weapon. I blackened my face with mud from the edge of the Lake.

Macitoc, a well-formed Mexica of middle height and one of Mocte-cuzoma's retainers, presented me with a short hunting spear, three wooden bows and ten stone-tipped arrows fletched with the black feathers of carrion birds. Unlike most of the pipiltin, who could not live without their feathered finery, Macitoc looked like a hunter. All he wore was his maxtlatl loincloth and a green stone in his lower lip— he was pleased that I wished to hunt like a Mexica. He caressed the black feathers of the arrows and spoke a single word, "*Miquitzli.*"

At this time, I could understand few of his words but his meaning was clear. *Miquitzli* is their word for death.

Reverently he touched the mud-covered scars of my face and spoke slowly that I might understand. "*We not like the others.*"

I wondered at his meaning as I flexed all of the bows. I chose the strongest although it did not compare with the one Señor Tamayo had fashioned from horn and wood. I flexed the weapons and I could see why cotton padding stopped Mexican arrows. If the Mexica had known the Moorish art of weaponry, their arrows would have pen-etrated not only our cotton but also our armor.

●●●

With a whoop and a shout and a blaring of conches, the line of In-dios surged forward. At first nothing happened and, I started to believe that the island had long since been hunted out. Then a hare—a large one—with protruding golden eyes, hopped from the cover. The animal stopped with his ears raised in disquiet. Moctecuzoma, to whom the right of first blood belonged, tossed a feathered dart with his beau-tifully carved atlatl. The hare was pierced through-and-through and whined like a baby. Despite the trailed dart and a ribbon of blood, the animal dragged itself into the brush.

An attendant jumped up to recover the hare but Moctecuzoma stopped him with a slash of his hand—he didn't wish to alert other beasts of our presence. Then there was a cracking of brush and—where there had been nothing—animals bounded and darted everywhere. Most were rabbits and hares but there was the occasional ciervo, a small wolf they call coyotl and *I* even a gato—a spotted wildcat. Arrows and darts flew and some of the beasts were struck but continued to rush on, doubling back at the edge of the island. One of my arrows struck a small-antlered ciervo behind the ribs and another hit the gato in his flank. I missed the coyotl but, despite the fact that the beast was running at full speed, Moctecuzoma neatly skewered him with a throwing dart. The beast, without slowing down, bit the dart in two. Both pieces of the bloody dart were found lying on the earth, later, but the coyotl was also found, dead and piled up in a bush.

A strange beast ran close to me. Dropping my bow, I struck with my spear and pinned it to the ground. The creature was fierce and hissed in fury but I leaned on the spear, not permitting it to strike me. Its snarls weakened as it died. I observed the animal in wonder. It was not large, but had needle-sharp teeth. It had whitish fur and the long naked tail of a rat.

"What is it?" I asked.

Macitoc, with six bloody rabbits and hares dangling from his waist, strode over and explored the creature's belly. Under folds of skin, eight pink and naked babies squirmed. Their eyes were covered by skin and their mouths were fastened to the creature's teats. Macitoc, laughing, pulled one off, threw it to the earth and ground it under his foot.

"*Tlacuatzin.*" He pulled off a second and offered it to me. For a moment I was confused but then I too crushed it into the earth. Macitoc chanted and, between us, we killed the last six. Clearly this *Tlacuatzin* was big magic and the killing of its offspring was imbued with importance.

The beaters arrived and searched through the bush, following the blood-trails of wounded animals. Twenty animals, including the wild-cat and two ciervos, were recovered. We then repositioned ourselves as two other drives were conducted. Each drive produced fewer animals but I was able to kill a large green and scaly lagarto—three cubits in length—with great wattles on its throat. Macitoc slew a deadly cascabel that he nearly stepped on. He also killed an armored animal that had neither teeth nor eyes and had the size and appearance of a fast-moving tortoise. For the rest of the afternoon, we simply watched as Moctecuzoma ordered his people to set up nets and drive animals to them.

"Are you not concerned," I asked Moctecuzoma, "that you will deplete this island of its game?"

The Emperor smiled his sad smile. "My ancestors have hunted this island for generations. *Huitzilopotchli*—the god of the hunt—has promised us that if the island is hunted no more than once a year and, if we give him an abundance of victims, there will always be many animals to honor him. I know it appears that we capture everything but the god is good, and always replenishes the island."

"Do all of your subjects respect the island?"

"Most Mexica respect the gods and would never dare trespass on one the god's reserves. It may be difficult for you to understand this—for you yourself are a teotl—but, in my land, there are some evil men who have no belief. If my guards should catch them killing their game, they receive especially worthy rewards."

●●●

Along with the game we had slain, we returned to *Tenochtitlan*. That night we had a special feast, eating the harvest of the hunt. The flesh of the liebres, conejos y ciervos had been sliced from the bone, covered with spicy salsa chocolatl—*molé*—and served on tortillas. We even supped on my great lizard—its flesh was white and, when seasoned by peppers, was tasty. I was offered meat of my sacred *tlacuatzin*—I was hesitant to eat it but found it to taste of sweet and tender but overly fat pork. Portions of the gato and coyotl were served and, despite the fact that my belly was full, I had to taste them. Both were quite delicious but, then again, they were covered in red and green chiles and fried tomates.

Chapter 9

Over time I became more familiar with the Mexican tongue and was even able to form simple sentences in Nahuatl. It was therefore politic that I attempt conversation with Moctecuzoma and the other captive chieftains during those times I was ordered to guard them. I did this out of interest and to counteract the actions of some of the other guards. Many of our Castilians were simple men who detested the pretense that they were attending to the needs of a sovereign prince. These soldiers insulted Moctecuzoma by making water in front of him, passing foul smelling wind and making crude gestures with their hands. Moctecuzoma gave two chalchihuitl to one of these men so that he might be grateful and show more respect. Instead, this low man, thinking that he might gain even more wealth, passed even more gas in the face of the emperor and left a great turd on his throne.

Despite my feelings about Moctecuzoma I did none of these things. Instead I tried to show him more respect than I truly felt. I also had many questions about his faith and the history of his people.

"Is it not wrong to sacrifice human beings?" I asked.

Moctecuzoma looked at me without blinking. "Is it wrong to sacrifice the grain of centli to grind into meal? Is it wrong to sacrifice the guajolote for the sake of our children's food? You teotoh kill in battle but do not honor the gods—you waste lives, honor and meat. A slave is no more than the property of his master but, when he goes to a flowery death, he is a striped-one—*uauanti*. When his heart is torn free, he is transfigured and becomes a *cuauhtecatl*—a sacred being. Thus, you can see, it is an honor for a slave to receive such a death."

"Quite an honor...but do these slaves go willingly to the gods?"

"Yes, except those who are from godless lands."

I asked an obvious question, "If a flowery death is such an honor, why do not your lords and priests and—for that matter—*you* volunteer?"

Moctecuzoma had an answer. "If it should be required, I will joyously accept. For now the gods are satisfied with my sacrifice. Do you not see my scars?" He proudly showed me old and fresh wounds on his earlobes and legs then lifted up his robe and showed me the wounds on his penis. "They are the badges of my *teohpouhcococ*."

At this point I was at a loss. I knew that the word *teotl* meant god and that *teo* meant godlike or sacred things. Yet I had also learned that the word *teopohua* meant to suffer pain and affliction. I tried to understand.

"Is pain godlike?"

He was confused by my question. "Pain is of the gods."

"Do the gods want for man to suffer?"

Moctecuzoma understood. "The gods rejoice in death, grief and pain just as they rejoice in life and pleasure."

Burgos, Castilla-León

"Here, Padre Mendoza, we see their logic. In that all things were of the gods, the gods must rejoice in them all. If they gave life they also demanded death. The Mexica were just helping them out. When I was guarding Cacama, the rightful ruler of *Texcoco*, he tried to explain it in another way. Cacama, like many of his ancestors, fancied himself as a poet and sang this song to me:

> *Ehecatl* blows the ruinous dust
> Many flowers
> Will I meet my grandparents again?
> In dark *Mictlan*
> All of the spears are broken
> The crystal shatters
> The blossom fades
> The Centli ear withers
> The Quetzal feather tears
> The Coyotl Warrior laughs
> with his woman
> The Ocelotl knight shouts
> his triumph
> but all must
> marry the Earth
> The soil is moldering flesh.
> Rain, the blood of victims
> The sun in its last cycle
> *Anahuac, ee-yaa, Anahuac*."

"I must say, Your Grace, that the Mexicans were no optimists. It's small wonder that Cortés tipped them over so easily."

"Yes," the old man agreed, "although they were successful enough over their Indio enemies."

Mendoza tapped his fingers on the table. "I'm wondering about the linguistic aspects. The Mexican word for divine things *teo* is suspiciously like the Latin *deo*. Do you not find it surprising that the meaning in both languages is exactly the same? Is it possible that there is a connection? Is it possible that Roman mariners visited Nueva España and left the nativos with the legacy of civilization, architecture and even, I might say, a taste for public homicide?"

"An excellent question, Padre Mendoza—it's possible, of course, that the similarities are entirely coincidental. On the other hand, the possibility of ancient maritime exchange cannot be ruled out. Another possibility is that both Latin and Nahuatl derived from a primordial tongue. Even though centuries may have passed, certain important words—especially words for God—may have come through virtually unchanged."

"Perhaps the language spoken before the attempted construction of the Tower of Babel..."

"Quite so, Padre Mendoza."

The Emperor continued his explanation, "I climb the mountain—*Coatepec*—and, with the sharpened bones of lion and tiger, I lance the skin of my ears, legs, lips, tongue and my godlike tepolli and sprinkle the droplets of the sacred blood on *Techcatl*, the altar of sacrifice. For, you see, the gods are thirsty for blood, especially the blood of the Uei Tlatloani."

I changed the direction of my questioning, "Where do the Mexica come from? Why do they rule over so many others?"

Moctecuzoma told a story that I heard with variations, all over Mexico.

"We came from *Aztlan*, in the north—it is the island of herons, the place of the seven caves—the place of the *Azteca*. We came as shapeless barbarians, dog people—*Chichimeca*. We marched to the south guided by holy men. We came to a place we call *Tula*, wherein there is the sacred mountain *Coatepec*. On the mountain suffered the goddess of the earth, *Coatlique*, who was heavily pregnant. Her numerous sons and daughters took offense for Coatlique was a widow and her impregnation filled them with shame. Her sons and daughters slew her—cut off her head. From her corpse was born *Huitzilopotchli*—the Hummingbird God—the god of the sun and of war. *Huitzilopotchli* was born full-grown and armed—born full of vengeance—he attacked all 400 of his brothers and sisters and he cast them into the sky where they became the southern stars. His strongest sister was *Coyolxauhqui*—she of the golden bells. She was strong but *Huitzilopotchli* prevailed, cut off her head and threw it into the night sky. There it shines as the moon with the golden light of her bells. *Huitzilopotchli* chopped the rest of her body into pieces and threw it from the heights of *Coatepec*, to the foot of the mountain. He then came to the people and led those who would follow him to the shores of this Lake. The others—the *Tolteca*—mourned for the slaughtered *Coyolxauhqui*. They stayed at *Tula*."

"And the Mexica, My Prince?"

"In *Anahuac*, the people—the Mexica—were not welcome. Hungry, ill clothed we wandered the shores of the Lake. The King of *Culhua* took mercy on us and gave us a poor place in the marsh. We fought his battles, gained him much territory and the king was greatly pleased. In his gratitude, the King gave his most precious possession—his only daughter—to be the bride of Mexica. The Mexica, in homage, paid the King and his country a great compliment. They gave the girl to *Huitzilopotchli* and to the high god, *Xipe Totec*."

"*Xipe Totec*," I said, "I know of this God from my woman. He is the Flayed..."

"Yes," Moctecuzoma continued, "he is the Flayed God who demands human skin. The King of the *Colhua* arrived late to the wedding ceremony and failed to recognize his daughter in her new divine form. Then he saw her, dancing on the summit of our first holy mountain. Her fresh skin was worn—inside out—by the highest of our teopixquia. To the sound of drums, whistles and conches the priest sang, danced and cavorted in front of our gods."

His voice dropped to a whisper. "The king of *Colhua* must have been mad for he ordered his warriors, who were not our equals, to wage war against us. Even so, at first things went against us and we were driven from our place by the lake. Unlike the king of *Colhua*, however, we *did* honor the gods. *Huitzilopotchli* came to his people and told us what we must do. He said that we must look for a great nopal cactus—one bearing the nest of an eagle devouring a snake. We would recognize the place by the many colored feathers of the birds that the eagle had devoured. We were also to look for two junipers and a spring bubbling water of two colors. When we found this place, the

Mexica must settle.

We found the place on this very island, here on Lake Texcoco. Here one group founded *Tlatelolco* and another group went a little south and founded *Tenochtitlan*. Here the Mexica were safe and waged many wars. In memory of the past, we raised a new *Coatepec* and consecrated it to *Huitzilopotchli* and *Tlaloc*—we put the image of the butchered *Coyolxauhqui* at the foot of this mountain. Because we did these things, the Tenochca defeated the *Culhua*, which is why we now call ourselves *Culhua Mexica*. For the honor of *Huitzilopotchli* and all of the gods, we defeated many others, including our neighbors, the *Tlatelolco*—we are now all one people."

Chapter 10

Cortés hoped to bleed an intact Mexico. To this end he made Moctecuzoma's captivity as pleasant as possible. He and other officers attended him in the mornings, asking if he had any orders. Afterwards, Moctecuzoma gave audience to his subjects who had petitions or who had lawsuits to settle. All of these transactions were recorded in colorful pictures, which is the Mexican manner of writing although these pictures are much given to obscenity. After all of his business was transacted Moctecuzoma enjoyed watching us engage in our routine military practice. It is in some ways surprising that Moctecuzoma—who had once been a warrior—showed no apprehension at our martial activities. He seemed to enjoy watching the Spanish military arts and never once did I hear him comment on the superiority of Castilian armor or weapons.

That was all to the good because the Caudillo was taking no chances. He didn't want us to get soft or bored—we drilled relentlessly and practiced mock combat. Even so there were disputes over gold and women and fights broke out. These unplanned for combats were more deadly than duels for someone, in his anger, would strike out at another, and then—there on the tiles—was a bleeding corpse. Formal duels were the result of boredom and the aggravation of being in close quarters. Cortés forbade them, of course, but there was no preventing them although they were conducted in secret. Once two of the Captains—Olid and de León—came to blows over some trivial matter. De León cut Olid across the back of the hand, which was no great thing, but after that they were no longer friends.

Frequently Cortés and Moctecuzoma would play a game called *totoloque* that is played with golden balls aimed at a target of gold. Bets were placed and both men cheated but it did not matter, for both men gave their gains to their followers. Now that he seemed to be getting on in such friendly terms with Moctecuzoma, Cortés announced the discovery of the treasury—he showed no surprise.

"These things belong to you, Malinche," he said. "I only ask that you leave those things that belong to the gods. I wish the treasure were greater but I have given much of it to you, already, in the form of gifts."

"I thank you, my Prince. We will only take those things we need."

●●●

Doña Francesca spoke quietly to me: "Rodrigo, you and I need to help one another. Word has it that Cortés won't permit us to take gold or jewels but he will let us remove feathers and mantles."

"What do you want me to do, steal some of the precious metal?"

"I wouldn't ask you to do anything that foolish. When the room is opened to the men, I want for both of us to enter and, working as quickly as possible, choose those feathered things of the finest workmanship. If my guess is right, we will get most of the better things. All the rest of the men want is more cushioning for their pallets, and they will be paying little attention to the quality of the feather work."

"Why should we go to the trouble?"

"It's because these beautiful things are worth *more* than their weight in gold."

I was perplexed. "Other than diamonds and rubies, few things are worth more than gold—certainly not a few fancy feathers."

"You're wrong, Rodrigo. The wealthy in Europe have their share of gold—what they don't have is this wonderful Mexican art. Unless I miss my mark, the things in the treasure room will be the best of the best. When the room was first opened I looked at the mats and tlamatlis—*magnificent*. There are designs and idols formed from thousands of beautiful feathers sewn more closely and with more art and care than did God use on the living birds. There are entire mantles made up of the green, blue and orange feathers of hummingbirds and finches—none of the soldiers, including Cortés, paid the slightest attention."

I wasn't convinced. "The men will enter that room like a plague of locusts and they'll grab everything for their personal comfort. I doubt we'll get more than a handful of things."

"I've approached some of our men and asked them if they would take a few extra items for me. Still, I need your help."

I must admit to being offended. My first thought was that Francesca had come to me out of friendship but now recognized that she was using me as she was using others. My feelings must have shown on my face.

She tried to suppress a smile. "You are *hurt*, Rodrigo."

"Absolutely not. We're just acquaintances."

She waited before going on. "Let me tell you something so that you don't misunderstand—my coming to you is very different than my going to others but why shouldn't I take advantage of male foolishness?"

"And my foolishness?"

"No, Rodrigo. Until this moment I had no suspicion that you thought about me at all. I came to you because you are the one man here whom I trust and I came to you to ask you to be my partner."

"Partner?"

"Before I ever left Villa Rica I prepared for potential valuables. Totonacs have built me secret storerooms in their country and I have engaged tamanes to transport our treasure there."

"Can you trust them?"

"With my life. They think I am a priestess and they fear my magic."

I was ashamed to ask the next question, "What's...in it for me?"

"Twenty-five percent."

"Done."

Burgos, Castilla-León

Two of the guards—one of whom was the grinning Ruben Villalobos—entered the room, bearing platters of food. Without fanfare, the skeletal Bishop helped himself to chopped meat, chiles, boiled squash and steamed potatoes. He poured liquid butter over everything. Mendoza, driven by hunger, did the same.

"Lunch, too," Mendoza said without looking up. "What drives you to such generosity?"

The ancient man chewed contentedly. "I'm a compassionate fellow, Padre. To be certain your efforts to leave my service tested my good nature but time is too precious to bear a grudge."

"Perhaps I have misjudged you, Your Grace."

The robe-covered skeleton looked up from his meal and—slowly—smiled his bony smile. "The cook certainly took her time, Padre, but you know how these Indios are."

"They have no work ethic." Mendoza agreed, as he swallowed a chunk of fiery meat. He followed up the meat with a flagon of red wine—he drained the cup. "Where are the servants who served our morning meal—not that I have any complaints?"

"I gave them the afternoon off. Tom—my Englishman—needs to husband his strength."

"Of course, Episcopus, a man in his condition *should* save his strength. In my lay opinion, he should be in an infirmary or, better yet, in a charnel house."

"You overstate the case, Padre, but he must take care of himself."

"Why might I ask?"

"I have decided to make him one of your keepers—the one who delivers your meals."

"*What?*"

"He needs the money for his physicians."

Mendoza considered arguing but, instead, poured another glass of wine and drained it down without stopping.

"I trust you are not a borracho, Padre."

"Far from it, but the wine cools the fire in the meat. Perhaps—if I am permitted a recommendation—your cook could go easier on the chiles next time."

The old man helped himself to more meat. "You always request the same thing, and my answer hasn't changed, Padre."

Mendoza finished another cup of wine and shoveled more meat and chile into his mouth. "Don't get me wrong. Your cook's art is great and I would certainly rather have this than nothing."

"Excellent, Padre Mendoza, I think you can be accommodated. Chiles—cultivated in Cuba—will be added to your daily diet."

With the Emperor's full consent, the vault was reopened—the soldiers and some of the women crowded into the room. Most of the men did nothing more than ogle the piles of golden idols and ornaments. Francesca and I, however, went right to work, removing beautiful works of feather work and passing them to nervous tamanes waiting outside in the corridor. Quickly, however, the soldiers turned from the gold and started to take as many feathered mats and mantles as they could fit under their arms—some even returned for second and third loads. I saw that a few of the men, despite the watchful eyes of our Captains, were using their collection of mantles to cover their theft of treasure. Mostly they pilfered small items that they secreted under their armor. Some of the officers and guards did the same.

By the time it was over, and adding the things that Francesca received from admirers, we had seventy-six tlamatlis, fifty-eight mats, and *all* of the quetzal tail plumes—soldados got all of the rest. Hundreds of packs of mats and tlamatlis were trundled off to the various quarters. The treasure room was then sealed again and a guard posted to prevent additional thievery.

I was still worried. "I hope your tamanes make it out."

"They should. They are dressed as slaves and their bundles are loaded in baskets. No one will bother them."

●●●

Cortés was dissatisfied with Moctecuzoma. "My Prince, you have already sworn your fealty to our Emperor, Carlos I, and it is now time to receive the same promise from your governors and chieftains. I will record their oaths both in your writing as well as our own."

"Malinche. I will call my Lords together."

It took days for the chieftains to arrive from the various parts of his Empire. Many had traveled day and night to make this appointment—an order by the Uei Tlatloani was taken seriously. When they arrived, many appeared haggard and some were ill. When they were all assembled, Moctecuzoma made a speech—a speech that Malinche prepared for him.

"The God who once ruled this land has now returned. The white teotoh have come over the Eastern Sea and have been sent by their master to reclaim his realm. I have sworn my loyalty to these Beings and demand that all of you do the same and give your annual tribute to them."

The pipiltin, many of whom lived on the periphery of the empire, were clearly shocked by the change in the order of things but not one raised a voice in protest. Such was the respect that they held Moctecozoma that—despite mutterings—they swore their fealty to their new emperor, Carlos I, as was duly documented and endorsed by the royal notary, Godoy. The document, of course, was to be sent to España as soon as possible for Cortés was determined to inform the King of our accomplishments.

"Now that your Lords have sworn their oath to Carlos I, it is well that they send gifts to our emperor."

"It will be done," proclaimed Moctecuzoma. "I will add the treasure of Axayacatl."

●●●

Treasure poured in from the empire, including silver, gold and the various commodities in which the taxes were usually paid. I visualized the Mexican tax collectors exacting tribute in their usual rapacious fashion. Contrary to Church law and contrary to what we had promised the Totonac chieftains, we were not putting a stop to this cruel taxation; we were now responsible for it.

On the other hand, scruples make poor fare for conquistadores and it was now time to reap the reward for all of our sacrifices. Cortés announced the subdivision of the gold, silver and precious gems. The royal treasury, which had been resealed after the removal of the mantles, was reentered and its full wealth was revealed to the entire army.

Most of the value was in gold although there were also silver and beautiful things made of chalchihuitl and pearls. The gold was in many forms—present were native nuggets and grains as well as solid ingots.

Other golden items were in the form of animals, toys, birds, insects, and flowers—all of which were exquisitely fashioned. Also there were golden and misshapen idols depicting all of the devils with which we were by now familiar. Some of these were of gods and men copulating and performing other disgusting acts with one another for—as the entire world knows—the Mexica had no concept of mortal sin. The gold was valued at one hundred and sixty-two thousand pesos de oro and the silver at five hundred thousand ducats more. Jewelry was more difficult to value.

"In its present form, the treasure will be difficult to carry," the Caudillo said. "We'll need to melt it down into transportable bricks."

Francesca, who was attending our meeting, disagreed. "Señor Cortés, many of these articles are entirely unique. In Castilla, they'll be worth far more in their present form than as featureless ingots. Besides, I know that you are concerned about the judgment of history—how can you consider destroying these marvelous things?"

"That is exactly the point, my Lady. I *am* concerned about history. We will be accursed if we don't render these things of the Devil into more worthy forms. Our men also need to receive their shares—the division of the spoils in their present form will be impossible."

"Impossible or not," Francesca said, "I prefer my share in its present state."

Cortés glared at her with a look of lust and hatred. "As you will, Doña Francesca."

Gems were picked from the gold and silver jewelry and the metals were melted down into portable ingots, each imprinted with the king's seal. Taking Francesca's lead, I made certain that my share was kept in its original state. I selected two especially evil-looking demons and a toy with moveable wheels. It was strange, I thought, that the Indios had wheels for their toys but not for transport.

Cortés spoke to me as if I were his servant. "I trust that you have not taken more than *your* share."

"No, I haven't," I said.

Cortés and his treasurer made their calculations. The Royal Fifth was subtracted and then Cortés subtracted his fifth and another large share for his investment. Quantities were put aside for Governor Velásquez, Francesca de la Barca and the other investors. The Caudillo's friends and Captains also received large shares. The caballeros, arquebusiers, and crossbowmen all received double shares—the common soldiers received only one hundred pesos apiece. Although I was an officer and a Regidor, Cortés allotted me only two hundred and fifty pesos.

"You have too much gold, Rodrigo. We'll melt it down and give you your appropriate share."

I spoke for the others. "One hundred pinches pesos for men who have suffered and died for you—keep my share of the gold. Your hunger, Caudillo, is greater than mine."

He smiled back, addressing all of his angry soldiers. "The division has been entirely fair and entirely according to our agreements—agreements which, I must remind all of you, have been duly recorded with your signatures and marks. But, if anyone here is dissatisfied, I'll gladly share my fifth with him."

Cortés reckoned that he had subdued his army as thoroughly as he'd subdued Moctecuzoma. He didn't expect any takers—he was dead wrong.

"I take you at your word, Caudillo," I shouted. "I'll keep the items I have selected. Their...excess... value can be subtracted from *your* share."

"It would be *you*," Cortés snarled.

Emboldened by my resistance, Mexía, the treasurer, spoke up. "Gifts that we have been receiving from the Tenochca seem to be missing and nowhere do I see the treasure from *Cholula*. By my inventory even many of the items that we first found in the room are now missing. The value of the treasure as it now exists is scarcely over two hundred thousand pesos de oro. By my calculations the value should be closer to seven hundred and fifty thousand. I don't wish to be impertinent but *where* is the rest of it, Caudillo?"

Cortés' eyes drilled through Mexía, and his words were soft but dangerous. "Who are *you* to question my division of the spoil, Señor Mexía? Some of the gifts, as you well know, were given to me personally and not to the army. The spoil of *Cholula* has been sent to Villa Rica and will be divided later."

An old veteran, Cristbal Piñeda, spoke—Piñeda was afraid of nothing, especially not Hernán Cortés. This was his mistake because Cortés later had him murdered. "Your *personal* property?"—Piñeda, as well as some of the other men, were in open rebellion—"*All* of the gifts and *all* of the spoil belong to the King and the army. Also, Caudillo, I see no provision for those who have died for you—wives and children will be left destitute. You, my trusted Caudillo, are a thief and a swine."

Cortés bristled, "*All* of *my* treasure has been returned to the coast."

"Convenient, señor." Mexía was now really angry and showed it. "Our emperor should be pleased."

"You think you can threaten me, Gonzalo?"

Mexía went on, mindless of Cortés' anger, "Where are the other items?"

"I wouldn't know. Maybe the men have lifted some of it."

"Might then I suggest a search of the men and their quarters—the search should include *all* of your Captains." Mexía knew something. "A search of our facilities in Villa Rica is also in order."

"You insult your fellow officers."

"*Insult, Caudillo?*" Mexía bellowed. "Then why is it that three of our men—men who stayed *here* during our hunting excursion—reported seeing your noble Captain—Don Javier de la Concha—enter the chamber and leave with gold. Is it possible, Caudillo, this is why you were so determined to go hunting and so determined to leave Javier here to *protect* our treasure?"

De la Concha, who had been standing to one side of Cortés, leapt forward knocking Mexía to the ground. I drew Bebidor and slapped him across the face with it—*hard*. De la Concha, falling back, drew his weapon and charged me. He was good but he was also wild with rage—I sliced his nose and then his throat. I knocked his weapon aside and kicked him hard in the side of his leg. He crashed to the ground.

"*Leave off, Rodrigo!*" Cortés shouted.

"*I'll have the bastard's gizzard!*"

Alvarado, Olid and even de León drew their weapons against me. Cortés never moved.

"Do as you're ordered! Let him go!"

I held the point of my sword at de la Concha's throat just where the chin meets the soft skin of the neck—Bebidor tingled in my hand. I looked up and saw the Captains arrayed against me.

I laughed, "One-by-one or all at once, it makes no difference to me. Either way de la Concha is a dead man. Does anyone here challenge me? *Caudillo, mi compadre*"—I drew out '*compadre*' and trilled the 'r'—"maybe you? Yes, my noble Caudillo, protector of our lives and fortunes, by all means *you!*"

I heard Francesca's whisper, "Go easy, Rodrigo."

The Captains were silent but Cortés snapped, "Put up your weapons, señores. We will have no more dueling in my camp."

As one, the swords crashed back into their sheaths. I kicked Concha's sword away and jerked him to his feet. "A few more fights with me, Javier, and you'll have as many scars on your face as I do. Now, Mexía tells us that you have lifted some of the treasure. I, for one, would like to see it. I would also like to know the names of the others."

Cortés looked unblinking into Concha's eyes. "It was only me." Concha lied. "I took a necklace for my amante." From under his armor he produced a necklace of gold and pearls.

"*Ah-ha, señores!* Mexía was right and Concha here—one of our Captains and a man of *infinite* honor—is nothing more than a thief—a cheap thief, at that." I snatched the necklace and held it up for all to see. "Just a five hundred peso bauble for one of his many whores. I have no doubt, though"—I looked *through* Cortés—"that there are others and I have no doubt that there is a great deal more. The honorable man that you are Caudillo, I trust that you'll deal with at least this one ladrón, appropriately."

"I will, indeed," he hissed.

Chapter 11

Burgos, Castilla-León

"I hate to question your testimony, Your Grace, but it is scarcely credible that you were so combative with your Caudillo."

The old man sat deathly still and waited.

Mendoza, not knowing what do, decided to rephrase himself. "I'm not saying that you aren't courageous but, it has been a very long time and perhaps your memory fails you. After all, *he* did have the power to punish flagrant insubordination."

The scars on the Obispo's face flickered. "Perhaps you should read between my lines, Padre. At this point of our invasion, he did *not* have the power. Bickering was constant and flares of temper common. I remember my actions well because they were *my* actions but others were equally—to use your word—*insubordinate*. The army was held together only by fear and greed and not out of respect for Malinche. Many times, soldados—and even some of our Tlaxcaltec allies—challenged Cortés to his face. If he had hanged them all, our enemies would have mopped up the others between dawn and dusk."

"You must be wrong, Excelencia. Everything I read confirmed that he had tight control of the expedition from beginning to end."

"That is only because Cortés was there both at the *beginning* and at the *end*. Between these times, trouble followed Cortés like vultures follow a dying beast. Also, Padre, let me tell you about courage. I'm *not* a courageous man."

Mendoza sat speechless not knowing how to reply to such a revelation. "You have your faults, Obispo, but cowardice doesn't appear to be one of them."

"Oh but you're wrong, Padre. I know myself perfectly and I *am* a coward."

"Inconceivable."

"I have little fear of death, Mendoza. I really never have. It is *that* which you mistake for courage. My cowardice is of an entirely different variety but it is cowardice of a *particularly* despicable type."

"What...?"

"That is for you to ponder, Padre, for I will *never* tell you for, you see, I am too much a coward to reveal my cowardice."

Now it was Mendoza's turn to sit silently.

The old man went on to another subject. "Padre Mendoza, from your previous research, can you tell me what happened to the treasure of Axayacatl?"

"I can easily recollect what I wrote for it has been reported by many others, including Cortés, himself. Most of the treasure was lost during the retreat of La Noche Triste."

"And buried in the mud of the Lake?"

"Yes, Your Grace."

"And how is it then that—although most of his surviving soldiers were left destitute—Hernán Cortés became one of the wealthiest men in Europe?"

"I never really gave it much thought, Your Grace. Those in command usually profit from it."

"Especially Cortés. As Mexía reported the original treasure—not counting that of *Cholula* and other sources—amounted to over seven hundred and fifty thousand pesos de oro. When the treasury was opened for general viewing the value in metal was a little more than two hundred and twenty five thousand. The amount allocated to the men and Captains was fifty five thousand, all of which was held individually in their quarters. Francesca de la Barca's share was five thousand, which she also kept. The King's Fifth was forty five thousand and Cortés' fifth came to thirty six thousand and the monies to all other investors, including Don Diego and Cortés, himself, came to eighty four thousand. Thus we can see that Cortés' share of even the reduced amount of remaining treasure was seventy six thousand pesos de oro—a very nice investment, considering that most soldiers received only one hundred pesos. Of course, it was far worse than this—over five hundred thousand had disappeared into thin air and into Cortés own pocket. He, no doubt, shared some of this loot with Alvarado and, perhaps, Sandoval, Concha and Olid but no one else—including the King—ever saw any of it. By my estimation, Cortés—by this end of the Conquest—personally amassed a minimum of five hundred thousand pesos de oro. Even then his greed was not slated—he ordered that all gold taken from the treasure room must stay with the men—they were not to gamble it away or hide it away in the earth."

Mendoza seemed perplexed. "Why would he insist on this?"

"He reckoned that, by fair means or foul, he would come into possession of the small amount of gold that the men had managed to acquire. Francesca, however, outsmarted the fox, and smuggled all of her gold to Villa Rica. She purchased plain cotton mantles from *Tlatelolco*, wrapped her gold in them and paid Tlaxcaltec tamanes to transport it to the coast—I added my small amount of gold to hers."

Mendoza groomed his hair with his hand. "What could have happened to the rest of the treasure—*assuming*—that there really was unaccounted for gold?"

The old man looked Mendoza in the eye. "It is important that we document the truth precisely because there have been so many lies—Cortés, with the complicity of a few of his officers—of whom Sandoval, Olid and Alvarado were the most important—smuggled the treasure out of *Tenochtitlan* over a period of months. By the end of the Conquest, counting the treasure subsequently stolen from the men and the Indios and counting the value in slaves sold"—the Bishop did the mathematics in his head—"and adding the bribes for encomiendas and the tribute extorted from the peoples of Mexico, Cortés' personal profit could not have been less than one million and probably closer to *two million* pesos de oro."

Mendoza was not impressed. "I've heard it all before. His enemies accused him of this and worse—but—none of it stuck."

"I don't know about *that*, Padre. Cortés *was*, if you can recall, stripped of the office which he held most dear. Despite his delivering all of Mexico to the emperor, the governorship was turned over to others."

"Yes, Excelencia, it was turned over to men more corrupt than Cortés."

"I cannot deny it, Padre—my point is not that Cortés was a thief but that his greed had no limit. After La Noche Triste, as one of many sorry examples, he seized the small amount of gold that he previously gave to the men. Think of it—he told the men that they could take all that they could carry. Some of our soldiers weighed themselves down with gold and paid for it with their lives. Then, the gold-carriers, of which there were but few survivors, had to give it all back. Justice according to *Santo Hernán Cortés*."

With the Emperor's acquiescence to the looting of the Royal Treasury, the Conquest of Mexico would seem to be complete. There was one item that should have troubled us deeply, if we had not been so blind—Moctecuzoma showed no hint of a religious conversion. Despite our example, and the constant preachments of Cortés and our friars, he never wavered. The same mind-numbing faith that permitted us to take over his capital now threatened our entire enterprise.

"Malinche, it has been many days since I honored my gods. I must go to their shrines."

Our Caudillo refused his request. "They are demons, Great Prince, and you should worship at our altar."

Moctecuzoma's eyes flashed and he clinched his jaw. "I *must* honor my gods or my lands will wither."

Cortés felt the strength of Moctecuzoma's determination—he relented.

"You may go but in the company of teules. Should you attempt to escape you will be cut down at once. There must be no human sacrifice."

●●●

Moctecuzoma, attended by one hundred and fifty of his chieftains and a troop of us Castilians, was carried on his litter to the teocalli. A magnificently attired nobleman, carrying a golden standard, marched in the advance. Despite the Prince's imprisonment, his pipiltin and teopixquia treated him with all of the deference due his station. Reverently, they lifted him from his litter and helped him up the steps to the top of the Mosque. There were the usual smoking braziers of incense and the priests—overwhelmed by the long-hoped for presence of their Uei Tlatloani—jumped and danced as if they were mad.

There was fresh blood all over for, during the night, victims had died. Other living victims stood at the foot of the *Templo Mayor*—there were four men and three women—naked except for stripes of red and white paint. Their mouths were rouged red as if already filled with blood and their eyes were blackened with soot. I could not help but notice that one of the women had been at one time, quite beautiful. She was pitifully malnourished but still had full breasts and buttocks. She, as well as the others, was hypnotized by the barbaric music of drums and flutes. The victims danced to the rhythm, swinging their hips and shuffling their feet. Breasts bounced and swayed.

Padre Olmedo spoke, "You may pray, Moctecuzoma, but you must not take a life."

On his own teocalli, the Emperor was transformed. "*I will do the bidding of my gods!*"

The first victim, who was a tall thin fellow, started to mount the stairs. He stopped now and then to dance his mournful dance. Some of us surged forward to prevent the sacrifice—Olmedo waved us back.

"Do as you will, Moctecuzoma, but know that the Gates of Hell yawn wide for you."

Moctecuzoma, feeling his old power, paid no attention to Olmedo—deeply, he breathed in the fumes of the sacred copal. Transported—the Prince's body swayed to the music—victim and executioner danced the same dance. The skinny man reached the platform where he was given a feathered fan. In front of the green stone of *Techcatl* he continued to dance. The five black priests moved as one. They picked the man up and bent his back over the sacrificial stone. Four held his hands and feet and a fifth held his head back by his long hair. Moctecuzoma lifted the sacred knife and incised the skin of the lower chest from the left to the right—the man's cries were those of a beast. Moctecuzoma regarded the victim with something that looked like—*love*.

Moctecuzoma's hand thrust under the ribs and seized the living heart. Blood spurted as he sliced the vessels that bound the heart to the body. Triumphant, he lifted the heart to the sky. Blood welled up into the mumbling man's chest cavity and spilled over onto the under-lying stone. As Moctecuzoma placed the still-beating heart in the altar of *Huitzilopotchli* the priests threw the body down the stairs. The body tumbled all the way to the bottom and came to rest on the great disc of the goddess *Coyolxauhqui*—she who was dismembered by her own god-brother. The carcass rested on the sacred disc for moments before it was carried away by teopixquia who were gathered there for that purpose. Six remaining victims continued to sway and dance.

The pretty girl was the last to climb the mountain. She sang her song, stamped her pretty feet and danced before Techcatl. I decided to test my friendship with the Prince.

"Lord Moctecuzoma, your god has eaten his fill. Give me the girl."

At the sound of my voice Moctecuzoma seemed to rouse from his trance. "You want me to make the sacrifice in your honor? A teoltl you may be but *Huitzilopotchli* is far greater than you."

"Malinche himself wants the girl alive."

"He cannot have her for, as you can see, she is already one of the *uauantin*, and the god thirsts for her blood."

I thought quickly. "Then why did *Tezcatlipoca* come to me in the night with the message that I am to take the last *uauantin* to Malinche."

Confusion spread over his face. "You blaspheme!"

"Then why does not *Tezcatlipoca* strike me dead?"

For moments no one moved—I thought I had won—then, in one abrupt motion, the dirty teopixquia swept the girl up and spread-eagled her across the bloody stone. Before I could move, Moctecuzoma ripped her open and tore out her heart. Moctecuzoma presented her heart to the sun, as the girl lifted her head to look at me with bewildered eyes. Then, like the first six, she was tossed down the steps where she cartwheeled to the bottom. My anger was great and with a quavering voice I cursed the Emperor:

"*Oh, Moctecuzoma and all of you teopixquia*"—I motioned toward the priests—"*you have disobeyed the God of Mictlan. Woe be unto thee!*"

All of the preachments of Padre Olmedo never produced the effect of my few words—Moctecuzoma, in all of his finery and with blood up to his elbows, quailed before me.

●●●

Moctecuzoma called Cortés to his chambers. Knowing what the audience must be for, I accompanied him. The Prince flinched when he saw me. I wasn't surprised. Rumors were spreading that he had been speaking evil of me and now called me *Chichtli*—the owl—an unholy spirit who flies by night.

"Malinche." He pointed at me. "I do not want Chichtli anywhere near me. Keep him from my sight and keep him far away. Better yet, *kill* him."

"Why is that?" Cortes looked surprised.

His face was taut with fear. "Spirits visit him by night. He is a *witch*."

"I'm sorry to hear you say that, My Lord. Rodrigo always speaks highly of you."

"He has bewitched you, Malinche and he is trying to bewitch me. Get him away!"

Cortés shrugged. "As you wish, my Lord. We wouldn't want him doing any witchery on you, would we?"

"Do not laugh at me, Malinche—I am not a child—I know what I am speaking of. His power is great and he has already bewitched Cacama of *Texcoco*."

"How so?" Cortés clucked.

"Cacama, who has borne you good will, now plans to attack you and me. Chichtli's sorcery has twisted Cacama's mind."

"Perhaps I can reason with him?"

"It will not be necessary, Malinche—my own priests and sorcerers have laid the necessary spells. We have lured Cacama into a false meeting and my people have taken him prisoner. Today, he will be brought to you bound in nequen as if he were but a slave. Do with him as you wish but, if you do not want more treachery, get Chichtli far from here."

The Caudillo took advantage of Moctecuzoma's fear.

"Continue the translation." Cortés nodded at the nearby Doña Marina. "I want our friends to learn how teules deal with witches." Cortés turned to me. "Rodrigo, how many times must I warn you that you are not to speak to ghosts and play with magic?"

"Many times, Caudillo." A ripple of disquiet passed through the room.

"Still you disobey me. Do you have any explanation?"

"It cannot be helped—the gods come to me by night—sometimes they only whisper in my ear"—Moctecucoma was stunned—"and sometimes they come to me in their full glory. *Tezcatlipoca* is beautiful and sparkles like a mirror but *Huitzilopotchli* is terrible beyond description. He wears a belt of bloody heads and a cloak of human skin—his face is full of wrath."

Moctecuzoma's voice was barely a whisper. "*What....what do they say?*"

"*Woe be unto thee, Moctecuzoma*. They say that I must tell you. Woe be unto thee and thy descendents for thou hast committed the sin of disobedience."

Moctecuzoma squeezed his eyes shut. "Get him away from here, Malinche."

"Absolutely, My Prince. You are confined to your quarters, Chichtli, and you must stop making spells. And now, My Prince, I would like to talk to you about Cacama."

●●●

The talk must have been productive because Cacama was brought to Cortes in the bottom of a canoe wrapped like a birthday present. With Cacama as prisoner, the Caudillo became kingmaker and ordered a new king—the brother of Cacama—to rule *Texcoco*. Still, despite his fall from grace, Cacama was thought to know where there was hidden treasure. Cortés ordered Pedro de Alvarado to return to *Texcoco* with Cacama as his hostage.

A little gold in the form of grains, nuggets and idols was located but Alvarado reckoned that Cacama was playing him false. Alvarado put him to the test by pouring scalding oil over his hands—Cacama became more talkative. By these and similar methods Alvarado extracted even more wealth from *Texcoco*. Cortés was pleased and rewarded Alvarado for his initiative.

Burgos, Castilla-León

Padre Mendoza stopped and pulled at the ends of his mustache before speaking. "I have written at length about the affair of Alvarado, Cacama and the gold. Later, there was even an ecclesiastical inquiry into the business—Alvarado was exonerated. At least one witness said that Cacama returned to *Tenochtitlan* with no sign of injury. Yet you disagree."

"I do. I saw the injuries myself and, at the time, there was no attempt to deny it. Alvarado said it was an...accident. Alvarado had a sense of humor."

"Why must you assume the negative against one of your most stalwart Captains."

"It's because I know Alvarado and it is because of the rumors floating through camp—I not only heard that Alvarado found a great fortune in gold but that most of this treasure was hidden away from the King and from the men."

"But to condemn your Captain, Your Grace..."

"Yes, I condemn him and I condemn the rest of us too. You never knew Alvarado but even *you* have traced his trail of blood. He was like a child never touched by the guiding hand of a parent. He was—at the same time—both innocent and terrible. Have you seen such children, Padre?"

"Children are innocent."

The old man's scars were livid in the flickering light. "Young ones are often the worst."

"But...."

"At one point in my life I had time on my hands, and liked to fish off the rocks of on the coast. When sitting there—with nothing better to do—I watched the children playing. The game was always the same—crabs skittered around the rocks and hid in the crevices—children, like cats, are excited by movement and would try to capture them."

"Certainly, children are playful."

"Yes, but the crabs were fast, and rarely was a child quick enough to capture one. At this point the game would *always* change. In their frustration, the children would strike the crabs with stones or batter them with sticks. This technique was more successful and some crabs were crippled. When crabs were disabled their fates were certain. The children would either kill them in novel fashions or they would take their pleasure in dislocating the limbs. Oftentimes, they would let the creatures survive with only two or three limbs so as to extend the torment."

"Crabs do not feel pain. If I thought they could I couldn't boil them alive."

"That's not the point, Padre. Children *are* into torment. Have you not seen them pitting one tribe of ants against another or feeding disabled grasshoppers to spiders. Do you not know what children—if left to their own devices—are capable of doing to a nest of young birds or to a litter of mice?"

"I do *not*."

"You haven't been observant, Padre, or perhaps it is because your relationship with children has been directed to...other things..."

Mendoza straightened his back. "I am a man of God and refuse to see evil where only innocence exists."

"Then I'll get back to my point. We are all born barbarians who must be softened by the hand of our mothers. In Alvarado's case—for reasons I don't understand—he remained a child and, as such, was an incredible monster. He reveled in pain and he enjoyed the anguish he inflicted on the Indios. His eyes would light up whenever he tortured a man or merely abused him. Alvarado tortured Cacama, Padre. It was part of his nature."

Chapter 12

"I have been appraising our situation." Cortés spoke to his assembled officers. "Thanks to you, my loyal followers, we have achieved the conquest of Mexico and now all that we must do is to consolidate our gains and reap our reward. It's important that we explore the country for gold and agriculture and exert our presence in other areas of the Empire." He went on, "Captain Velásquez de León, my friend, I would like you to take one hundred and thirty troops to the mouth of the *Rio Coatzacualco*, sixty leagues to the south of Villa Rica."

"*Si, Caudillo.*"

"I want you to search the area for a good harbor. Once you determine the best location, I want to establish a settlement." I smiled to myself for de León had been one of the strongest Governor's men. Now, against all of Don Diego's interests, de León would be setting up his own colony.

Cortés went on, "In addition to protecting yourself from the indígenos I want you to explore the land for gold." Again I smiled to myself. It was *always* gold.

"Rodrigo?"

"Yes, Caudillo."

"Stop daydreaming. I have tasks for you, too."

"I wasn't..."

Cortés wasn't listening. "Moctecuzoma tells me that most of his gold was mined in *Zacatula*. I have decided to send an expedition there commanded by Gonzalo de Umbria. Pick four other worthless soldiers to go with him."

I couldn't believe the order. De Umbria's foot had been amputated in Villa Rica by order of the Caudillo.

"He can't walk."

"He got this far didn't he? Besides, he is a man who can be spared."

Cortés dug at his crotch. "You, Rodrigo, are to organize an expedition to *Oaxaca*."

"How many men shall I take?"

"You're staying here. I only want you to put it together. It shouldn't be too difficult because the only man going is Hernán de Barrientos."

This was an open death sentence. Barrientos was a likeable fellow with a mop of yellow hair and funny gray eyes. He was also a bulwark in battle. Unfortunately, while in *Tenochtitlan*, he and Cortés had had a disagreement over one of the Emperor's daughters. Cortés now planned to murder the man.

"What is Señor Barrientos supposed to achieve?" I asked.

"He's to lay out a Crown Plantation. He may recruit as many nativos as he can and experiment with crops and animals. In his spare time he can do a little gold prospecting."

Cortés must have been surprised when, over one year later, he discovered that not only was Barrientos alive but he had set up his own fiefdom and developed a broad expanse of fertile ground. He was respected by the Indios and was rich in all things—especially big-breasted women.

Still a fourth expedition, with one hundred and thirty men, was sent under Antonio Rangel. Along with Diego Pizarro and Andrés de Tapía, they were sent to *Panuco*, to the north of Villa Rica, to check for evidence of gold and for evidence of a hostile invasion from the islands.

At first, Cortés ordered me to go with de León. Before departure, however, he reconsidered his decision, and told me to stay and defend the palace. In my case and, in the case of some of the others, he was determined to keep an eye on me—he and I despised one another. My only solace was that he knew full well that many of the men also hated him. If he started to eliminate all of these, he was finished.

Still, during this period of the Conquest, the land was peaceful. Cortés was usually out of sight, attending to his many women, and cheating Moctecuzoma at tlatoloque. Our various expeditions traveled the country in complete safety. More than that, the natives willingly provided food and shelter for our exploring parties. Some of them even gave golden gifts to the Castilians. This profitable situation may have gone on indefinitely but Cortés, from overconfidence, miscalculation or simple boredom, gambled with our success. In so doing, he assured the deaths of hundreds of our men and the doom of a civilization. Surely, the Caudillo was in league with Satan.

● ● ●

As an officer, I had my own room where I lived with Amelia. The room was large at ten paces square and the ceiling was twice my height and as blue as the sky. The walls were painted in vivid colors, showing scenes of fishing and hunting but also the sacrifice of men and animals. Unholy monsters, bearing partially eaten victims, stalked through verdant meadows.

The floors were of red tile, partly covered by cotton mats and animal skins. Garlands of flowers—replaced daily—hung from the doorways and walls. What little light there was came by way of skylights, cleverly protected from the rain. At night, light came from candles of our own making. The fat for these candles came from Mexican fowl, dogs and—I'm ashamed to say—sacrificial victims.

Amelia tried to perform all the household functions of a wife but, in that we had an army of servants, there was little to do. Still, she tried to do the best she could and— more than once—I saw her trying to repair damaged clothing but she wasn't much good at it. As the child-bride of a god, she had never been taught sewing or other simple household chores.

She was considerably better at bedtime. It was as if she sensed our danger and tried to compensate for it by her passion. Even after we were sated, she whispered strange words in my ear and clung to me as if she could hold me forever. After she fell asleep, I enjoyed running my hand over her body—she was a beautiful doll. Unlike a doll, however, her body trembled and she oftentimes moaned in her sleep—I wondered what monsters filled her dreams.

When I had time, we practiced our Nahuatl and Castilian and, I must say, that she had a better ear than mine. Francesca had been correct—Amelia was not only intelligent she was endlessly inquisitive. When I was not around, which was much of the time, Francesca took Amelia under her wing and helped her with her Spanish as well as with friendship. It was good arrangement; otherwise, both women would have been very lonely. Our other Castilian women had no time for Amelia and the Indio girls were frightened of her. She was, after all, dedicated to a god.

"Rodrigo," Francesca surprised me one day. "Cortés has done us both a great favor by giving Amelia to you. She is such a treasure."

I didn't know what to say but said it *anyway*. "...I had my doubts—but—I've learned to...like her. Besides, it would have been a shame to let her be sacrificed."

She moved a little closer to me. "You know, I really don't get along with the other white women—most are common sluts. Those Ordaz sisters are a little too friendly to suit me."

"They are a little...different."

"That's an understatement. I prefer Amelia's company."

"How about all of your other admirers?"

She laughed. "You might not have noticed it, Rodrigo, but I am *very* particular. I would never consider a campesino and the hidalgos on the expedition are aristocrats in name only. Any nobility they might have possessed was lost long ago."

"Cortés?"

"Oh, he is intelligent enough, but I wouldn't trust him with a female goat."

I couldn't help but grin. "That describes almost all of the soldiers."

"It doesn't describe you."

I looked at my feet. "I thought that Amelia..."

"Hardly. You are the only man in the army who has not been with fifty women," She shook her head. "Our mujeres are even worse—some of them have been doing it with Indios in exchange for a few chalchihuitl and a little gold. María Estrada is the biggest whore in the army. She is getting rich."

"I'm not like the rest of our women." ~She brushed my scarred cheek with her lips. "I wouldn't want you to break faith with Amelia but...I get lonely."

I was confused and embarrassed. The truth be known—I wanted to run my hand over Francesca, too.

Burgos, Castilla-León

"Did you do it, Obispo?"

"Do *what*, Padre?"

"You know full well '*what*'."

The old man's icy eyes, which had been staring into space, now focused on Mendoza. "I see that now I must read between *your* lines, Padre. You wish to know whether I had a relationship—a *romantic* relationship—with the Lady."

"Something like that, Obispo."

The old man thought for a long time. "Is it possible that I've missed something in you, Padre. Is it possible that your interests extend beyond small boys and self-abuse?"

"It's not that at all, Your Excellency. I merely prefer to include all pertinent details of your story. You have already told me how this dissolute woman threw herself—multiple times—at your feet."

"Then...I will answer your question. We *did* have a romantic relation—from the first time we saw each other."

"You mean to tell me, Obispo, that you...that you were...that she was..."

"You must be more specific, Padre."

"...You were quite detailed about your fornication with the woman in Italy."

The ancient man grinned a bony grin. "...And now you want me to give chapter and verse on Francesca."

"Absolutely."

"From the first time we saw each other—even though neither one of us knew it—we were bound to each other."

Disappointment clouded Mendoza's eyes. "Then you didn't..."

"A gentleman keeps his own counsel, Padre."

Mendoza struck his head with the palm of his hand. "*Gentleman, Obispo*? You weren't nearly so fastidious in your tale about your Italian peasant." He tapped on the manuscript. "I have it all here."

"That was quite different, Padre. She was indeed a peasant but Francesca was a Lady—an aristocrat. Besides, I wanted to test your reactions with my tale about Angela in Italy—you were perfect *thus* I find it unnecessary to lay the same snare."

"A trick?"

"A trick, Padre, and you gulped it up like a hungry dog."

"You *lied* about it?"

The old man leaned forward, his lips barely moving, "*Lie, Trick?*" —he shrugged his shoulders—"It's for you to distinguish the difference."

"So you refuse to go into detail about...this...this...*Francesca?*"

The Bishop got up and paced back-and-forth. "There are low men—childish, stupid or depraved—who enjoy boasting of their accomplishments with women." He stepped over to his chair, put his hands out and supported himself on the wooden back before continuing. "These men delight in telling other men of their conquests because they naively think it gives them masculine status...it doesn't. It only serves to make them less significant than they already are."

"Then, Obispo, you are telling me that men on your expedition boasted of Señora de la Barca?"

"I am telling you nothing more than this, Padre. In my opinion, many men get *more* pleasure talking about it than they do in the act itself."

"Your point?"

"Telling another man—the *details* of physical romance—is but another way for one man to *diddle* the other man. The woman is but the go-between."

Mendoza sensed the insult but couldn't put his finger on it. "Then you *won't* tell me."

The old man took his seat. "No, Padre, I certainly won't tell you. Besides, every Paladin must have his Fair Lady."

Chapter 13

Cortés confronted Moctecuzoma. "Great Prince, we are no longer willing to worship our God within the walls of the palace. We must worship him in the open air where all of your people can see the Glory of our God. The best place for this would be in one of your shrines on top of the *Templo Mayor.*"

He was shocked. "Malinche, why do you request a thing that will surely bring down the wrath of my gods and stir up an insurrection among my people. They will never endure this profanation of their holy place."

"It is not me, Great Lord," he lied, "but my followers are insistent. Should you refuse, they will take *Coatepec* by force and topple your false devils."

Moctecuzoma said nothing, knowing that Malinche would do what he wished.

Cortés went on, "Mighty Prince, I will not inflict unnecessary pain upon you or your people and, if you will give your permission, we will leave all but one of your gods in their places but—but I must insist—the horrible image of your false rain god, *Tlaloc*, will be removed. I am prepared to be generous. Your priests may place it elsewhere as long as you promise that no more human lives will be sacrificed to him. The temple of your other idols—*Tezcatlipoca* and *Huitzilopotchli*—will stay intact, and you and your priests may continue to worship them there. The *Tlaloc* temple will be cleansed and, once sanctified, we will build an Altar to Our Lady. No longer shall we be disturbed by the unholy throb of Tlaloc's serpent-skin drum. Where you move it doesn't matter, just as long as we Christians never hear it, again."

"Malinche." Moctecuzoma looked as if he would weep. "I so order it."

●●●

When the word was given, the Castilians gave a shout and mounted the stairs of the *Templo Mayor*. The teopixquia, who knew of the order, stood by in silent hatred as we pushed the child-killing *Tlaloc* off of his pedestal. After this was done, Tlaxcaltec and Mexican slaves labored to clean off the blood that was caked on the floor and walls of the templo. The walls, although stone, were deeply stained with ancient blood so a layer of whitewash was applied. We then raised a crucifix and a portrait of Our Lady and the shrine was decorated with beautiful flowers. It was an interesting contrast—in one templo the foul-smelling priests sacrificed to the terrible *Tezcatlipoca* and *Huitzilopotchli* and, in the other, we Castilians held mass and took the Holy Sacrament. This situation could not last forever.

●●●

Moctecuzoma, who had been pliable and outwardly friendly turned cold and aloof. He called Cortés into his quarters.

"Malinche, because of my love for you I must warn you. Our gods have been offended by your violation of their holy place. They tell my priests that they will leave *Tenochtitlan* unless you teotoh are driven from the city or sacrificed upon our altars."

"This comes as an unpleasant surprise, My Prince."

"I have only to raise my finger, and every Tenochca will rise in arms against you. Should you fail to heed my warning none of you *will* leave here alive."

Cortés—recognizing this as real trouble—was conciliatory. "I would like to depart but unfortunately my ships rotted out and had to be destroyed. It will take weeks before we can set to sea, again. Even so, we will leave but I love you so much that I cannot stand to be deprived of your companionship. You will have to travel with us."

Here Moctecuzoma had the opportunity to demonstrate manhood but—predictably—he didn't.

"If I should send workmen, will it be possible to build your vessels more quickly?"

"Of course, My Lord." Malinche had won.

"Then we will stay in my Capital until your boats are completed."

●●●

Moctecuzoma ordered hundreds of laborers to the coast. Supposed Castilian shipbuilders led them but impeded the construction. Boards were cut the wrong size or at the wrong angle and work proceeded at a snail's pace.

In *Tenochtitlan*, things were going from bad to worse. The previously apathetic Mexica were no longer quite so apathetic. Knots of unhappy Indios gathered outside of our quarters. Their faces told the story—we were no longer welcome. No longer were we to be permitted to go where we pleased and travel the city at will. Now, after Cortés' humiliation of the Tenocha religion, everyone had to stay in the palace for fear of open rebellion. We stayed in our armor night and day, vigilant against the possibility of attack.

When we believe that things cannot get worse, they oftentimes do—*cuando menos piensa el galgo, salta la liebre*. So, it should come as no surprise that even more alarming news reached us from an unexpected quarter...

Narvaez
Burgos, Castilla-León
March 9, 1581, 8:15 A.M.

"Because of all the time that we've wasted, we will dispense with breakfast."

"Not even a few eggs...?"

"No, not even eggs. Besides, I know that you've already had your breakfast."

"Si, Excelenia, but only Mexican atole and a dab of sauerkraut—I detest sauerkraut—it gives me gas."

The old man wrinkled his nose. "I've noticed. Let me think. I didn't have much more than you did. Fried fish roe, breaded flounder, pickled eel and steamed corn cakes. Not much."

Mendoza looked pitiful. "Is there any left?"

"No—I gave the leftovers to the poor. Let's get to work."

"When will we be served lunch?"

"We won't. I'm bloated from this morning's meal. We'll dispense with lunch."

"Then, of course, we'll have a nice supper?"

"No, Padre. I'm trying to watch my weight. Besides, we are behind schedule and I don't like interruptions."

"Schedule?"

"That's right, Padre Mendoza. We need to finish the manuscript before I drop dead of old age or before—God forbid—something unfortunate happens to you."

"But, Episcopus, I haven't had a decent meal since our last session together and I find it increasingly difficult to concentrate on our work."

"*Concentrate, Padre, Concentrate!* It may be your salvation."

PART 2

"Good news, Malinche. Other teotoh have arrived to carry you back to your own land."

"*What?*"

"I can see that you do not believe me, Malinche, but here is the evidence." Moctecuzoma's attendants unrolled paper scrolls on the floor. The colors were vivid and showed eighteen ships, five of them wrecked on the sand. The pictures also showed strange figures of things that may have been men, horses and cannons.

Cortés fell to his knees as much in terror as anything else. He pretended, however, that his kneeling position was because of his gratitude to the Lord. "Blessed be the Redeemer for all of his Mercies! We are delighted by this wonderful news. We will now leave your kingdom and report your loyalty to King Carlos."

"Is it possible these new teotoh serve another lord, Malinche?" Moctecuzoma knew something.

"All Castilians, My Prince, serve the great Emperor Carlos. It is possible, however, that these new people are a low form of human—really beasts—known as Basques—they are neither teules nor white men. If they are these, Great Prince, you will need us more than ever for they are filthy creatures that will bring bad luck on the land for they are all thieves, murderers and adulterers. Do you know how many have arrived, My Prince?"

Moctecuzoma hesitated before giving his information. Later, however, we learned that he did not lie. The Great Prince spoke, "My spies have counted one thousand along with seventy of your great beasts. There are many tepoztli and other things. *Look!* See how some carry maquahuitls and spears and others carry the small tepoztlis that make killing smoke and my spies have painted others that carry the bows that shoot by magic. If they are your brothers you need not delay your departure. *When will you leave?*"

"Soon, my Prince, but first I will need to send my ambassadors to the coast to meet with these new people. If they are indeed teules and not Basques, we will then depart."

Moctecuzoma, who expected our immediate departure, looked slightly less than relieved. "Do as you will, Malinche. You are welcome to stay here as long as is necessary."

●●●

Cortés discussed the situation with his officers, "These ships on the coast can only mean one thing—Velásquez has flanked us. We need more information but, for the moment, it's wise to make Moctecuzoma think that we are deceived. Señor Ordaz, order all of the men to shout loudly and fire their mosquetes in celebration."

The situation remained in uncertainty until two days later when a messenger arrived. He reported that our men in Villa Rica were sending six captive Castilians from the new armada. They were enemy emissaries who had tried to obtain Sandoval's surrender but Sandoval was alert and loyal to our cause. He lured these cabrónes with false promises then slapped them in irons.

Sandoval then decided to have some fun. Even though his prisoners were Castilian he bound them securely and wedged them into crates of rough wood—crates which were then strapped to the backs of especially strong tamanes. Accompanied by Sandoval's men, the crates were transported by teams of tamanes all of those many bone-jarring miles—through forests and up and down mountains—all the way up to *Tenochtitlan*.

Cortés, when he heard of Sandoval's packages sent orders that the prisoners be released from their crates. It would not do for the Mexica to see any teules humiliated. These traitors would march into the city as proud free men. It is well that our Caudillo was so cautious for our hold on the City was fragile and any small thing could tip the balance against us.

●●●

The prisoners were released but, sore and stiff from their ordeal, they limped into our palace. Cortés, with a look of concern, greeted them as if they were old comrades. The men were, in fact, an interesting group and included a priest and an escribano.

"Mis amigos," the Caudillo said, "I don't know what could have gotten into Gonzalo to have treated people such as yourself so shabbily—I'm determined to make up for it. I'll make sure that you have a good bath and have an excellent meal—I'll even see that you get a new set of clothing. To make amends for Gonzalo's actions, I even have a few gifts for you."

The prisoners, expecting hanging or at least a flogging, looked pitifully relieved.

"I'll meet you at dinner, señores," Cortés said.

Dinner was nothing less than a banquet with fish, fowl, tamales and delicate canine tidbits. There were tropical fruits and all of the vegetables of Mexico. After the meal, Cortés presented each man with a golden chain. In addition he gave medallions to the enemy priest, Padre Guevara, and the notario, Antonio de Amaya. Not one man of us failed to notice that each these prisoners was given more gold than us soldiers who had been here for months and fought in all of the battles.

"I trust you'll enjoy your accommodations."

"We already do," spoke the priest. "I don't know how we could have ever believed Narváez' lies."

"Narváez?" Cortés asked, "If he's the man I know—he has courage. Isn't he the renowned conquistador who fought against the nativos in Española and Cuba? When he was done not many were left alive."

"Yes, Señor Cortés, that's him." Pánfilo de Narváez—he's the one appointed by the Governor to lead the fleet," he went on in a lower tone of voice. "I'm afraid the Governor has empowered him to take your command."

Our Leader didn't react. "If he has the Royal Documents, I'll readily relinquish command and follow Don Pánfilo's orders."

The notario, de Amaya, spoke up, "He does not have Royal Authorization; he relies on his own authority as the King's Adelantado."

"Quite so," cooed Cortés.

"But from everything we see here," the notario made a broad gesture with his hand, "you are even now acting in the interests of our Emperor. In my legal opinion, the Velásquez' edict is a shell that has no validity—no validity whatsoever."

"You don't say?"

"Yes I do. What do you think, Padre?"

"Don Hernán is doing God's work and nothing must interfere with it. I am willing to return to the coast and promote the Caudillo's cause amongst Narváez' soldiers. Of course, a little gold would make my arguments even more persuasive."

Amaya was not about to be outdone. "If you will have me, I volunteer my services for the same purpose."

"Accepted, señores, but don't go too hard on Gonzalo—he's young and impetuous. You may tell Pánfilo that I want peace between us. I would be willing to consider"—Cortés' hesitation was imperceptible—"a *joint* command."

"We will, Caudillo, but I don't think he'll listen. He's fortified *Cempoala* and gained the support of this very fat cacique. He has branded you a traitor and threatens to hang you—he also knows your dispositions. Shortly after landing on the coast he was approached by several of your own men—I'm sure that they are just malcontents but it seems that they are unhappy with the way you divided the spoil—they are actively helping Narváez. They seem to hate you and are looking for revenge."

"I don't know what could have happened to have made them so unhappy." Cortés shook his head in wonderment. "On the other hand, there's no accounting for treachery."

Hearing of the presence of a rival Spanish force, Cristóbal Pineda, who still fumed over the distribution of the treasure, deserted the palace. His absence was detected and Cortés sent Tlaxcaltec assassins with orders to kill him. Pineda's corpse was brought back in a hammock.

●●●

After two or three days of fat living, our newfound accomplices were sent back to the coast with a horse loaded with gold. Once they arrived, they tried to convince Narváez to make peace but the man was obstinate. He told them that he would not compromise his agreements with Governor Velásquez. They *must* support him. He went on to tell them that he had been in contact with Moctecuzoma who promised the support of an army of warriors. In exchange, Narváez would return the Prince to his rightful position as Uei Tlatloani of the Mexican state. Cortés and many of his followers would be honored with public executions.

Here, of course, Narváez lied—Moctecuzoma would have fared no better under Narváez than he had under Cortés. Moctecuzoma, his empire and people were doomed when the Great Admiral—Cristóbal Colón—first put his boot on a beach in San Salvador.

In order to best accomplish their mission, our spies swore their fealty to Narváez. Their oath was false, however. Secretly, they worked on Narváez' soldiers, telling them of Mexico's great wealth and of the largesse and sweet nature of Hernán Cortés. Quietly, they distributed gold to Narváez' soldiers in the name of the Caudillo. Narváez officers soon became restless—some even suggested a peaceable fusion of forces. Narváez refused to listen and laid his plans to march inland and attack our force in *Tenochtitlan*.

●●●

The Caudillo, who usually reveled in turmoil, found himself in a situation even more perilous than usual. De León and Rangel were engaged in distant missions with one hundred and thirty men each. Sandoval, in Villa Rica, had one hundred men, many of whom were old or sick or injured and we in *Tenochtitlan* were occupying an unsettled city with only two hundred soldiers. In the unlikely event that we could combine forces, we could only hope to muster five hundred soldiers. We could not hope to match Narváez' one thousand troops nor could we match Narváez' seventy horse or his great superiority in big guns and other armament.

As usual, Cortés gambled. He ordered both Rangel and de León to join us in *Cholula* with all of their forces. This was a double gamble—Rangel and Velásquez had been sent from *Tenochtitlan* because of their potential for disloyalty. Velásquez was a kinsman of Governor Diego of Cuba and had led the rebellion against Cortés in Villa Rica. Equally bad, he was also the brother-in-law of Pánfilo de Narváez. If Velásquez turned against Cortés, *El Diablo* couldn't save the expedition.

Cortés rolled the dice yet again—he refused to abandon the City. He did the unexpected and something that competent officers condemn—he split our force. He left one hundred and twenty men behind. Disastrously, he left Pedro de Alvarado in command. The rest of us—an overwhelming force of eighty men—marched toward the coast.

Before he left, however, Malinche met with Moctecuzoma.

"It is necessary that some of us march to the coast, My Prince. I fear that it may be necessary for us to protect the Totonacs and your Mexica from these new arrivals who I fear are the thieving Basques."

"Malinche, all you have to do is ask, and I will send one hundred thousand warriors as well as thirty thousand slaves to carry your equipment."

Cortés smelled the trap. "It will not be necessary, Moctecuzoma. We teules are protected by our God and, no matter the situation, always prevail."

"Then I will take measures to make certain that your shrine is protected."

Chapter 15

We needed to travel light and fast so we were obliged to leave our cannons behind. In *Cholula*, we were relieved to find that both de León and Rangel were loyal. They had arrived with men that swelled our force to three hundred and fifty. Cortés then received bad news.

He sent to *Tlaxcala* for two thousand Indios, but they refused to come. They were willing to fight the Tenochca but they had no interest in fighting Castilians again. Besides, how could they know which group would prevail? When the gods fight, it is best to get out of the way. All of the tribes weren't so fastidious, though. Using fast runners, we communicated with the Chinanteca, a tribe to the south who were hostile to the Mexica and were renowned for their great two-headed spears—longer than those used by the Germans in Italy. Cortés ordered three hundred of these weapons and he ordered them to be tipped with copper rather than itzli—their purpose to fend off the Narváez' horsemen. Sandoval, Tapía and sixty other men also reinforced us. Sandoval himself was reinforced by Pedro de Villalobos and other deserters from the Narváez' camp.

In the meantime, there was an exchange of messages between Cortés and Narváez—he demanded Cortés' immediate obedience. Our Caudillo, in turn, demanded to see Narváez' articles of Royal Authority. Such articles were not forthcoming because, as Cortés well knew, no such articles existed. He dictated a letter to me, written out by me in the legalisms of the Salamanca school of law.

"*In that you, Don Pánfilo de Narváez, have failed to comply with the rightful request of one Hernán Cortés, Captain-General of the community of Villa Rica de la Vera Cruz, as to the production of Articles of Royal Authority, this same Hernán Cortés is empowered to hold you in contempt of Royal Authority and, as such, you will henceforth be regarded as a rebel against His Majesty, Carlos I, Emperor of the Netherlands, Spain and Germany. This same Hernán Cortés is empowered to take all means to secure your arrest even if it should lead to your death.*"

Signed by those of us designated as officials of *Villa Rica*

● ● ●

Our Caudillo sent me, Olmedo and de León to the Narváez camp with a message of peace. Narváez—a large florid man with red hair—read the message in silence and, as he read, his flushed face grew even more flushed. He turned to Velásquez de León.

"Brother-in-law, this Cortés thinks he is above the King. I have been considering matters and believe that—after I capture the cabrón and hang him—you are the best man to command his force under me."

De León said nothing, as if considering the matter.

"And you Don Rodrigo, I would like you to command two companies...let's make that three companies of my foot soldiers."

I was also silent.

"Padre Olmedo you shall be chief chaplain of the army—the Church will receive ten percent of any treasure taken and"—Narváez winked—"you may personally take all you wish—for your expenses, of course—from the Church share."

Olmedo spoke, "Whatever decisions are made, Don Pánfilo, it is most important that the Indios see no evidence of Christian disunity. If they do, your efforts here may prove a disaster to the Holy Cause."

Narváez was agreeable. "You are wise, Padre—I propose that we negotiate with Cortés and lure him to us. In this way it should be possible to take him without a fight. What do you think, gentlemen?"

De León—intemperate at the best of times—rose from the table, knocking his stool over.

"I've had enough of you, Pánfilo—you always were a slimy worm. That my sister should have married you is bad enough but here you are trying to command men better than yourself."

Narváez, not to be outdone also leaped to his feet, drawing his great two-handed sword. "If you were not a relative, Don Velásquez, I would make you regret your words. As it is, all of you are ordered from camp. May God help you when I catch you again."

On the road back, I spoke to Fraile Olmedo. "Well, that didn't go very well, Padre."

"Better than you think, Rodrigo. I was able to bribe Narváez' gun master, Rodrigo Martínez. He will stop up the touch-holes of the cannons with wax."

● ● ●

We rejoined our little force and advanced toward the banks of a river known by the Indios as *Chachalaca* and, by us, as the *Río de las Canoas*. This river was the only obstacle between Narváez' larger force and us. Satan was left with an agonizing choice—Pánfilo de Narváez or Hernán Corteés—Satan raised his hand. He caused the skies to darken and for the winds to howl. The heavens erupted with sheet lightening and there was continuous thunder. Rain came down in torrents and the river became a cataract. It was no longer possible to cross. Cortés, not knowing himself whether *El Diablo* had judged for or against him, decided to give a speech:

"Narváez has come here to punish us, señores, and to steal all that we have gained. We are but one-fourth the size of the enemy but we have the experience and we know that God is with us. It is now up to you. Remember the words of the immortal Rolando, 'A mas honor, mas dolor'—the greater the pain, the greater the honor—*Arriba y Adelante!*" The camp erupted in cheers.

Our force was divided into five companies—sixty men, under Diego Pizarro were to take out the artillery. Eighty, under Sandoval and Concha, were ordered to take or kill Narváez. Velásquez de León, with a third group of sixty men, would seize his own cousin, Diego Velásquez, the younger. Ordaz, with a fourth company of one hundred men, would strike against Salvatierra. Cortés and the rest of us would remain in reserve, ready to strike wherever needed.

● ● ●

Despite the raging waters, I scoured the banks looking for a crossing. A great fallen tree had become stuck across the torrent, slowing the onrush of the waters. Cortés viewed the crossing with a critical eye.

"What do you think, Rodrigo?"

"We can make it. We *must* make it. If we can get across in this storm, we'll catch the cabrónes with their pants down."

"How would you do it?"

"A living chain to break the force of the water."

"Who goes first?"

"Me."

Rope that was used for the animals was taken and looped at one end. I placed the loop around my waist and stepped into the torrent. Fighting the torrent and shuffling with my side to the current—I crossed. Three times I came close—too close—to losing my balance. I knotted my rope around the base of a strong tree on the far side and waved to the others. Frightened men followed, holding the rope, linking their arms and making a chain. With this human barrier in place, the army made its crossing. *El Diablo* smiled down on us and exacted the price of only two men—two of our smaller soldiers. I knew both these men and they were both exceptional soldados and more than a match for the mightiest savage but here in the cataract that was the *Río Canoas*, height was everything and strength was nothing. Their cries were lost in the roar of the river.

●●●

Later, we discovered exactly how fortunate we were. Narváez—learning from a deserter that we were close—ordered his army to deploy in our direction. When the storm broke, he reckoned that he had nothing to fear and countermarched to his base in *Cempoala*—which was his fatal mistake. We therefore caught Narváez completely unprepared and, in the dark, we charged into his sleeping camp shouting "*Viva el Rey, Spiritu Santo!*"

Sandoval attacked the teocalli where Narváez had his headquarters. Narváez fought with his great montante, killing two of our soldiers, but he and his men were forced back into one of the templos. A thrown firebrand produced a shower of sparks and the templo's thatch went up with a roar. Narváez was struck in the eye by a glancing ballesta bolt then—thinking he was killed—surrendered. He was held in irons with Salvatierra, Gamarra and others as the battle continued. Some of the cannons were firing but, in the darkness, their shots went wide. Pizarro and his men charged them with a whoop and a rush and captured their crews.

Narváez' horsemen were better organized and made a desperate charge in the dark. For a time the fighting was deadly as mounted Castilians charged us. I unhorsed one of them with my copper-headed lance and then speared another horseman through his throat. The remaining caballeros surrendered.

"*Viva Cortés! Viva La Victoria!*" Our men shouted even as the rest of the enemy force surrendered. Only nine men were killed, five of Narváez' and four of our own.

The chastened Narváez spoke to the Caudillo afterwards, "You must be proud that you have captured me."

Cortés' voice dripped with *sarcasm*. "It's the least thing I have done in Nueva España."

Burgos, Castilla-León

"Truly a remarkable victory, Your Grace, considering the impossible odds against your small force, which again, is evidence of God's favor."

"And He didn't favor Narváez, Padre?"

"The facts speak for themselves."

"And if the battle had gone against, Cortés? We'd be having a very different conversation, wouldn't we?"

"But he didn't and we aren't," Mendoza said smugly.

"Very good, Padre! Totally irrelevant but quite good."

Mendoza decided to press his advantage. "All of your men, all of your soldiers were quite...*masculine*...I'm sure."

The ancient man fixed the Priest with his cold stare. "Not all, but certainly the majority."

"...And all—*quite voluntarily*—joined your expedition fully expecting to leave their women, and—the pleasures of feminine company—behind, for months even years?"

"Yes, Padre, men frequently leave their women to pursue their chosen occupations. There is absolutely no mystery to this."

Mendoza slammed his fist against the table. "Yet, I who have felt myself dedicated to God since I was a child, have piously eschewed the company of females and, *for this*, you persecute me. It seems to me that—no matter the Divine Hand that guided you—the whole lot of you were nothing more than a band of *queers*."

Mendoza knew he'd gone too far as he watched the Bishop's face. First it went dead white then flushed, reddened and turned purple. His eyes bulged and seemed to burst from their sockets. His scarred lips were fixed and immobile then proceeded to go from sneer, smirk, twisted smile and unholy grin. He started to choke and his hands clutched at his throat. Mendoza couldn't believe his good fortune. The old man was having a stroke.

The ancient Bishop fell forward onto the table and slammed it with his palms. Sounds arose from deep in his chest. He choked, rasped, giggled and cackled. He slapped the table and laughed so hard he couldn't breathe. He looked up at Mendoza and laughed still more. Tears ran down his face and he laughed even harder.

"Oh My God, Padre," he wept, "that *really* was a good one. Our noble Band of Brothers was just a Gang of Queers! Cortés wasn't trying to put down the practice of sodomy, he was just trying to get in on the action!"

Mendoza had to wait for the Bishop's laughter to die down before he could respond. "I'm pleased that you find me so humorous, Excellency."

"You should work in the circus." He cackled even more, "...*A Company of Queers!*"

"Perhaps I overstated the case."

"Don't apologize, Padre. I haven't laughed like that in years. It cleaned some of the dirt from my system."

"I'm glad I amused you."

"But you do make a point, Padre, and one I've wondered about myself."

"And what might that be?"

"The *most* masculine of men are precisely those who are more likely to strike out into the wilderness or go off to war without the prospect of a soft woman."

"You must admit, Excelencia, that it is a little strange."

"Men with more feminine makeups avoid these things at all costs. They much prefer the soft breasts and thighs of a woman."

"I'm *sure* you have an explanation, Obispo. You always do."

"Then I must disappoint you, Padre, for I have no explanation. It is simply an observation."

"Perhaps then, Your Grace, I wasn't entirely wrong. These so-called masculine men may not be truly masculine."

"No—more likely that overcharged masculine energy requires worlds to conquer. If I am right, may God help us when earthly frontiers are pushed back to nothing. These men will then conquer one another."

"But surely, Your Grace, some men whom you regard as effeminate sometimes embark on adventures..."

"Reluctantly, yes, but they will desert or find a woman at the first opportunity. They cannot tolerate being away from female flesh. They are needy and their need masquerades as manhood."

"I don't understand."

"I don't understand it myself but it is worth consideration. Are not both of us are—in our different ways—historians."

"Correct."

"Do you know the history of the Northmen?"

"That they were queer?"

"No, Padre. *Do* you know their history?"

"What do they have to do with the subject at hand? I know that these unholy pagans ravaged Christendom for three hundred years."

"What happened to them?

"Killed off. Their few survivors retreated to the wastelands of the far north."

"Wrong, Padre! They injected their seed into the peoples of Europe. They wrested land from the craven Franceses and renamed it North-man Land now called Normandy. They conquered England and Ireland, colonized the islands of the North, ravaged Europe, took Sicily and laid claim to North Africa. Still other Northmen attacked to the east and became the powerful tribes of the Russ and named their lands Russ Land."

"Your point, Obispo?"

"The people of the north took their most aggressive and masculine men and *threw* them against the rest of the world. Deprived of this blood, the north was left with the stay-at-homes—men who can't be parted from their women—and their lands stagnate with peace."

"Peace is not stagnation, Your Grace. It is God's ultimate plan."

The old man ignored him. "The lands that received the most attention from these pagan raiders are those that benefit from their masculinity—Normandy, for example. As the Normandos send their most aggressive men off to battle, other lands benefit and Normandy stagnates."

"Perhaps, but..."

"Inglaterra was conquered by the pagan Northmen followed by French speaking Christian Northmen—the Normans. Mark my word, Padre, the Inglés *will* be formidable rivals in the future. There *will* be a bloody contest for the Americas."

"I disagree with you, Excelencia, for God has decreed that the Americas will be Spanish."

"Even now, Padre, we Españoles are feeding our most aggressive men to the huge American stomach. I don't know what will come of it but I will predict this—España will stagnate."

Chapter 16

We consolidated our victory and incorporated the defeated soldiers into our army but then we received terrible news from *Tenochtitlan*—the entire city was in revolt. The brigantines had been burned and Alvarado's force was under siege. The Mexica had assaulted the palace and killed five Castilians. Despite weariness, fear and grumbling, Cortés ordered an immediate countermarch on *Tenochtitlan*.

There were hardships during the journey but once we reached *Tlaxcala*, there was abundant food. From *Tlaxcala* we received reinforcements of two thousand native warriors. We now had approximately one thousand four hundred Castilians, one hundred horse, one hundred arquebusiers, numerous crossbowmen and multiple culverins and a few even larger cannons. With the addition of our Tlaxcalteca, we were becoming an unbeatable force—or so we thought.

After organizing and resting in *Tlaxcala* we marched west between the volcanoes. As we entered the *Valle de Mexico*, we had another unpleasant surprise. All of the pueblos and villages that had previously been so friendly were now depopulated. Those few people, who were present, kept their distance.

●●●

On the march we learned from our Indio spies what had happened in *Tenochtitlan*. It was the custom for the Mexica to celebrate a great May celebration—*Toxcatl*—in honor of *Tezcatlipoca* and *Huitzilo-potchli*. The greatest ceremony was held in the *Plaza Mayor* where it was celebrated by sacrifice of a youth who was the incarnation of the god—there were to be religious songs, the music of drums, flutes and conches and snake dances. The participants were many of the priests and chieftains—the common people were observers. The presence of Moctecuzoma was also required.

Alvarado—or so he claimed—grew suspicious when the Tenochca stopped delivering as much food as usual. A washer-girl was found hanging from a rafter, although this may have been because of fear of pregnancy. Tlaxcalteca said that the black fingerprints of Mexica priests had fouled the portrait of Our Lady in the old temple of *Tlaloc*. They also said that there were plans to destroy our Christian altar and place *Tlaloc* back into his original position of honor—they also reported that the Tenochca would stage a revolt in ten days.

Alvarado seized three slaves who were waiting for sacrifice in front of the *Templo Mayor*. Using Francisco, a converted Mexica, as the interpreter, Alvarado put the slaves to the torture. He burned pine logs and put the flames to their feet. One refused to talk so Alvarado had him thrown from the wall. Predictably, the other two confirmed that there would be an attack. Not satisfied with the words of slaves. Alvarado tortured two of the Emperor's relatives who were held in the palace. They also agreed that there would be an attack in ten days.

I knew this Francisco, the supposed interpreter. His knowledge of Spanish was nonexistent. To all questions we would smile and answer '*Si.*' Alvarado knew this so he also knew his tortured confessions were worthless. He only received the answers he wanted to hear.

"Will there be an attack in ten days?"

The tortured man screams.

Francisco agrees, "*Si.*"

Alvarado also ordered that Moctecuzoma and all of his noble attendants be placed in iron leg-braces—Moctecuzoma wouldn't attend the festival because Alvarado had a plan and his plan didn't include the death of the Prince.

On the day of the celebration, six hundred chieftains and priests arrived to honor their god—thousands more came to watch the festivities. Alvarado, remembering our noble actions at *Cholula*, decided on a cheap victory. In this way he believed that he would win the praise of his Caudillo, his King and the favorable judgment of history.

All of the Captains, including the custodian of the treasure, Alonso de Escobar, and our criminal fraile, Juan Díaz, supported the action—only de Tapía opposed it. Francesca de la Barca who, along with the other women, had remained in *Tenochtitlan*, heard of Alvarado's plot.

"Are you *mad*, Pedro? The Tenochca are already at a flashpoint—if you do this, may God only help us."

"Women should stay out of men's affairs." Alvarado flashed his usual grin. "They don't have the intelligence for important decisions. If, on the other hand," he fondled her hair, "you permit me to visit you tonight, I'm certain that we can work things out."

Most women were enchanted by Alvarado—but not Francesca. Reportedly, she produced a small knife. "Try it, and I'll make it shorter by half."

●●●

Alvarado was not deterred—in a duplication of the Caudillo's marvelous triumph at *Cholula*, Alvarado's men, along with a few Tlaxcalteca, nonchalantly made their way to the three entrances of the *Plaza Mayor*. The soldiers, with smiles and sometimes imitating the steps of the dance, infiltrated the feathered revelers. Alvarado himself gave the signal.

"*Mueran!*"

The blood of the chieftains ran like water—some fled to the gates but were caught on the pikes of the defenders. It was *Cholula* all over again, only worse. Caballeros, infanterias and Tlaxcalteca showed no mercy—there were no prisoners. The width and breadth of the Plaza was slippery with blood. Castilians and Tlaxcalteca killed, killed and killed again.

Having butchered six hundred chieftains, their blood lust was not sated. They turned their attention to the observers. Thousands died but some escaped by climbing the walls, hiding in the recesses of templos or hiding under the piles of dead. Alvarado saved some of the higher-ranking chiefs, whom he later ransomed for gold.

The soldiers, all of whom had been dissatisfied with Cortés' distribution of the spoil, now rectified things by stripping the gold and gems from the dead and looting the shrines. In a coordinated move, the Castilian jailers fell on the nobles chained in the palace. Cacama, the ruler of *Texcoco* was slain, as were most of the other pipiltin. Moctecuzoma was saved, as was his brother, Cuitlahuac, who was the governor of *Iztalapan*. Itzquauhtzin, the governor of *Tlateloloco*, was also left alive. My friend, Macitoc the Hunter, broke free leaving two Castilians and three Tlaxcalteca dead in his wake.

●●●

The Tenochca, who had been so passive, surged onto the offensive. All over the City secret armories were opened and warriors were armed—the newly replaced Great Drum boomed from the heights of *Coatepec* as outraged warriors attacked Castilians looting the dead. They drove them from the Templo precinct, through the gates and up to the walls of the palace. Alvarado was struck in the head by a stone and knocked to the ground—and was barely rescued by a Tlaxcaltec fighter. He, along with the others, retreated and closed the gate. Stones and darts rained into the enclosure, as frenzied attacks came in waves. Some of the warriors scaled the wall and were pushed back only at the last moment. Thatch and other flammables ignited—Alvarado, frightened and covered with blood from his wound, rushed to the chained Moctecuzoma.

"Look what you've done!"

"I have done nothing, Tonatiuh." Moctecuzoma moaned, "I have done *absolutely* nothing."

"You are responsible."

"You have murdered the nobility of Mexico and you hold me responsible? You have ruined yourself, Tonatiuh, and you have surely ruined me."

Alvarado unsheathed his knife and held it at the Prince's neck. "You will order your people to go home or I'll cut your dirty throat."

After seeing what had happened to the other chained nobles, Moctecuzoma knew he would do it. Once again he betrayed his people.

"Take me to the wall."

Now that his attendants were dead, Moctecuzoma had to adorn himself in his own finery—he was slow and clumsy at it. Once finished he was taken to the wall. The fighters below recognized him at once and stopped their rampage, although, according to Francesca, the wails of grief from all points of the city were heart-rending.

"Lay down your weapons, countrymen. You are no match for the power of the teotoh. All you can do is die and leave your helpless babies and old people to starve. Burn our dead with honor in front of Coatepec and then go home. Let there be no more destruction."

●●●

There were shouts of protest but most of the warriors simply walked away. During the next days there were limited raids. From the *Plaza Mayor*, a huge column of black smoke rose skyward as the dead were incinerated. The palace, however, was blockaded as both food and water were cut off.

Alvarado's men, desperately thirsty, dug into the gardens. They found a seep—digging deeper the flow became better although the water tasted of salt. Food stores, however, were depleted and every man and woman was put on quarter rations. Alvarado, realizing how Cortés must react if he abandoned his post, put off his retreat to the last minute. He was too late. He ordered his troops to board the brigantines—the Mexica attacked. Soon the ships were ablaze and the survivors were forced back to the palace.

●●●

Marching to Alvarado's relief, we passed along the causeway from which we had originally entered the City. This time, however, there were no crowds nor were the waters filled with canoes—the only boats seen were occasional canoes hovering ominously in the distance. Our march encountered no resistance although we had to stop and repair destroyed bridges. Cortés dismounted, pushed two hard-working Tlaxcalteca aside, and labored beside me. Together, we pulled a barricade apart with our hands—it was five cubits tall and composed of loosely piled timbers and chunks of masonry. We freed each piece and cast it into the lake below.

"This is too easy, Caudillo."

Cortés grunted as he pulled a large timber free of the pile. "Don't worry, Rodrigo. With the number of men we have, the Mexica will be as tame as sheep."

The Caudillo led by example. As I got to know Cortés I knew that his example was not that of philosophy. It was the by-product of his overcharged energy. He had to be moving and was incapable of simply commanding.

"I hope you're right because it'll be impossible to keep this many men supplied during a siege."

"We'll just brush them away like we always do." Cortés picked up a ragged chunk of masonry and flung it into the water.

I watched Cortés from the corner of my eye and though he was covered with filth, he was confident, even buoyant.

I pulled the last timber free and toppled it into the water where it bobbed like a fishing cork. "Maybe we should leave a garrison—skirmishers, really—on the causeway just to be on the safe side."

Cortés went to his hands and knees, pushing the last remaining trash over the side, "I've already thought it through—this causeway, if it should come to that, is too long to defend. We'll garrison one of the northern causeways to insure an open road to the mainland."

●●●

Other than for this manual labor, our entrance into *Tenochtitlan* was uneventful.

The streets were deserted and the only sounds were the tramping of our feet and the mutterings of our soldiers. As we neared the besieged palace, we could see the debris of combat. There were broken spears, feathers, arrows and occasional great smears of dried blood.

Alvarado met us at the gate, a look of relief replacing his usual grin.

"Thank God, you've arrived, Caudillo—Moctecuzoma has incited the Tenochca to rise against us."

He glared at Alvarado. "Your stupidity may have cost us everything."

"It's not my fault, Caudillo. What could I do?" He was the picture of innocence. "Moctecuzoma ordered an attack—it was just like *Cholula* all over again."

"*Attack?*" the Caudillo questioned.

"The Tlaxcateca reported it."

Beyond anger, I entered the conversation. "*Cholula*, Pedro? First, the Tlaxcalteca hate the Mexicans and things that they say against them can't be trusted. Second, we entrusted our women with you and you gambled with their lives. Third—*culero estúpido*—you don't share the same language with these Indios—we kept our interpreters with us."

"Francisco can speak the language."

Cortés shoved me aside. "Francisco? That imbecile? I won't call you a liar, Pedro, but you *have* disgraced yourself."

Malinche's anger was great and extended to Moctecuzoma. Cortés refused to meet with the Prince.

Chapter 17

Our force now totaled over one thousand Castilians with three thousand allies—ominously, the Mexican barricades closed behind us. Our numbers, which seemed such a strength, now became a weakness. For days, the streets were deserted with no Mexican delegation begging for peace. Our stores were running low and we were placed on half rations. We tasted hunger.

"Moctecuzoma wishes to speak to you," the page, Orteguilla, informed Cortés.

"What have I to do with this dog of a king who suffers us to starve before his eyes."

Andrís de Ávila corrected him, "If it were not for Moctecuzoma, the Mexica would have already overrun us."

The Caudillo didn't agree. "Did not the dog betray us in his communications with Narváez? And does he not now suffer his markets to be closed and leave us to die of famine?" Cortés then turned to the few surviving attendants. "Go tell your master that his people *must* open the market or we will do it for them." He softened his words. "Also tell him that I will release his brother—Cuitlahuac—as a gesture of friendship."

I had learned some Nahuatl from Amelia and was therefore ordered to release Cuitlahuac. He was a younger version of the Emperor but there the similarity ended. Unlike his brother, Cuitlahuac was defiant. Even so, he thought I had come for his life.

"I am ordered to release you. I am to tell you that Malinche has punished Golden Tonatiuh. You must also tell your people this: '*Malinche desires peace and is willing to make amends.*'"

Cuitlahuac smiled a crooked smile. "I hear your words, O *Chichtli.*"

●●●

His release was a mistake. Cuitlahuac immediately joined the rebels and became their ruler in the stead of Moctecuzoma—our situation was worse than ever. Shortly afterwards, a soldier who had been sent to *Tacuba* to retrieve one of Malinche's mistresses—a Moctecuzoma daughter—returned covered with wounds and blood. He had failed in his mission. The Tacuba causeway was thick with armed Tenochca who demanded the Princess. When the soldier refused, they attacked him. To save his own life he dropped his weapon and ran, leaving the girl in the hands of the enemy.

"Our situation is precarious, gentlemen," the Caudillo lectured the soldiers. "We must consider the possibility that the Mexica let us reenter the city, only to better destroy us."

"*Imbecil!*" shouted a voice from the back of the crowd.

"*Vamanos!*" shouted another.

He went on as if nothing had been said. "We need to know exactly what the Mexican intentions are. I have ordered Captain de la Peña, along with other good men, to scout in the direction of the southern causeway. With luck, it should be possible that a show of force will reduce the city to its previous level of calm."

●●●

Cortés ordered Diego de Ordaz, Hector Herrera and me to take a force to scout the route to the causeway. We were to take infantry and, to discourage attackers, most of our crossbowmen and musketeers. Our force was potent but still we didn't want to attract undue attention. Ordaz ordered that we refrain from unnecessary noise and these precautions seemed to work. The streets were empty, echoing only to the tread of our feet.

Like smoke, clouds of armed warriors billowed from canals and behind houses. Others appeared on the roofs. The volume of their whistles and screams was deafening and momentarily shocked us into inaction. Thousands of the same people who had previously been so passive, charged us from the alleys, canals and temples. Heedless of their lives, they smashed into our column with spears and maquahuitls and shot into us from barricades, rooftops and even from canoes. Eight Castilians were slain in the first assault and the rest of us were wounded. Ordaz himself received three wounds. My armor and shield protected me from the shower of missiles—a blur to my left and I was hit in the cheek by an arrow—the itzli point striking my teeth. I broke the shaft and drew the broken end out through my mouth.

We fought back with the strength of terror. The Mexican fighters got in behind us and threatened to turn our flank. I circled my sword over my head as a signal. Our signalmen, desperately waving their flags, transmitted my order up and down the line.

"*Dar de vuelta!*" was repeated to my right and left. Despite the force of the attack our line curved until the ends finally met to complete the circle.

"*Fuego!*" Muskets exploded, spitting balls of death.

"*Recarge! Fuego!*"

The battlefield became a pall of smoke and screaming wounded. In front of me, the head of a warrior dressed as a great falcon, exploded. In a flash of time, I could see the skin of his scalp collapse onto the base of his skull.

"*Quedensen unidos!*" The espadas pulled closer together. I drove Bebidor's point up through the chin of a warrior who was only a boy. The force of my blow lifted him off of his feet and, for a moment, only my blade supported him.

Crossbowmen and arquebusiers fired at warriors but an arm's length away. We infantrymen protected them with our shields, stabbing through the flimsy Mexican shields and into the enemy's unprotected bodies. Unable to advance, we fell back towards the palace leaving a trail of death in our wake.

Closer to the wall we could see that the ambush was but part of a larger Mexican attack. The transformed Tenochca attacked the palace killing another twelve Castilians and wounding another forty-five. My own force lost another six men as we forced our way back to the gate. The man next to me—a Greek from the island of Cyprus—was struck senseless by a large stone thrown from a rooftop. I tried to protect the unconscious man, but was unable to keep him from the grasping hands of the enemy. They dragged him off with shouts of triumph.

The gate was opened to receive us. Before I could enter, a chieftain armed with a bronze-headed club struck my shield with such force that it shattered in my hand. The man was quick and before I could retaliate, he grabbed my arm, dragging me away from my compadres. I encircled his neck with my left arm and, with all of my power; I drew his face close to mine. I bit into his cheek, removing a chunk of flesh. Surprised, the man relaxed his grip. With room to move, I thrust Bebidor into his belly driving it completely through him, turned and escaped through the gate. Afterwards, I was soaked with sweat and it was a long time before my body stopped shaking.

Dozens of Tenochca scaled our walls but all those who reached the top were knocked off or killed. Blazing arrows and darts fell like burning rain and set the remaining thatched and wooden structures ablaze—if it were not for the fact that most of the palace was made of stone, we would have been lost. The battle lasted all day but subsided after nightfall. In the dark, we bound our wounded and repaired our defenses.

"What do you think, gentlemen?" Cortés was trying to sound calm.

"Retreat to the north." Diego de Ordaz advised.

"But the causeway is cut."

"Fill in the gaps or bridge them."

Cortés scratched his beard before speaking, "I don't think we're to that point, Diego. Do I hear any other ideas?"

Pedro de Alvarado, who had regained all of his old confidence, spoke up. "Take it to them, I say. Now that we've got the men and horses let's go on the offensive and teach them a little respect."

Cortés looked for me in the ranks of wounded soldados. "De la Peña? Are you still alive?"

I was, but barely. "If we're not going to retreat, Pedro is right. To stay bottled up here in the palace is only to delay our extermination."

Cortés nodded his head. "Agreed. Tomorrow we go on the offensive. Organize your men, señores."

●●●

As expected the Mexica advanced in a tightly packed mob. When they were close enough we fired our cannons cutting down dozens. The rest of us sallied forth along with several thousand Tlaxcalteca. The enemy was forced back but their ranks solidified and they held us. Undaunted, we banged the hilts of our swords against our shields and charged again, knocking the Tenochca back. The enemy broke, fleeing with screams of terror. Seizing our victory, we shouted our old battle cry "*Santiago!*" and pursued. The enemy, however, surged in from the sides—hundreds more appeared on the rooftops.

We were caught in their ambush and had to fight our way out of it, killing thirty or forty with every charge. In their rage, they never seemed to feel it. We did feel the damage they were doing to us.

We burned houses, hoping that we could start a general conflagration. The houses were separated, however, by water and we could only burn one house at a time. Our efforts to fill in the broken canals were equally hopeless. Mexican missiles always drove us back. I have seen many battles in Italy and have faced French cannon and German Landsknecte but never before have I faced the unadulterated violence of the Mexica warriors. We fought our way back to our quarters but it was a very near thing.

That night was a horror of screams and whistles—the heads and body parts of some our killed soldiers—illuminated red by hundreds of torches—were thrust up from the Mexican barricades. The night was pierced by even more terrible cries. Captured Tlaxcalteca and Castilians were dying slowly and horribly. I recognized the white-bearded head of old Hector Herrera borne on a pole. Just as he had predicted—he'd made his last fight.

●●●

The next days were a nightmare of Mexican assaults. We retaliated with attacks out into the streets. We tried to break up the Mexican companies and to kill as many as possible. It was never enough. The Tenochca were not stupid—feeling the effect of our cannon, they confined most of their attacks to the long-range bombardment of arrows, sling-stones and darts. These missiles punished us when we went on the attack. Even in our defensive positions—behind the palace's wall—missiles still lobbed in with the occasional soldier hit or killed.

Given the Mexican tactics, most of our charges went into thin air and only afforded the enemy a chance to get better shots at us. During the few times that the Tenochca assaulted in force, we inflicted losses that, to most enemies, would be catastrophic. The Mexica, however, were made of better stuff. No matter how many died, their numbers were always replaced. Our force, however, was whittled down hourly.

●●●

"We lost fourteen more today. I don't understand it." Cortés had been wounded during the day's fighting and was despondent. "I thought the Mexica were cowards."

"They were never cowards, Caudillo," I said. "They were merely disciplined which is why they are now so dangerous. They were acting under the Emperor's orders but now, they are acting under the orders of Cuitlahuac."

"I don't believe it. That swine Moctecuzoma has ordered the attacks."

"You're deluding, yourself, Caudillo. Our great prize, Moctecuzoma, is now worthless."

He considered this reality. "If you're right, Rodrigo, we must take possession of the *Plaza Mayor*."

●●●

The Caudillo was right. Much of the fire that we were receiving was coming from the *Plaza Mayor* and especially from the heights of the teocallis. These structures were crowded with thousands of howling savages. The most bothersome of these buildings, because of its height, was *Coatepec*, the *Templo Mayor*, itself. On its steps and top were hundreds of armed Tenochca who kept up a constant torrent of long-range fire against us. Because of this incessant punishment, our situation was becoming untenable—we had to put an end to it. Escobar—along with one hundred men—was ordered to clear the steps of the temple.

Three times we charged into the Plaza, and three times we were driven back. It's strange the things that stick in one's mind. I remember picking up an enemy copper-tipped spear, driving in into an enemy warrior and impaling another on his far side. Both writhed on the same pole before the farside Indio pulled himself free. The warrior—the target of my thrust—forced himself along the weapon to get at me but, while still reaching out, he gurgled blood, slumped and died.

I left him with my spear. He'd earned it.

Cortés, protecting his wounded hand with his shield, led the next attack with forty horsemen, three hundred Castilians and many more Tlaxcalteca. Two horses slipped and fell on the polished tiles—their riders instantly seized and carried away by triumphant enemy warriors. Nevertheless, we succeeded in scattering the defenders in front of us and charged up the steps of the Great Mosque, *Coatepec*—the summit packed with painted fanatics. The Mexica had the advantage of height and, along with their usual stones and darts, they hurled down burning timbers. Castilians and allies were crushed and burned alive, and many others were wounded. Others went down, slipping on the blood-coated stairs.

A fist-sized stone struck me in the chest and knocked me back—I couldn't breathe—recovering, I continued up the steps. I fought my way up to the top where the combat became even more desperate. Warriors—sacrificing their own lives—seized some of our men, clutched them close and rolled over the sides. Two naked Mexica seized the Caudillo and dragged him to the edge. José Maldinado speared one and, picking up a broken tile with both hands, crushed the skull of the second. If it were not for this, Cortés would have tumbled to his doom.

At first we prevailed and even dislodged their idols and fired their templos. Slicing and stabbing in all directions, I wounded two wild-eyed Mexica and forced others over the precipice. We killed many teopixquia and took two prisoner. Then it all turned around—hundreds of fresh warriors appeared. Down the steps we stumbled, faster than we had ascended them. The onslaught forced us back through the plaza to the shelter of the palace but even here the victorious enemy kept coming. They scaled our walls but, feeling our steel, they backed off.

After the fighting subsided, we counted our losses and found that we had lost forty-five more Castilian dead. Mexican savages, gaudy in their body paint and feathers, lashed the bleeding and mutilated bodies to spears and paraded them before us in triumph. The orange glow of their torches flickering on the dead faces of our friends made the scene all the more Hellish.

Burgos, Castilla-León

"It is an interesting thing about memory, Padre, especially about things from those far away days—it is difficult for me to remember if something actually happened or was simply related ..."

Mendoza dropped his plume and regarded the old man with something like contempt. "Do you mean to tell me, Obispo, that this."—he tapped the manuscript—"is but an exercise in futility?

"Not at all, Padre. I was just expressing an opinion. Much of what we think we remember was related to us by others. More often, however, our distant memories are but the *memories* of lost memories."

"Another one of your contorted philosophies, Excelenica..."

"We forget many things, Padre, but sometimes we remember the memory itself."

"Perhaps."

"Let me tell you something else interesting about memory. The most vivid things are *not* the emotion of confrontation; the beauty of a sunset; the crawling fear of battle or even the sensual pleasure of the love of a woman."

"Then, Obispo, might I ask what—*for you*—what are the most tangible memories?"

"*Smell*, Padre. The scent of flowers in the air; the odor of an infant; the sour smell of a Mexican pueblo and especially the smell of battle."

"Battle has its own smell?"

"Sweat, gun smoke, hot blood, shit and spilled guts."

"Not very appetizing, Obispo."

"*It* is the smell of *fear* and, if very close—so close you can see the pores in your enemy's face—smell his sweat, smell his foul breath—see his grimace when he feels the blade; see the light leave his eyes..."

"Perhaps, Your Grace, we should get on with your narrative."

Lost in his memories, the old man wasn't listening. "The French smell the worst. They stink of the foul things that they call food."

Mendoza was growing increasingly uncomfortable but tendered a question. "The Indios, Obispo?"

"Better than Europeans—the savages don't wear heavy clothes and, the rags they wear, they wash weekly."

"No doubt a primitive ritual..."
"No doubt, Padre."

Chapter 18

Malinche was now desperate. "Then I have no choice. I'll have to go to that cabrón and get him to talk to his people."

"Too late, Hernán," Olmedo told him. "Moctecuzoma has no power."

Cortés approached Moctecuzoma but at first he didn't speak. Moctecuzoma's voice was so faint it came as a whisper. "What more does Malinche want of me? I neither wish to live or to listen to him. He is responsible for all that has happened."

Padre Olmedo, who had been unable to turn the Emperor from his gods, had nevertheless become his friend. He spoke softly to the unhappy man. "Thousands of your people are dying, My Prince. If you would but speak to them, they might still listen."

Moctecuzoma, even at the end, had no spine. "Maybe if you had asked me earlier it might have helped but now it is too late. Nevertheless, I will try."

Accompanied by Cortés and Fraile Olmedo, he mounted the parapet so he could stand on the wall and speak to his people below. As warriors rampaged in the streets below, Gonzalo de Sandoval and Javier de la Concha, standing to the right and left of the Prince, protected him with their shields. The Mexica, recognizing Moctecuzoma, lowered their weapons. He began to speak: *My relatives and subjects, I want you to put up your weapons and to go home....*

One great feather-clad chieftain shouted his contempt, "We will not listen to you, whore of the Spanish! Cuitlahuac is our leader now. You have deserted your people and deserve only death."

Stones and arrows flew like a swarm of angry bees and clanged from the protecting shields. Concha pulled his shield towards himself, leaving Moctecuzoma exposed. He dropped as if pole-axed—three stones hit him—one of which struck him hard in the temple. His subjects, seeing what they had done, fled, leaving the streets empty of all but the dead. The unconscious man was carried back into our quarters but, on recovering consciousness, he refused any help.

"Leave me," he said. "My people have done right. For my friendship to you I have betrayed my own country. It is best that I die."

●●●

The Caudillo, seeing that our enemies had run away, ordered us to hold our defensive positions until the Mexica made their intentions known. We were not long in suspense for the Tenochca quickly reassembled their forces and began a relentless long-range bombardment. It was clear to me that our defensive posture was bound to lead to our utter defeat—our only chance of salvation was to take the battle to the enemy. I searched my memory. Most of our losses and defeats came from enemy fighters who had the advantage of height from the rooftops of adjacent buildings. In the dust I diagramed my idea to Cortés.

"I've seen this done in Italy—it's a simple engine called a *mantalete*—it's a wooden tower built as two big boxes, one on top of the other. The height should be such that arquebusiers can fire directly at or even down on enemy warriors fighting on the rooftops."

He was interested. "*No hay mejor maestra que la necesidad*—there's nothing like a little fear to sharpen our minds. How does it move?"

"Axles and wooden wheels. The engine will be pulled into place by our Tlaxcalteca."

"They will take heavy casualties."

"Regrettable," I said.

●●●

Our carpenters built three of these mantas out of wood scavenged from the palace. Each engine was designed in such a way as to hold twenty-five soldiers. Loopholes were cut for the use of arquebuses and each required a force of hundreds of Indios pulling on attached ropes. Although I would have liked to see them taller, additional height might have caused them to topple. Nevertheless, our engines were formidable and the mere sight of them gave our soldiers hope. I was reminded of the horse of Troy.

We manned these machines and marched forth. I armed myself

with an arquebus, climbed a ladder into the machine and took my position seated on a narrow board. In the rear and to the flanks of our engines we positioned infantry along with crossbowmen. Tlaxcalteca, pulling with nequen ropes and pushing from behind, moved the protesting engines through the streets. To my distress I found that my engine swayed, dangerously—missiles banged into the side. It reverberated like a huge drum. Enemy fire was intense and Tlaxcalteca tumbled from their positions on the ropes. The survivors pulled the mantas to a broken down bridge while, at the same time, Castilians and allies filled in the canal with debris taken from ruined houses.

It was a rare experience to actually be looking *down* on the enemy. I pointed my musket at a fat man throwing stones from the roof of a house. He was bald with a naked chest that was painted in blue and pink circles—the range was not over three arm-lengths.

"*Fuego!*" The sound of twenty-five arquebuses going off at one time within a confined shell is why I can now barely hear—my ears still ring as if there are whistles inside of my head.

The rooftop fighters either died on the spot or jumped to the street below. As the smoke cleared I could see that my man was on his back with four great wounds on him. I was not the only one who thought the circles made good places to aim.

New Tenochca replaced the dead and, for a time, we shot them to pieces but there were nearby buildings taller than our mantletes. There was a great crash, and a stone came smashing through the roof, crushing a soldier and bending his musket. His body fell to the street where it was pulled free by a door that I had provided for just that purpose. Then there was second crash and a third. Then there was daylight overhead and the man beside me was replaced by a splatter of blood. Through the opening in the roof I could see a nearby building packed with warriors throwing stones and flaming darts.

We quenched the numerous fires while others continued firing their weapons at the enemy. The inside of my mantalete filled with choking smoke and showers of sparks. One of our musketeers exploded. The powder at his hip ignited, blowing his genitals away. We let the screaming man down and continued the battle. We fought all day but finally the bombardment became unbearable.

"*Retrete!*" Our Captains shouted. Our Tlaxcalteca, who had sheltered from the onslaught by hiding in ditches and rubble, resumed their positions on the ropes. Under a storm of fire and taking many casualties, they pulled the mantaletes back to our palace fortress. As we retreated I could see that the Tenochca were busily digging out the canal that we had filled in with so much effort and blood.

● ● ●

That night we repaired our mantas as best we could, and, at first light, we sallied out again. We changed the direction of our attack and fought our way along the avenue to the west, leading to the causeway at *Tlacopan*. Not expecting an attack in that direction, the Mexica had few defenses and we caught them by surprise. By a combination of infantry defense and fire from our mantas, we filled in seven breaks in the canals—we reestablished our connection to the western mainland.

After two days of fighting our mantaletes were riddled with holes and, in places, fires had damaged the basic structures.

"What do you think, Rodrigo?" the Caudillo shouted up to me.

"Time to abandon them, Caudillo."

"Then get the men out and burn them. We don't want to give these savages any trophies." As it turned out, we did not have enough wood or time to build any others.

● ● ●

We were overjoyed when the Mexica proposed a truce. All they required is that we release two of their priests we had captured on the top of the *Templo Mayor*. The Caudillo agreed, hoping that the Tenochca might lift their siege. We couldn't know it but our release of the priests was one of the worst things that we could have done. One of these men was their great high priest—*The Teoteuctli*—and was necessary for the coronation of their new emperor—Cuitlahuac—the man who had sworn to destroy us. The Mexica redoubled their attacks, driving our garrisons from the canals and breaking them open again.

Cortés—trying to maintain our only avenue of escape—charged out with both caballeros and infanterias. We smashed into the enemy and drove them back from the canals. We burned nearby houses and used their rubble to—once again—fill in the reopened canals. The Mexica, who knew how high the stakes were, reassembled and struck us with a cloud of arrows.

A tigre-clad man, swinging a long-handled club, attacked the Caudillo. The blow hit him in the side, almost striking him from his horse. He lost his lance but, by hanging onto his horse's neck with both hands, he managed to hold on. The warrior now turned his attention to me. He feinted at my head and, when I raised my shield to defend myself, he aimed a blow at my legs. I jumped back—not in time—something cracked in my leg. I hit the ground hard and looked up to see the Tenochca raising his club to deliver the final blow.

He stood there for seconds as if thinking it over. Then, as by magic, blood poured from his mouth and he collapsed on top of me. Macitoc stood there in his place, a bloody hunting spear in his hand. He nodded towards me, turned, struck a Castilian down and disappeared into the mass of fighters.

I struggled to my feet but, unable to use my injured leg, I hopped behind our shield wall. I was unable to fight and, as long as the enemy was between our force and the palace, I was also unable to retreat. Terrified, I had to watch the battle over the shoulders of our infantrymen.

The fighting was deadly and later it was reported had that St. James—*Santiago* himself—was in the midst of the fight. Some also said that *la Virgen Santisima*, clad in her white robes, was seen throwing dust in the eyes of the enemy. These rumors were false. I saw the mounted Alvarado fighting bareheaded, his sword slashing like that of Achilles—golden hair glowing like a halo. I also saw a Mexican woman, clad in a white tunic, fighting on behalf of her countrymen. These mortal human beings were confused with St. James and the Virgin.

●●●

Moctecuzoma, whose wounds had not seemed dangerous, was dying. Totally dejected, he had refused food and water and had given himself up to his terrible gods. Padre Olmedo, raising the crucifix over the emperor's head, offered to take his confession.

"I have but a few moments to live and will not at this hour desert the faith of my fathers."

"But your soul will burn in Hell."

Moctecuzoma, his eyes wide and lustrous, stared at the ceiling. "I have tried to obey the gods, and I will go to my place in *Mictlan*, but you, my friends, will be the ones who roast in Hell." He went on, "I would speak to Chichtli."

I limped to his side. "Chichtli I have offended *Huitzilopotchi* and I am paying his price. Now I beg of you, speak to the god and tell him that I meant no evil. Ask him to save my people and tell him that I will be his slave in *Mictlan* from this day until the end of eternity."

"I will tell him—but—he is a god."

Moctecuzoma whispered, "I know." He turned his head and died with his eyes wide open. The date was June 20, 1520.

● ● ●

In hopes that the enemy might desist in their attacks, the Caudillo gave Moctecuzoma's body to his people. A truce was called and, in a gesture of conciliation, twenty Mexican lords were released and departed with the body of their emperor. Some of the other chieftains that we still held were put to death—I can't remember why. That night something happened that had never happened before. Hundreds of Mexican women, bearing torches in the darkness, came to look for the bodies of their dead that had been accumulating at the foot of our wall. The weeping and screams were more terrible than was the onslaught of their men. Listening to the intensity of the wailing, I recognized that there was no way that we could ever again make peace with these people—the hatred now ran too deep.

Gustavo Müeller—a short, muscular man—was guarding the wall. He had a colorful history and, to hear him tell it, he was outlawed by the Germans for public indecency and manslaughter and by the Italians for seduction of nuns, sacrilege and theft of Holy Relics. A step in front of the authorities, he fled to Catalonia where he made himself unwelcome by looting two cathedrals in Barcelona. Now—with absolutely nowhere else to go—he was guarding a wall in the heart of a hostile city located at the ends of the earth. He called out to me, "Have you seen the Hell and the lament down there, Rodrigo. If you haven't seen it, you can do so from here."

He gave me his hand and, by using a crutch that I had fashioned from two Indio spears, I was able to climb to the top. By the light of flickering torches, I could see people moving over the street that had become a battlefield. Weeping women, finding the bodies of their husbands and sons, threw themselves down on swollen, stinking, leaking bodies of warriors who had been dead for days.

"We had better get out of here, Rodrigo." Müeller was ordinarily as solid as a rock but what he now saw unnerved him. " Even if we could defeat their men, we will *never* defeat their women."

I agreed, "Now that Moctecuzoma is dead..." I didn't have to end my sentence.

I signaled to Francesca, who was waiting below. "Come see this."

We both pulled her up—Múeller handled her more than was strictly necessary. Francesca never noticed and stared on the scene in silence. Then she whispered, "We'll never get out of here."

Later, we heard that Moctecuzoma did not receive the rites of a dead emperor. Ordinarily there would be days of mourning, and then the body, along with sacrificed jesters, attendants and concubines, would be cremated with full honors. In the case of Moctecuzoma, however, his corpse was tossed onto a garbage heap and permitted to rot.

La Noche Triste

The Caudilllo, who now had fallen into one of his periods of gloom, bent to the will of the army. One of our men, a sooth-sayer, by the name of Botello, influenced his decision. He was a tall, skinny fellow with a limp who was known to favor the abandonment of *Tenochtitlan*. This scoundrel managed to avoid combat by doing favors for our Captains by foretelling their golden futures. He claimed that he had been astrologer to the Pope in Rome and, shortly before that deadly night, he told Andrís de Ávila that he had consulted the stars.

"I tell you, señores, the stars are right for it. Jupiter and Saturn are in alignment and Mars crosses Orion's belt. Tonight is a favorable period for high adventure."

"Whose adventure, Señor Botello," Francesca asked, "ours or the enemy's?"

"Ours, of course. These *ignorantes* don't know the stars."

I was unconvinced. "One question, señor. How do you know the position of the stars? It has been solid overcast for over a week."

"*Ahh!* That is a craft secret. Suffice it to say that I have a valuable instrument from the Orient for astral alignments, divination and interpretation of ancient manuscripts."

Cortés was listening in. "Tonight, you say?"

"Yes, Caudillo. Tomorrow night will be too late. Jupiter will have moved out of its ideal position. Anything might happen."

"And if we go tonight?"

Botello smiled confidently. *"Success!"*

Cortés, who had previously been impervious to all appeals to leave, now abruptly changed his mind.

Burgos, Castilla-León

"Your Grace, I previously reported on Botello's influence in my book—no matter what else may be said against him, Cortés was a practical man. Why do you think that he heeded the words of this mystic when he had already rejected the same suggestion from some of his Captains?"

The Bishop pondered the question before answering. "Cortés was, despite his other qualities, superstitious as any other man. Despite all of his calculation, deceit and determination, he felt that our ultimate success was in the province of a higher powers. On the other hand, *if* we had been safe in the City and, *if* Cortés had not been in one of his funks, he would have dismissed Botello's words without a second thought. Yet, we were besieged and growing constantly weaker. Even our Caudillo came to realize that retreat was our only alternative. Botello's words merely speeded up the process by a day or two—for the worse, I might add. If our retreat had been more carefully considered, our losses would have been fewer."

"On the other hand, Your Grace, astrology is a science that must be respected."

"Only in the sense that some of the practitioners of astrology are also agents of Satan—Botello, for example, also dabbled in the black arts. In my opinion, Satan was determined to draw the last drop of misery not only out of Mexico, but also out of our soldiers. Botello spoke the words but Satan softened Cortés' mind, and made him listen. La Noche Triste was the hideous result."

As Francesca and Amelia were tending the sick and wounded, I called them aside. They knew why I came.

"Has Cortes made his decision, Rodrigo?"

"Tonight."

Amelia's large eyes grew even larger.

"I just learned of it myself. I'm sure he wanted to keep the information from Mexica spies so he is leaving little time for preparation."

"Stay with us!" Amelia begged.

"I will be commanding my company and will be in the van. We should be able to provide adequate protection for both of you and some of my men's other women. Do you have your weapons?"

During the previous months I had trained both Francesca and Doña Amelia in the rudiments of the sword and the short Mexican hunting spear. Francesca had become an expert but Amelia, because of her size, was hopeless.

Francesca responded, "I'll get our weapons and armor?"

"No metal armor. If you get knocked off the causeway or into a canal, you'll sink and drown. I'm only going to wear cotton padding to fend off arrows. Go light as possible."

"*Si, Señor.*"

"We'll be leaving at midnight...Cortés is gambling that the Tenochca are exhausted with today's battle and will post no guard. It is a huge gamble but it is a gamble we'll have to take. Fortunately, the night is overcast with rain and thunder. This should help to cover the sounds of our retreat."

Francesca surprised me. She stepped forward and shook my hand. "Rodrigo, I only wish we'd had more time to get to know one another better."

"There will be plenty of time later," I stated without conviction. "I'm even thinking of money. The Caudillo says that after the King's Fifth has been loaded onto horses, the treasure room will be opened and we can take all we want."

Francesca stepped back and eyed me dubiously. Amelia, who understood my words, started to weep.

"No, I'm not that stupid," I said. "Those who load themselves with treasure tonight may find that they die rich....and soon. I'll enter the room, get all I can and bury it in a place I know in one of the gardens. That way, if we are victorious, we can recover it later. If we should lose...well...it won't matter, anyway."

"We'll help you."

"No. I want you two to get your weapons and wait for me with the army."

I kissed them both quickly and made my way to the treasure room.

PART 3
Chapter 19

In anticipation of our flight, Cortés ordered construction of a portable bridge adequate to support the weight of marching men, horses and the cannons. He planned to move the bridge from back to front, in this way leap-frogging the army to safety across all of the open gaps in the broken causeway. He also ordered that our tamanes carry long bridging planks that, in the case of disaster, men on foot might escape. The horses' hooves were muffled in cotton padding and the army was ordered to retreat along the *Tlacopan* causeway to *Tacuba*.

The southernmost causeway would put our force much closer to our friends in *Tlaxcala* but its greater length, and more numerous broken bridges, could prove fatal. Better, he calculated, that the army enter the mainland at *Tacuba* and fight its way to the north and then down the eastern side of the Lake, which would put us in range of our allies. Two hundred men would be in the vanguard including most of the Captains including Sandoval, Concha, Tapía, Olid and Lugo. Our frailes would also be in the van along with Doña Marina and Pedro de Alvarado's mistress.

The center was commanded by the Caudillo himself and included one hundred men, all of the cannons and the surviving nobles including one of Moctecuzoma's sons and two of the dead monarch's daughters—both of whom were Cortés' mistresses. The King's gold would also be traveling here, guarded by Alonso de Ávila and Cristóbal de Guzman. The rear guard, which was the bulk of the infantry, was, unfortunately, placed under the command of Pedro de Alvarado.

As you know, Cortés later testified before the Royal Tribunal that the King's gold was loaded on one sound and another lightly wounded horse. He also testified that both of these horses were lost during the retreat on the bridges.

Burgos, Castilla-León

Mendoza stopped writing. "You are skeptical of his testimony?"

"You're correct, Padre. Two horses could never carry that much weight.

"Do you claim that Cortés recovered this gold?"

"No. He never recovered it because he never lost it. The King's Fifth was loaded onto four horses, *all* of which were strong and completely intact. Two of these horses were lost but the other two survived."

"Then how is it, Your Grace, that this never came out during the inquiry?"

"It's because the Officers of the Royal Court were bribed and because the Captains were complicit."

Mendoza chuckled. "Ah, Your Grace, *excusa no perdida, la culpa manifesta*—you have just delivered testimony against yourself."

The old man winked at the younger priest. "But it will never matter, Padre, if you know what I mean."

Mendoza quickly picked up his quill.

To be certain, the retreat started out well enough—Cortés' initial calculation was correct. The Mexica, as exhausted by the day's fighting as we were, had not left a single man to watch for an attempted escape. The weather also seemed to be on our side, for there was unusually black with a constant drizzle, accompanied by rolls of thunder. Unfortunately, the storm was just overhead and the lightning flashes were brighter than daylight.

The gates were pushed open at midnight, July 1. The men and horses shuffled out, no man speaking above a whisper. The army marched twenty abreast and managed to cross all of the canals within the city without drawing attention despite the unavoidable clatter of armor.

As the army splashed onto the causeway—disaster struck. A Mexican woman, drawing water from a canal, spotted the army during the flash of an especially vivid bolt of lightning. Her screams woke nearby warriors who quickly relayed the warning to others across the city. Teopixquia shouted for the warriors to take their canoes and attack the fleeing enemy. At the same time the great serpent-skin covered drum of *Tlaloc* boomed out revenge.

●●●

Within the city, the shouts and cries grew to the volume that exceeded that of the thunder. Fearing the inevitable, our soldiers broke ranks and began to run. The first open ditch was encountered, which delayed the terrified soldiers. The bridge was laid down and the disorderly retreat continued but now the shadows of the first canoes appeared accompanied by the whir of occasional arrows and darts. The army hurried on but was stopped by the next gap and it was not possible to travel forward until the rear guard had cleared the portable bridge. The army was thus squeezed between two gaps as the canoes increased in number and Mexican fire increased. When the rear guard finally cleared the bridge, it was pulled up with difficulty and then it was dragged to the front—*through* the mass of panicked soldados and Tlaxcalteca—where it was laid down, yet again. By now the surrounding Lake was thick with canoes and individual warriors, eager for glory, leaped onto the causeway and fought the Castilians and Indio allies, man to man.

The army—no longer an army—groped its way forward but was stopped yet again by another open canal. This time, due to the ferocious Mexican attack and due to the fact that most of the designated bridge carriers were dead or captive, it was not possible to again deploy the portable bridge—it was wedged so tight that it couldn't be pried up. Increasing numbers of Mexican darts clattered against armor and occasionally chunked into flesh. Enemy warriors, oblivious to danger both in the front and the rear, jerked both Castilians and allies from the causeway and into the water. Dozens of prisoners were pulled into their canoes.

The army was thrown into total confusion, as all order was lost. Cannons toppled into the water, horses were slain, and men, who in the daylight would have been heroes became cowards. Alvarado, in charge of the rear guard, abandoned his horse and then, to his eternal disgrace, even his men. He threw a great plank over an open water gap and, teetering, made it to the other side. His men were not so lucky and died by the hundreds. María de Estrada fought off knots of the enemy with the sword of one of her lovers.

Men, in their terror, tried to escape by pressing on the men in front of them. The men, in front, toppled into the water gaps, like sheep going over a cliff. Soldiers weighted down by armor and gold, were either drowned in the water and mud or were taken captive by the victorious Tenochca. The only soldiers who had much chance were those who, anticipating what could happen should their flight be detected, had removed their iron armor. Some of these men were able to swim the gaps and finally made it to the mainland.

At one gap, the men died in such numbers as to completely fill it with bodies. Some of the men following were able to keep their feet dry by stepping on the dead. Cortés and others made it to the mainland but turned back. Even Cortés, however, could make no headway and was finally driven back.

Later, I was told, the Caudillo although badly shaken, never faltered in his determination of final victory. He tried to minimize his casualties, marched to the north and later to the east. Even he, however, could not disguise the enormity of this Noche Triste. He had lost over one half of our force, including most of our horses and all of our cannon. He had only four hundred and twenty soldiers remaining and had left more than eight hundred others dead or prisoners. Some of these losses could have been avoided, however, had he only better planned his retreat.

Cortés, to the destruction of most of his force, believed in Botello's prediction. He therefore moved so abruptly that some soldiers defending one of our other strong points never learned of it until our main force had already left. With no alternative but capture and death, they tried to retreat the same direction of our main force. Consequently, when the alarm was raised they were caught in the streets of *Tenochtitlan* and were captured and killed to the man—over two hundred and seventy more *were* lost here.

Despite the loss of more than half of the force, I find it suspect that most of Cortés' Captains survived. To be certain some important men were lost, including Velásquez de León, Botello, Lares, Terraszas and the popular el Pulido. Moctecuzoma's son and daughters were also lost. The few Mexican lords we still had with us also died or disappeared. We also lost the brave Francisco de Morla.

Burgos, Castilla-León

"It must have been a terrible experience, Your Grace, but is it not possible for us to now take a break. My fingers are sore and my backside is numb. I fear that if I don't stand up soon, I may never stand up again."

The old man didn't budge. "We still have a lot of work."

"But, Excelencia, just a few minutes."

"When we finish you will get all the rest you need. Who knows? I might not return for a month."

"A *month?*"

"Or two months, depending on the Suprema."

"Why not twice a week?"

"My life's not my own, Padre." The old man's laugh was more like a wheeze. "It belongs to Holy Mother Church."

"Perhaps if you let me leave the prison at night—with guards, of course."

"No."

"I won't try to escape."

"No."

Excelencia, I still have a little property...in...in...an assumed name."

"How much property?"

"Two thousand riales of rich crop land in Castilla Vieja."

"Go on."

Mendoza leaned over the table, his voice dropping to a whisper, "Perhaps if I put the deed in your name?"

"It's worth consideration."

"And then you would release me."

Now the old man leaned over the table. "No."

For good or ill, I was not a party to the retreat—I have recounted the events as they were told to me later—I was unconscious and nearly dead when the army retreated. After my departure from Francesca and Doña Amelia and realizing that heavy metal and water don't mix, I kept Bebidor but buried my armor in a place the Mexica were unlikely to find it. The same principle applied to gold—there was no way to swim away with it.

Many of the casualties suffered were the result of decisions by Cortés and the treasurers. The gold had been melted into ingots that weighed more than half of one hundredweight and was stamped with the Imperial marca. He did this to comply with Royal Law and to make it less likely that a single soldier would steal any gold. The weight of one ingot would have simply been too great for one man to walk very far with.

Malinche would have been better off leaving most of the gold in its original state, because most of the objects, although remarkable, were delicate and not heavy. Once he decided to melt the gold down, it would have been better had he made them into smaller bricks. Now, however, the weight of these ingots doomed many men and guaranteed the loss of most of the treasure.

I will not underestimate my own greed but it was tempered by reality. My only chance to keep any treasure was to secrete it here in the palace and hope that, at some future time, we would recapture it. I had anticipated the retreat and had already dug a deep but narrow hole in a private place in one of the gardens. From the treasure room, in two trips, I collected two ingots of gold. I placed them in the hole and planted a nopal cactus over my cache, getting hairlike thorns in my hands in the process.

Nearby, I had already dug up another cactus in readiness for additional spoil. Because of my leg injury, I had to use my crutch so my progress was slow. By the time I returned to the treasure room, there were only twenty—maybe less—ingots left and these few were being stuffed under armor of half a dozen gleeful soldiers. There were still a few pearls and two boxes full of chachihuitl; however. I took all of the pearls and fistfuls of blue-green stones. I made my way back to my hiding place by a round about route because—even in our grim circumstances—I feared the greed of our men.

I don't remember hearing anything. There was the flash of a face in the torchlight, a stunning blow on my head, and the taste of metal. All was darkness.

Chapter 20

Burgos, Castilla-León
March 17, 1581 7:30 A.M.

"I trust that you have been using the hours that you spend in your quarters to organize our discussions and put them into a readable form."

"I do my best, Obispo, but I find it difficult to work when I think only of food. I am considering leaving the priesthood and becoming a cook."

"Nonsense, Padre. Not only have I cured your gout but you look like an entirely different man."

This statement was quite true. Mendoza, when he had entered the prison, had been plump and sleek but now his skin sagged and he appeared fifteen years older than his actual age.

"To answer your question, Your Grace, I have succeeded in completing the first chapters of our new historical effort. When you have time, I would be glad to show you what I have."

The old man nodded. "Excellent, Padre, as soon as this session is over I *would* like to see it. I anticipate great things from our collaboration—a complete history of the Conquest of the New World."

Mendoza jerked forward. "*What!* I though we were rewriting the history of the Conquest of Nueva España—*only*."

The old man's eyes glittered in the flickering light. A serpent—deadly, timeless and buried in white Dominican robes—coiled sinuously in front of Mendoza. He felt himself suffocating...

"That's right, Padre," it hissed, "only Nueva España. Let us continue."

I don't know how long I lay there but I became aware of a roar as that of a great wind. The sound grew louder as I regained my consciousness. One side of my head was without feeling and the other side throbbed with an unbearable pain. I was lying in a puddle of very sticky water. As I became more conscious I realized it was blood. I also knew that I was alone. In the distance I could hear the faint pop of muskets and the less common roar of cannons. At first I didn't understand what had happened but then it came to me. A thief in our ranks had clubbed me. I lifted my hands up. My fingers were still clasped around the chalchihuitl and pearls. If thief it was he must have been scared off. Then again, why rob me? The treasure room contained many more of these gems. Then I remembered the face...

Reality washed over me like ice water. I was abandoned—wounded—in the middle of *Tenochtitlan*. Unless I could think of something—and quickly—I was dead. As long as I could move, however, I was still alive. I found my crutch, crawled to the wall and pulled myself up. I felt my head and could feel the lump. My hair was matted with blood and there was a great tear in my scalp. At the same time, I felt a stinging pain in my right side. I explored my cotton armor and found a small perforation. More fearful than ever, I pulled the material up and explored myself with my fingers. Underlying the perforation in the cotton, there was an identical perforation in my skin. Not only had I been clubbed but, once down, my assailant had knifed me.

If the blade had perforated my guts, I must surely die. If it pierced my lung, I was still probably finished—but—a wounded soldier usually coughed blood. My breathing was normal so I suspected my lung was intact. I didn't stop to consider esoteric medical matters, however—I had to do something, and do it immediately. I considered following our force but knew—now that the enemy was aroused—not even an army could make it.

My possibilities were narrowed to one. I must find a hiding place. At the same time I knew that if I couldn't stop the blood, the Mexica would track me no matter how secure my refuge. I looked for something to staunch my bleeding. It wasn't hard to find—debris left by the army was scattered everywhere. While looking for something to pack my wounds I came on two other soldiers. One had his skull crushed and the second had a sliced throat. I knew both of them. One was Enrique Presa—one of the men who had openly argued with Cortés over the division of the spoil. The other was Bernardino de Soría—the man who had informed against his fellow conspirators in Villa Rica—a man Cortés wanted dead.

To make dressings for my wounds, I stripped the cotton armor from the dead men and packed it against my chest. I took another piece and held it to my head. It was still oozing and, to reduce the chance of leaving a trail, I kicked off my bloody sandals and replaced them with the sandals of one of the dead men. Satisfied that I wasn't leaving a blood trail, I hobbled to the center of the palace.

In the direction of the gate to the *Plaza Mayor* I could hear Mexican voices—the first Tenochca searchers. They had entered the palace, no doubt looking for loot and Castilian stragglers. I didn't have much time.

The palace was single-storied but centrally there were two levels. I found the steps and, while trying to avoid the walls with my bloodied body, I limped upward to a hall that was flanked by multiple rooms. Moctecuzoma and his attendants occupied these rooms during happier times but they were now full of refuse and equipment that our men had abandoned. I found an opening to the outside and stepped out onto the roof of the first story. It was flat and tiled but in places there were planters containing flowers, shrubs and small trees. Still other areas were channeled for run-off water. Moreover, the roof was not all of the same level, reflecting the height of the underlying ceilings. Because of this there were occasional recesses and alcoves. I found one barely large enough to fit a small man, and squeezed myself into it.

For the first time since my assault I could breathe more easily—not that it made any difference. I was still wounded, perhaps fatally, and I was still in the heart of the enemy's city. I had no water but I wouldn't die of thirst because it was only a matter of time before the rooftop was thoroughly searched. My situation was hopeless but—listening to the cries in the distance—not as hopeless as that of many others. From my hiding place I could see the top of the great teocalli—*Coatepec*. The light of torches illuminated shadowy figures moving on its summit. The great drum of *Tlaloc* beat on monotonously. I also noticed that the sounds of gunfire had ceased although the distant shouts and screams proved that the battle went on. Probably, I thought, our arquebusiers were so pressed by the enemy that they didn't have time to reload their muskets. The sounds of combat went on for a long time but I was unable to stay awake. I roused as the light of the sun struck the *Templo Mayor* and the buildings around it.

●●●

My first thoughts were not thoughts—there was only pain, weariness and a terrible sickness in my stomach. Even my sickness was unreal and I was back in Italia on my belly beside an icy stream drinking buckets of delicious water but then—a physical blow—the terrible truth hit me again. I listened. The drum still throbbed but the sounds of battle had disappeared. The top of the Great Mosque was crowded with men, some of whom were black teopixquia and others were pipiltin resplendent in their colorful devices and plumes. What had happened? Had the army escaped? I didn't have time for speculation—I heard footsteps nearby. I pulled myself tightly into my compartment thinking that the searchers were not wasting time. The footsteps came closer—stopping—*close!*

I wondered if I left any blood—a single drop would betray me. The footsteps came closer yet and the next thing would be exultant Mexican faces. I would be hauled out, bound and placed in one of their cages, waiting my time for a flowery death on their altar—my captor would feast on my flesh. I was still armed, however, and, despite my wounds, I considered crawling out and facing death on my feet. The footsteps stopped but an arm's length away.

I heard the sounds of a rough struggle. There were the sounds of a blow and then words shouted in Nahuatl and another voice in Castilian—I shuddered—if this was another man's choice of a hiding place, would other Mexica come to search here? Still I wondered who my unfortunate companion was. He must have heard me as I wandered there in the dark but he would have had no way of knowing if I were friend or foe—I wondered again if I had left a telltale drop of blood. As the sounds of the struggle subsided, I could hear the Mexican captor chanting the doggerel that they always recite to their victims. High-pitched sobs and prayers to Our Lady accompanied this pagan chant. Then the only sounds I heard were of footsteps disappearing behind me.

For some hours I was afraid to move but then my heart jumped into my throat as I heard a scraping sound but a short distance away. The noise was on the rooftop in the direction of the *Templo Mayor* but away from the two-story apartments where the footsteps had disappeared. Denial is a powerful impulse and I dismissed the sound as that of a carrion bird. Then I heard it again and there was no question that it was the sound of metal scraping on the roof tiles—I froze—I heard a clanking sound and then a curse whispered in Castilian. "*Madre de Díos! Silencio!*"

I eased up and found myself looking at the backs of two heads, one black and the other red. I wriggled forward.

"*Quienes son ustedes?*" I asked. Both men nearly fainted

Regaining their wits, they jerked around to face me. "*En El Nombre del Diablo quien eres tú?*" I had seen both of them but didn't know them. They were some of the Narváez' men.

"Rodrigo de la Peña. I was wounded in the palace before the army ever left. I had no choice but to hide here on the rooftop. I had no idea I would have so much company."

I looked at the two men—neither one of them appeared to be wounded. Except for their helmets they were both wearing full armor that glittered dangerously when they moved. It was the noise of their armor against the roof tiles that had given them away. Both men had been lying flat in a rain gutter and now, confirming my identity, they flattened out again. When the Tenochca came again—as they certainly would—these men were dead.

"I am Manuel Paulino," one of them whispered, "and this is my friend, Angel de Turbe. Our company was betrayed and the two of us barely made it here alive."

"Betrayed? What sense does that make?"

"It makes sense if you are that bastard, Cortés. Our Captain Molino should have been alerted to the withdrawal but nobody told him. We didn't even know we were left behind until we heard the shooting. Then, with the entire city full of screaming savages, we tried to try to cut our way out—may Cortés roast in Hell—he sacrificed our men to distract the Indios and save his gold."

"He's capable of anything," I whispered, "but even he wouldn't ruin part of his army as a diversion. Still, I've been knifed and not by the Indios. I saw who did it—it was one of Cortés' pigs."

Paulino was trembling. "I wanted to get rich but right now I'd give up everything I have to be back in Santo Domingo. Did you hear what happened to Rico?" He gestured in the direction of the captured Castilian.

"Yes—they'll be back, you know."

Paulino's teeth started to chatter. "We've got to get off this roof."

I agreed. "I'd like to go with you but I would only slow you down."

Paulino went on. "I'm sorry that we will have to leave you alone but you can see how it is."

"Claro," I said. The truth is that I was safer with them gone.

The three of us shook hands. "We'll wait until dark and drop down over the side."

● ● ●

I repositioned myself in my hiding place and, from where I was hiding, I could see the beginning of great festivities on the top of *Coatepec*. The top steps were garlanded with flowers and huge multicolored banners snapped in the wind. Although I couldn't see it, I could hear the trampling of many feet and I could hear melodious voices—young girls—chanting their pagan songs. I must have fallen asleep now it was night, illuminated by the fires from the tops of templos. My newfound friends whispered their farewells. "Good luck to you, Rodrigo. May you live to see the shores of España again."

"*Buena Suerte, señores!*" I said out loud. Then, under my breath, "You're *definitely* going to need it."

There was a scuffling of feet and I heard the sounds of two heavy bodies hitting the tiles below. Then I heard no more.

My pain, but not my fear, had subsided a little—the knife wound was not fatal—it had been deflected by my cotton armor and had only traveled under my skin. Not that it mattered. I was pinned down in the center of *Tenochtitlan* and my discovery was only a matter of time. My only hope was to get what rest I could and slip out of the city along one of the canals—even that seemed impossible.

By raising my head a little I could see the *Templo Mayor*. There were dozens of priests on its platform and, by raising my head a little more, I could see the other teocallis, templos and even the ball-courts—they were packed with thousands of people. This was that night I saw things that I will never see again.

Chapter 21

Hundreds of captives were bound and waiting for sacrifice. All were either naked or clad in simple loincloths. Some had been painted red and white and still others appear to have had their eyes blackened with soot. All appear to be shocked and, with the exception of the occasional victim who cursed and screamed, all did exactly as they were ordered. Most of the victims were Tlaxcalteca, but also present were Españoles, a few of whom I was able to recognize. From here I could recognize the stooped figures of Velásquez de León, Francisco de Morla and Alfonso de la Madrid. I could not see the expressions on their faces but they were as docile as the others.

Also present were rows of the dead laid out as neatly as are the carcasses of partridge and hares displayed by one of our great lords after a successful day in the field. The dead had all been stripped and, despite frightful wounds, had been cleaned of excess blood. The Tlaxcaltec dead were separated from those of Castile. Also present were the carcasses of at least twenty horses. Mexican pipiltin and commoners were held back from the bodies by a cordon of Mexican warriors. Even so, the occasional Tenochca broke through the ranks and, screaming, sometimes weeping, attacked the dead with knife and club. I saw no attacks on the living prisoners. To my way of thinking, the living were the property of the gods and were therefore beyond mere human revenge.

Revenge or not, the dead could still serve as trophies. An army of priests—Workers from the Pits of Hell—decapitated the dead and pealed the skin and flesh from the skulls. Still others, using great drills of bronze, bored holes into and through the sides of the skulls and scraped the gelatinous gray brains from the skull cases. The skulls were then strung on the *tzompantlin* like so many white and pink pearls. The dead horses underwent similar indignities. In these cases the teopixquia were less familiar with the anatomy, and they struggled to free the heads from the carcasses. Once they had been decapitated, however, they were treated just as were the human heads. Skins and flesh were removed, the skulls were drilled, and the skulls were then strung on skull-racks of their own. The animals were also flayed and their skins were then staked out to hang like sodden banners.

I looked closer and could see that some of the horses were not actually dead—some of them lifted their heads and whinnied. Many squirmed and tried to kick free. Their efforts were to no avail, for their legs had been bound securely. I wondered how the Mexica had performed the feat of downing and tying these powerful animals. I also wondered how they carried them to this place. I imagined the strength of the Mexican attack. To subdue and take horses alive would have taken dozens of determined warriors. If they had the numbers to waste on the capture of horses, they would have mustered enough strength to sweep our army from the causeway.

I tried to calm myself. Francesca and Amelia weren't there and, although there were hundreds of dead and prisoners in the plaza, they were fewer than a quarter of our entire force. My fear chilled me again—the Tenochca would hold back some of their captives to die over a period of days. The ones below could very well be a minority of those taken—I wept bitter tears—the entire force had been lost.

To the rhythm of drums and the trill of flutes, girls sang their hymns and warriors danced their wild dances in front of the victims. The ceremony unfolded as the first victim, a Tlaxcalteca—a maxtaltl-clad war chief—flanked by priests bearing incense burners—marched up the steps. The man knew how it was supposed to be done. He mounted the steps with an arrogant tread and, with every step, he shouted his hatred. This was a climb like no other for, at the summit of his mountain, a priest adorned with a headdress of green, yellow and red feathers handed him a resplendent fan fashioned from the green tail feathers of the sacred quetzal. To the rhythm of the drum and the shriek of whistles, he danced his very last dance and, from what I could see, he didn't miss a beat. Five muscular teopixquia picked the victim up and threw his back across the sacrificial altar. Four restrained his arms and legs and a fifth pulled his head back by its long hair.

The stone knife flashed and then the presiding priest held the still beating heart for the hushed crowd below to see. The heart was then placed in the burning bowl—*Quauhxicalli*—sacred to *Huitzilopotchli*. The soft tissue of the neck was cut with precision and then—with two of the priests holding the body—the head was twisted, the body convulsed, and the head came free—all in one smooth motion. The head and body were then tossed from the teocalli. The body tumbled but the head rolled and bounced like a misshapen ball. The bloody corpse fell directly on top of the moon disc of the goddess, *Coyolxauhqui* who, in a like manner, had been dismembered and thrown from the mountain by her brother *Huitzilopotchli*.

The next victim was a Castilian. From this distance and covered with paint, it was difficult to identify him but he bore a resemblance to Botello, our sooth-sayer. Before he could mount the steps his courage failed him and he fell to his knees begging and praying. Two warriors, clad only in loincloths and feathered headdresses, seized him by the head and dragged him up the staircase to the altar. Botello tried to stop his progress by wedging his hands and feet against the steps—it was no use and he only managed to make his ascent more painful. The crowd waiting below hooted.

The victim shrieked as he was picked up and bent back onto the sacrificial stone. His hair was too short for a good hold so his head was pulled down with a double-handled yoke. The high priest held his knife high and chanted unintelligible words. The knife plunged down accompanied by Botello's frenzied howls.

Blood squirted higher than the priest's head, covering his face with blood. The teopixqui sprang back holding the palpating heart overhead. He added it to the smoking brazier. Again the head was cut off more quickly and neatly than I could do with the sharpest knife. It was hard to tell from this distance but I thought, or maybe imagined, that the lips of the decapitated head still moved and the eyes blinked. The still quivering body tumbled to the foot of sacred *Coatepec* where the head and body were recovered by two separate groups of priests.

The broken head was carried to a platform close to the great skull rack—*tzompantli*. Reverently, teopixquia made cuts in the scalp and peeled off the skin. At this point, however, the skull was not treated in the same way as the skulls of those who had been killed on the causeway. The skin of the head and face was then elevated on a stake and the skull was placed in a great boiling pot. Care was taken that this particular skull would be spotlessly clean when it was displayed on the skull rack.

At the other side of the plaza, at the place we called *Infierno*, priests butchered the body but not like we would do a sheep, cow, or pig. Rather than disemboweling the carcass, they simply disarticulated the arms and legs leaving the torso for the feeding of tigers, wolves and lions in their great menagerie. The limbs were skinned back and the flesh was removed from the bones. Some of the meat was placed on braziers; other pieces were placed in boiling pots and still other pieces were awarded to the two warriors who had dragged their unwilling captive up the stairs.

●●●

The next victim was one of the horses. Heavy ropes were attached to the animal as teams of Mexica labored at dragging the struggling animal up the staircase. On the teocalli platform, the teopixquia acted with even more ceremony than they had with their human victims. One of these foul men—the *Teoteuctli*—gave a long speech. His words were sometimes directed at the crowd below, sometimes to the shrine of *Huitzilopotchli* and sometimes to the horse itself. He then took a stone knife—longer than the one he used on his human victims—and held it over his head so that all of the spectators could see it. He studied the horse carefully, as if trying to determine where best to strike. Deciding, he made a long cut in the horse, just behind its ribs. The volume of the horse's screams caused the teopixqui to draw back. The huge animal jerked and struggled, but still the priest sliced deeper.

Suddenly, the animal's entrails slid out. Undaunted, the priest reached over the guts with both of his hands, one of which held his knife. Unaccustomed to such a huge beast, he was initially unable to find the heart—he made more internal cuts. He then thrust his arms up to the shoulders into the cavity he had created. He made more cuts and huge volumes of blood surged from the cavity, totally soaking the *Teoteuctli* from head to toe. Victorious, he moved back displaying the huge and palpating heart in his hands.

The same Tenochca, who had hauled the horse up the staircase, now toppled it down the stairs. The dead but still struggling carcass tumbled to land on the great moon disc of *Coyolxauhqui*.

●●●

Too horrified to take my eyes away, I watched the ceremony far into the night. Once, one of the horses—a roan with a white blaze—broke free of his bindings. Guts dragging, the animal leaped from the temple platform and down the steep staircase. Halfway down, he stumbled and went down head-over-heels. Still fighting, and trying to run on broken stubs of legs, the horse stumbled into the surrounding crowds. Masses of people attacked the ruined horse, halting it before it went any further. Dozens of warriors covered the animal—when they retreated the horse was still as were two members of the crowd.

All of the captives were not sacrificed. De León, Franciso de Morla, de la Madrid and the Negro, Gilberto, were held in reserve as were, I also saw to my great distress, my recent acquaintances—Manuel Paulino and his friend, Angel. Exhausted, I fell asleep but something woke me again. Across the way, on the steps of *Coatepec*, a victim was climbing the steps. Unlike others who shamed themselves, she was going to her death without an escort of guards. Back straight, she looked towards the summit and her ascent up the steps was a delicate dance. My heart stopped. The woman was heart-wrenchingly small and she was naked except for garish red-and-white painted stripes. Despite the black soot around her eyes and despite the distance, I would have recognized her anywhere. She was my poor Amelia.

Burgos, Castilla-León

"Would that I could tell you, Padre Mendoza, that I leapt from the roof, charged into the Plaza with my sword flashing, a shout of defiance on my lips. I would like to tell you that I saved the girl with an act of godlike heroism and, if I could not tell you this, it is better that I not be here today—far better had I died. I'm ashamed to tell you that this isn't what happened. Instead, like a miserable sniveling coward I lay there and did exactly nothing—I didn't even have the courage to watch. I hid my eyes and wept like a child. I sobbed until I could feel nothing."

Mendoza stopped his writing and stared at the emaciated old man as if seeing him for the first time. He spoke very softly,

"Your honor is not compromised. There was nothing you could do."

Now it was the old Bishop's turn to be silent—then he spoke. "I wish that were true—but—it's a lie." The Bishop's voice dropped to a hoarse whisper. "My life has been a lie." He clenched his fist rapidly, three times. "*I am a lie.*" For long moments that withered old man didn't speak, visualizing the nightmare sixty years earlier. "I had the opportunity to die like a man. May the God of Moses and Abraham help me—I chose to live."

Mendoza looked intently at his feathered writing instrument as if it had suddenly become very interesting. He looked up. "If you are unable to have pity for yourself, how can I expect any mercy?"

"That, my friend, is a very good question."

I awakened to a burning thirst. The sun was well up and the rooftop was a furnace. Even so, there was nowhere to go. I decided to bear my discomfort until nightfall but no longer. Like a bird transfixed by the eyes of a serpent I couldn't turn my head away. I again watched the Plaza. Judging by the fresh blood dripping from the great altar and the waiting line of captives, the ceremony had started again.

It is a remarkable thing about the mind; even the most terrible things can become routine. More concerned for my thirst than I was for the lives of my comrades—I watched as dozens went to their fates. I learned why the Mexica referred to it as a *flowery death* for when the vessels of the heart are first severed, blood spurts forth like a red flower coming into bloom. Such is the logic and beauty of ritual murder.

Chapter 22

The rites on the great teocalli subsided as another ceremony was enacted down on the Plaza, itself. The center of this activity was an elevated platform into which was carved a vision of their terrible demons. Next to the platform were two lines of men—one was a line of captives and the other Mexican warriors clad in magnificent costumes in the form of eagles and Mexican tigers. The first captive, a skinny Tlaxcalteca, mounted the platform. In the center of the platform was a hole in which there was a nequen rope. The rope was fastened to the ankle of the man in such a way that he could move freely over the platform, but no farther. An Eagle-clad Tenochca circled the platform—he was armed with a beautiful feathered buckler and a maquahuitl—its itzli blades flashed in the sun. A teopixqui lifted the Tlaxcaleca's weapon up to him. It was also a maquahuitl but, rather than itzli, it was armed with golden feathers. The victim was not given the benefit of a shield.

The priests chanted their prayers that were, in turn, echoed by the two combatants. The Mexica circled the platform from below even as the Tlaxcalteca moved at the end of his tether, keeping as much distance as he could between himself and his enemy. The Tenochca's strike was a blur—a streak of blood appeared on the Tlaxcalteca's lower leg. He instantly retaliated and struck the Tenochca hard across the head. The blow almost knocked the man down but he recovered and struck back. One blow was parried but another laid the Tlaxcalteca's thigh open. Seeing his advantage, the Tenochca struck again and again. The Tlaxcalteca fell to his knees. Itzli flashed again, and his worthless weapon was knocked away. Four black-robed priests, who had been waiting in the background, moved forward quickly. They seized their victim's bloodied limbs while a fifth removed his heart.

The next combat involved a Castilian clad, like all of the others, in only a loincloth maxtlatl. I recognized the man. He was Alfonso de la Madrid and, under other circumstances, a very good man. His opponent was a warrior clad in a costume resembling a Mexican tiger. The surrounding crowd murmured in dissatisfaction. Madrid didn't know the words and he didn't know how he must act to satisfy the gods. He merely slumped, dejected, and made no effort to defend himself. The warrior tried to goad him by poking his butt and then slicing him with his maquahuitl. It was no use. Madrid was completely defeated and wouldn't move. Disgusted, the Tenochca flicked his wrist. The maquahuitl ripped through the large vessel in Madrid's leg. Blood spurted in pulses as, weakening, he let the maquahuitl slip from his fingers. He stood there looking completely bewildered as his life's blood poured out. He sagged to his knees but, before the priests could move, he fell face forward—dead. Nevertheless, they removed his heart and head.

The third combat centered on Velásquez de León. Like Madrid, he faced a tigerman and, like Madrid, he merely looked down at his feet with disinterest, his feather-armed maquahuitl held loosely in his hands. His Mexican executioner shouted but de León didn't react. The Tenochca strutted around him, poking him contemptuously and making insulting gestures. He turned his head to the crowd as if to speak an apology for de León's poor performance. It was a stupid mistake. Suddenly—unexpectedly—de León slammed the end of his maquahuitl hard into his enemy's face. Even from my location I could hear the bones break. The tigerman's weapon clattered onto the platform as, all with one motion, De León picked it up and struck, almost severing his enemy's arm at the shoulder. His next blow struck the neck and the Tenochca collapsed, his head held by a tag of skin. The priests dragged the body out of range of de León and proceeded to remove the heart and head of their slaughtered countryman.

Now the Mexica had a problem. Although tethered, de León was fully armed and dangerous. They could have attacked him, en mass, but that would have disgraced the god. Instead, they continued with the ritual. De León killed three more and wounded two others before, he himself, went down in defeat. I later noticed that de León's skull was awarded a place of honor on a special skull-rack of his own.

Gilberto, perhaps because of his black skin, was afforded a special honor. Ropes tied to a massive vertical rack immobilized his arms, legs and head. Starting with a long cut down the middle of his back—he was skinned alive. Manfully, he refused to cry out but there are limits to courage, and by the time they started on his legs, his screams were those of a trapped and tortured beast. He weakened and died before they started on his face. His skin was laced to the rack the same as we stretch the hide of a goat and his naked corpse was butchered and disarticulated.

● ● ●

By the time the Tenochca had finished with Gilberto's and de León's body, it was nearly dark. In the heat of the day, my thirst had increased to the point that I was beyond the point of caring. I considered dropping off the roof to the ground below as my unfortunate friends had done, but rejected the idea because of the injuries to my leg and chest. Also, within the palace of Axayacatl, I knew the place where we had found water, and hoped that the place would be unguarded. I reckoned that as long as the festivities continued, the palace of would be empty.

As it grew darker, torches threw their flickering light over the rooftop. I reentered the upper floor and descended the stairs to the ground level. Pine-resin torches illuminated most of the rooms and quick observation showed that the Mexica had already cleansed the apartments. Slowly, carefully I unsheathed Bebidor. I crept along trying to remain in the shadows. I heard a faint rhythmic sound and then I heard the whispers of a woman and then of a man. Two lovers, also expecting to have the palace all to themselves, were having a very private tryst. I didn't disturb them.

I made my way to the garden where the spring had been found. The garden was ruined by the tread of Castilian feet and broad areas had been dug up for latrines and the entire area still stank of it. The spring was at the other end of the garden. The soldier who discovered the place had been a farmer in Castilla and recognized, from the dampness of the ground, that there was an underlying seep. At the time, Alvarado's force was under siege and the Tenochca had cut off the water from the great aqueduct. His men were desperate for water and, when the seep was reported, a well—a very deep well—was dug in the garden. Remarkably, the water had less salt than the surrounding lake. Otherwise the army would have perished.

The Mexica had not only failed to fill in the spring, they seemed to have already improved it. Water, which had been several feet from the surface, now filled the well. I tried to control myself but my body was taking control of my mind. My parched throat contracted painfully as

I looked at the water only a body length away. On the other side of the garden, two old men played at a game of thrown bones using cacao beans as their bets. These men must have tired of the revelry outside and retired to this quiet place.

From around a doorway, I watched the two men. I had no way of reaching the water without alerting them and there was no way that I could leave without drinking. Both men were intent on their game and occasionally sucked from a shared gourd. It must have contained octli because both men were very drunk. This simplified my task. The first viejo died before he knew that he was dead and the second was dead before he could shout the alarm.

I thrust my head into the well and drank. I filled my stomach, buried my remaining pearls and chalchihuitl and marked the location in my mind.

● ● ●

Escape from the front entrances, given the outside activities, would be nearly impossible. An escape from the roof, as Manuel and Angel had attempted, was hazardous but was probably my only alternative. Before I took that route, I decided to check on a door in the back of the palace that Cortés had walled up during the siege. Originally the door had been used by servants and, with a great deal of luck, the Mexica may have opened the door again.

I could have wept with relief. Not only was the door open again, it was not guarded. Looking to one side and keeping in the shadows, I stole out onto the city streets—I had a plan. I eased myself into the waters of the nearby canal. The water was cold but, after the initial shock wore off, it was tolerable. With only my nose and eyes above the water I felt my way along the bottom always moving farther from the *Plaza Mayor* and my crime in the Palace. Several times I had to dive and swim under the water for, despite the attractions of the adjacent festivities, I heard the voices of people on the streets above.

● ● ●

Crawling through the mud with all of its filth, I put distance between the palace and me. I finally found what I wanted, a small canoe overturned on the bank with its paddle laying under it. There were two nearby houses but both were dark and I couldn't see or hear anything stirring. I righted the canoe and dragged it into the water. The canoe was heavier than it looked and its bottom scraped on the bank. Nearby, one dog—then another—rushed to the bank, yapping wildly. With the canoe still resting on the bottom, I climbed into it, nearly swamping it. I pushed off with my paddle.

The canoe was tippy and difficult to maneuver. I propelled my vessel into the middle of the canal but it kept going and grounded itself on the opposite side. I pushed off again and was aware of movement in a nearby house. I tried to control my craft with a mixture of paddling and sculling and had some success at guiding the craft. To be certain, I was unable to maintain the straight course that the Mexica always achieved, for my craft veered to the left and then to the right.

I was making progress, however, but whenever I heard a nearby canoe, I stopped my paddling, bent down and let my canoe drift. At one point—from the darkness—words were directed at me in their language. I grunted back and continued my paddling. After I had continued for some time in this way, the canal widened as I entered the open lake. Far behind me I could hear shouts of distress—someone's canoe was missing.

●●●

Using only the stars I paddled to the east. It was here that Moctecuzoma said that he had a hunting refuge—I reckoned this might be a place of very few people. I was weak from loss of blood and lack of food so I was obliged to stop paddling and drift with the wind. Despite my sickness and fear I could still appreciate the sheer magnificence of the scene. The night was moonless and the sky was ablaze with stars. Behind me the torches on the templos and teocallis lighted the city. The horrible, beautiful *Templo Mayor* was brighter than all of the rest. The monotonous beat of its huge drum echoed over the water and penetrated my soul. Its message was clear—I had abandoned the women I had sworn to defend—Angela, Amelia, Francesca—abandoned and destroyed them.

Twice I turned back, determined to throw myself at the enemy—I ached for the self-immolation—the relief of self-murder. Then I remembered my oath and my father's words, "*You are condemned to hardship and loneliness.*" I gritted my teeth, bore my grief and struck out for the east.

Burgos, Castilla-León

Mendoza put down his plume and flexed his hand. "You actually considered a return to the enemy capital?"

"That's *exactly* what I'm telling you, Padre. Once I escaped the City and was in no immediate danger, I lusted for self-destruction."

"You make no sense, Excelencia. If you had seriously considered the sin of suicide you would have done so earlier. You were beaten, stabbed and trapped—you were semi-conscious and miserable with pain, thirst and fear and then—to top it off—you were forced to watch the Mexican blood rituals and witnessed the death of your mistress." The younger man shook his head. "Madness."

The old man's eyes glowed with its blue light. "Madness, perhaps, but a human madness, Padre. The closer we come to death, the stronger the pull of the flesh."

"I don't understand, Excellency."

"Those in the most hopeless circumstances seldom chose self-destruction. At these times the soul may be weak but our animal nature fights back and overcomes spiritual weakness. Suicide is a greater risk when the soul is stronger than the flesh."

"I still don't..."

The old Bishop suppressed his irritation. "Once I was on the Lake—removed from immediate danger—my soul once again took charge of my body. I considered the release of certain death at the hands of the enemy. "

"One time, Your Grace...."

"One time, Padre? Every hour of the day and every day of the year I consider my dishonor. Years ago I would have fallen on my sword if it hadn't been for my promise to my father."

The wind—an easterly wind—came up and slowed my progress—I paddled most of the night. I could see the torches from other cities along the bank and could therefore determine the location of Mocte-cuzoma's refuge for, in that area, there was a broad expanse of shore and dark forest where there was no light. My canoe scrapped bottom just as the first hint of daylight appeared. I dragged the boat up onto the beach and back into the forest. I covered it with dead branches and brushed out the drag marks on the shore. I hoped the gamekeepers were far away, for they were man-hunters skilled in locating the sign of lake-borne poachers.

I worked my way inland. I found a mountain creek and walked in it, always heading upstream into the mountains. The water was freezing but by doing this I avoided leaving a trail and always had available water. I didn't stop until the sun was overhead. Great boulders surrounded the stream and I was able to limp from rock to rock leaving no trace of my passage. I reckoned that if the gamekeepers did hit my trail and found where I entered the stream, they would also deduce that I had traveled in it and search for me nearby—I, therefore, put several hundred paces between the stream and me and held Bebidor at the ready. I found an overhang in the rocks and spent the day sleeping with one eye open.

●●●

I relocated the stream by the gurgling of its waters. I kept going until the ground grew too steep for my continued passage. I think that it was at this point that I first had the luxury to consider my options. I was now well clear of Mexico and believed that my presence on this mountain had gone unnoticed but where should I go from here? My biggest problem was that I didn't know if any part of the army had survived. Another problem was that one of Cortés' Captains—Javier de la Concha—for it was his face I had seen, had tried to kill me. If he survived the flight from Mexico he would surely try to murder me again.

If Cortés were alive, he had suffered a terrible defeat. In this condition, his nearest safety would be in *Tlaxcala*. On the other hand, if the army were completely destroyed or greatly disabled, it was likely that the Tlaxcalteca would regard any surviving Castilians as no more than sacrificial offerings. Nevertheless, I had to take the chance—although I would do so carefully.

As close as I could determine I was north of the lakeside pueblo of *Chimalhuacan*, a tributary of *Tenochtitlan*. *Tlaxcala* should be almost due east—maybe a little south. The problem was that between the Lake and *Tlaxcala* there was the sierra—and I didn't know how far these mountains extended nor did I know the difficulty of the terrain. I considered the possibility of traveling south to take advantage of the passage between the two great volcanoes but the route was heavily traveled. I disregarded the idea.

There was only one choice and that was to penetrate the mountains—even then I must travel by night and avoid trails to mountain villages. I would have to stay in the most rugged and remote country while keeping water nearby. I regarded the shadowy mountains above me. If I rounded their summits and stayed out of the passes, I should go undetected.

I struck out to the east and upward, feeling my way between boulders and twisted trees. By first light I could look back and see the Lake with all of her gleaming cities—from a distance, it was not possible to tell that we had even been there.

●●●

I found a crevice in the rock and spent the next five days trying to recover my strength. Famished, I dug for roots and found wild onions—*cebollas silvestres*—sprouting in the rocky meadows. I built traps of twigs and stones and was able to kill a large rat and an animal like a small rabbit but without a rabbit's long ears. There were also small tasteless red berries and I consumed as many as I could although I paid the price with vomiting.

Still sick but improving, I continued my journey for two nights, stopping again to forage and trap for food. I even found a large serpent, similar to that found in the Mexican menagerie. The creature was fierce, coiling its body back like a spring and whirring its castanets in a high-pitched buzz. I struck the serpent with Bebidor, cleaving it into two parts. Both parts continued to writhe but the rear portion did so without direction. The front end, however, tried to crawl forward but without success. The head was still quite alive, however. It snapped like a dog and yellow venom squirted out on the stones. I struck off the head and was amazed that the head, even without its body, continued to bite in a hopeless rage. No wonder that the Mexica honored these serpents in their templos.

I had heard both the Indios say that these serpents were good to eat. The thing didn't smell good, however—it had a musky odor. Nevertheless, with an empty stomach I couldn't be particular and I peeled off the skin as easily as I would peel off my stocking. The meat is, in fact, white and quite delicious although it would have been better cooked. Eating such foods and sleeping in caves and crevices in the day, I slowly made my way east. It was fortunate for me that it was summer because, even so, I was chilled by the wind. I could sleep only by pulling pine boughs and sometimes loose earth over my legs and body.

Chapter 23

After days of travel, I peered down from the heights and saw the fires of a city that could only be *Tlaxcala* but now, I warned myself, I must be especially cautious because the Tlaxcalteca would either be my saviors or—if I miscalculated—my executioners. That night, I crept into a field that was undergoing cultivation. I waited until daylight.

As I had hoped, a single man—an old man with white hair and wearing a dirty maxtlatl—limped into his field and began working with a digging stick. I had two choices—seize the man or simply approach him. In any event, if his answers were wrong, I'd need to kill him. I approached him openly.

My sudden appearance startled him—he raised his stick to protect himself. I raised my hands with my palms forward.

"Greetings, friend." I said in their language.

He didn't lower his stick. "Greetings."

To show him that I meant no harm, I sat on the ground, although I was prepared to spring on him. "I am one of Malinche's men escaped from the Tenochca. Do you...do you have news of our army?"

Relief spread over the man's weather-beaten face. "They are to the north—along with our heroes they have defeated the Mexica at a place called *Otumba*. Our gods protect Malinche."

I'm certain that relief showed on my face, too. "I am Chichtli. Have you heard of me?"

"No." He raised his stick higher. Sorcerers were suspicious characters even in *Tlaxcala*.

"It's just a name, my friend—just a name." I looked to the north. "Malinche says you must help me. He says you must give me food and drink. He says you must take me to *Tlaxcala*."

●●●

The man—Nacatl was his name—led me to his thatched one-room home. It was built of twigs and saplings chinked with mud. His wife sat in the dirt and ground centli into a meal on a worn stone metate. Two girls watched her work as four other children played in the yard. Two of them, a boy and a girl, were busy pounding a tortoise open with a stone—Nacatl paid no attention. Another child pursued a terrified pato with a crooked stick held as a spear.

Nacatl delivered a blow that would have stunned a grown man. The child tumbled across the dirt but jumped up as if nothing had happened.

"Stupid boy," growled Nacatl, "he never learns. He is worse than coyotl." He turned to his wife who, by now had stopped her work to stare at me. "We are honored to have a white man—one of Malinche's teoltl—as a guest in our home. Get us some food and water."

The woman, who was bursting with curiosity, obeyed without protest. I seated myself, cross-legged on the dirt. Soon, I was served tortillas, frijoles and chiles on a flat platter of wood. The children watched wide-eyed, as I pushed the frijoles and chiles onto the tortillas and ate everything that was put in front of me. Even Nacatl watched as I ate.

"*Ay-ee, Chichtli*, I did not know that teoteoh ate like men." He turned to his oldest child, a boy of about ten, the same one he had punished. "Xamania, this is a special occasion—bring us a fowl."

Soon the boy returned with a duck, the one he had just been chasing. His mother took it and twisted its neck—flapping—it squirted its filth onto my food. The children, laughing, seized the bird and plucked it. Soon it was quartered and roasting on the fire.

Unable to take my eyes off the bird I spoke to Nacatl. "How far to *Tlaxcala*? You must guide me." I didn't need someone to show me that way but I reckoned that the presence of a friendly guide would protect me should any of the locals be tempted to take advantage of a lone Castilian.

"Half a day—no more. I will lead you for we must pass through the land held by the Otomi. Unlike me, they have no love for you teoteoh." He pointed to a scar on his atrophied leg, "The Tenochca have crippled me—otherwise I would be helping Malinche."

His wife served me large pieces of the sizzling fowl. Just before serving it she sprinkled coarse white grains over the flesh—salt—already the presence of the teules had improved the lives of the Tlaxcalteca.

The flesh was tender but I could consume no more than two quarters. Nacatl ate the rest. I watched as his wife cleaned out the tripas and then began to prepare a caldo for her and the children. She tossed the bird's head and feet into the stew, too. I had no doubt that their meal was richer than usual.

Nacatl farted. "I am content, Chichtli. I have lived to see you teoteoh come and I will live to see *Tenochtitlan* in ruin. My life is complete." He sat as if thinking things over. "Would you like the use of my wife?" Startled, his wife looked up at me.

"That won't be necessary."

"Perhaps you would like one of my children?"

I couldn't keep the anger out of my voice. "No, that will also be unnecessary."

He sat in silence, contemplating the mystery of the teoteoh. "Then I shall delay you no longer. We can reach *Tlaxcala* by dark."

●●●

In *Tlaxcala* we were surrounded by dozens of pipiltin and war chiefs.

"*Ay-aa!* We are happy to see you Chichtli." One of them whooped. I recognized him from our days in *Tenochtitlan*—his name was Oztoman and was best known for his flashy feathers and his dislike of combat. "Everyone say you die but you are Chichtli and now you are alive. We welcome you back from *Mictlan*."

"Are any other teoteoh here?" I asked.

"No, you are first. Some of our fighters come but Malinche still fight in the north—soon he come here, too."

So, I thought, the army *would* come and soon I must kill de la Concha.

"I would like to inform Malinche myself of my resurrection when he arrives. It will give me pleasure to see the happiness in his eyes."

Doubt clouded Oztoman's face. "Too late, Chichtli—we already send fast runner to tell Malinche the good news. We beg your forgiveness."

I couldn't afford to let the Tlaxcalteca know of my revenge—so I laughed. "There is nothing to forgive—Malinche will be happy and that makes me happy, too."

● ● ●

The Indios gave me a grand tile-floored apartment complete with monstrous paintings. They also gave me two women but I wanted nothing to distract me from my plans. Squatting in the corner, I tried to think.

A simple assassination was not a consideration—Concha would be too alert—besides, I wanted him to see it coming. I considered making an accusation in front of Cortés but he would protect his friend no matter what he'd done. I really had only one choice—spread the word of Concha's crime and then challenge him to an open duel. Cortés would fume but, with the weight of opinion on my side, he wouldn't be able to prevent it. I drew Bebidor from its sheath and studied it. I caressed the blade and spoke to it as if it were alive—as indeed it is. "I apologize to you, Slayer of Warriors. You must soon taste the blood of a pig."

● ● ●

Two days passed in comfort. My clothes were useless rags and were replaced by Indio garb of maxtlatl, tlamatli and cactli. I traveled the narrow streets of the city and had a chance to compare it with *Tenochtitlan*—the city was not nearly so grand. Its buildings were low and its plazas small and crowded with vagrants. There were, of course, no canals although a creek passed through one corner of the city.

Unlike the Mexica, the *Tlaxcalteca* were and, no doubt still are, a dirty people. Refuse was dumped from windows into the streets and great clouds of buzzing moscas filled the air. The smells were even worse than the plaza in Tlatelolco and to the odor of human waste was added that of rotting garbage.

There were the usual templos and teocallis—they were just as numerous but smaller and less adorned than those in *Tenochtitlan*. Most of these places were doing a deadly business. Accompanied by jubilant guards, there was a steady stream of prisoners-of-war streaming in from the north. These prisoners were the fodder for nonstop human sacrifice—there were hardly enough priests to do the job. Human flesh was so abundant that poor people, who rarely got to sample this delicacy, carried sacks of meat back to their families.

A few of the Indios were unfriendly. One old man—an Otomi by his dress—was staggering drunk on octli. He tried to strike me with his fist. I retaliated with my cuchillo, slicing his face. Seeing the glowering looks around me, I laughed as if the whole thing were a great joke. Soon the spectators—including Otomi spectators—were laughing, too. After this, I resolved to stay close to my quarters until our Castilians arrived.

●●●

"What's going on here?" I asked an armed warrior standing just outside my door.

He pointed at three nearby armed men. "We protect you."

"I don't need protection."

The man, who was wearing a headdress of black feathers, straightened his back. "We protect you—stay here."

I pondered this unpleasant change of events. "By whose orders?"

"*Malinche*—he sends word that we must watch you until he arrives. He does not want anything bad to happen."

I considered arguing but it would do no good. I also considered fighting my way out but—what then?

"Malinche loves me well. I will gladly await his arrival."

●●●

I was under arrest but—why? The obvious thought was that de la Concha, learning of my survival, told a lying story of my treachery. An even more troubling thought was that Concha might be the agent of Cortés—if so, my fate was sealed.

Then again, why would he want me dead? Time and again I had proven myself useful to him. Of course, there was the business with Francesca, but that was a long time ago and Cortés had put it behind him. Or had he? Or could it have been my complaints about the division of the gold? But many had complained and he had singled out no particular enemy—I excluded Cortés as a danger. Then again, Cristóbal Piñeda, who had complained to Cortés, was brought back to *Tenochtitlan* in a sack.

The Indios neglected to disarm me, a situation that Malinche would no doubt correct. When my guards were sleeping I threw back the maguey rugs, pried up bricks and buried Bebidor in the underlying earth—I kept my knife in case of emergencies. I was just in time—I awoke the next morning to find my guards replaced by Castilians.

●●●

"*Buenas dias, senores.*" I said as nonchalantly as possible. "Thank God you've come."

"*Buenas dias, señor.*" The soldado swept his helmet from his head and made an elaborate and unnecessary bow. The soldier was Chico Máfuez, a man with an evil look—he'd had the misfortune of losing his nose in a knife fight in a *casa de putas* back in Extremadura. I knew his two comrades by face but not by name.

"Where's the Caudillo?"

Máfuez' answer was curt. "You'll see him soon enough."

"I'm sure he's busy." I considered my next question. "My friends—Paco Migues, José Maldinado, Juan de Alva—did they make it?"

"All dead. De Alva died honorably enough—killed on the causeway—that's what Sandoval said." He made a noncommittal gesture. "It seems a very expensive luxury to be one of you friends, cabrón. Migues and Maldinado were hanged for it. Besides they were hiding gold."

The blood drained from me. "Hiding gold? But the Caudillo said...."

Without warning Máfuez struck me across the face. "You question our Jefe?"

Stunned, I felt hatred rise in my throat. "In the street, Chico..."

He stared at my hip. "I'd oblige you, de la Peña, but it seems you have thrown away your sword—*cobarde.*"

"Swords, knives, teeth—it makes no difference to me."

Máfuez glanced at his comrades. "Grab him."

They seized me, knocked me to the ground and searched me for weapons. They found the knife tied to my leg.

Máfuez was delighted. "I see that our noble Don keeps a cuchillo tied to his calf like a common pimp. Who were you going to use it on, cabrón? The Caudillo?"

They bound my arms and legs and dropped me on my belly—hard—in the middle of the room. "Orders of the Jefe, Don Rodrigo. He wants to make sure you are good and safe." Máfuez kicked me in the side of my head. "By the time he gets done with you, you'll have a *real* headache."

●●●

That night my worry was only exceeded by the numbness in my hands. Unable to get up and relieve myself, I urinated on myself and had to lie in my own water. Sleep, when it came was full of nightmares—I was jerked to my feet. Sunlight streamed through the door.

"Have a nice rest, Rodrigo?" Máfuez laughed. "It should be good practice for what you have coming." He cut my bonds but I was unable to stand. Rough hands steadied me and pushed me out of my room and into the street.

"You're so fortunate, de la Peña." Máfuez said. "You have a *special* audience with the Caudillo—stand straight—you don't want these Indios to know that you're just a piece of shit."

Supported on both sides, I was pushed and pulled down the street. Slowly, agonizing life came back into my hands and feet but I saw no opportunity for escape. Six armed men escorted me and the street was filled with hundreds of curious Tlaxcalteca.

"Get out of the way," snarled Máfuez at the wide-eyed Indios. He muscled two men aside and struck a woman with the flat of his sword. "Out of the way, dogs."

We moved down the street until we came to a low building covered by glistening white stucco and frescos of red and blue demons. I was pushed through the door and fell sprawling to the floor. I looked up to find myself confronted by a dozen men seated at a long table. I knew all but one—they were my fellow officers of the principality of Villa Rica—Alvarado, Olid, Ávila, Sandoval, Concha, Mexía, and all the others were there. Cortés sat in the center, dressed in velvet finery that had somehow survived the retreat from Mexico. The others were dressed in dirty cotton clothing and rusty armor. The friars, Olmedo and Díaz were there, as was a stranger—a pale-faced Franciscan.

The Caudillo spoke *first*. "You could have dressed better for the Tribunal, Don Rodrigo."

I was relieved by his jest. "Sorry, Caudillo, but I left my fiesta costume back at my estate in Cuba."

He barely smiled. "Very amusing, Rodrigo, but when you hear the charges against you I suspect you will be less amusing."

I raised my voice so that no one would have trouble hearing me. "Come now, Caudillo, my sense of humor has no limits. For instance, when Javier de la Concha knocked me unconscious—and *stabbed* me—just prior to our retreat from *Tenochtitlan*. I almost laughed myself to death."

"Javier?" Cortés raised his eyebrows.

"I saw his ugly face."

Mexía and Ávila glanced at one another but Cortés only smiled. "Your case, Rodrigo, is not helped by lies. You stand accused of deserting your command during time of war—the penalty is hanging."

That stopped me a moment. "*Deserción?*" I pulled up my tlamatli and pointed to the unhealed wound. "De la Concha's cuchillo." I pointed to the fresh scar on my scalp. "Concha's club."

De la Concha, who was seated beside him, responded with a crooked smile. Some the other men, however, looked less certain. Cortés' reply was as smooth as silk.

"You could have collected these scratches anywhere, Rodrigo—they might even have been self inflicted. What other proof can you present before we pass sentence?"

I smiled back at Concha. "First, there is logic, Caudillo. What fool would leave the army while in the midst of the enemy?"

"You were born a fool, Rodrigo." Cortés said.

"Not *that* much of a fool, besides, I have proof."

Now, Cortés and de la Concha *weren't* smiling.

"Beside me that night were the bodies of Enrique Presa and Bernardino de Soría. Concha hated them both and both had their heads smashed in. If even one of these men is still with the army—then you know I lie. If, they are both missing..."

Cortés retaliated, "I fought beside de Soría that night on the bridge—I *personally* saw him fall." He paused to let his words sink in. "Rodrigo, not only are you a deserter, you are also a perjurer."

So, I thought, Cortés *had* ordered my death!

"I'm not through, gentlemen. When I was hiding in the palace I came on two of our men..."

"More deserters...." he said.

I didn't stop. "Their names were Manuel Paulino,"—here I had to stop to remember—"and Angel de Turbe—they told an interesting tale.

They said that they were with a detachment led by Capitán Molino and that he was not informed of the retreat..."

Cortés leapt to his feet, his face contorted by anger. "*That's a lie!* Everyone was informed of the retreat—if Molino didn't make it, it's because of incompetence."

I'd finally hit the hot spot. "That's not what I was told. They said that *you*, Hernán Cortés—*El Jefe, Caudillo, Capitán, el Líder Magnífico*—misled Molino to create a diversion." I looked around the room. "Tell me who is lying, gentlemen—me or the Caudillo? Where is Molino's troop? Dead to the man, I'll warrant."

Now, it was Alvarado's turn to stand. "Hold your tongue, cabrón, or I'll skewer you where you stand."

I laughed in his face. "So you're in on it, too, Pedro." With nothing to lose I pointed at all of the men. "How many of you are in on it?"

There was a long moment of silence and then Mexía, Ávila and Olmedo shouted their innocence.

"There you have it, Caudillo—your own tribunal knows the truth of it—*you* stand convicted of false witness and murder."

Alvarado, sword in hand, jumped over the table but caught his heel on the edge—it tottered and Alvarado fell at my feet. I kicked him right in the belly and then stomped his hand. I scooped up his loose sword and pointed its tip at the startled Cortés.

"Who is the liar, Caudillo? Let's put the issue to God."

I ached to push the espada up to the hilt—I should have.

Cortés recovered his composure. "I think not, Rodrigo—you haven't heard the rest of the evidence."

"More evidence—I can hardly wait." I helped the doubled-up Alvarado to his feet, broke his sword against the floor and kicked him in the backside.

Cortés looked at me with unvarnished hatred then turned to the strange fraile.

"Let me introduce Padre Pedro Melgarejo de Urrea." He nodded to the new friar, "He is a recent arrival on a ship piloted by Diego Díaz. He is a special envoy from the Royal Court and comes with *Bullas Cruzadas*, signed by the Pope for forgiveness of sins committed by our soldados in Nueva España..."

"Then my difficulties are over." I said, "I'll purchase one of those

Tolerancias and walk away a free man."

"No, *Tolerancia*, no matter how dearly purchased, will secure your freedom." Cortés lisped, "Read the accusations, Padre."

The Franciscan unrolled a parchment—he knew the words already:

"Rodrigo de la Peña, son of Jorge and Ínez de la Peña—condemned heretics—stands accused of acts against God and the Holy Faith. He has, with his own hand, slain two officers of the Holy Office both of whom were priests of the Dominican order. He is also accused of fleeing España to escape the justice of *Santo Oficio y Autoridad Real*."

So they caught up with me.

"Where are your witnesses, Padre?" I asked.

"Witnesses will be produced on our return to Castilla."

Someone may have seen me in the vicinity of the killings but no one had seen me committing the acts.

"Whom am I supposed to have killed?"

He checked his notes. "Padre Benito de Luna and Renato Medina."

I gave the Padre my best grin. "I never heard of them."

He stood up from his chair: "You," he pointed at me, "were seen in the vicinity of both crimes."

"Hardly evicence, Padre," I said.

"Besides you have a motive." The friar went on, "You and your family are Jewish swine."

"If that's your evidence, Padre, you'll have to arrest our Caudillo, too. The way I hear it, his father's grandfather—twice removed—was one-quarter Jew."

"*Silencio!*" Cortés roared. "You are speaking to a man of God."

I bowed from the waist. "It seems you have a problem, Caudillo. Either you hang me now for the false accusation of desertion or you wait until a ship is available to return me to España for a trial by an ecclesiastical court. In that I am completely innocent of all charges—I'd prefer to take my chances back in Castile."

"I'm sure you would," Cortés threatened, "but as Commander of the Army, *I* have jurisdiction." He turned to his assembled officers. "A compromise is in order."

"Compromise with a felon?" spoke Díaz. "Have you lost your senses?"

"Careful, fraile." Cortés hissed. "I am not above hanging you from a rafter even if you are a supposed Padre." He slowed down. "By compromise, I didn't mean that we would compromise for de la Peña's freedom. I meant that we should compromise with his punishment—deserters are hanged but heretics are burned. I propose that Rodrigo be suspended upside down with his head warned by a very small fire."

Everyone, with the exception of Mexía, Olmedo and the new friar roared their assent—de la Concha was especially vocal. "I'll take care of it, Caudillo."

The Franciscan stood up and pointed a finger at Cortés. "This malefactor deserves the flames but only after a proper trial by authorized Inquisitors. The prisoner is to be remanded to *my* authority."

Cortés also stood up, so angry he couldn't speak. When he finally found the words it came as a whisper. "Challenge me, Padre, and you'll share de la Peña's fate."

The fraile sat down.

He turned back to me. "Now, my good man, you will be returned to your cell where you will be held for one week prior to the execution—seven long days to consider your sins—seven days to consider the smell of your hair burning just before your brains burst through your ears."

Chapter 24

Cortés warned my captors to keep tight guard on me at the price of their own lives—he also made the mistake of returning me to my old apartment. For the first two days I did nothing but plan my escape. I had no doubt that, with the help of Bebidor, I could escape my immediate confinement but—how to get out of *Tlaxcala*? Once my escape was discovered, every person would be searching for me—my detection was inevitable. My only hope was to escape into the hills and even this seemed a slim hope.

If I could live long enough, more ships would come and there was a chance—a bare chance—that I could enlist in a returning crew. Even if

I succeeded I was still a wanted man and my situation in Cuba or España would be little better than here in Nueva España. Nevertheless, I couldn't afford to remain inactive—in five days I'd be dead.

Still, I pondered—my acts in had been against a despised foe and, as such, were justifiable. Now, however, I had no chance of escaping lest I slay my guards—and the guards had done nothing more than obey orders. Even Máfuez only persecuted me because he believed me a traitor.

My life or their lives? Was it cold-blooded murder? Still, I reasoned, it wasn't *exactly* murder. If I managed a bloodless escape, Cortés would hang the guards, anyway.

I waited until my guard—one always stayed in my room—nodded off to sleep. I throttled the man while muffling the sounds of his struggle with my own body.

"What's going on in there?" said a sleepy voice.

"*Nada,* I replied, *"una pesadilla."*

I lifted up the bricks, removed Bebidor and dusted it off.

"Chico," I managed a hoarse whisper, "I need to shit—watch the prisoner for me."

I heard the sound of cursing but shortly the figure of Máfuez filled the doorway. I stuck him exactly as you would stick a pig, right at the base of the neck. I put my weight behind it and felt the blade sever his spine. He dropped right where he stood.

Crouching, I stepped outside. The two other guards were curled up at the foot of the wall, one sleeping and the second just waking up. I gave the waking man a heavy blow with the hilt then—just as you would a chicken—I chopped at the second man. Blood rose from his neck in a fountain.

Without stopping to clean my blade, I crept out into city. The streets were empty and, because of my Tlaxcaltec garb, the few people I did encounter never gave me a second look. I soon found the outer wall, which I scaled by climbing onto the roof of an adjacent house and leaping to the ground. The wall was low so, except for a bruised ankle, I made the jump without injury. After that it was a matter of heading east, in the direction of the coast.

I skirted Indio farms and forded two small streams. First light caught me in the open. I found refuge in a field—a *milpa*—of centli and calabazas. The crop was not yet ripe but, faint with hunger, I gorged on the grain and even found the pith of the centli stalks to be sweet. Twice during the day, I heard Indios calling to one another—their words, however, were only greetings and contained nothing threatening—nevertheless, I burrowed deeper into the undergrowth.

At nightfall, I ventured out—again heading east. The country climbed and the air grew more frigid. As I traveled I turned and watched the lowlands behind me. Once, in the distance, I saw small moving lights—torches? I picked up my pace and entered steeper country with boulders and occasional trees. Once—twice—I thought I heard something behind me but there was nothing. Then, there could be no doubt of it. There was the sound of fast moving feet over the leaves. With Bebidor drawn I turned to confront the threat.

Shadows—shadows ghosting through the starlight—no form or substance—the sound of fast breathing. *Perros!* They were upon me before I knew what they were. One bowled me over—a second went for my throat. I thrust my fist into his mouth and into his windpipe—his teeth closed on my arm. With my free arm I slashed with Bebidor. My first blow struck a leg and the second sliced ribs. Still, neither of us released the other—his jaws locked onto my arm and my hand jammed into the back of his throat. The second dog, confused by the melee, attacked his comrade. This distraction gave me time to change my grip on my sword. I seized it part way up its blade and, like a needle threading cloth, *pushed* it through the mastiff's skin. I then seized the sword closer to its hilt and repeated the process—in this way I pushed Bebidor deep into the beast's body. There was a convulsion that almost tore my arm off—the dog went limp. I turned to the other dog whose teeth were still locked in the rump of his friend. I split his skull—he died without a whimper.

There were more shadows behind me but this time I was prepared. Two powerful mastiffs came in fast but were unable to close. Howling, both dogs retreated, one missing part of its jaw and the other dragging his guts.

I waited to see if there would be more dogs or men but all I saw was the outline of trees and all I heard was the wind. The dogs had far outrun their handlers, which gave me time to continue my flight. I looked around and could see that, to the north, the sierra climbed almost to the sky—this would be my best and probably my only chance of escape. If either men or dogs came at me they would have to approach me from below and the advantage would go to me. On the other hand, I was injured. My left arm and hand were lacerated—I couldn't tell how badly. I could barely move my fingers.

Daylight found me far above the plain, picking my way through boulders and, using my good hand, climbing rocky ledges. I was afraid to look at my arm. The skin was torn with four or five punctures that penetrated to the bone. Still, the bone seemed intact although I couldn't make a fist. I remembered my wounds from the leopard and I remembered the mortification. I found a rivulet of water and cleaned the lacerated flesh. I was appalled that the water flowed completely through the wounds. Despite the pain, I cleaned them of blood and dirt.

Now, I could rest. I found a vantage point and surveyed the country below me—nothing. I doubted my tormentors would give up the chase until I was dead. I continued climbing until I was in country so steep and difficult that even the most agile dog would be unable to follow.

●●●

For three long days, I moved toward the east. I backtracked and angled north and south to throw off pursuers and to disguise my intentions. Tlaxcaltec trackers, if they divined my plan to reach the sea, would simply move back-and-forth until they picked up my sign, making my efforts pointless.

Famished, I was forced to descend into lower country to search for food. I found fruits and berries as well as skinny lizards and fat grubs. Twice, I found culebras—scaly serpents—stretched out on rocks and another time I found a small cocodrilo lurking in a scum-choked pond. I slew it with a single blow and peeled the hide from its tail—its flesh was stringy and tasted of bad fish. Another time, I encountered a beast the size of a cat hanging upside down in a tree. I knocked it down and was amazed to find that the animal had sludge for blood. All of its motions were painfully slow—green moss grew from its fur. Despite its diseased appearance, I devoured and found it edible but not good.

I penetrated the coastal forest, taking care to take pains to walk in water-filled swamp or on the branches of fallen trees. I knew these Indios—they could follow a mouse over a tile floor. Taking no chances,

I lay hours in ambush but saw nothing more dangerous than the occasional bird or lizard. Barefoot, my clothes in tatters, and keeping off the trails, I finally made it to the beach. I heard the waves before I saw the water.

After the gloom of the forest, my eyes were dazzled. The sand was blinding white, the sea emerald green and south, towards Villa Rica, the furled sails of four ships glinted in the light of the noonday sun. Three were brigs that Cortés saved from destruction and one was the caravel that brought *la Inquisicion Sagrada*, in the person of Fraile Pedro de Urrea, to Nueva España. Soon, I told myself, more ships, more priests and more soldados and adventurers would arrive. The more the better. Then, but only then, could I consider escape. A ship's captain—one who didn't know me—might welcome the addition of an extra hand. I knew it would be a long wait—weeks maybe months. I wondered if I had the luck to survive that long.

Shelter must be inconspicuous. The best I could find was a great tree that had fallen taking smaller trees with it. The tangle of exposed roots supported the truck. The growth around the overhanging trunk formed an open grotto. It was a natural shelter but I tried to make it better. I wove long swamp grass into mats which I used for the walls and flooring. I used the same grass and fronds for thatch and waterproofing.

It wasn't enough—the tropics, unlike more temperate zones, have two seasons—the dry and the wet. It was my misfortune to arrive on the coast during the rains. I was unable to build a shelter adequate to exclude crawling vermin and the inescapable wet. Fire would have helped but smoke could have been seen from a distance. Fire was impossibility in any event because everything was soggy and rotten. That clothing that I had remaining fell from my body. I went naked except for sandals I fashioned from the tree bark and the skin of a slow cocodrilo.

During the next days, three separate ships—one from the north and two from the south—arrived in front of Villa Rica. From a distance, it was difficult to see what was happening. One thing was obvious, though. Within days, each ship was systematically dismantled—the same as we had done with our original fleet. Cortés was taking no chances—no ship would be allowed to return to España or the Islands.

My spirits, which had been low, fell to nothing. I considered throwing myself into the sea.

Burgos, Castilla-León

Mendoza stopped his transcription. "Why should you have been in more distress than the natives? Did they not thrive under these same conditions?"

The old man paused. "I am not an Indio, Padre. As a soldier I was used to hard living but I was not used to the constant wet. Also, Indios did not build their villages in the forest—they built their huts in clearings and fincas. They were, also, better craftsmen than was I and, although they experienced the full force of the rains, the thatching of their hovels was tight, enabling them to keep dry. In addition, my movements were restricted to the dark hours and, even then, I had to take pains to cover up the signs of my passage. My diet was limited to fruits and tubers and to things I found on the beach—things like the great tortugas that left broad trails from the sea to their buried eggs. I slew one of these creatures with Bebidor but then found that I was incapable of opening the shell to get at the flesh. I was reduced to lapping its blood like a starving cur. Thereafter, I learned to leave the adult turtles alone but would backtrack them to the place they had secreted their eggs under the sand. I dug these up, lay on my back, tore them open and sucked down their contents, one by one."

"Obispo, I wouldn't turn down a few eggs even those of a turtle."

"Yes, Padre, they are indeed delicious. I can still taste their wonderful richness on my tongue and the back of my throat. Their delectable flavor is truly unique and wonderful. Clams..."

"*Clams*, Your Excellency?" Saliva was running from Mendoza's lips into his beard. "Did you say *clams*? Surely clams can have no impact on my gout."

"You're right, Padre, clams are not only delicately delicious, they are permissible in the treatment of gout...Unfortunately I do not have a supply of them and don't expect to in the foreseeable future. You will have to be satisfied with your usual menu. But on the coast of Nueva España clams—*almejas*—were not a problem when the tides were low. Sometimes, however, night and low tide did not coincide and then I went hungry. I scoured the beach and found the occasional dead fish or gull. Once I found the corpse of a small whale—*ballena*—and sliced some flesh from its body. I removed meat next to its backbone—only here did the meat smell fit to eat. I devoured it uncooked but paid the price for my hunger..."

"Perhaps we can discuss *my* hunger, Excelencia."

"You know nothing of *real* hunger, Padre." The old Bishop said grimly, "...Belly cramps, vomiting, bloody diarrhea. I was ill for days and, even on recovery, I was too weak to search for food. My skin, especially over my hips and elbows blistered and sloughed off. I was dying, one piece of me at a time."

"...But you lived."

"I lived." The old man smiled. "Through no fault of mine. A voice in the wilderness beckoned me towards life."

"I don't understand...."

"I don't either," the Bishop said. "As a rational man I tell you that conscience has a voice.

The priest was doubtful. "Whose voice, might I ask?"

"Angela."

"Angela...wasn't she the slut you abandoned in Italy?"

The old man held his temper. "...The poor girl I abandoned..."

"What more is there to tell—you threw her to the dogs—that's enough."

"More than enough, but I haven't told you everything. There was a soldier with Pánfilio de Narváez—he was wounded during our assault. I saw him lying in the mud, his life's blood draining away. I recognized him from Italy. I asked him what he knew of Angela."

"Angela—the pretty one with the big eyes?"

"That's her."

"She had a baby,"—he winced with pain—"a boy. We were defeated—not much food—many of us starved. Where in Hell were you, de la Peña?"

"The girl?"

"The child died first, then the girl." The man choked, producing a froth of red bubbles. "She died begging your forgiveness."

Mendoza's lips curled. "*You* think you can come to *me* for absolution? You are more deranged than I thought you were."

The old man's face turned lifeless. "There is no...absolution. Angela's only crime was innocence. She thought that *she* was the one who had trespassed against me. May God help me. I left her with guilt for *my* crime." The old man stood up and started to pace. "Guilt can drive a person mad."

"If you wish to alleviate your guilt, Excellency, you would improve my diet."

The old man wasn't listening. "In the forest, lying in my own filth—I heard Angela's voice. She begged and beseeched me—sometimes she cursed me—she drove me from my bed of self-pity. She drove me through the forest—don't tell me how–cajoling, laughing, threatening, weeping–I took paths never trod by human feet. I splashed through swamps crawling with unspeakable creatures and treacherous with sucking mud. When I could no longer walk, I stumbled and when I could no longer stumble, I crawled. Angela was always there, whimpering for our dead son and–always, always–forcing me on."

Mendoza leaned back in his chair. "A curious phenomenon, Your Grace—helped by a lost soul." Mendoza stood up and seemed to enlarge. "You *must* admit the existence of God."

The old man stopped his pacing. "I am flagellated by guilt...*punished* by it. Do you understand?"

"There is nothing to understand. You have earned it."

"Angela's ghost, Padre, may have been nothing more than a conjunction of my conscience and my starving body."

"But..."

The Bishop held up his hand. "On the other hand, her voice *saved* me. I do not rule out the possibility..."

"Christ redeems sinners."

"Even you, Padre Mendoza?"

"I am a believer."

"You are repentant? You have been forgiven of your sins?"

"Absolutely."

The old man's lips turned white. "Do you not feel *guilt* for...?"

"My conscience is clear."

The Bishop relaxed. "Then, Padre Mendoza, you are in precisely the right place for you are dangerous, indeed."

Mendoza had to fight down his hatred. "You are avoiding my question, Obispo. I'll put it to you another way. If you were actually aided by a departed soul, does this not *prove* the existence of God?"

"Even if I were to accept the possibility that Angela was..." The old man shook his head as if he were trying to free it of an unwanted thought. He started over, "Have you considered, Padre, that there might be an afterlife without God or that there could be a God without an afterlife? To God, we may be less important than grains of wheat or motes of dust." He reached into his garments, searched around with his hand and then held it up with something between his index finger and thumb. "No more important than this insignificant creature that sucks my blood."

"Not only are you a heretic, Excelencia. You are ridiculous."

The old man cracked the louse between his nails. "For your sake, Padre, you'd better be right."

Chapter 25

I don't know how long my journey through the forest lasted—but—then it was over. I was in high country-far from the forest and I was hungry and freezing. Below, clinging to the walls of a narrow valley, was a village. I waited until dark and, as silently as my weakened body would permit, I crept down to steal an ear of maíz and maybe a blanket. I wasn't quiet enough. A noisy small dog—little more than a puppy—rushed towards me. He ventured too close and was silenced forever. Defeated—exhausted—I leaned back on a large rock. I would be no match for the most inexperienced Indio.

Strangely, however, the village remained still. Once, when the wind blew in my direction, I detected the odor of death. I investigated the nearest hut and found it to be occupied by three swollen corpses—by their sizes, two adults and a child. The stinking dead occupied two other huts but five others were abandoned, although all of the articles of daily life were still present. Just outside of the village was the body of a woman. In her agony, she had torn off most of her clothing. I drew back in disgust. Her skin was pocked with sores I had seen too many times before. As a child, the disease had passed through our village like a wolf through a flock of sheep. I suffered from it myself and barely survived. It was *La Viruela*—the Scourge of...."

Burgos, Castilla-León

Mendoza stopped writing and jabbed his finger in the direction of the old man. "Smallpox is one more proof of divine intervention on behalf of the Conquest—Our conquistadores were spared but the heathens were not."

"I suspect that God might disagree with your interpretation, Padre. The Indios—who were innocent of this plague—were decimated which *did* simplify the task of conquest. At the same time, however, it deprived Emperor Carlos of hundreds of thousands of subjects and slaves. The most immediate proof of this was that it destroyed most of the Taino Indios necessitating the importation of thousands of Negroes to the Islands."

"What harm can possibly come of it, Your Grace? Blacks are not only natural slaves but, unlike the fragile nativos, are all but immune to hardship."

The ancient man started pacing again, his robes dragging the floor. "I don't know what harm can come of it, either but—like our conquest of Nueva España—there will be a price." The old man turned to face Mendoza. "Satan has already announced that the price will be high."

Mendoza couldn't contain himself, "To my knowledge, the Evil One has made no such recent pronouncements."

"Padre, you are a Jesuit Priest but never learned to listen with the ears of your soul. I will spell it out for you. An African slave with the Narváez expedition—one Francisco Eguía by name—introduced *La Viruela* to Nueva España. It seems that an epidemic had been raging in Española but Pánfilo Narváez took precautions to exclude anyone who might be harboring the disease. Narváez' physician missed the early lesions of *la Viruela* because of Eguía's black skin. Eguía was Satan's unwitting instrument in the transmission of his unholy pestilence."

"As usual, Your Grace, you confuse Satan with God."

"It seems that we have gotten off the subject," the old man said. "I was telling you how I found myself in sole possession of a village populated only by the moldering dead. This proved to be my salvation—I was able to gain shelter, food and warmth. In order to improve the air I would have preferred to have incinerated the bodies in their own dwellings—I didn't have the courage."

"Courage, Your Grace?"

"I wasn't that *stupid*, either, Padre. Funeral pyres would have been seen for leagues."

"Ah."

"Nevertheless, I prepared myself for visitors and gathered my strength. After a time, even the odor became tolerable."

"Yes?"

"Have you noticed, Padre, that as a corpse nears the end of its process of dissolution, the odor changes from foul to musty."

"No."

The old man lectured on to his unwilling student. "As the viscera and flesh dissolve to nothing, there comes a time when all that is left is bone and shards of drying skin. The odor, while still unpleasant"—the old man spread his hands out in explanation—"becomes tolerable."

"Fascinating, Your Grace."

The Bishop leaned close to Mendoza's ear. "As the English say, '*Ashes to ashes, dust to dust*.'"

Mendoza grimaced.

The old man nodded. "...Sometimes, it's good to be reminded of the *limits* of our...relationship."

Mendoza didn't speak.

"Good then, Padre, let's go on, I heard—or felt—Angela's presence only one more time. She whispered advice...she urged me to go to the Mexica. She *formed*,"—the old man clenched his fist—"the thought in my mind that my only salvation lay with the enemy."

Mendoza couldn't contain himself. "...*Imposible!*"

"Perhaps there is a God, Padre. Perhaps he, in his wisdom, prepared me to be an inside witness to the destruction of Mexico. Perhaps He was preparing me for our current enterprise."

"Nonsense."

The Bishop went on. "I was, after all, a *mercenary*. What did it matter who I fought for or against? I was fighting for personal profit, not for faith. In Italy—for money—we slew Germans, Swiss, Italians and mountains of Frenchmen. What difference should it make if I killed a few Castilians or, for that matter, if I died by Christian hands."

Mendoza still looked doubtful. "Obispo, you have already told me that you had long anticipated the Mexican defeat. Why should you have expected anything more than a stay of execution?"

"As they say, where there is life, there is hope," the old man explained. "The longer I lived, the longer I had to effect a plan for long term salvation. Such was my thought then and, as you can see, I calculated correctly."

"But your friends?"

"Ah, Padre, but they were mercenaries, too."

Having regained much of my strength and clad in the raiments of a poor Indio, I traveled until I encountered signs of Mexican outposts. Approaching one of these directly would have been suicidal. I decided on a more indirect approach. I watched the trails and found one that was traveled by warriors carrying the feathered symbols identifying them as messengers. I captured one of these men as he trotted along toward the west. I forced him down, wrested his weapon from his grasp and put the itzli blade to his throat.

"Do you travel to *Tenochtitlan*?"

"*Do you kill me?*"

"Not if you are wise, my friend. Do you travel to *Tenochtitlan*?"

"Yes."

"Good. I mean you no harm." I pressed the blade into the skin. "Do you know of *Lord Macitoc*—Macitoc the Hunter?"

"He serves *Cuauhtemoc—Uei Tlatloani*."

"But is not Cuitlahuac Emperor?"

Despite the blade, my captive was relaxing—perhaps he had given up hope.

"Only in *Mictlan*—he is dead of the Holy Disease. Cuauhtemoc is Emperor." My captive knew full well from the color of my eyes and my misuse of his language that I was one of these enemies. I admired his courage.

"Well, my friend," I lowered the knife. "I am no longer your enemy. I wish for you to deliver this message to Macitoc and to your new Uei Tlatloani":

"*I am Chichtli and I offer my services to the Mexica. Lord Macitoc must meet me here, at this very place, in ten day's time. He must come alone.*"

I asked the messenger to repeat my words, which he repeated with perfection. I then sent him on his way. I knew that my message would be delivered. There was no guarantee that my message would be favorably received, however. I knew that there was an excellent chance that my next visitors would be a Mexican war party. Taking no chances, I made my camp in a cave a full league from the proposed meeting place. On the day of the meeting I planned to watch from a high peak and assure myself that Macitoc came alone.

●●●

My hiding place did not include an abundant food supply. The first seven days passed slowly—my boredom relieved only by gnawing hunger. On the eighth day I awoke to find that I was no longer alone. Silhouetted in the early light was a squatting figure.

"Have no fear, Chichtli. I am your friend. I wait while you sleep." It was difficult to make out the man's features but I knew his voice.

"It is I, Macitoc. I bring you meat." He gestured to an animal laying between us. "I know you not eat good—I bring *temazatl*." The beast was a small red ciervo with short spikes for antlers. "I also bring you these," He tossed a bundle towards me. There were three human scalps. "These," he pointed at the scalps, "are Tlaxcaltec coyoteh—they follow your trail."

A thrill of fear ran through me. Despite my pains to cover my trail, Macitoc had found my hiding place. Far worse, Tlaxcaltec assassins—probably fielded by Cortés—had tracked me for leagues, maybe all the way from the coast.

Sitting up, I tried to sound calm. "Thank you, Macitoc. The death of these enemies fills me with gladness. Malinche has condemned me to death."

Macitoc nodded. "Spies tell me this thing. Cuauhtemoc welcomes you as a friend and I, Macitoc, am your brother. We are forever joined in *teyotl*—faith. Before the foundation *Anahuac*, *Tezcatlipoca* decree you fight beside me."

"Yes, my brother, I *will* fight beside you but I will not deceive you—Malinche is but the sharp end of a heavy spear." I scooped up a palm full of sand and let it trickle between my fingers. "The white men are more numerous than these grains of dust. Soon they will be irresistible."

"It is no ....." Macitoc searched for the words.

"*Cenca cualtic–important?*" I filled in the words, wondering at his clumsiness of speech. Nahuatl, at least the Nahuatl of *Anahuac*, was not his first tongue.

"It is no...important. Mexica fools—I tell them to finish Malinche but they stop kill captives. They *not* my people."

I was confused. "What?"

"I, *Lipan*, not Mexica." He straightened his back. "Macitoc's people fight Mexica—much killing. Captives given," He slapped his chest. "I fight."

I was starting to understand—Macitoc was a hostage of the Mexica but he was a hostage on a long leash. "But why do you fight for these enemies of your blood, Macitoc? Walk away and never look back."

"I am promised, Chichtli." He stroked the coat of the dead temazatl. "When Mexica swept away, I leave—now I fight. Come with me, Chichtli, and we make great names for ourselves. In the end, we go north,"—he pointed into the distance—"my people."

"But what will *I* do there?"

Macitoc smiled wider than before. "*Ey-ya Chichtli!*" We hunt, we fish, and we eat *peyote*. We live like men."

"What then?"

"These *xolotameh* the teotoh ride—they are animals?"

"Yes, Macitoc, they are only great beasts."

"Then they have fawns like other xolotemeh—when the time is right let us steal them and take them to my people. We use them to hunt the great bulls of north. We use them to defeat our enemies, the *Huichol. Ey-ah Chichtli!* We take their fat women."

The prospect of a lifetime away from my own people was unappetizing but I no longer had a people—probably never did. I remembered my father's last words—'*never forget, never forgive.*' Besides, I'd already made my decision.

"You and I, my brother, will make great names for ourselves."

Hummingbird God • 203

Chapter 26

The way back to *Tenochtitlan* might have proved impossible had it not been for Macitoc's help. The land was no longer under the control of the Mexica. Time and again we had to hide from Tlaxcaltec war parties. We traveled through narrow gorges and we climbed high passes known only to vultures.

During our journey, I questioned Macitoc about his knowledge of Cortés.

"Malinche take *Tepeaca*. Those not killed—*tlacohtlin*—slaves."

"Many?"

"More than leaves in the forest. Our spies say much trouble—teoteoh keep pretty girls but Malinche say 'No'. All branded on faces and sold."

"But where is the market for all these people?"

"The Tlaxcalteca and other traitors buy them—their temples red with blood."

Burgos, Castilla-León

Mendoza stopped the narration. "I'm sure you are mistaken, Obispo. Cortés certainly did enslave rebellious Indios but he would *never* permit them to be used for human sacrifice."

The Bishop tapped his fingers in irritation. "Believe it, Padre. Cortés—as miserable as he was—underwent a transition after la Noche Triste. He no longer made a pretense of religious zeal. He realized that he must conciliate the Tlaxcalteca. If he had not done so, even they may have risen against him—not one Castilian would have survived. From that time until the final reduction of Mexico, he turned a blind eye to the practices of his allies. When on the march, hundreds of captives were sacrificed—sliced up and eaten—within sight of our noble conquistadores. It is said—although I did not witness it—that some Castilians participated in the heathen rituals and even tasted human flesh."

"Impossible."

"I do not require that you believe it, Padre, only that you document it."

"Christians would never commit such an atrocity."

"You overestimate the quality of our Spanish troops, Padre. Many were capable of the lowest depravity."

Macitoc captured a skinny guajalote in an abandoned village—it was pecking at human bones. We killed the bird and carried it to a place in a nearby scrub. We rested but did not build a fire until well after sundown. Macitoc spoke as we grilled the bird over the embers.

"Malinche rules land from *Tlaxcala* to coast," Macitoc said.

"The Mexica are unable to block his reinforcements?"

He shook his head. "More teoteoh, xolotameh and tepoztlin. We defeat them at *Calpulalpan*—I lead attack. We take plenty white men and women. We take six great xolotameh."

"Where are they now?"

"Women and most of men have honored the gods. A few saved" —he spat in the dust—"xolotameh sacrificed—fools."

"Where is Malinche, now?"

"His men take *Texcoco*—use fire." He contemplated the sizzling flesh. "*Ey-ya Chichtli!* They burn temples. Pretty amatl pictures of Azteca now"—he blew into the palm of his hand—"smoke."

Cortés, I thought, was nothing if not thorough.

"What more?"

"Malinche kill many in *Texcoco*—others dig big ditch between *Texcoco* and Lake," *Macitoc* laughed. "Malinche drain water and get to *Tenochtitlan* on dry ground."

This was as close as he ever got to a joke. I returned the favor. "Not unless Malinche knows how to make water flow uphill."

He grinned at my jest. "Malinche block river—river close to *Huexotzinco*—close to *Tlaxcala*. He make big water. He make acallin—boats." Macitoc looked doubtful. "Christian God, strange God, he like sacrifice acallin."

"Sacrifice?"

"*Eee*-acallin on sea and new lake—teoteoh pull them apart the same as we pull apart,"—*Macitoc* tore a wing from the bird—"*cuauhtecatl.*"

I remembered that *cuuauhecatl* was the corpse of a sacrificed victim. "How do you know this, Macitoc?"

"The same as I know trouble you and Malinche. Some Tlaxcalteca fear Malinche more than they hate Tenochca."

I pondered this mystery. "Do you know who among the teoteoh does these things?"

"Our spies say Malinche make Señor Lopez high priest. He make slaves cut trees on mountain."

Martín López was the same man who built our brigantines in *Tenochtitlan.*"

"Do your spies say how many acallin were built in *Tlaxcala?*"

Macitoc showed me all ten fingers then four.

"How big are these boats?"

He paced off fifteen steps. All I could do was whistle. Even for Cortés, it was a remarkable undertaking—tackle from the ships we destroyed on the beach in Villa Rica was probably, even now, being brought up from the coast. Under the watchful eye of Martín López fourteen small brigs were under construction. They would be tested on Cortés' new reservoir, carefully disassembled and transported by an army of allies to *Anahuac.* There they would be reassembled next to Cortés' new—very well fortified—canal—close to *Texcoco.*

Macitoc squatted and tore meat from the bone with his teeth.

"The teoteoh do not make sacrifices of acallin—they build them for war," I told him. "Their pieces will be carried to *Texcoco* where they will be rebuilt on Malinche's new canal. Malinche will attack *Tenochtitlan* from the land and the water."

Macitoc dropped the wing. "*We stop Malinche!*"

"If we still have time."

●●●

We descended into the Valley using trails only Macitoc knew. He remembered the exact location where he hid his canoe and found it without searching. A hard wind with gusts of rain was blowing in from the west and the surface of the Lake was a froth of choppy waves. Nevertheless, we paddled out onto its surface and, after hours of cold, wet, backbreaking labor, made the shelter of the canals of the great city.

I looked around me and could see that little had changed. The tinampas were still green gardens; children still played and laughed and women ground centli on their metates. The temples still gleamed in the sun and smoke still rose from each teocalli. Traffic in the canals was still heavy and the canoes were piled high with the products and tribute of Mexico.

We landed next to the Great Plaza, close to the very place I had fled many months ago.

"Give me maquahuitl." Macitoc pointed at Bebidor.

I didn't like it.

"Give me maquahuitl." He pointed toward the crowds thronging the Plaza. "Mexica must think you my *tlaantli*—captive."

I still didn't like it but, surrounded by hostile Tenochca, I had little choice. I handed Bebidor to Macitoc who stroked it appreciatively. He then bound my neck with a strong leather cord and led me across the Plaza.

●●●

Despite my garb, I was identified as a hated teoltl. Warriors eyed me with hunger and Macitoc with respect.

Macitoc led me to a room in the palace decorated with the scenes of the chase and the skins and horns of beasts. I was amazed at the size of the antlers hanging there—they were three times the size of those of the largest ciervo rojo I had ever seen in España.

Macitoc returned my espada. "You wait here, Chichtli. I find Cuauhtemoc."

Macitoc returned shortly and led me to the Uei Tlatloani. He was adorned in the green feathers and gold and jewels of office. His head-dress gave the false impression of height. He was, in fact, shorter than the average Mexica. His eyes were large and luminous and he would have been handsome if his ear lobes, nostrils and lower lip hadn't been disfigured by the usual jade and golden jewelry. Later, when I got a better look at him, I thought that he looked younger than his reported twenty-five summers but, for now, his expression was forbidding. I averted my gaze and prostrated myself on the floor.

I lay there unnoticed as he attended to minor affairs of state. I remember ruing my decision to put myself in his power for I remembered what Macitoc had told me about the ruler. The new emperor was an even more determined enemy of the white men than had been his predecessor, Cuitlahuac. It was he who had led the Mexica forces against the Castilians on the sad night. On the other hand, it was Cuauhtemoc who had called off his victorious Mexicans when victory was certain. Macitoc reported his words to me:

"The gods have smiled on us, Macitoc—if we do not honor them now they will visit disaster upon us. We have given too many Mexica souls to the foul spirits of the night. When Tonatiuh shines down on us, we will finish our work with these unbelievers."

And so—as I witnessed, from the rooftop of Axayacatl's palace—the gods were abundantly honored. Still, in the field of *Otumba*—under the golden rays of *Tonatiuh*—Malinche delivered a smashing defeat to a massed Mexican army.

Cuauhtemoc, however, failed to interpret the divine message. On the death of Cuitlahuac he seized power. He slaughtered all who stood in his path—friends, relatives, nobles and priests died. It was said that he killed not only those who would compromise with Cortés but also those with whom he had private quarrels. Now, like a fool, I had placed myself in his power.

●●●

"Arise," he said. "It is not fitting that a teotl should abase himself as if he were a common man."

Not knowing what to expect, I slowly rose but still averted my eyes.

"You must look at me, Chichtli, for you are a sorcerer who knows many things."

I looked at him directly. Dried blood covered his earlobes and, I had little doubt, his shins and his penis. He had been offering himself to his gods.

He spoke, "My people have given your woman to the *Huitzilopocht-li*—if I had known, I would have saved her for you. She now dances in *Mictlan*."

"An accident, My Prince."

We stood in the throne room of Moctecuzoma's old palace. Unlike the first time I saw it, however, the place was run-down. Even the pipi-ltin and teopixia looked beaten. The new Prince leaned forward on his throne. I could see that he was recovering from *la viruela*—his skin was covered with sunken scars.

"The gods have forsaken us, Chichtli—they send a punishment more terrible than Malinche—they send the Holy Disease." Cauahtemoc clinched his jaw. "*Tezcatlipoca* shoots his arrows into our midst—offerings make no difference."

I tried to explain in terms the Prince would understand. "Your sacrifices will not help for the disease is *not* of the gods—Malinche's men have brought it with them from lands over the seas."

Cuauhtemoc pondered my words. "Chichtli, you have great power—will you help my people?"

I was on dangerous ground and knew it. "I am the Owl, O Cuauhtemoc. I cannot make miracles. Only time will stop this plague."

Cuauhtemoc again stopped to think. "Can you then help us in our war against Malinche? Can you make a spell to kill him?"

I drew Bebidor. "This is my spell."

A muscle under his left eye twitched. "What must we do, Chichtli?"

I thought before speaking, "The teoteoh you see before you now are but the first stones of a great avalanche—they will come in unstoppable numbers and you will be smashed. Negotiate for the best peace you can."

Cuauhtemoc stiffened. "I have slain those of my priests and lords who have spoken this treason..."

I was silent.

"...But, Chichtli, you are no common mortal—you speak to the gods. Tell me now what will become of me should I heed your words?"

Not knowing where the questioning was leading, I told the truth. "You and your nobles will be replaced by a Castilian Governor—perhaps Malinche, himself."

"And our lives, Chichtli?"

"If you prove useful and compliant, you may live. Otherwise you will surely die."

"And what of our faith, Chichtli? What of our gods and customs?"

"My Prince, the Christian Gods are jealous Gods. They will tolerate no others."

"And how many Gods do the Christians serve?"

"Three, Great Lord. God, the Father; God, the Son; and God the Holy Spirit."

"Three, Chichtli? So few?"

"Four if you count the Holy Mother—the Sacred Virgin. Five, if you count Satan."

Now Cuauhtemoc leaned forward and spoke in a whisper. "Perhaps this Holy Mother is the same as our Earth Goddess, *Coatlicue*, and Satan is *Xipe Totec?*

"I doubt it, My Lord."

"And perhaps the others are the same as *Tlaloc, Huitzilopotchtli* and *Tezcatlipoca?* Perhaps Malinche is *Quetzalcoal?*"

"No, My Lord. The white priests say that your gods are devils."

Cuauhtemoc sat back. "Two of Malinche's messengers came to me with soft words of peace. They said that we would be permitted to worship our gods in our old ways. They swore that my dynasty would continue to rule in the name of Carlos. You confirm what I already know. *They lied!* Now their white skins are draped over a rack in the Great Plaza. If you lie to me, Chichtli, you will share their fate."

Incredibly, my fear evaporated—I was suffused with power. "Moctecuzoma also threatened me. His miserable soul wanders eternally on the far side of dark *Mictlan*. Moaning, hopeless, alone—it weeps for its sins against me."

Cuauhtemoc's eyes widened. "I do not threaten you, Chichtli, but I must know if you will you help in my war against, Malinche?"

"Then, Cuauhtemoc—despite my warning—you are determined to resist?"

He stood up from his throne as if he would strike me. "*You refuse me?*"

I delayed my words so that they would have more effect. "I promise only blood."

The Prince seemed to deflate. "It is enough. We have known that we were doomed before we ever heard of Malinche—long before our ancestors fled *Aztlan*, before they left the Seven Caves—our teopixia have always predicted it. Will you help me, Chichtli, make the passing of the Mexica a thing of memory?"

I had survived.

"For the sake of love of you, My Prince, and for my hatred of Malinche, I will help you."

Tenochca

Cuauhtemoc provided me with the black robes of one of their filthy priests—I refused to wear them. I also refused to have my ears, nose and lip pierced to permit chalchuitl ornaments. I agreed to wear the garb of a warrior-pilli with seven captives to his credit. With a sharp flake of itzli I shaved off my beard.

I still have some memory of my finery—a soft cotton maxtlatl hanging to my knees and bound to my waist with a sash fashioned from the velvety skins of moles and mice. My old leather belt secured Bebidor. A tlamatli fell to my ankles. It was made of cotton but embroidered with brilliant feathers of tiny huitzlin. My feet were protected by leather cactli and the top of my head was covered by the flattened head of a small *cuetlachtli*—wolf. The rest of its skin hung behind me with its tail dragging on the ground. In my left hand I carried a small wicker shield—*chimalli*—adorned with rabbit fur and parrot feathers. Its purpose was purely decorative—it wouldn't have afforded protection from any but the lightest arrow.

To increase the effect of my facial scars I painted them red, black or white before participating in pagan rituals and before entering battle.

Macitoc added the skin of a spotted *ocelotl* to his usual maxtlatl. He eyed me critically. "Good, Chichtli, but for wrongness of eyes, you are Tenochca."

●●●

We patrolled the city looking for signs of Tenochca preparedness—there was little. People thronged the streets going about their usual activities but the signs of stress were there. The temples were busy as hundreds of victims—poor people and slaves—went to their fates. The avenues, which had been so immaculate, were now littered and filthy. The people seem to have lost purpose—many were listless with the lesions of *la viruela* scarring their skins. The beautiful gardens were unweeded and the beasts in the menagerie were neglected. Warriors who should have been shadowing Cortés strutted around intimidating the town folk.

PART 4
Chapter 27

We attended a meeting between Cuauhtemoc and his Generals on the summit of the Tlatelolco teocalli. Most of the session was wasted on discordant music, dancing and the killing of quail. The military discussion was rote and ritualistic—most was too rapid for my ear. I interrupted and asked them to slow their speech so that I could follow. One of the pilli—Inantzicatl—objected to my presence. He was dressed like his namesake, the coral serpent, but whereas the serpent has scales, Inantzicatl was adorned in a stunning display of red, yellow and black feathers. Inantzicatl, also like the coral serpent, was short with a deadly reputation. It was he who had led the attack on Alvarado's rear guard on the terrible night.

"Who is this teoltl to spy on us?" He turned to face Cuauhtemoc. "Take him from us, O Prince, and give his heart to *Tonatiuh*."

Cauahtemoc held his ground. "Chichtli hates Malinche. He will be my sharp knife."

Inantzicatl challenged Cuauhtemoc. Against all of the custom of Mexico, he looked directly into his Lord's eyes. "Chichtli slew my brother and nephew. Chichtli made the spell that sickened my daughters and me."

Cauahtemoc should have ordered his death on the spot. His power, however, must have been too fragile for him to do so. Instead, he turned to me.

"Will you swear an oath on the blood of your gods, Carlos and Jesus Christ?"

I had no problem swearing on the blood of any of them. "Not only theirs but I will swear an oath on the blood of my own father."

"That you will be loyal to Mexica?"

"I will be loyal to *Mexica, Tenochtitlan* and *Cuauhtemoc*."

Cauahtemoc took a step closer to me. "That you will kill the other teoteoh?"

"I will slaughter them."

Cuauhtemoc gestured to one of the priests who bounded down the steps and returned with a struggling child.

"The blood of this child is the blood of your father and the blood of your gods."

The victim was a little girl and small for her age—she couldn't be more than four years.

The child, I rationalized, would be sacrificed one way or another, still I didn't want the child to die for my sake.

I steeled my voice. "The blood of a child is a weak thing for an oath of this power. I will swear an oath on my iron maquahuitl—a weapon that was forged in *Mictlan* by *Tezcatlipoca*, himself."

With nothing to lose, I drew Bebidor from its sheath. The chieftains drew back. Cuauhtemoc and Inantzicatl stood firm.

I grasped the hilt with both hands, raised the blade and, with every fiber of my strength, brought it down in a scything slice. Inantzicatl's head, neck and right shoulder were separated from his torso and went tumbling down the steps. What remained of the body lay quivering in a spreading pool of blood.

"Now, My Prince," I bowed respectfully, "my oath is sealed with the strong blood of a warrior." I pointed Bebidor at the other pipiltin. "Does anyone here wish to challenge your Uei Tlatloani?"

All were silent except for Macitoc who chuckled at my joke.

"Now," I said, "let us waste no more time—Malinche never rests and Malinche never sleeps. While you dance and paint your faces, Malinche plots your destruction. Where is he now?"

"We must honor...." said an old man known as Ipantli.

"Honor *our* gods with the hearts of Malinche and all of his treacherous allies. Until then, you will honor the gods by making remorseless war—*where* is Malinche?"

There was silence.

"*Where is he?*"

Ihocochin—a tall man of austere bearing, spoke. He would have been imposing if he were not dressed to resemble an armadillo. "We have defeated him in the mountains, on the shores of the Lake, and in the low places where the frogs and serpents live. The gods glut on the flesh of his slaves."

I ran my finger down Bebidor's blade. "Then, how is it that Malinche sacked *Tepeaca* and *Texcoco?*"

The eagle-chief, Omeceli—the man who had been responsible for the defense of *Tepeaca*—answered. "Trickery, magic and treachery."

I bent close to his face. "Or your treachery, brother? We have just returned from the coast and see no evidence of Malinche's defeat. He controls the country and enslaves your allies. What is the truth?" I pointed to a dark man with the feathered emblems of many victories. His name, as I learned later, was Pechtli.

"Malinche receives reinforcements from the sea—many teoteoh and tepoztlin."

"Tell me more," I insisted.

"His teoteoh control the land east of the mountains—but—to the south and around the Lake we are victorious." Pechtli looked doubtful. "In the north, Malinche has been driven from *Xaltocan* and *Azcapazalco*. In the south, we have forced his retreat from *Chalco*. He attacked *Xochimilco* but, as the teoteoh lay drunk on octli, we breached the dike and flooded the city."

I read his mind. "Malinche's feet got wet."

Pechtli hung his head.

"And you contaminated your fresh water lake with salt."

"It was a good plan—our teopixquia promised..."

"Let me tell you about priests." I said. "Malinche has his own. Should they tell Malinche to jump off a mountain, he will not jump. If they tell him to attack when he knows he will lose, he retreats. If they tell him to retreat, when he knows to advance, he will attack. Malinche listens to his priests only in matters of God; in all other matters he takes his own council. Still, perhaps our teopixquia are stronger than Malinche's."—I looked around, knowing the truth—"How many teoteoh have been captured—*how many?*"

Pechtli's chest swelled. "We have sacrificed and killed over one thousand Tlaxcaltec fleas."

"White men?"

"Macitoc took forty-five at *Calpulalpan*. We have killed and captured sixty in other places."

Pitifully few, Cortés would have more than made up for these losses by new arrivals from the sea. Still, I hoped, if the Mexica collected more allies....

"I know that the people of *Tlaxcala*, *Cholula*, *Huexotzinco* and *Taras-*

cala have joined Malinche. Who else has joined your enemies?"

Cuauhtemoc replied, "The Tzentalteca, Zapoteca and the Mixteca have proved false. Those in *Texcoco* are slaves of Malinche. The cities of the Lake support us. Our friends—the Lords of *Michoacan* and *Tomatlan*—send us warriors as do the *Wariho, Zacateca* and *Akwa'ala*."

Some of the cities of the Lake had, by the pilli's own admission, been ruined by Cortés. Those lakeside cities still intact were vulnerable to attack or subversion. The others peoples were either forced allies or were from far distant pueblos and provinces—they could offer little help.

Burgos, Castilla-León

Mendoza winced and stopped writing. "A cramp—you must give me a moment."

The old man shrugged.

Mendoza rubbed his forearm while flexing his hand. "From my own research, it seems that your tale is incomplete."

"No doubt."

"You mention nothing of Cortés' conquest of *Cuernavaca*—one of the most important cities of the Mexican Empire."

"You mean *Cuauhnahuac?*"

"Yes, if that's the heathen pronunciation."

"Have you been there, Padre?"

"My travels—because of my ecclesiastical responsibilities—have never extended to Nueva España but I have read it is a full fifty leagues south of the southernmost end of Lake Texcoco."

"What's your point, Padre?"

"Cortés wasn't defeated. He—ah—pacified all of the country to the north and the south."

"You should be a politician, Padre."

"It puts the lie to the Mexican claim that they drove Cortés from all other lakeside cities."

"It wasn't a lie, Padre, not exactly. In part, they were telling Cuauhtemoc what he wanted to hear. In part, they misunderstood tactics. In truth, Cortés was conducting a reconnaissance in force. He penetrated to *Xochimilco*, but then was forced into withdrawal when the Tenochca breached their dike and flooded the city. Cortés lost nothing more than a little face—the Mexica wrecked *Xochimilco* and ruined their water supply."

I kept talking, both to gain time and gather my thoughts, "Now tell me, my friends, of Malinche's canoes—the ones he sacrificed in the mountains. What do you know of them?"

Ihocochin answered, his forehead wrinkled in doubt. "Malinche has carried their pieces to *Texcoco* where he now rebuilds them. Perhaps, he plans a new sacrifice?"

"Are they complete?"

"Our spies say most are finished."

I made a spiral in the air with Bebidor's point. "Malinche throws his coils around *Tenochtitlan* the same as a serpent strangles a bird. He has been testing your weakness, laying waste to the country, enslaving the population and gathering allies. He diverted your attention from the real threat—the acallin from *Huexotzinco*. While you were pursuing Malinche's army, he brought his boats to your Lake without opposition."

"We sent some warriors..."

I raised my voice, "*Fools!*" Once these canoes are complete Malinche will blockade the causeways and sweep *our* canoes from the Lake. We will starve."

Cuauhtemoc raised his eyes to the firmament. "This is why *Huitzilopotchli* brought you to us, Chichtli—to lead us from sin."

"Time is late, My Prince." I pointed to the noonday sun. "Gather your forces—no matter what the cost—we must burn Malinche's canoes. Where is Malinche *now?*"

The pipiltin glanced at each other.

"Nearby?"

Yolmitoc the Elder whispered, "*Tacuba.*"

"*Tacuba*"—I shook my head—"*Tacuba* should have been his grave."

There was silence.

"Maybe it's not too late." I pointed to all of them. "Malinche's teoteoh are not divine. Do you not know they are men like all others?

Also—listen carefully—you are playing into Malinche's hands by taking prisoners alive. Can you not hear Malinche laugh?"

Yolmitoc could stand it no longer. "We are not stupid men but our gods..."

I slashed down with Bebidor. "Who here will fight to kill?"

The priests—the filthy black priests—tried to shout me down.

I pointed at them. "These teopixquia lust for defeat but what do the war chiefs want?"

Macitoc, Ipanti and Pechtli stood forth but only Pechtli spoke. "My brothers are dead of the white man's metal and my wife and children are dead of the white man's sickness. These teopixquia are the ones responsible for our misery"—he glared at the priests—"from this day forward, I fight to *kill*."

"Good, now what has been done with the white men's weapons?"

Yolmitoc answered, "They are in the temple of *Quetzalcoatl*."

"They have honored the god enough. Now they will be used against their makers."

Chapter 28

Burgos, Castilla-León,
March 28, 1581, 6:45 A.M.

"Excelencia, I do not wish to be ungrateful but I must protest. My diet of bread, water and fish soup may alleviate my gout but it is destroying my soul."

The morning's light filtered through the small window and illuminated an area on the floor. Mendoza was clad in the usual vestments. As the months dragged on the priest had grown careless of his personal grooming. His clothing had smudges of mildew and his mustache and beard were overgrown and unkempt. His skin was sallow and waxen and his eyes were bloodshot and sunken.

The ancient Bishop, who always looked like cold death, was unchanged. His vestments were immaculate and the large silver crucifix at his neck was polished. His Bishop's ring glinted like a splash of fresh blood.

The old man clucked in sympathy. "Perhaps, we have overdone things—I will order breakfast."

Mendoza fairly salivated. "Thank you, Your Grace."

"I'm hungry myself. I feel like herring—salt herring—and bread soaked in milk."

"Obispo, may I respectfully suggest a slab of bacon and a little wine...?"

"Your gout, Padre—besides, it's bad for your stomach."

"But I need real food. *Mira!*"—he wiggled a front tooth—"My teeth are falling out."

The Bishop looked surprised. "I had no idea things were so serious. I'll order something more substantial. '*Guard!*'"

One of the guards entered the room and snapped his heels—the Bishop addressed the man without looking at him.

"Tell the cook that *I* want salt herring, roe, and a well-seasoned bowl of tripas—I'd also like a cup of cold water. For the Padre here...hmm...a bowl of atole seasoned with peppers and lemon juice. He'll also want a cup of fresh water and two slices of bread covered with lard."

The guard, who was entirely unmilitary, replied with another sharp heel click. He turned to leave.

"*Manteca, Excelencia?*" protested Mendoza. "*Posible queso y mantequilla...?*"

The Bishop rolled his eyes. "Cheese and butter, Padre? You are a hard man to satisfy. No bread and fat, guard, just the porridge."

The guard slammed the door on the way out. At first Mendoza's face registered shock but then he broke into tears.

"Buck up, Padre," the old man consoled, "your meal will be here presently."

Mendoza, whose dignity had utterly failed him, begged like a child. "Please, Your Grace, please! For the sake of common humanity I *need* herring and milk. I'll even accept the lard..."

The old man cackled like a chicken. "Too late, Padre—*Carpe diem quam minimum dredula poster*—you must seize the moment and not trust to the morrow."

The Bishop leaned back, enjoying Mendoza's reaction. "Ah...here is your atole, Padre. You have fifteen minutes."

Chieftains representing ten thousand warriors appeared before me. I presented them with Castilian armor recovered from the waters along the northern causeway. "Give the armor and weapons to your best men—those who will not hesitate to kill. I will train you in the use of these things but first, let me tell you this. Malinche's most powerful weapons are *words*. With words he wins allies; his words confuse your people; his treacherous words defeat you before you go into battle. Still, if you know their tactics and weapons, his words will lose power." I lifted Bebidor. "This is what the white man calls "*espada*." It is but a better kind of maquahuitl, and the ones you have captured—and capture in the future—must go to your best maquahuitl men. Unlike the maquahitl, it is for killing not wounding. Like the maquahuitl,"—I sliced at the air—"it can be used to slash but must be used with power." I jabbed to the front. "For the cut must be deep and disabling. Unlike the maquahuitl, the espada is pointed and can be thrust to penetrate shield, armor and man."

"The white man's lanzas"—I picked one up—"are but a version of your own *tlacochtlin* but must be wielded differently to produce a lethal wound. These are ballestas." I picked up a crossbow. "They have no magic and are but a different kind of *tlahuitolli*. They require special skill to use but any one of your warriors can learn to use them and learn to use them well. Here is its *totomitl*." I displayed a crossbow bolt. "It is short and tipped with the white man's metal. We will need more of these points and we need larger points for spears. I order our men of metal to melt down both the large and small tepoltzin—the ones of gray metal—and make all the points we need."

"Destroy them?" asked a chief clad as a common warrior. "Shall we not use these tepoltzin against their makers?"

"We do not have the fiery food that these weapons eat."

I had an afterthought. "Give me a sling-shot ball."

Omecetl, a chief who led the slingers, produced a round ball from a pouch at his waist. The ball was fashioned of oven-baked clay.

"Your men of metal will also make us many metal balls from the tepotzlin made of yellow metal. They will be heavier than these and will strike with more force." I doubted that they would injure the armor-clad Espanoles but they should make an impression on Cortés' allies.

●●●

There were Castilian captives held as exhibits in the menagerie. With the consent of Cuauhtemoc I interviewed them—they were naked and crowded into one tiny cell used to house uanantlin prior to sacrifice. Thinking me a Tenochca, they regarded me with sullen indifference.

"Señores," I addressed them, "you have an opportunity to save your lives."

Their shock was matched only by their relief.

"Qué?"

"You will be permitted to live under one condition—you must provide assistance to the Mexica."

"Against our own people?" The speaker was emaciated—his skin was smeared with excrement and his hair was caked and filthy.

"I didn't say, mind you, that your assistance had to be enthusiastic—just enough to keep you from being killed."

"What must we do?" said the man.

"Train them in Castilian tactics and weapons—you don't have to train them well."

"But when the Caudillo takes *Tenochtitlan* he will hang us for traitors."

I told a great lie. "The Caudillo is a compassionate man—he'll understand."

●●●

All five prisoners volunteered to save their lives. After they were cleaned up and fed I visited them again. I took one of them aside and spoke to him privately. He was a short man with yellow hair and hailed from the border country of the Pyrenees.

"What's your name?"

"Yuste—Juan Yuste."

"How long have you been a prisoner...?"

"I don't know—months."

"How were you taken?"

"*Díos!* We were all but wiped out in a place called *Capulta* or something." Tears welled in his eyes. "We had four women with us—the cabrónes served them on maíz cakes and forced us to eat them."

I put my hand on his shoulder. "What do you know of the Caudillo? Was he receiving reinforcements?"

"Oh yes! By the time we left, sixty survivors from one of Garay's failed expedition arrived. What choice did they have but join up? We also received two brigs and one caravel from Las Islas and another big caravel all the way from España—all together, two hundred men with plenty of horses, big guns and small arms."

"By now he should have more."

"I hope. Why all the questions, anyway?"

I shrugged my shoulders. "I just want to know when to expect deliverance."

"Me, too, hombre—I can't thank you too much for saving our skins." He sat quietly thinking things over. "But why are you dressed like these salvajes?"

I looked around as if fearing eavesdroppers. "I want to trick them into thinking I'm with them in spirit as well as body—they're so stupid. In the meantime I'm giving them bad information and stabbing them in the back. They way I see it, we can help the Caudillo a lot more here than we could on the battle line."

"*Increíble!* I hadn't looked at it like that. If I can talk them into it, I'm going to dress up like an Indio, too."

I slapped him on the back. "That's the right attitude—besides, it's not like you have much choice. As far as training goes—just make a good show of it. Show them how to adjust the nut and bowstring on the ballesta and show them how to point it. The ignorantes will probably shoot themselves."

●●●

I outlined my plan to Cuauhtemoc—it was very simple.

"We must conserve our strength for we will need every man in the defense of the Capital. Here, on the island, each warrior will equal ten on the mainland. Still, these will not be enough. Malinche has a vast army of allies and each day he grows stronger."

Cuauhtemoc was grim. "All Mexica will remain loyal to the Triple Alliance."

"Malinche is a serpent, My Prince. He has already conquered *Tex-coco*..."

"...and her people have fled to our protection."

"Yes, but most of those still alive stayed behind and now help Malinche. This is his strategy—he will force those he defeats to fight for him and he will tempt those he has not defeated to join in the looting of your Empire."

"Is there nothing we can do?"

"It is late, My Lord, but you must shore up your allies. Tell them that the fight is a battle of faith; the white men will destroy their good way of life and the gods that they love."

"They know this, Chichtli."

"Tell them again—this won't be enough, though—tell your subject cities and pueblos that they need not pay your taxes. Tell them that they will no longer be required to provide victims...."

Cuauhtemoc grimaced. "But *Tenochtitlan* will become impoverished and our gods need blood."

"Feed the gods with the blood of your enemies. As for poverty—how poor will you be should Malinche sack the city and burn her temples."

The Prince was silent for long seconds. "If I order all of these things can you promise victory?"

"I can only promise piles of your dead enemies."

●●●

"How does it go?" I asked Juan Yuste.

In fact, it was going much like I knew it would. What had started as a ruse had become something quite different. Yuste and the others had become friendly with their captors and were taking a professional interest in their training.

"*Bien, bien!* Too bad, Enrique tried to escape. I warned him but he wouldn't listen." Yuste went on. "To tell you the truth, Rodrigo, if I had a little gunpowder..."

"But we don't."

"Too bad. Have you heard news of the Caudillo?"

"He's ruined a few farms and burned four or five pueblos." I shook my head in feigned sorrow. "Unfortunately, the Tenochca caught Sandoval between *Texcoco* and *Chalco* and took a handful of Castilians and hundreds of Tlaxcalteca."

I failed to tell Yuste that I led the Mexica force. When Sandoval counterattacked, we retreated to our canoes and escaped without a single casualty.

"*Infierno!*"

"I've also learned that the Caudillo had problems with his foremost Tlaxcaltec war lord, Xicotencatl the Younger. Something about a woman. Cortés cooked him over a slow fire."

Yuste struck his forehead.

"He replaced him with Chichimatecatl."

"But everyone knows he's a coward."

"Worse yet—there's been big trouble over division of loot—there was a rebellion."

"I shouldn't be surprised," he said. "The old veterans told me that the Caudillo grabbed the treasure that he gave to them before the retreat from *Tenochtitlan.*"

I bent closer to his ear. "That cabrón, Alvarado, was mentioned as one of the plotters."

"But the Caudillo's alive?"

"He lives a charmed life."

"Thank God. He may pull it off yet, but what will the Mexica do to *us* when Cortés wins..."

I was worried about the same thing.

"That's negative thinking, Juan. If you can convince the Mexica that you are with them body and soul, they'll leave you alone. Besides, we'll soon have reinforcements."

"What?"

"The Mexica picked up twelve deserters."

The deserters surrendered to a very surprised Mexican farmer on the road between *Texcoco* and *Chalco.* These Españoles, most of whom were strangers to me, told me that Malinche had thwarted another plot within the army and they were fleeing his vengeance and had no option other than going over to the enemy and hoping the Mexica would accept them in a role other than that of sacrificial victims.

They told me that this latest plot against the Caudillo involved over two hundred Castilians including some of the Captains—Lugo, Marín and Ircio. In an attempt to imitate Brutus, they were to fall on Cortés and stab him to death. Cortés' great friend, Pedro de Alvarado would then take command.

Unfortunately, a turncoat betrayed the scheme and one of the ring-leaders—Antonio de Villafana and his pilot, Diego Díaz—were tortured and hanged without trial.

I questioned one of the captives. Not surprisingly, perhaps, it was Gustavo Müeller. I questioned him closely. "Villafana's dead, you say, but how about Alvarado?"

"Cortés hasn't touched him."

"It doesn't make sense," I said.

He shrugged his shoulders. "He spread the word that Alvarado wasn't party to the rebellion."

"What? Alvarado would take command but knew nothing of it?"

"Of course it's a lie," he said. "Everybody knows that Alvarado was more deeply involved than Villafana. Word is that Cortés has"—he made an aggressive gesture with his fist—"special feelings for Alvarado."

"How did you escape?"

"Bribed the guard."

"You say there were two hundred rebels—Cortés can't hang them all."

"Only a few of us were to be an example. Even so, he travels with a bodyguard of armed men."

España would conquer all Mexico but Cortés walked a tightrope of death.

I stepped closer to the prisoner so he could see me better. "Do you know who I am?"

He regarded my Mexica attire then laughed. "I'd know you any-where, Rodrigo—even under all that war paint."

"You and I, friend, are here under the same circumstances." I gave him time to consider my words. "Cortés will kill us should we return. The Mexica will reward us should we assist them."

"That's what I'm counting on, Rodrigo."

"You don't have to help them too much."

"I plan to help them plenty. With luck, I'll personally cut off Cortés' shrunken balls."

"You *hate* him that much, Gustavo?"

"The bastard cheated me, Rodrigo—took everything I had—but, I don't hate him. I'd just like to make a coin purse from his scrotum."

"You'll have to fight me for it, Gustavo."

"You'll have to fight all of us, then, Rodrigo. Every one of us has sworn a blood oath against the pinche cabrón."

●●●

Burgos, Castilla-León

Mendoza tapped his fingers. "I cannot dispute that you helped the heathens—it's something that a man of your character might do. I cannot accept, however, that others Christians joined the enemy. Besides, as a scholar, I find no record of it."

"Have you not read Bernal Díaz' account?"

"A mountain of lies."

"He recorded that Christians fought with the Tenochca although he got the numbers and circumstances wrong."

"Ridiculous."

"No, Padre, it's not ridiculous at all. Disaffected and terrified men *always* defect to the enemy—even to an enemy bound to be defeated. Most men make decisions based on the proximity of death..."

"Not good Catholics."

Chapter 29

Cortés positioned himself in front of *Tacuba* facing the Tlacopan causeway—the same causeway on which he had retreated only eight months previously. He had the gall to attack us in broad daylight. We repelled him, killing six Castilians and taking five others captive. I was able to convince four of the captives that their best interest lay in joining my small force of white men.

In the following days, Malinche crouched in *Tacuba*, undecided whether to renew his offensive or whether to retreat. Tlaxcaltec and

Mexica fighters taunted each other and challenged each other to duels. Neither side interfered as Indio combatants sparred between lines. I had the opportunity to watch one particularly interesting contest.

"*Tlaxcala is the home of dung beetles!!!*" shouted a broad-chested Tenochca known as *Canautli*—The Duck. He strutted between the lines wearing a tlamatli made from the gray and red furs of coyoteh. Four tails of the same beasts dangled from his shield. His right hand bore a short hunting spear with a solid iron point—my metal workers had been busy. The spear was attached to his wrist by a nequen cord.

Apparently, dung beetles are not well thought of in *Anahuac*—the insult prompted a response by a Tlaxcaltec chieftain, *Nexicoli*, serving in a regiment led by Chichimecatl. He swaggered out to confront his enemy.

"*Mexica smell like lizards!*"

This was killing talk. Both fighters approached one another with affected, stilted strides. The spectators whooped for their champions. I couldn't help but notice that the Tlaxcalteca was the better armed of the two. True, his shield was of similar make but he bore a Castilian espada and looked like he knew how to use it.

The Mexican was the first to try but his spear went wide by almost a forearm. With a twitch of his wrist the spear was back in his hand, again. Nexicolli jumped forward striking at Canautli's head but missed by a fraction. Warily, the two fighters circled one another. Clumsily, the Tenochca tried a toss but again missed by a wide margin. Nexicolli shouted his contempt and pressed his advantage. Time and again he almost succeeded in striking his over-matched enemy.

The terrified Mexican continued to miss wildly—Nexicolli grew even more confident. Canautli drew back, measured his enemy, and drove his spear again. Nexicolli, expecting another bad shot, barely moved to defend himself. The spear struck him directly in the groin and protruded beyond his buttock. He dropped his espada and dropped to his knees. His Mexican victor chanted the usual dirge as slaves appeared and drew the defeated Tlaxcalteca into our ranks.

"*Tlaxcaltec women fuck monkeys!*"

Our Mexica champion defeated five more chieftains—the Tlaxcalteca went wild. In an undisciplined mob, they attacked our line where we butchered them like the dogs they were—I killed two myself.

Thwarted, the Tlaxcalteca took their revenge on *Tacuba* and, despite Malinche's efforts to save the city as a base of operations; it nearly burned it to the ground. The next morning, fifty Tlaxcaltec bodies hung from the walls of the city. Cortés had put down the riot in his usual way.

●●●

A single Castilian, under green and white banners of peace, entered the ground between the two forces. With great courage, he walked within fifteen paces of the assembled Mexica.

"Show yourself, Rodrigo! I know you're there!"

Cortés, of course, knew of my presence in the camp of his enemies—prisoners were bound to have reported it. I ordered a servant to run back to the city and return with things that would tempt Malinche.

I stepped from the Mexican lines—scarcely ten paces of bare ground separated me from my enemy. Unlike at our last meeting, we had *both* dressed for the occasion. His head was uncovered but his attire was sumptuous—he was dressed in purple velvet and brocade covered by polished chest armor. My attire was even more striking. In addition to a red and yellow patterned maxtlatl, I was wearing chain mail covered by a tlamatli made from the skins of small mountain cats. My polished metal helmet was decorated with green and black feathers that trailed down my back. My face was painted—the left side white and the right side black—the scars on my face, blood red.

"You've changed, Rodrigo—have you put on more weight?"

"It's difficult to stay thin, Caudillo, when one's diet consists entirely of fat Castilians."

"Very funny, Rodrigo, but have you considered the penalty for treason?"

I laughed out loud. "Exactly the same as it would have been for your false charge of desertion."

"If you'd taken your punishment like a man, Rodrigo, you would not be killing your friends and countrymen.

"Hernán, *you* have killed most of my friends. As for my countrymen—you think like a civilian. I *am* a mercenary"—I let my words sink in so that he could absorb the full implication—"*exactly* like some of your other men. They don't care who they are fighting—just as long as they're paid. Your payment, Caudillo, has been—shall we say—*minimal*.

The Mexica pay me with honor and gold.

"*Oro?*"

"That's right, Hernán. Gold! Think of it. *Gold!!!* Treasure rooms full of the stuff. Cuauhtemoc is so grateful to me, he's giving me a king's ransom and I'm hiding it away in places you'll never find."

Now this was a lie—Cuauhtemoc was rewarding me but he wasn't stripping the coffers of Mexico to pay me. As Cortés once told me, fear can be useful thing and, of the things that he most feared, the loss of gold was the greatest.

"Perhaps I have been too hasty, Rodrigo—maybe you and I can strike a bargain. Your life for—let me see—three-quarters. *No!* Make that only *half* your gold."

I held my hand out and slowly clinched my fist. "As soon as I am in your grasp you will s-q-u-e-e-e-z-e me for the other half."

"You're a hard man, Rodigo, but I think I have something that just might soften your heart—half your gold for your life and the delight-some person of Doña Francesca de la Barca."

"A bad joke, Caudillo." I measured the ground between us. If I calculated correctly, I could kill him before he reached the Castilian line.

"No joke, Rodrigo. I've got her."

"She died..."

"Not quite—I managed to save both her and Doña Amelia during the holocaust."

"Then show them to me!"

"They're in *Texcoco* but I can arrange to present her to you as soon as possible."

"*Fool!* I *saw* Amelia die on the top of their mosque. "

He didn't even slow down. "I don't lie to Christians, Rodrigo. May-be you saw a different woman." He shrugged as if Amelia's life were a trifle. "Maybe I'm mistaken. The Señora, however, is very much with us. I've seen and spoken to her many times."

"Then you've seen a ghost."

"Not so, Rodrigo. I may have been wrong about Amelia but not about Francesca. I know you were—*close*—to her." He thought for several long moments. "I am even prepared to present you with pa-pers—witnessed by Padre Olmedo—that not only is she alive but she is completely untouched."

My mind was a whirl of emotions. What if she *was* alive? But then, I *knew* Malinche—he wove a sticky web.

"Keep your documents, Caudillo, and I'll keep my gold. The trouble between us"—I slid Bebidor from its scabbard and thrust its blade into the earth—"goes deeper than the memory of a dead woman."

"My, My, Rodrigo, I thought that you were a practical man. You'll never live to enjoy your mountain of gold.

"That remains to be seen, Cortés, but what is certain is that you will never see it, either."

I gestured to my servant who had just returned breathless from the city. I removed a heavy object from a bag that he carried.

"Here's a sample, though—it belongs to you—it even has the Royal Mark on it. It was recovered following your glorious retreat from *Tenochtitlan*." I walked closer to him and laid the ingot on the earth. "I give it to you, Hernán. You must only give me one small thing in return."

Malinche's gaze was riveted on the gold. Without looking up he replied, "What do you want, Rodrigo?"

"At night I have trouble sleeping—my head hurts."

He glanced up. "Yes?"

"...Give me Javier de la Concha."

"He's my friend, Rodrigo."

"That ingot's worth five thousand, maybe seven thousand, pesos de oro."

"My officers will revolt."

I upped my offer, "Two ingots, Hernán."

"For two ingots of gold—you can keep your miserable life and I'll throw in the bitch."

"Concha or nothing."

"*Nada.*"

"Then I will adjust my offer, cabrón. Does not Javier boast that he has slain eleven men in duels?"

"He's the best I've ever seen."

"*Bien. Muy bien.* My offer is two ingots in exchange for the opportunity to exchange blows with the cabrón. If you're right about your champion, you may add the gold to your pocket—and—you may feed

Hummingbird God • 229

my carcass to the ravens."

"And the gold you've hidden away?"

"Search for it."

He considered the alternatives. "Two ingots of gold....I will leave the rest to Javier's honor."

I'd judged my man correctly. "That's all I ask for, Cortés."

●●●

Malinche convinced de la Concha that he should confront me in combat—he told him he could thus assuage his honor and remove a threat to the army. He never told him that by risking his life, that *he* would turn a profit of over ten thousand pesos de oro.

The duel was to be private—a secret place in an overgrown garden outside of the walls of *Tacuba*. Cristóbal de Olid would serve as Concha's second—Macitoc was my man. Cortés had been previously paid one ingot of gold with guarantees for the remaining gold after the duel—no matter the victor. Cortés was not present. He sent armed witnesses, however—Pedro de Alvarado, Gonzalo de Sandoval and young Bernal Díaz.

To prevent intervention, I brought my own-armed escort—all bearing Castilian armor and weapons. Pechtli was there, as were chieftains from *Tomatlan* and *Oaxaca*. Guards roamed the perimeter of the garden, wary of intervention by forces from the opposite side. Should the alarm sound, combat would cease and the contestants would flee in opposite directions.

●●●

I watched de la Concha the same as a lynx watches a hare. He was discussing the fine points of swordsmanship with Alvarado. It had been months since I'd seen the bastard but was struck by how much he resembled an oversized rodent. He was a well-equipped rodent, however. His helmet had sidepieces that protected the sides of his face and his plate armor was nearly spotless. His legs were hidden by metal greaves and metal-studded leather gauntlets protected his hands.

I was wearing my old helmet and chain mail. A thick leather hauberk protected the back of my neck. By previous agreement, both of us were armed with shields, throwing spears and swords.

"Nice seeing you, Rodrigo," Concha said. "Too bad our re-acquaintance will be of short duration.

"Shorter than you think, Javier."

His smile was forced. "Before you die, you should know how much we enjoyed your *amante*. The Caudillo played with her first but when he grew bored with her—he gave her to the men." He waited to see how I would react then bowed from the waist. "I've had the privilege of putting it to her myself. *Hombre!* She loves it. She's a regular whore."

I removed my helmet and then my armor.

Concha held up his hand. "This is supposed to be a duel—not suicide, *culero*."

"Our contract calls for us to fight with similar equipment. We're going to fight without armor."

Concha looked around him for support. Alvarado shrugged. "He's right, Javier. Now kill him and let's get out of here."

Shamed, de la Concha stripped himself of his armor. I noticed how thin his chest was without its metal plate.

I laughed at his nakedness. "Now, Javier, I want you to know that the Caudillo—your noble friend, protector and Judas—has *sold* you to me for 30 pieces of silver."

His face fell but tensed, again. "*Lying, cabrón!*"

"You're a leaf in a whirlwind, Javier—a pig for the slaughter. You're the only one not in on the joke. I'm going to kill you today—butcher you—and *everyone* knows it."

Concha fought back. "I fucked that bitch with half a hard on. That's all she's worth."

"You are Cortés' *puto*, Javier, and now that he's tired of you," –I thrust my spear towards him—"*I'm* going to *put* it to you."

"*Pinche cabrón!*"

"You're dead, Javier." I grinned my best grin. "You're already dead—dead, stinking and bloated. See how the vultures circle."

Involuntarily, Concha's eyes turned up, scanning the skies.

"Are you ready, Javier? Ready for Hell?"

He didn't answer. Shield up, he sprang forward and started to circle.

Spears quivering, bowstring taut, we stalked one another. I saw the sweat running down his face and chest and I could smell the stink of his fear. Twice de la Concha nearly threw but held back when I dodged. On the third time, however, I was too slow—his spear flew and struck my shield. I tried to pull the spear out but couldn't—I threw the shield down. Concha drew his sword, bent forward and charged.

I put all of my strength behind my throw—I knew it was a good one. My spear clanged against his shield just a little right of center. I stepped aside to avoid his rush. De la Concha, however, didn't counter my move. Shield fixed to his body, he ran right past me and through the ranks of my Mexica friends. He dropped his sword and fell to his knees, clutching the shaft of my spear.

I shouted in Nahuatl, "Take him to *Tenochtitlan*."

Concha was seized by my people and, before the Captains could react, was bound and packaged for his savage journey.

●●●

The Castilian Captains stood arrayed against my Mexica chieftains. I put up my hand.

"Tell Cortés that if he wants the rest of the gold, he must meet me here at first light. Tell him that with de la Concha punished it should be possible for us to strike a bargain. Tell him that he must come alone and unarmed."

Sandoval, who was little more than a child, had the rough voice of an old man. He objected, "The agreement was that the gold be delivered on completion of the duel."

"A technicality, Gonzalo—I'll be here in the morning."

"The Caudillo would be a fool to meet you here unarmed—you hate him as much as de la Concha."

"Then he may come armed if he if thinks that will protect him—but—he must come alone. Tell him that it's a test of courage—the risk of death versus"—I placed my hand flat at eye level—"a pile of gold."

●●●

That night I went to Cuauhtemoc. He was sitting on his throne toying with the wounded Javier de la Concha. My spear had penetrated the man's shield and entered his belly below the ribs. The spear had been pulled through Concha's body and Cuauhtemoc was tormenting Concha with the same filth-covered weapon. He moaned with each jab.

Seeing me, de la Concha begged, "*Mata me! Finish me!*"

I ignored my enemy. May he broil in Hell.

Cuauhtemoc looked up at me. "I tire of this teoltl—perhaps you would enjoy sacrificing him to your god of the Smoking Mirror—*Tezcatlipoca?*"

I chuckled. "....And insult the god with *this* thing who tried to be a man.... I will return him to Malinche."

The Prince was suspicious. "Why do you return your enemy to Malinche? Do you betray me?"

"No, My Lord, far from it—I have a plan to betray Malinche. My return of this man is part of my plan."

"He is dying—why should Malinche want him back?"

"My return of this man, even though he is dying, should confirm to Malinche that I have had a change of heart." I hesitated to tell Cuauhtemoc the rest of my plan for I knew that the Indios could not keep a secret.

"Do not betray me, Chichtli."

"I must convince Malinche that I am his man."

A light shined from his eyes. "You have done well by us, Chichtli. You have earned my trust."

Chapter 30

I waited on the bleak plain of *Tacuba*. An unarmed Malinche appeared from the mist. De la Concha—belly green and swollen—lay between us. Fly covered guts protruded from the gaping wound in his groin. Cortés never looked down at him.

"Where's the gold, Rodrigo?"

"Just as I promised, Hernán." I passed a heavy nequen sack over to him. "One bar of gold and—to show my good faith—an ingot of silver."

Concha started to groan as Cortés lifted the ingots from the sack. "If you'd been killed I would have been cheated."

I had to laugh. "You knew I wouldn't lose, señor. You condemned de la Concha as surely as if you'd put a cuchillo through his liver. You should have seen his face when I told him that you *sold* him to me."

Cortés wasn't listening. He was too busy hefting the precious metal.

I continued, "There's a lot more where that came from—which is why I wanted to talk to you." I gave the dying Concha a shove with my foot. "This culero was the cause of the trouble between us."

He smiled but his eyes didn't. "That's right, Rodrigo. De la Concha has been a troublemaker since the first day of our adventure. Now that he's gone, there can be peace."

"That's the way I see it, too, Hernán—besides, I have no love for these Indios. After you conquer their City, I'd like to be able to return to España in safety and even a little wealth and—with you as my backer—my problems with the Holy Office might dry up and blow away."

But problems with *Santo Oficio* never dry up and blow away.

He ran his fingers through his beard. "I'll guarantee it! Now, let's talk about the gold...."

"I've got more hidden in the City and, even better, I know where Cuauhtemoc has hidden the Royal Treasure."

"*Donde?*"

I clucked my tongue. "All in good time, Hernán. You don't mind if I use your first name?"

"No problem—*the gold...?*"

I put on my warmest smile. "These stupid Indios trust me—I'll deceive them while searching for more treasure." I bent forward and whispered, "The little bit of gold that we've got thus far is *nothing.*"

I thought he would urinate on himself.

"By all means, Rodrigo, stay in the enemy camp. Disrupt them and confuse them but never let them know what you are doing." He stepped closer and jabbed me in the ribs with his elbow. "*Demonio!* Even if you must wipe out a few of our own men..."

Cortés was feeling good despite the fact that his friend was dying at his feet.

"When we find all the treasure you get ten percent—minus the King's share, of course."

"Thank you, hombre. I'm so grateful."

He thought for a moment. "May I give you some advice, Rodrigo?"

"By all means."

"Don't let our Castilians know that you are among the enemy."

"They already know."

"Most don't and—those that do—I'll order to keep their mouths shut."

"Why *shouldn't* they know?"

"It's a matter of security and morale. They might not understand the—*subtlety*—of what we're doing."

Cortés was magnificent—he planned to keep his men *and* the King ignorant of any gold I discovered.

"You're right, Hernán. They wouldn't understand."

"Also, your meeting with me here is bound to have aroused Cuauhtemoc's suspicions—what did you tell him?"

"I told him that I was double-dealing you."

He slapped his thigh. "Did the fool buy it?"

"I've staked my life on it."

"Here's what I recommend—become as much as a Tenochca as possible—give them no cause to mistrust you. Eat their food, sleep with their women and pray at their altars—*La Puta Santisima*—dine at their cannibal feasts. Fight alongside of them but you must not place yourself in danger."

"I plan to avoid combat."

"Not good, Rodrigo—they may start to suspect you—simply avoid the thick of the fight."

"I think I can arrange that."

"If Cuauhtemoc should ask your advice—give it—and make it believable, too. Just give it a twist—a very, very little twist..."

"I'll do all I can."

"I know you will, Rodrigo." He slapped me on the back. "You're going to be my sharpest knife."

Chapter 31

Cuauhtemoc called a council of war. "What is our best course?"

Quiahuatl, warrior-priest of *Tlaloc* stood forth. "We put more faith in our weapons than we put in our gods—we must prove our faith. Call in the warriors for a demonstration of devotion. We must reconsecrate the great teocalli—more victims than for its first dedication—slaves, captives, criminals, those too old to work and those affected by the gods. *Tlaloc* will be grateful and wash away the teoteoh."

Many were in agreement with his words.

"Quiahuatl eats too many mushrooms," I said.

Cuauhtemoc spoke, "Then what must we do?"

"We wait for Malinche—he will soon move. When he does, we must take his canal and burn his acallin. I want long wooden sticks—thousands of sticks. They are to be three times the length of a spear and sharpened at one end."

"Are the women and children to fight?" Macitoc said.

"Not yet. We will plant the sticks in the mud of the Lake in those places that Malinche's boats will strike them. They may not sink the boats but they will slow them and make them vulnerable to attack."

I continued, "Mark my words, brothers. When Malinche strikes he will advance along the causeways. I propose that the women, children and the old be organized into squads armed with tools to break stone and move earth—one division of workers for each causeway into the city. The workers must break the bridges and then—should the white men and their slaves fill in the breaks—the workers, even the very old and very young, must reopen the breaks and make them even wider."

Quiahuatl was livid. "To defend our city with women is an insult..."

I raised my voice, "The ruin of our Empire is the greatest insult. Besides, do not the warriors have the responsibility of combat? Four divisions of warriors will be organized, each defending a separate causeway. The divisions will be organized into land and lake fighters—the tactics will be ambush with defense from rooftops and behind parapets. Lure the enemy through the breaks in the causeways then hit them and hit them hard. Wound his xolotameh and push his tepotozlin into the mud."

Initl, leader of the men of *Michipan*, spoke, "The men with white man's weapons—will they fight?"

I had been thinking about the possibilities. "We will keep a reserve of our strongest fighters including Tenochca trained with white man's weapons—our white men allies will join them. This company will be used to stiffen our lines and to take advantage of Malinche's mistakes."

I waved down a protest. "This will not be enough—we need good information. I will travel to the white man's camp to spy upon them."

There was no wind and a half-moon illuminated the waters of the Lake. Fish slapped the surface as I paddled through the milky water. Wearing the clothing of a dead Castilian, I traveled alone. The donor of my garments had been a very tall man and I was forced to trim the pantalones and sleeves—I hoped that my alterations wouldn't cause suspicion.

I needed to contact Malinche but I was worried about his soldados—some would remember. They would remember my condemnation, my killing of the guards and my escape. Still, there was no other way.

I hid my canoe in a reed bank and struggled through the tangled vegetation to the dry land. A Castilian patrol heard the commotion and challenged me.

"Who goes there?"

"A spy from the enemy camp—my name is for the Caudillo."

"*Adelante!*"

I took a few paces forward until I could see their faces. They were three strangers—Thank God. They searched me and even looked in my mouth. One of them fingered my frayed sleeves and another discovered the stitched tear under my right arm—despite washing, traces of old blood remained.

"These rags belong to someone else."

"I'm a poor man, señores. They are all I could afford."

"Anyway, you're unarmed. You must forgive us, compadre, but there have been attempts on the Caudillo's life."

"No offense taken—you're doing a good job. I'll tell the Caudillo about it."

The youngest man was pleased. "Thank you, señor."

One of the men conducted me to *Texcoco*. Our trek paralleled a newly constructed canal, which was over half a league long. Towards the end—the end closest to *Texcoco*—brigantines were moored. There was also an army of Indios—mostly unhealthy looking Texcocans—laboring by torchlight. Nine boats were already complete—others were partially built. Sections of hulls as well as pieces of bracing, ringing and masts were lying next to the canal waiting for reassembly. Not for the first time I was astounded by Cortés' vision.

Of as much interest as the brigs were the defenses. Parapets of earth protected the canal from both the landward and lakesides and cañónes were emplaced in the best positions. Fifty, maybe seventy-five soldados were quartered within the fortifications, as were hundreds of armed Tlaxcalteca. I noticed that the Indios had set up a shrine—a small teocalli made up of earth and stone right next to the Castilian camp. Its steps were stained with blood.

We entered the walls and I saw that *Texcoco* was largely ruined. Macitoc was right. Malinche had indeed failed to control his allies. It was hard to imagine that *Texcoco* had once been a magnificent place—the loveliest city in *Anahuac*—with beautiful gardens and palaces. Its destruction was an act of criminal vandalism. The town had been entered peacefully enough but the Tlaxcalteca had ignited the city. The great libraries—all the history of Mexico—had burned to the ground. I thought of the great library of Alexandria burned down by Roman legionnaires, people who deemed themselves civilized. The Tlaxcalteca also claimed civilization but they were, at best, miserable barbarians and chronic incendiaries. Bebidor, at my side, lusted for their blood.

●●●

Cortés was quartered in a palace that had escaped much of the damage. He was waiting in a room that he had been turned into an office complete with a large desk of polished wood. He wore a red cap with a long green feather, the tail feather of the sacred quetzal, symbol of Mexican Royalty. Polished plate armor protected his chest and back. Two bodyguards, equipped with two-handed montantes, stood close to the door. Cortés sat at the desk while three Indio girls—twelve, maybe thirteen, years of age—attended to his comfort. One rubbed the back of his neck—the other two were under the desk massaging his thighs.

He didn't bother to get up or shake my hand. "I was afraid you might have forgotten about us, Rodrigo."

"I keep my word."

"Excellent, but I trust you haven't compromised yourself. How did you explain your departure from *Tenochtitlan?*"

"I told Cuauhtemoc that I had a plan to give you false information."

He readjusted his legs so that the girls could position themselves better. "Did he believe you?"

"Cuauhtemoc trusts no one. He finds me useful and he believes me a traitor. He believes that I serve his purpose."

"Good—then what do you have to report?"

"The Mexica are massing forces to the south—close to Cuauhnahuac. Their intention is to push to the north and the east, destroy Villa Rica and cut off your communication to the coast."

"*Hijo!* That complicates things. My brigs are nearly ready. I'd hoped to move directly on the City but now I'm forced to delay things a little. Do you know how many warriors and their direction of march?"

I shrugged. "My position is sensitive—I try not to appear too inquisitive. You know all that I know."

"And the gold?" He rubbed the head of the youngest girl.

"It's in the old palace."

"Do you know where?"

"Like I said, I try not to be too inquisitive but one of the servants said it was hidden under the tiles..."

Cortés jumped up. One of the girls bumped her head on the underside of the table. "A *hole* under the floor?"

I tried to calm him. "Don't worry, Hernán. I'm told that there are rooms—*four rooms*—under the floor. They've been there since ancient times—dug for defense." I leaned forward and whispered, "They are *stuffed* with treasure."

Cortés sat back down, the color in his face slowly returning. "Big rooms?"

"From what I'm told—*big.*"

He spread his legs again and repositioned one of the girls. He closed his eyes in satisfaction. "*Jesus Dulce.*"

"Don't get too comfortable, Hernán. They'll have a plan to move the treasure should they face defeat..."

Deception should involve an element of doubt. I had no idea how much treasure Cuauhtemoc possessed and I had even less idea where it might the stashed. I planned to be far away when Cortés learned the truth.

He snapped back from his revery. "I'm more than a match for this Cuauhtemoc."

"I trust you're right, Caudillo, because he's already prepared a special rack for your head."

"Premature of him, don't you think?"

I changed the subject. "I didn't believe you when you told me that Francesca was still alive."

"You should have more faith in your Caudillo, Rodrigo."

"She's alive?"

"Of course."

"Concha said things..."

"Combat lies, Rodrigo." Cortes' laugh came from deep in his belly. "He was trying to rattle you. As it turns out, you *rattled* him more."

"Have you—have you...?"

"...Touched her?" Not me and—to my knowledge—nobody else. She keeps to herself."

"I want to see her."

He withdrew his hand from the child. "There's not enough time."

I bent closer. Behind me both guards became alert. "I want to see Francesca."

He never changed his expression. "Let us first discuss military matters—you always give good advice."

He stood up and walked up to a wall decorated with a large amatl painting showing Lake Texcoco and the surrounding country. The map was marked with a confusing assortment of multicolored devils.

Cortés went on, "Now that the Mexicans are on the move, I propose to muster half of my Castilians along with most of my allies then make a forced march along east and then the south shore of the Lake."

He traced a route that would place his army close to the edge of Lake Texcoco—vulnerable to attack from its waters. "From here I will march south through these mountain passes and take," and here he mispronounced the Nahuatl name of the city, "*Cuarna...Cuarnacaca* by assault."

He was giving me more information than was necessary.

"Your army will be vulnerable here, here and here." I indicated the edge of the Lake and the narrow gorges. "I recommend a more inland and circuitous course."

"Too slow—with the Mexicans moving, I need to move fast."

"Then put out a strong flanking force."

"You think me a fool, Rodrigo? Once *Cuernacaca* is reduced I will divide my force with one detachment circling east, through the mountains, striking at those pueblos in revolt against us and at these garrisons"—he stabbed his finger against the map—"south of *Tepeaca*. The other detachment will move northeast toward *Tlaxcala* and link up with my first force—*here*." He indicted a point north of *Tepeaca*. Do you have suggestions?"

Cortés wasn't foolish enough to trust me—his instruction was nonsense to test loyalty. His true plan was yet to be learned but I doubted that it included a division of his forces. Moving against *Cuauhnahuac* made sense. There he could watch for the Mexican reaction and decide on the best plan of action. If the Mexica moved against his supposed division of forces, he would learn that I was a traitor.

"A bold plan, Malinche." He looked up to me sharply but I continued as if I had not noticed. "If you execute it perfectly you should catch the Mexicans in a sack. The problem will be timing. If you don't get it right the enemy will escape—he might even defeat you."

"Not likely, Rodrigo. I'll bring Mexico to its knees."

"Now, Hernán, if I might visit Francesca?"

His face registered irritation. "Make it short and don't tell her too much—*ah*—I'd like to speak to you again before you leave."

●●●

Francesca was quartered in a ruined part of the city occupied by soldados newly arrived from the Islands. She had been warned of my arrival and was standing at the entrance to her hut as if blocking the door. She was dressed in a shift of unadorned Texcocan fabric and her feet were bare. The room behind her was austere with cotton mats piled in one corner.

She looked older than when I had last seen her—older and more careworn—although it only accentuated her beauty.

"What have they done to you?" She wasn't impressed by my appearance, either.

I ignored her question. "Did you know I was alive?"

"I was told in *Tlaxcala*..."

"Where I was imprisoned?"

"...You betrayed us to the enemy—you killed our men—you abandoned us." She looked through me. "Dear God—Amelia was captured...."

I took in a breath and let it out slowly. "...Dead—*Sacrificed*—Dead..."

She clenched her jaw, "But you still live—*mi bravo*."

I squatted in front of her. I picked up a handful of pebbles and let them drop slowly, one at a time. I watched them without looking up at the woman. "You believe what they said about me?"

"You are an Indio," she whispered.

"Yet I walk in the Christian camp under the Caudillo's protection—an interesting thing."

She shook her head as if trying to clear it. "*Too* interesting, señor."

"Yet you survived too, Francesca."

She glanced up. "Cortés moved me to the front of the column."

"And *you* left Amelia in the center."

"I tried—he wouldn't..."

I dropped another pebble. "I would have died to protect *both* of you but I was felled by de la Concha." I dropped still another pebble. "Malinche wanted you alive for his own purposes—he cared nothing for Doña Amelia."

She blinked fast, holding back pent up tears. "You blame *me* for Amelia's death?"

I dropped all of the stones but couldn't lift my head to face Francesca—my tears wet the soil. "Blame you, Francesca? For what? For *my* dishonor—for my own stupidity and greed? Blame you for my own shame and weakness? I think not. If you feel guilt, it is on your own shoulders. I carry enough around for the two of us."

She broke down completely. "I hated you, Rodrigo—my hatred sustained me. Now you come back to me and leave me with *nothing*." She struggled to control herself. "Couldn't you have seen me earlier—even a message?"

I rubbed my sleeve across my eyes and looked up. "I thought you died on the causeway. Today is the first day that I *knew* you lived." I stood up slowly and brushed dust from my knees. "It's good that you survived even if Amelia didn't."

"Rodrigo, if I had only known..."

"My fault, too, Francesca...I should have tried harder. On the other hand—you knew that I lived, even if in the camp of the enemy. Did you have to assume the worst about me?"

"What was I to think, Rodrigo? You were with the savages. I was wrong to think that you had abandoned us but—try to be fair—what was I to think?"

"I'm going to be fair so I'll do you a favor, cielito."

Her grief was now mixed with confusion. "A favor?"

"Let's just say that I owe it to you."

"You owe me nothing."

"No, Francesca, I don't. Nevertheless, you are the beneficiary of a debt owed."

"*What* are you talking about?

"You must tell me the truth—your survival depends on it."

She looked even less certain. "The truth?"

"Have you been with Cortés?"

She was caught by surprise. "How could you ask such a thing—*No!*"

I nodded as if in agreement. "I'll explain it to you—I'm valuable to the cabrón. He'll do whatever it takes to maintain my loyalty. He's sworn to me that he's never touched you but—if he has..."

"Well, he hasn't."

"But if he has...he'll fear that I'll learn the truth and betray him. He'll see you dead before he runs that risk."

"Risk? You're talking to me now."

"Yes—and he's ordered me to return to him after I speak to you. He will ask me what you've told me. If you are telling the truth, and you've not been with him, you're safe. If you're lying he'll kill you to prevent me from learning. If you were with him and I confront him with it, I run the risk but you are safe."

"What can I say...?"

"If you should admit that you"—I struck my palm with my fist—"*succumbed*, I'll feign outrage but let myself be placated by his usual empty promises."

"You're trying to trick me."

"Why should I want to trick you?"

She licked her lips. "*What else was I to do?* We were defeated, discipline collapsed and I needed protection."

"I don't judge you, Francesca."

"No, Rodrigo, I'm sure you don't." She was just getting started. "After the things we shared, after the confidences we exchanged and you...you don't even care. Why should I feel guilty? *Why?* Now you come here, after all this time and blame me for doing what I had to do. By the Mother of God..."—She caught herself—"Why should I care what you think about me—you don't care about anyone, not even yourself."

"...And de la Concha and the others?"

Her eyes flashed. "I would *never* degrade myself..."

"Yet Javier said it was true—they were his last words. Don't worry, though. I defended your"—I paused briefly—"chastity."

"You? I heard he died in a duel but—you?"

"Me."

"Well, I'm glad he's dead—but—I was never with anyone except Cortés and with him only three times."

"Three?"

"Just enough to satisfy his curiosity..."

"*Curiosity?*"

"...His vanity."

I could hardly believe what I was hearing. "*Vanity?*"

"...and—may God ever help me—to *revenge* myself against you."

Chapter 32

I ordered two thousand warriors south toward *Cuauhnahuac*—laying waste to those pueblos that sided with Malinche. Cortés took the bait and marched out of *Texcoco* with most of his Castilians and a great host of savage allies. He, in his turn, reduced those villages that favored the Tenochca, enslaving them or giving them to his allies for sacrifice and cannibal feasts.

To keep up the appearances of a major Mexican effort, the passes were fortified and avalanches set off by our men killed many Tlaxcalteca and a few Españoles. Still, Malinche moved south—deeper into the country. When he had fully committed himself, I turned my attention to his brigantine fleet in *Texcoco*. I had drawn up a map on return from my trip to Cortés' headquarters—I reviewed it in detail.

The defenses were formidable and, knowing Malinche, he would have strengthened them before his departure from the city. A frontal assault—even if massive—was not a possibility. All it would produce was a host of Tenochca dead with no damage to the fleet. I decided on an indirect approach—a large-scale assault but not on the canal, itself. The attack would be staged by a mixed force of Mexica and allies against the north wall of Texcoco. The attack would serve as a distraction against the more important target—the new canal and the ships, themselves. Our assault force would be small and come from the Lake. First, however, a picked force of trained assassins was to silence enemy outposts guarding the approaches to the canal and the lakeshore. Cuauhtemoc disapproved.

"Chichtli, there is no honor in this—to kill without warning."

"Malinche is not fighting for honor. He fights for victory. We must do what we can to survive."

The Uei Tlatloani was insistent. "I—not you—am the leader of my people. I *will* send my challenge to *Texcoco*."

I stood firm. "If you compromise my plan by warning the enemy, I will do nothing to help you."

Cuauhtemoc had to make a choice—he chose to compromise. "I will tell the white men of our attempt against *Texcoco*. I will say nothing of your attack on the acallin."

"You are wise, My Prince. Let them further strengthen the defense of the city and weaken the defense of the canal."

●●●

Macitoc led the attack on the wall and I led the assault on the canal. My canoes glided through the dark waters and waited in the undergrowth opposite *Texcoco*. In the distance there was the din of battle—whistles, conches and the throb of drums. Screams from thousands of throats cut through the dark. There were the steady pops from mosquetes and the occasional boom of cañónes.

I sent twenty of my young men—the pick of warriors—those who had no compunction to kill. They had been trained in the use of knives made from the iron of captured tepotzlin. They slipped into the water and, as silently as eels, slithered through the muck.

There was no way to know if they were successful but, as great fires rose from the northern quarter of *Texcoco*, my main force went the way of the first twenty. There was no opposition, only rumpled bodies and pools of blood glistening in the light of the rising moon. We came to the first parapet—a long mountain of rubble. Eighteen indistinct shapes squatted in front of it—the survivors from my first wave.

"Did you get them all?" I asked their leader.

"One escaped."

"Which direction?"

He gestured toward *Texcoco* away from the canal. "There is a spear through his belly."

"Still, we may not have much time." I listened as the shouts grew louder. I could hear the crackle of flames and I could smell the smoke. I had two hundred and fifty warriors armed with iron weapons and four Castilians with crossbows. The attack must be sharp and decisive.

"*Move forward!*" I whispered.

Two hundred and fifty men mounted the parapet—we could see the dark trench of the canal beyond. "*Axca!*" I roared. "*Attack!*"

War cries shrilled from two hundred and fifty throats. The warriors rushed down the reverse slope to confront thousands of startled Indios.

"*Macamo tlaantlin—No captives!*"

The enemy, many of whom were simple laborers, broke and scattered. My own warriors, thrilled by their success, stopped to gather prisoners. I lost half of my force in this fashion. They stopped fighting to lead their prizes back to our canoes.

My remaining fighters surged through the next barrier into a party of fifty Castilians. Now the fighting grew desperate—jab and hack in the dark at the foe. Musketeers fired into the faces of my warriors and my crossbow-men returned the favor. Bebidor drank deeply that night—I slew five of my own countrymen. I seized a flaming brand from a fire and pushed my way to the first brig. I leaped onto its deck and applied my torch to its furled sails. A Castilian—florid in the red firelight—moved to stop me. I shoved my blade through his face. Others, carrying more fire, joined my attack on the ship.

A berserker's madness surged through me; I leaped from the deck into a mass of defenders and fed them to Bebidor. They went down as if they were children. "*Fire!*" I screeched in Nahuatl, "*More Fire! Bring More Fire!!!*" as the flames roared up around me. Heat, blood, flame, lust—eternal sacrament of hatred. My strength was the strength of the bear and my soul exploded. "*Kill, kill, kill, kill—No Prisoners!!!*"

Then it was over. A gang of white-faced, musket-bearing Castilians appeared in the darkness. Someone barked out the orders: "*Prepare! Apunte! Fuego!*"

There was a numbing concussion and I was thrown to the deck. Chastened—crawling with pain—I struggled up and joined our defeated warriors retreating toward the Lake. One man, a crossbow man by the look of him, supported my body—my right leg was useless. He dragged me through the mud and pushed me into a canoe.

"Hold on, señor. We depend on you." I knew Gustavo Müeller's voice.

●●●

My wound was serious—the ball took me through the wing of my right hip and lodged under the skin of my buttock. The removal of the ball was no problem—a Tenochca healer, after the usual incantations and the burning of copal, slit the skin and removed the flattened piece of lead.

Macitoc came to me. "You live, Chichtli, but not fight again."

"I *will* fight again. How went your side of the battlefield?"

"We kill many Tlaxcaltec and Texcocan traitors. We break the wall and burn many houses—we do as you order."

I waited as a surge of pain passed through my body. "I did not do as well, my friend. The enemy fleet is untouched."

"Chichtli you do good. Three acallin burn—two sink. If warriors obey you, Malinche need walk *Tenochtitlan* over water."

I knew better. "I should have trained our warriors better—if only they had not stopped to take victims..."

"It hard to break old habits, brother."

"Yes, Macitoc, they are hard to break but *you* must break them."

"What I do?"

I remembered the ancient Roman practice of *decimation*—every tenth man. I doubled the quota.

"Arrest every man on the raid who returned with a prisoner. Line them up and proclaim their stupidity to all of *Tenochtitlan*. Count them out and select every *fifth* man. On the summit of *Coatepec*, in the presence of all our warriors, the unselected four shall seize their comrades and *beat* them to death."

Macitoc understood perfectly, "The eighty shall slay the twenty?"

"It is a small price to pay."

●●●

My wound did not heal well. For weeks I knew nothing. I had terrible dreams. As if from a fog, I saw a great ruined city ringed by ten thousand crucified men. Then, this awful scene disappeared and was replaced by a stooped old man clad in a ragged gray cloak. I looked closer and found him disturbingly familiar. His face was scarred and one eye was missing.

Despite the old man's frailty, he was armed and alert. Both of his hands were locked around the pommel of an old-fashioned sword. I remember the harsh cries of ravens and the hoof-beats of a six-legged horse. Out of the mist bounded the enemy—a monstrous wolf with glittering teeth. There was no hope. The rest I don't remember, only a confusion of hallucination, pain and terror.

●●●

During my illness, Malinche captured *Cuauhnahuac* and then turned northwest to attack *Xochimilco* on the south shore of the Lake. Here, he was almost taken captive but, again, Satan saved him. He sacked *Xochimilco* and burned as much as he could. He continued to move north along the western margin of the Lake. He was slowed by the loot he carried and by mud from the constant rains. The Mexica and their allies attacked him—defeated him. The young pages who served Cortés were taken and—delirious as I was—I couldn't help them. Both of the boys were offered as a special sacrifice to *Tlaloc*.

Cortés reached *Texcoco* without further losses but was outraged to learn of our raid on his fleet. His anger was assuaged when he learned that Martín López—with but two brigs totally destroyed—had repaired much of the damage and was ready to sail. He also must have been pleased to learn that three hundred more men—and weapons—had arrived from the coast.

At the same time the Tenochca grew stronger in numbers. Peoples of the north and the west, forgetting old grievances with the Mexica, allied with them in a common defense. The Tenochca were responsible for the defense of the Lake and the Capital, itself, and our allies would attack the enemy flanks from the mainland. *Cuauhtemoc* hoped to catch Malinche in a vice and crush him.

●●●

The Malinche's army was on the move, circling the Lake. Alvarado and Olid were reported in the north—Alvarado destroyed the aqueduct of *Chapultepec* and lay siege to the causeway at *Tacuba*. Olid occupied the entrance of the causeway at *Coyoacan*, more than a league and a half to the south. Sandoval marched from *Texcoco*, along the east shore of the Lake, and camped at the entrance of the southern causeway of *Iztapalapa*.

Malinche was now in a position to inflict terrible harm on *Tenochtitlan*. On June 1, he sallied out with his brigantines while, simultaneously, his land forces assaulted the three causeways. *Cuauhtemoc* attempted to counter the Castilians with a canoe fleet of his own. It was a mistake that almost succeeded.

The flagship—La Capitana—became grounded on some rocks and was attacked by dozens of canoes. Cortés lost his courage and—according to all reports—tried to surrender. If he had done so, the result might have been the same as the retreat of Cleopatra at *Actium*. He and his fleet would have been destroyed. Martín López, however, was determined to protect his labors. He picked up a sword and repulsed the Tenochca. He then ordered the rest of his fleet to attack our massed canoes.

The Tenochca were able to do little for the decks of the brigs were much higher than their own canoes. The Castilians slaughtered them with volleys of crossbow and musket fire. Those canoes that attempted to flee fouled one another and were run down by the brigantines. Hundreds died and the lake turned red. The destruction of our fleet was but part of Malinche's plan. The brigantines sailed on until encountering the *Ixtapalapa* causeway close to its junction with the causeway of *Coyoacan*, which was also the location of the fortress of *Xoloc*. Cannons were offloaded and used to pound the defenses. Cristóbal de Olid's horsemen, attacking along the western causeway, flanked

Xoloc. The fortress fell and its defenders were forced into the City.

Tenochtitlan might have fallen there and then, had it not been for Gustavo Müeller. Dressed and armored as one of our Castilian enemies, he penetrated their battle line and single-handedly attacked a squad manning two cannons. In an act that—depending on the nature of God—atoned for all of his previous misdeeds, he applied a torch directly to the enemy powder supply. There was an enormous explosion, knocking a great gouge in the dike and wrecking two nearby brigs. Müeller was blown to pieces. The gunner and four of his comrades died, as did Malinche's hopes for a *coup de main* against *Mexico*.

Chapter 33

I lay in the temple of the women so sick I couldn't rise.

"Priests say you better."

"I don't feel better, Macitoc. Food tastes like poison."

Macitoc regarded me with his black eyes. Malinche kill Tenochca—canoes not move. Soon we need go north."

"But I am crippled."

"I not leave my brother."

My mind was clearing. "Where is the enemy?"

He told me and I was appalled by his words. I thought of a solution—not for victory—but to delay defeat until I was well enough to move.

"Now is the time of our women, children and old people." I told him. "Have them break the causeways and build up barricades to protect our warriors. If the enemy should fill them in, return at night and break them open, again. We must work and fight by day and night."

"We break causeways plenty. Malinche's acallin kill women, old people."

"Then now is the time to use our long stakes—plant them deep in the mud next to the causeways."

Macitoc faded from sight as sleep overwhelmed me.

●●●

The Mexica put on a brave fight, even if it was hopeless. Allies of the Tenochca ambushed the Castilians and I was pleased to hear that Alvarado suffered the greatest losses. Close to *Tacuba* Alvarado was humiliated—thousands of his Indio allies died. Alvarado was forced back to protect his landward communications. The Tenochca responded with an army of laborers. Working all day and night, they dug gaps in the levies and broke down bridges. Alvarado counterattacked and filled in the gaps with rubble. Mexican workers returned after dark and opened the gaps, again.

The most effective tactic was false retreat and ambush. In this way Alvarado was again defeated. Against orders, he pursued a party of warriors through a break and was trapped on the City side. Three hundred of his allies died and fifteen of his white soldados were captured. Malinche was outraged. He almost replaced Alvarado with Ircio—he should have. That night, the captured Castilians died on the *Tlatelolco teocalli* Alvarado's troops were close enough to see their comrades die screaming deaths.

●●●

Weeks passed, the battle dragged on, and I was getting better. I was gaining weight, advising Cuauhtemoc, and I was even starting to walk with a limp.

"I grow weary of inactivity, My Prince. I wish to join the struggle."

"You cannot move fast enough to avoid the enemy."

"In a canoe propelled by your warriors I can move fast enough. I have a plan to defeat the white man's acallin."

"Go if you must, Chichtli, but you will not join the fight."

I planned my ambush. In a southeast arm of the Lake, hemmed in by the shore and protected by shallows, my warriors set out stakes. Fifty war canoes with one thousand warriors vanished into the reeds. Pretending to be a nativo casting a net, I watched from a two-man canoe. Three big canoes—the kinds used to transport food and supplies—paddled back-and-forth across the opening to the inlet. Twelve powerful warriors—dressed in simple loincloths—manned each of these vessels.

Four brigantines, sails glinting silver against the sun, appeared from the north. They spotted my three canoes and, catching the breeze, heeled over. Like birds of prey they bore down on the Mexica vessels. The bait taken, my warriors pulled away towards the bank. They paddled into the inlet with the brigs in close pursuit. With crunching and snapping sounds the brigs came to abrupt stops. Two men fell overboard and others were knocked off their feet. The Castilians, recognizing their peril, tried to back off the stakes—too late. Fifty canoes burst from cover. The fight, even from a distance, was brutal.

Cañónes boomed but the crews were overwhelmed and slaughtered. Even so, such was the strength of the Castilian fire, we captured two brigs and damaged the third—still burning, the third brig managed to outdistance her pursuers. Most of the Castilians, including Pedro Barba, leader of the crossbow men and an old friend of mine, were killed or captured.

Later, six of the survivors—also crossbow men—volunteered to serve us although this was from fear, not conversion. I ordered ten recalcitrant captives—against the protests of my warriors—executed on the spot. By example, I wanted to break the bad habit of seizing prisoners for sacrifice. My warriors, hard fighters one and all, were inexperienced in the art of quick executions. I almost got sick. I saved Barba for the last.

"*Please, Rodrigo, Please!*"—Barba begged—"You can't do *this* to a comrade."

I flexed Bebidor and let it spring back, again. "You *are* a friend, Pedro, so I'll do the honors, myself. It won't hurt...*much.*"

"Rodrigo, *don't.*"

I cocked back for the blow that would have taken off his head.

"I've changed my mind—I'll join you."

I tapped him on the head with the flat of my weapon. "Well met, *Caballero, Pedro.* I anoint thee '*El Defensor de Mexico.*'"

●●●

The Castilians learned to be wary of Mexican tricks and it became more difficult to lure them close to land. Still, my stakes sometimes found their marks. Twice, vigilant spotters discovered brigantines low in the water, nearly sinking. I led a party against one of these and took and burned the vessel. By these measures we eased the strangulation of *Tenochtitlan* but couldn't stop it. Shortages—especially of food and good water—were felt everywhere.

The causeway battles were inconclusive. For each gain there was an equal loss and the war was more backbreaking work than a glorious struggle—the seesaw battle went on for months. I was reminded of Troy where the battle ground on for ten long years. Just like Troy, men sallied forth and pounded each other on a daily basis. Arrows, darts, crossbow bolts, musket balls, and slingers' rounds darkened the sun only to be spent uselessly against the bulwarks of the opposite side. Opposing work crews labored against one another, one side filling in breaks and their opponents breaking them open again.

The work was accompanied by incredible noise. There was a constant screeching and keening accompanied by the boom of drums, the trill of whistles and the clack of missiles clattering against stone. Still, people get used to anything. Just as the sound of the surf crashing against the sand disappears in the depths of the mind, the constant noise of battle vanished into the depths of the ordinary.

●●●

My Castilian fighters were doing good work, although most had been killed during my illness. I had twenty left including Juan Yuste. I regarded Barba and other recent captures as unreliable. Even so, they were essential for my defense.

Under the cover of night, Sandoval moved to *Chapultepec*. He made a breakthrough and threatened the city. With no alternative, I was forced to use my Castilian reserves. A handful of Mexica held up the advancing enemy. There were hundreds of the cabrónes, most of them Tlaxcalteca in paint and feathers but with a hard core of Castilian crossbow-men and arquebusiers.

I threw in my fighters. A few of the Tlaxcalteca enemy, seeing that they faced white men, threw down their weapons and ran to the rear. The Castilians behaved differently. They let out a howl of rage. My ballestas, who were half of my white force, fired their bolts—some were deliberately high. Yuste punished Barba on the spot. He split his skull down to the chin.

After this it was us against them. Protected by earthen bulwarks we inflicted more casualties; Castilian and Tlaxcalteca dead and wounded piled up in front of us. The enemy climbed the bulwark of bodies and fired into us. Poor Juan Yuste was one of the first to fall—a musket ball entered his mouth and removed the side of his head. We would have been utterly defeated had not Macitoc arrived with two hundred people. Some of his people were warriors but most were women and old people. With the strength of desperation, they pushed the enemy back.

I was crippled but I couldn't stay still when I saw that old women were fighting like warriors. Then, I was in the forefront of battle with the great god, *Tezcatlipoca*, at my side—shining, beautiful, terrible—enemies falling like ripe fruit. My vision cleared and I could see that it was only Macitoc clad in an iron breastplate and swinging a great two-handed montante.

Terrified enemy fighters pushed one another off the dike in their desire to flee. Some were not cowed—caballeros, astride their horses with lanza points down—faced us with unflinching courage. They came at a canter and then a full charge. Macitoc's montante flashed and the first horse went down without a leg and the second without a rider. I wounded my man in the leg and took him captive; the fourth galloped back toward the mainland.

●●●

Still, the city groaned under enemy pressure. Houses built on the causeways were either destroyed by the enemy to produce fill for the gaps or by the Mexica to produce barricades for defense. Enemy brigantines attacked and burned crops and homes on the tinampas. The displaced inhabitants had no choice but to retreat deeper into the City. At the same time, people from the mainland who were fleeing the enemy's wrath, also crowded into the City. By order of Cuauhtemoc, homes that housed single families now housed many. Still, it was not enough. Ragged refugees slept in the corners of gardens, in templos and in the streets.

Starvation was everywhere. Living skeletons wandered the streets begging for food and digging through the garbage. The desperation of others was even greater—the shrubs in the gardens were dug up and their roots eaten. Bark was stripped from trees and chewed to ease the pangs of hunger. The torsos of sacrificial victims were no longer fed to the beasts in the menagerie. The bodies were now given to the poor who devoured them totally although they had to do so without the fuel to make cooking fires. No longer were skulls impaled on the tzompanitlin—the heads were cracked like eggs for the brains. Finally, even the menagerie was not safe—the beasts were slain and devoured. There were exceptions, though. The Huitzlin and sacred Quetzalin were saved, as were the coyoteh and oceloteh.

La viruela, which had subsided, became even more terrible—the starving poor died by the hundreds. Then, to add to the misery came an even more terrible plague—those who had appeared to be well in the morning were dead before the sun went down. The very young were those taken first, then the old and those who were starving—but no one was safe from the scourge. Entire households died.

At the request of the teopixquia, who knew not what terrible curse the gods were inflicting, I visited the afflicted. There was no wound or blemish on the victims. Instead there was an outpouring of excrement with the consistency of thickened water. The victims had a great thirst and would—if they could—crawl to a canal and drink volumes of bad water. It was never enough for their eyes became sunken and their skins loose. Death found them next to the canals but many never got out of their houses. Sometimes, the dead and living were in the same room, lying in pools of watery filth.

Burgos, Castilla-León

"I was helpless against such a plague, Padre, but I did what little I could do."

"What might that have been, Obispo?"

"I ordered those who had recovered from this dread malady to administer to those who were ill with it. I also isolated those dwellings where the inhabitants were dead or dying. Workers knocked out bridge connections to the most affected areas. Still it was not enough and the disease showed its hideous face in all parts of the City."

"So your efforts were pointless."

"Indeed they were, Padre, but the sufferers didn't think so. I became a Holy Man—a Healer—to the people."

Mendoza placed his feathered pen on the table. "Did you purchase your post from the Mexicans the same as you purchased you Bishopric?"

"Now *who* is being cynical, Padre?"

"Then I'll rephrase myself. Did you *bribe* the Mexicans the same as you *bribed* corrupt Church Officials?"

Mendoza expected an angry retort but the old man just cackled. "No indeed, Padre Mendoza, but I find it a capital idea. Fortunately or unfortunately, depending on your point of view, my post simply found me."

"How so?"

"I was *Chichtli*, a sorcerer who communed with god. Also, despite the fact that I fought on their side, I was still a teotl, a holder of unknown powers. My mystery was compounded by the fact that I *voluntarily* deserted Malinche to save the Tenochca from their fated doom."

"Fascinating."

"Perhaps not fascinating, Padre, but inevitable. Every Tenochca in the City could recognize me on sight. To be certain this was not entirely a good thing because the priests *hated* me for my influence—not only was I a greater healer than were they, but they knew I despised them as fools."

Mendoza nodded. "They were ignorant barbarians working for Satan."

"They weren't ignorant, Padre. They were the most highly educated men in the land—much like our own clergy. The problem was that almost all that they had learned was false and their false philosophies led to the destruction of their land. Still, the teopixquia were a minority and my warriors feared but respected me. The common folk—thinking I could save them—truly loved me."

"*Santo Rodrigo!*" Mendoza looked up and raised his hands to Heaven.

"As Holy as any other Saint," the old man retaliated.

"But before your *conversion*—when you were still fighting with Cortés—you *personally* slew many of these people."

The old man slowly smiled, "Just like the Jew—Simon...St. Paul—on the road to Damascus. He had been a famous Christian Killer but he saw the light and converted to the Christian enemy. All Catholics now revere him."

"And the Mexica revered you?"

"Not only that, but crowds of these poor people thronged to me whenever I deigned to walk amongst them. There were the lame, the halt and the blind but far more numerous were those crippled by combat wounds; those suffering the after effects of *la viruela* and those who hoped for a cure from our most recent plague. These sufferers clutched at me, hoping my touch might cure them."

"I'm sure your magic cured thousands of them, Excellency."

The old man ignored Mendoza's barb. "Hundreds obstructed my passage, singing my praises and throwing maize kernels and flower petals in my path—starving people throwing away scarce food to win my favor. They were *transported* by my presence. I will never forget their faces. Picture in you mind, Padre, the faces of people in the last throes of deathly disease lighting up with an ethereal radiance."

"*Jesus with the lepers*—you are both heretical and sacrilegious, Obispo."

"No, Padre, unlike Christ, I was but a miserable imposter with no power to heal. Yet, there is redemption in hope and I cannot rule out the possibility that the hope I gave them saved the occasional sufferer."—the old man shrugged—"saved for death by *Malinche*."

"No one was saved, Obispo?"

"No one was saved, yet this long suffering people—hopeless beyond grief and desperate beyond hope—came to me, fell to their knees and worshipped me as God. Dirty people, ragged people, starving people, diseased people and dying people put their hands out, hoping for a blessing. These—the same people whom I had hated, despised and butchered—yet they loved me all the same. They came to me for deliverance even as flowers—delicate, sweet smelling flowers—gathered at my unworthy feet."

Chapter 34

"Your City is dying around you, My Lord. It is time to speak to Malinche."

He stiffened. "If *Tenochtitlan* must die, it will die. I do not surrender."

"But what of your people, Great Lord?"

"Chichtli, the people no longer matter. Those who die will go to *Mictlan*. Those who live will be forced to give up their good ways—they will worship Christian Gods. They will still look like Mexica but they will no longer be Mexican."

I could see that the Prince had lost weight, for he refused to eat more than the allowance for his warriors. He went on, "My people die but I live. My warriors fight but I hide—it is time I join the battle."

I couldn't disagree.

"Then, My Prince, it is right that you lead us in a final effort. I propose a meeting with Malinche..."

His eyes flashed fire. ""I told you no surrender I will not even compromise."

"No surrender, no compromise—a meeting with Malinche to convince him of things that are not true."

"Do you have a plan, *Chichtli?*"

"My plan is to meet with Malinche."

I released one of our Castilian captives with a message that I would speak to Cortés and soon a released Tenochca returned with a message that he would meet me on the southern causeway. We met in the open—he with fifty armed men and me, bare-chested, wearing a plain maxtlatl.

"It's been two months since I saw you, Rodrigo—*where* have you been?"

"One of your musketeers gave me a present."

"Yes," he grinned. "I can see you have developed a list since I last saw you. Is it serious?"

"Not bad. I now come as Cuauhtemoc's,"—I paused so that he might detect the irony of the situation—"*emissary.*"

His smile disappeared. "I trust you don't serve him too faithfully."

Now it was my turn to smile. "Faithfully enough to give you some useful information."

"Is the cabrón ready to surrender the City and the treasure?"

Not just yet. He has sent me here to negotiate a prisoner exchange. It seems you have two chiefs that he is fond of. In return he will give you four Castilians and sixty Tlaxcalteca."

"Surely, Rodrigo, you didn't call me here to discuss such trivia."

"I didn't call you here, Hernán. I only encouraged the Prince to do so. I thought that during our...negotiations...we could discuss other things..."

"Go on."

"Like a plan to take the City."

"I *have* a plan."

"I've seen your plan in operation. At this rate it will take another year to reduce Mexico." I held out my hands. "Besides, I miss Francesca."

He shook his head. "My plan is working. *Tenochtitlan* is dying of hunger."

I raised my eyebrows. "My reports are that your army is in worse condition. It's riddled by disease and dissension according to prisoners."

He didn't deny it. "What do you suggest?"

"You *are* right, Hernán. *Tenochtitlan* is weak—starvation is rife and thousands die of plague. Her defenses—even those on the causeways—are paper-thin. A sudden offense along all of the causeways will put you in the heart of the city."

"Too dangerous, Rodrigo."

"...Before you try it, Hernán—I recommend that you make another peace offering to Cuauhtemoc."

"Will he accept?"

"It's worth a try. Much of *Tenochtitlan* is still intact—it would be a loss to destroy it utterly."

"Your plan, Rodrigo?"

"I will bring your offer of peace to Cuauhtemoc. Even if he doesn't listen he will be lulled into complacency—tonight you will receive your answer. If you see a great fire on the summit of *Coatepec*, you'll know the answer is 'yes.'"

"And if the answer is '*no*?'"

"An attack from all quarters—especially here along the southern causeway. The City should collapse like a house of cards."—Then I baited my trap with a cheese that Cortés could not resist—"If you pull it off, you may take the treasure before Cuauhtemoc can hide it."

Malinche's eyes glistened with greed. "*I like it!* Within the week the City and all its treasure will be mine."

As I moved to turn away, he stopped me. "Cuauhtemoc is an ignorant savage—he will be impressed by the written word."

He shouted orders and one of his men came up bearing a green plume, an amatl scroll and a candle. He spoke the words as he wrote:

> "I, Hernán Cortés, offer peace to Prince Cuauhtemoc, Uei Tlatloani of Anahuac-Mexico. In exchange Prince Cuauhtemoc promises loyalty to Emperor Carlos I and promises loyalty to his servant, Hernán Cortés. Should Prince Cuauhtemoc not agree to this generous offer, one Hernán Cortés—as agent for Emperor Don Carlos—is empowered to reduce Tenochtitlan to rubble, seize her wealth and enslave all of her inhabitants."

> Cortés folded it, melted wax on it and impressed his seal ring into the soft wax.

> "I have no doubt that these scribbles will impress him more than a mere oral offer—read it to him." He thought for a moment and then removed the seal ring from his finger. "Give him this as a sign of my love—make sure that he compares its design with the mark on this letter."

●●●

That night there was no flame on *Coatepec*. We prepared instead, for Malinche's assault. Warriors on the causeways manned their forward positions with but few skirmishers. More powerful barricades with larger forces were established closer to the City. The exception was the southern causeway where Malinche would personally attack. There, he would be permitted into the City, itself.

For three days little happened except for minor fighting. Before first light on the fourth day, the enemy surged against our first deliberately weak defenses. The first barricades were overrun but the enemy was stopped at the edge of the City. Malinche's force broke through the second barrier and crossed a broad bridge. Heady with victory and concentrating on killing, he failed to notice that the bridge had been prepared for his arrival.

Still crippled by my injury, I watched from a rooftop as Malinche and his men charged on to glory. "*Castilla! Aragon! Andulacia!*" they screamed, heads down, sighting along their lances, horse hooves thundering. Behind the mounted men, Indios and Castilians crowded together in their eagerness to participate in the final kill. Many of the Tlaxcalteca threw down their weapons to take up firebrands from hearths of nearby houses—their jubilation was beyond containment. My own excitement mounted to unbearable proportions. *The enemy had lost all organization! Now!* I signaled for the props to be knocked from under the bridge. It shuddered and collapsed with a roar. The dust cleared revealing an expanse of empty water, deeper than a tall man and fifteen cubits wide.

This was the moment. Cuauhtemoc—his standard-bearer waving his green and red Royal Banner—broke tradition by personally leading our main force into the battle. It was a thrilling sight—a wedge-shaped formation of eagle and ocelotl knights with Cuauhtemoc in the fore-front, *slammed* into the triumphant Castilians. Macitoc was there lead-ing tall-plumed warchiefs bearing Castilian weapons and a platoon of white men with ballestas.

Hidden warriors fired a cloud of darts from the tops of the teo-callis and templos. Even more burst from behind buildings, beneath bridges and up from the canals. Stunned, the horsemen reined to a halt. They were immersed in a sea of Tenochca and many went down. I watched as Cuauhtemoc attacked Malinche all by himself. Cortés didn't recognize the Prince and rode him down, knocking him sense-less to the pavement.

Even without Cuauhtemoc our warriors were victorious. Howling, screaming—hacking and stabbing with Mexican and Castilian weap-ons—they forced the enemy back to the gap. The enemy, unmanned by the miraculous disappearance of the bridge, panicked. Hundreds died in frenzied efforts to cross the bloody gap.

The cry went out that Cuauhtemoc was down. Tenochca, who mo-ments before had been in hot pursuit, milled about in confusion. With our victory in peril, I screamed my hatred and entered the fray. I picked up a banner from the lifeless hand of a Cuautemoc retainer and waved it overhead.

"*Yaoquizquin, ma xiquichehuan!!!*"

I hobbled toward those still fighting at the gap and was joined by a host of warriors. They surged against the enemy, killing them like sheep and pushing even more into the gap. Within moments, the wa-ter was filled with a bloody froth of dead and wounded men. As our men drove in for the finish, the crush became unbearable. Living and dead men were borne up and carried forward by the crowd. I couldn't keep my footing. Pushed from behind, I toppled into the water.

Beside me were struggling fighters, both victors and those soon to be vanquished. Everyone was covered with mud. In the writhing, *squirming*, confusion, it was impossible to distinguish friend from foe. An armored man—a Castilian, I think—threw himself on top of me and tried to hold me under. I locked my arms around his neck and held him down. He kicked, clawed and tried to bite me. I held him until his body relaxed.

Horses—unrecognizable mud-covered monsters—screamed and lashed out with their hooves. One of their dismounted riders was helpless in the hands of three warriors who were attempting to drag him from the water. With a shock, I realized that I was looking at a totally defeated Malinche and he was only an arm's length away.

Cristóbal de Olea leaped into the water and, slashing with a knife, wounded two of Cortés' captors. Then, turning like a cornered rat, he attacked and slew the third. A fourth, a maquahuitl-wielding warrior, attacked him, in turn. He slashed Olea's face, seized him by the shoulder and dragged him towards his doom.

Malinche was so spent that he could not lift his arms to defend himself. A child could have slain him. Covered with mud, however, our warriors didn't recognize him. As they battled more vigorous enemies, I dragged him to the Castilian side of the causeway. I made sure he recognized me.

"You almost had them. *What happened?*"

He couldn't speak. He could only vomit up dirty water. I pushed him into the arms of two Castilians.

"Take him. He's our Caudillo."

I could see confusion on their faces.

"No questions—move!"

●●●

We had a great victory—although it was to be our last. Cuauhtemoc, however, was in no condition to enjoy it. He was semiconscious, attended by his priests and his women. It was up to me to give the orders.

"Do you know how many have been taken?" I asked.

"One thousand Tlaxcalteca," Omitl answered. "Two hundred Tex-cocans and two hundred from other cities. In the south, we have taken seventy-six of Malinche's men and thirty on the other causeways."

"Of these, how many white men are dead?"

"Fifty. They lay in the Great Plaza."

"Let me see these bodies," I said.

●●●

Over five hundred naked corpses were neatly arranged on the tiles of the Great Plaza. Mobs of starving citizens waited until permission was given for them to take the bodies away. I looked at each Castilian corpse seeking for old acquaintances. Two men, both horribly mutilat-ed, lay staring at the sky. One had been in my original troop when we fought in Tabasco, one million years ago. Another was Arnufo Sepul-veda, a man who used to play the guitar and sing love songs. I soon found what I wanted—a man who could pass for Cortés. I then found a man with fair hair and beard. He would be my Pedro de Alvarado. Another resembled Gonzalo de Sandoval and a third, Cristóbal de Olid. One battered warrior with a scarred face resembled—me."

"Remove these heads." I indicated the bodies.

"Also remove these." I indicated others.

I watched as priests wielding itzli blades cut through the skin and tendons and dislocated the heads from the bodies.

"Now find me strong warriors—those with powerful arms."

So it was done. Bleeding heads, including one with yellow hair, were thrown into the air so that Malinche's men on the southern causeway could see them. From the shadows so that no one could see me, I shouted out threats in Castilian and then Nahuatl.

"We have killed Tonatiuh, Sandoval and Chichtli, the traitor! Soon, we kill and eat you, too!"

At Chapultepec, six heads were displayed on a parapet. "We have killed Malinche, Tonatiuh and Olid! You will be next!"

Into Pedro de Alvarado's ranks on the Tacuba causeway the heads of the false Cortés and others were tossed into the air.

"We have killed Malinche and soon we will devour your flesh with tomates and green chiles!"

●●●

Counterfeit heads and false words were delivered to Olid's men as well. Despite the fact that Malinche countered my efforts with messengers, it was more than his Indio allies could stand. Most of them, including the Tlaxcalteca, packed up and returned to their homes.

I could barely believe it. The Tenochca, who had teetered on the verge of total defeat were now close to victory. The bulk of their enemies—the vast majority—were gone. Terrified Castilians huddled behind their own defenses praying for divine intervention. They got what they prayed for—but it was not from Jehovah—it was from Satan in the guise of a Mexica demon.

Chapter 35

Cuauhtemoc regained consciousness and, although in much pain, took control of the affairs of state.

"I had a vision of the great god, *Tlaloc*. In ten days time he will cause a sacred storm and wash the white men away."

I was appalled and should have slain him on the spot. "Perhaps, My Prince, but is it not best that we keep this prophecy to ourselves?"

He was in the grip of religious ecstasy. "I have told my teopixquia—they have had the same vision. I have sent messengers to spread the word throughout *Anahuac*." He gestured to a servant who pulled him to his feet. "After this mighty miracle happens, all *Anahuac* will know that Chichtli is not the only one who speaks with God."

I tried to control my temper. "Remember the night when you drove Malinche from *Tenochtitlan*? Had you then pushed your attack and given the teoteoh no peace, Malinche and *all* his white men would have been dead *long* ago." I bowed to him as if in respect. "Now, O *Cuauhtemoc*, the gods have given you one final chance. Now is your opportunity—your last opportunity—to defeat Malinche. Attack him with all of your strength—take no count of losses."

The Great *Teoteutli*—a familiar of *Tlaloc* and jealous of my influence—stood behind the young emperor. He whispered in his ear and *Cuauhtemoc* nodded.

"You will not deprive *Tlaloc* of his victory nor me of my glory. *No!* Fight to keep Malinche out of the city—not more."

"Then you, Prince Cuauhtemoc, condemn your people."

"No, Chichtli, I save them."

It was hopeless. I staged some small raids on the Castilian forts and, I was even successful in burning a brigantine. In ten days time, however, there was no sign of *Tlaloc*. Indeed, it was one of the most perfect days I ever saw in Mexico. Knowing the falseness of the prophecy, our own allies abandoned us and joined Cortés. Countless Tlaxcalteca and many other tribes streamed in from all directions, reinforcing the enemy camps.

The relentless enemy with his numberless fighters advanced along all of the causeways, razing houses and temples and using their debris to fill in canals and breaks in the causeways. The festering dead—thousands of them—paved the plazas and choked the canals. The air was green with the stink. Hundreds of vultures circled above and clouds of blowflies clogged our nostrils.

"Chichtli, my brother," Macitoc said, "Mexica finished. We go north."

"You go. Wait for me in the ruin of *Teotehuican*. I will bring the horses."

I rejoined Malinche but before I did, I put my plan in motion. I got the idea when Malinche wrote his final ultimatum to Cuauhtemoc. I never bothered to show his message or his ring to the Prince—I kept them for my own purposes. Now, I wrote a letter on plain paper that I had removed from the body of a dead Basque. Using the letter to Cuauhtemoc as a guide, I penned out the message.

"My Dearest Wife Catalina,

I apologize for not writing more often but the difficulties of conducting a military campaign have prevented me from doing so. The war is now coming to a successful conclusion and I request your lovely presence here in Nueva España. You will be the greatest lady in this new country."

I was tempted to write more but feared my forgery might be detected. I signed it with a flourish almost as handsome as that of the real Cortés. I folded the letter, dripped molten wax on it and impressed

Malinche's own seal ring upon it. Later, on rejoining the army, I put the letter in the hands of a trusted messenger who, in turn, was to put it in the hands of a pilot returning to Cuba with news of the Christian triumph. It all went better than I ever could have hoped.

Burgos, Castilla-León

"You don't intend to leave me in suspense, Excelencia?"

The Bishop frowned. "Suspense?"

"Yes—this business of the forged letter. Are you trying to tell me that Catalina's arrival in Mexico was a product of your connivance?

"Connivance is such a nasty word."

Mendoza paused long moments before going on. "There were rumors about her death."

"More than rumors, Padre."

"The unfortunate woman had an attack following a fiesta—she died quite suddenly."

The ancient man stroked the scars on his chin. "Come now, Padre, you know more than that."

"Some malicious people hinted that Cortés may have been party to her death but these were just lies."

"It seems, Padre, that lies follow Cortés like flies follow horse shit."

Mendoza said nothing.

"Then, Padre, I will tell you what happened. Señora Catalina responded immediately to my letter. She arrived in Villa Rica and was in *Anahuac* before Cortés even knew about it. She discovered him there surrounded by a seraglio of women. She was *less* than delighted."

"I'm sure she wasn't happy, Excelencia."

The old man leaned back in his chair. "Cortés may have been a sultan among women but he was a coward in front of his wife. He promised to give up his harem and live the monogamous life of a Spanish gentleman. Of course it was a lie. He could no more give up women than a borracho can give up the bottle. There were endless fights both private and public. Finally, there was the fiesta you mentioned. Both Hernán and Catalina got drunk. He called her a slut and she called him a cur. He ordered her to her room then followed himself. Shortly afterwards, white and shaking, he called for his physician, Rolando Puente, who found Catalina lying on the bed. She was already dead. There were bruises on her neck and her windpipe was crushed. The physician was paid to declare her death natural but—as in all such cases—the truth will out. Years later, after Cortés had passed from the scene, Puente told it all."

"If you are telling the truth, Your Grace, you have much to be proud of—the death of an innocent woman."

"No, Padre, I am not proud, neither am I ashamed. I did not plan the lady's death and I certainly didn't commit her murder. That thieving cabrón—your paragon—Hernán Cortés, did it. The truth be known, I never considered that my forgery would lead to murder. Even I didn't think that he would stoop that low. I only hoped to make Cortés a little more miserable."

"And your plan, Excelencia, to join wild savages—you didn't actually go through with it?"

"Why not, Padre? If the white men had any sense, they all would have joined the savages."

"More nonsense..."

"Not at all, Padre. Civilized man leads a life of drudgery. Savage men lead lives of ease and pleasure."

"They lead lives of dirt and barbarity."

The ancient Bishop shook his head. "Think of the beauty and simplicity of it, Padre. Women do all the work and the men spend their time hunting and fishing."

Mendoza spit blood, placed his fingers in his mouth and removed a discolored tooth. *"Oh My God—my teeth are falling out!"*

The Bishop smiled. "Oh my God, you're right."

Chapter 36

I scrubbed the paint from my face and discarded my feathered regalia. I returned to the fold of the army as plainly clad as the lowest soldado.

"You've done great work for us, Rodrigo," Cortés boomed. "Thank you for saving my life."

"*De nada, Caudillo*," and he meant it.

"It's just a mop-up operation now but we haven't taken Cuauhtemoc—it won't be long now."

I looked out over the ruined Capital. Most of its buildings were rubble and those that weren't soon would be. Smoke curled into a leaden sky from a thousand ruined houses and temples.

I reinforced the impression of loyalty. "Cuauhtemoc has fled his palace and is hiding in the northeast district of the City. He has his family with him. I think he has some of the treasure, too."

"Do you know exactly where he is?"

I pointed toward some still standing buildings in the near distance. "There."

He thought about it. "*Infierno!* If he gets away he could raise a rebellion. I might never find the treasure. Rodrigo, I was impressed by your mantaletes—maybe you could frighten him with a catapult."

"Why do you need a catapult when you have cannons?"

"They're not *mortars*. Besides I don't want to kill him—not yet—I want him to surrender."

I shook my head. "Caudillo, I was in Italy but two and a half years ago. Our forces are a *modern* army with cannons and everything else. I don't know anything more about catapults than what I've read in books."

This was a lie—I had seen catapults of Italian design but had no desire to help Malinche more than necessary.

"Rodrigo, my boy, you've got your orders."

"Thank you, for your confidence, señor."

I consulted Martín López, the ship builder. We considered several possibilities including an arbalast—a giant stone-throwing crossbow. Our calculations showed that such a device wouldn't have the proper trajectory—besides—I didn't have a source of springy wood for the huge bow limbs. We settled on a catapult built like a gallows. A swiveling crosspiece, twenty cubits in length, was attached. One end of the crosspiece was long, the other short. I recognized that this engine would be subject to wood-breaking stress so I used the heaviest timber remaining. A team of Indios supervised by López, actually did the construction. They bound the structure together with fiber and strips of rawhide cut from dead horses and men.

A nequen sack was attached to the short end and, within it, we placed a great stone of three or four hundredweight. We cleared away the corpses and mounted the machine on the edge of the plaza within range of Cuauhtemoc's strong post.

I eyed the completed catapult—it looked like a great insect. "What do you think, Martín?"

"It'll probably snap in a dozen places. I don't know why the Caudillo gave me this dirty job. I'd rather be killing Mexicans."

I smiled to myself—López was one of the greatest troublemakers in the army but he was also one of the most useful. To insure his loyalty and to get him to finish the brigs, Cortés had assumed a kingly prerogative and knighted López in front of the assembled army. I was now dealing with *Caballero Martín López de Texcoco*—and a very sticky knight he proved to be.

"Caballero," I bowed from the waist. "Hernán gave you this job because you are the best engineer in the army—nobody else could accomplish it—certainly not me."

López addressed me as if I were a peasant. "If this thing doesn't work, it's your fault. You're the catapult expert—not me. The beams aren't right and the ropes will probably need to be shortened. It's going to shoot backwards or even straight into the ground."

"Maybe you're right," I said, "but go ahead and give it a try."

After aiming, a team of fifty Indios pulled the long end down by means of a rope. At Lopez order, they released the device. The sack ripped from the timber and the stone went straight up. It came down hard, barely missing the catapult and crushing one slow-moving Indio.

●●●

Cortés, who was watching the demonstration, lost his temper. "You promised me..."

"No, Jefe," I argued, "I promised nothing but ...."

He struck a pose. "You've had your chance—I'll tell Pedro to go in and take Cuauhtemoc by force."

"I'll give it a few more shots," I said.

Behind me, *López* was shortening the throw rope.

Cortes turned red. "I liked you better, Rodrigo, when you were with the enemy. I just gave you a *direct* order."

I grinned at him and slashed my hand down. The catapult snapped forward and a stone sailed into the distance.

"*I'm warning you, Rodrigo!*" he screamed. "You've had your chance." He pointed at the nearby Alvarado. "Pedro! Take your men in."

Alvarado who was grinning, as usual, shouted back, "Not with those locos shooting that thing."

"*Let her fly!*"

The stone sailed high and splashed into a canal in Cuauhtemoc's district.

"Got her range now, Hernán!"

"So you have, you insubordinate cabrón, but I *ordered* you to cease fire."

"*Fuego!*"

The stone went up in an arc and crashed into one of the buildings occupied by the Mexican resisters.

"*Uno mas!*" Another direct hit. López and I shook hands.

"I have an idea," López said. He trimmed the sack and, with the help of three Indios, loaded it with the corpse of a freshly killed warrior. Cortés watched in speechless rage. López, however, was beyond containment.

"Let it go!"

"The body flew up, head first, but quickly caught the wind. Spread-eagled and spinning slowly, it made a graceful arc and crashed directly onto a small teocalli in our target area.

"*Extraordinario!*' Martín beamed. Even Cortés was impressed.

"*Uno mas!*" I directed the Indios.

Another dead man smashed into the teocalli. The Caudillo, no longer arguing, watched the proceedings with interest.

"*Fuego!*" Dead men exploded against walls, tumbled along plazas and splashed into canals.

Cuauhtemoc and his chieftains, impressed by the dead dropping from Heaven, had enough. Alvarado, who had climbed to the summit of the great cue of *Tlatelolco*, gave a high-pitched whoop. "*There they go!"*

From my position on the plaza, I couldn't see the Lake. I clamored up the steps of the teocalli to see the final act. A fleet of large canoes cleared the stronghold and, knifing through the water, headed north. The brigantines, which had been waiting for just such a break, adjusted their sails and bore down on the Tenochca like a gathering storm. Even from this distance, I could hear the bangs of muskets and the louder crashes of culverin.

"Estupidos! Cortés shrilled, *"No tiren!"*

We climbed higher and—unable to affect the outcome—watched the battle unfold.

Malinche almost collapsed. Several of the distant canoes capsized and others went dead in the water. Still, the brigs continued to fire. The sound of the shots attracted several other brigs that had been busy destroying houses on the outskirts of the City. By the time the reinforcements reached the scene, the battle was over. Prisoners were dragged into the brigantines. Those canoes not capsized or sunk, drifted in the wind.

The brigs, under full sail, scudded back towards *Tenochtitlan.* I could see that the smallest—the *Nube*—was in the lead. *España,* under full sail and captained by Sandoval, closely followed *Nube* and, at one point, crashed into its stern. I trembled to think of the consequences if Cuauhtemoc were killed...

Both brigs—the *España* still banging into the stern of the *Nube*—pulled into the largest canal adjacent to *Tlatelolco.*

"What happened?" Cortés shouted. "Where's Cuauhtemoc?"

The master of the *Nube*—García Holguín—didn't speak, he pointed. In the bottom of the *Nube* twenty men and women lay bound together. Piled next to them were small idols of gold, copper and clay.

"Cuauhtemoc?" Malinche asked again.

Holguín tapped Cuauhtemoc with his foot. I barely recognized him. He was wearing a filthy maxtlaltl and his head was covered with a headdress with broken black feathers. He was dressed in the traditional rags of defeat.

I whispered in Maliche's ear, "You've got him. You've got the cabrón."

Burgos, Castilla-León

Mendoza looked up. "I know that Holguín, Sandoval and Martín López claimed credit for the capture."

"True, Padre. Did you also know that Cortés—arguing his own case before the Royal Commission—actually received credit for it? The capture of a king was embossed on his family's crest."

"You hate him, Excelencia, yet you have no problem with your getting the credit?"

"My antipathy for the man has nothing to do with it. If any man deserves full credit, it was Hernán Cortés. He was quite right to claim that no one else had the qualities to achieve total victory. I will not deny it. Only our Caudillo was both intelligent and ruthless enough to pull it off. None of the rest of us—including myself—had this combination of talents. Many of our conquistadores were just as ruthless as Cortés, but none of these were as intelligent. A very few, such as Martín López, were as intelligent but did not have Cortés' purity of ambition. *No one had Cortes' luck.*"

"But Holguín actually captured Cuauhtemoc."

"True, but without Cortés, it would have never happened."

"And Cuauhtemoc, what became of him?"

"Cortés pampered him. He petted both him and his family. He gave him empty sovereignty over the ruin that was *Tenochtitlan.* Later, of course, he had him tortured to extract treasure. Unfortunately, for both Malinche and Cuauhtemoc, there was little treasure to be had. Finally, during one of the inland expeditions, Cortés had him executed."

"I read that he died of a tropical illness."

"*Tortured* and executed, Padre. He outlived his purpose so Malinche eliminated him. Also..." The old man smiled sardonically. "Cortés took a fancy to his young wife."

"I don't believe it, Excelencia."

"Believe it, Padre. Believe it."

"Release the Prince!" Cortés ordered.

272 • Ron Braithwaite

I bent down and cut *Cuauhtemoc's* bonds.

"...You, Chichtli..." Cuauhtemoc hissed.

"I can still help you, My Prince."

Cuauhtemoc refused to look at me. Instead he turned to Cortés. "Malinche, I have done all in my power to defend my people and my empire. I have failed. Take your dagger and thrust it into my chest but...spare my family."

"What does he say, Rodrigo?"

"He says that you'll never find his treasure."

He struggled to control his temper. "Tell him that I will give safe passage to him, his wives and as many retainers as he requires—but he must turn the gold over to me."

"O Cuauhtemoc," I mis-translated, "Malinche says you have a beautiful wife."

Cuauhtemoc clutched the girl that was tied beside him. She was his favorite wife and was indeed beautiful—she reminded me of Amelia.

"Malinche cannot have her," he said.

"He is stubborn, Hernán. He says no gold—you can do what you want with his family."

Cortés reached his flash point—he *exploded*. "Then tell him that if he doesn't give me his treasure I am fully prepared to hang him up by his heels and skin him alive."

"*Ay-ah*, My Prince! Malinche says he is angry at your resistance in *Tenochtitlan* and will not compromise. There is nothing you can give him that will prevent him from hanging you up by your heels and skinning you alive. Then, he says, to spit on your memory, he will have sex with your wife in front of his army."

"Is there nothing I can do, Chichtli?"

"Malinche lies. As long as you tell him nothing—especially about hidden treasure—your wife is safe and *you* live. As soon you as give him what he wants, you die. To save your family and your life—say nothing."

"Then, Chichtli, I will say nothing."

The date was August 13, 1521.

Chapter 37

Something was wrong. It came as a shock to realize what it was. It was the silence. For months the din of constant battle with its background of gunfire, drums, conch trumpets, whistles and screams had filled the air. Now it was gone and its absence was a thing more tangible than was the noise, itself. Now all that was left was the drone of countless flies and, at night, even that ceased. The only sounds then were the yips of coyoteh frenzied by the smell of tainted meat.

The City itself was a smoldering wreck. The palaces of Moctecuzoma and Axayacatl were smoking ruins, as were all the templos and teocallis throughout the city. Except for a few houses on the periphery of the city, all had been pulled down and pushed into the canals. Those trees still standing were only spikes. All were missing their bark and leaves for the Mexica had stripped these to slate their hunger. The same was true of the lawns and gardens. The grass and shrubs had been pulled up and devoured.

The streets and the plazas belonged to the dead. Uncounted thousands lay in the streets, plazas and gardens. In the *Plaza Mayor*, the *Plaza de Tlatelolco* and other open places it was possible to walk on the dead without putting a foot on the tiles below. Yet, there was life of sorts in the City. In those few houses still standing, there were those Tenochca who still clung to life although too weak to move. The Tlaxcalteca had their own solution. They sloshed through the filth and butchered people too sick to lift their heads from the putrid floors. Perhaps it was a mercy.

I looked over the scene and was reminded of the destruction of Jerusalem by Titus and the incineration of Troy by Agamemnon. Españoles and Tlaxcalteca picked through the ruins searching for loot, occasionally digging at a likely spot or stopping to slay someone clinging to life. Sometimes I saw the glint of a knife. A few of our soldiers were opening corpses hoping for swallowed treasure. I rejected the idea of Troy or Jerusalem. The tragedy of *Tenochtitlan* surely dwarfed the others—I was overwhelmed by it. I was witness to an event that would either be honored or condemned by history—maybe both.

Cortés woke me from my reverie. "Rodrigo, I'm ordering our men back to *Tacuba*. I want you to get up a gang of Tlaxcalteca and dig into the ruins of the palace."

"Why me?"

"You speak the language and you have knowledge of the treasure rooms...."

"Only that they're under the floors of the palace—and the palace is *huge*—everything is covered by rubble. Besides, the treasure is gone..."

"Why didn't you tell me earlier?"

"You didn't ask me."

The veins on his forehead bulged. "*Where* is it then?"

"I wish I knew—I heard some of his people say that not one feather or chalchihuitl was left behind. They said that most was smuggled out of the City and some was dumped in the beds of reeds."

"What about *your* gold, Rodrigo?"

"Gone." I lied. "Cuauhtemoc seized everything I had. I knew that I'd outlived my usefulness when he ordered it seized. That's when I decided to rejoin the army."

"Are you telling me that there's nothing left?"

"It's there, Hernán. You'll just have to work for it."

"Then I give *you* the responsibility of searching out the reed beds."

"There are a lot of reed banks. Can you be more specific?"

"Interrogate your old compadres—their stinking lords and priests. Be persuasive and use your knife. They should give you some useful information as to where to look. Take some Texcocan divers with you—they'll do the dirty work."

"But there are still knots of resistance..."

The stench of the place was affecting Cortés' mood and it showed on his face. "Cuauhtemoc promised to stop hostilities."

"Yes," I nodded. "He said he would stop hostilities when we stopped *our* assault. How do you propose to get our allies to stop the killing?"

He pointed to a nearby catapult. "Simple. Any who continue the killing will hang. I will hang just as many as necessary even if I have to destroy the entire thieving Tlaxcaltec race. I'm leaving you in charge with authority to act in my behalf."

Now that the battle was over, Malinche no longer required extermination. Those allied Indios incapable of accepting this new reality suffered immediate retribution. My catapult supported the weight of eighteen murdering Tlaxcalteca. I hanged them all in a row.

●●●

Chichimatecle, following the execution of his rival, Xicotencatl, had become general-chief of the Tlaxcaltec armies. This high office, if possible, made him even more intolerable than he had been previously.

"Chichtli, you insult me by hanging my warriors. From where the sun now stands"—he pointed skyward—"you will not touch my people."

I looked him over and was not impressed. He was short and fat with a receding chin and a flat forehead. I pointed to the Tlaxcaltec bodies swinging from my catapult. "*You* must put an end to the killing!"

He set his face in a ferocious mask. "Two of my chiefs take over one hundred heads each. I want to see who is greatest head-taker."

I stood close to the cabrón, my nose not a hand's width from his. "Malinche has ordered me to hang any man who continues to kill."

"Malinche and I are brothers." He clinched his two hands together. "He will not offend me. You will not to touch my warriors!"

To emphasize his point he moved his hand to the hilt of his Castilian espada.

I fondled the hilt of my own weapon. "I will eat your flesh with tomates and green chiles."

Chichimatecle looked into my eyes and knew it wasn't a bluff. "Do not tempt me, Chichtli, for my hand is as strong as my word. My warriors will kill *all* of the Tenochca. Obey me or suffer my wrath."

I removed my hand from the hilt of my sword. "Do you indeed have a strong hand, Great Lord?"

Without warning, I seized him and wrestled him to the ground. It was easy for he was as weak as a girl. In front of his shocked chieftains I bound his hands and feet and then drew them together with a single cord.

"*Martín!*" López and others were standing nearby with their weapons unsheathed. They protected me from intervention by Chichimatecle's men.

"Let's load him up." I pointed to the catapult.

López grinned and pitched in to help. "I've been wanting to do this for a long time."

Chichimatecle, who fancied himself future ruler of *Tlaxcala*, was now nothing but another projectile. After cutting the dead Tlaxcalteca down, we loaded the screeching man and, at the point of our swords, forced his astounded chieftains to draw the catapult back.

"*Fuego!*"

"*Whaa-Bam!!!*"

Chichimatecle screamed all the way up and all the way down. It was an especially good shot and the Great Lord of *Tlaxcala* splattered beautifully against the wall of a ruined temple. Even the Tlaxcalteca chieftains were impressed. The killing stopped.

Chapter 38

A woman clad in a long white dress appeared on the far side of the plaza. She was coming in my direction, stepping over and around the swollen dead. Her body swayed gracefully—*un baile de muerto*. As she came closer I could see that she was not an Indio—she was Francesca de la Barca. She had taken pains to look beautiful—a flower in a sewer. Her long hair was glistening and tied back in braids and her lips were reddened. Kohl made her large eyes seem even larger. Indio warriors and white men turned to lust after her.

"*Rodrigo!*"

"This is no place for you, Francesca. The Tlaxcalteca..."

"I need to talk with you."

I should have been pleased but...

"You should have waited for me in *Tacuba*," I said.

"After our last meeting, I was afraid you'd avoid me."

"Then, I thank you for visiting me." I bowed.

"I almost turned back—the stench of this place." She wrinkled her nose.

I'd actually forgotten about the odor. "The Tlaxcalteca have been throwing bodies into the canals but it doesn't help much."

"No...it doesn't. Can we speak in private—somewhere that smells better?"

"Of course," I shrugged. Side-by-side we climbed the teocalli until we stood on the temple summit.

She looked out over the ruined city. "Do you remember the first time we saw this place?"

"I can hardly remember."

"It was wonderful, Rodrigo—the most wonderful thing I'd ever seen."

"Perhaps it will be beautiful, again."

"Not like it was. If it rises from the ashes it will be an Spanish city—a city of conquistadores and their bastard offspring."

"Is that what you came here to tell me?"

"No"—she gazed into the distance—"I wanted to see you one last time."

"You're leaving for the coast, Francesca?"

She turned to me. "No, Rodrigo. You're leaving."

"I'm happy in the Caudillo's service."

She turned to face me. "You won't be."

"No?"

"Last time we met, Rodrigo, although I didn't realize it then, you were trying to do me a favor. I don't like to have outstanding debts so now I'm returning the favor."

"I'm listening."

"Cortés is convinced that you lied to him about your own gold."

"Well, he's wrong."

"Wrong or not, Rodrigo, your hours are numbered."

"How do you know this, Francesca?" My voice dropped, "Does he *confide* in you?"

"You still mistrust me, Rodrigo, even when I am trying to save you." She shook her head. "Maybe I deserve it...no...Cortés doesn't talk to me. He confides only in Doña Marina. Doña Marina trusts me. She thought I would be happy to learn of Cortés' plans for you."

I tried to think of a way out—I couldn't. "Have you heard when I'll be arrested?"

"He's ordered a victory celebration in *Tacuba*, tonight—everyone is ordered to attend but I don't think that he will spoil the mood with an arrest. You won't be arrested until tomorrow or the day after that."

"Then this will be the last time we see each other, señora."

"I will be at the fiesta, Rodrigo."

"But I won't be."

She again looked out over the City. "What I told you before about hating you, wasn't true. You are never out of my thoughts—never have been. I think of you—worry about you—night and day." First her lip quivered then she started to weep. "I thought I'd never see you again."

"I wish I had known, Francesca."

"Would it have made a difference, Rodrigo?"

I wasn't sure it would have but I acted the gentleman. "I've been alone these many months—if I'd known you cared? Yes, it would have made a difference."

"But where will you go?"

"I don't know. Somewhere that the water runs clear and the grass grows green."

She glanced down at the corpse-strewn plaza. "Does such a place exist?"

"In the north."

She looked again into the distance. "Come to the fiesta tonight, Rodrigo—you have time. Afterwards, I want to be alone with you. I'll never have another chance."

"We've run out of time, Francesca."

She looked in my eyes. "Then I'm calling in *my* debt—now *you* owe me, Rodrigo."

I hesitated before answering, "I'll be there but late. I have some things to do."

"Don't disappoint me, Rodrigo."

I looked down on the stricken city and north towards *Tacuba*. "I'll bring you to the mainland. This is no place for a Lady."

●●●

That night there was only a sliver of a moon, making visibility difficult. I soon found what I wanted, however—a remuda of horses. Three sleepy Tlaxcalteca guarded them.

"*Aquin tehhuatl?*" questioned one of the guards.

"A messenger from Malinche."

"Then come to us, teotl, and state your business."

I stepped forward and could tell by their reactions that I wasn't recognized. "Malinche is having a grand fiesta tonight to celebrate his victory," I said. "He wants to share his joy with you." I produced two large flasks. "He wants you to drink and be happy."

"Only the old are permitted to drink octli," one of them said.

"Tonight is different," I laughed. "*Tenochtitlan* is no more, *Cuauhtemoc* is in chains and everyone is happy. Malinche orders you to be happy, too."

By now all three had gathered in front of me. Even in the dark I could see they were smiling.

"I will take the first drink." I took a long drink but the liquid was warm and bitter. I swallowed little. I passed the flask to one of the Indios who also took a long drink.

"I've never tasted it before." He lied. "Good." He took gulp after gulp until forced to yield to a second man.

Each man swallowed the bitter liquid without protest. Soon both flasks were empty. "Wait here, friends," I said. "There's more where that came from."

I returned with two more flasks and watched them get very, very drunk. One became amiable, one passed out, and one wanted to fight. I silenced them all then turned my attention to the horses; there were at least sixty and most were mares or geldings. Using soft words and moving slowly, I cut out two stallions and eight mares, three of them had foals at their sides. I bridled them, saddled three and separated my horses into two groups, each with its own stallion. I tied each group together.

I mounted one of the saddled horses—a pinto—and led each group away from the main herd and into the dark. I found what I was looking for—two large trees close together—I hobbled the horses and tied each group to separate trees. It wasn't as easy as the writing of it but I managed it.

Chapter 39

The fiesta was a disgraceful affair with much music, dancing and whoring. Everyone drank too much. Cortés, who was usually in such control, vomited and passed out on the floor. That night, enemies became friends and friends became enemies. Challenges were placed and, in their drunken states, brave men died at the hands of cowards.

"*You're late!*" Francesca whispered. "I thought something went wrong."

"I had things to do."

"At least you're here now. I was afraid you would abandon me."

"I keep my word, Francesca."

"Your word, Rodrigo, nothing more?"

"I don't know what you mean, Francesca."

Her voice returned to its usual tone. "You know exactly what I mean, Rodrigo."

But I didn't.

She looked around the room. "I never hated our men as much as I do tonight. Now that the danger is over...Look at them...pigs."

"Our men may be conquistadores but they are not heroes," I said. "They are but common men caught up in a great enterprise. Those who follow us will reap the reward of our folly. I am sick of it."

"And Cortés?" She pointed at the drunken man with her chin.

"May his most loyal Captains cut his throat."

She turned to look at me directly. "Not you?"

I stroked her cheek. "He is not my responsibility. Besides, he'll only be replaced by someone just as greedy but with less style."

"You admire him, Rodrigo."

"As I admire the perfection that is a leopard, a venomous serpent or...a mosquito."

"Have you been drinking, Rodrigo?"

"A little."

"Then it's time that we leave."

●●●

Her room was a cubicle in the far-end of a ruined palace. I was touched to see there were bouquets of fresh flowers, and flower petals were scattered on the floor. A pallet of furs lay in the corner. I was perplexed to see that her belongings were tied into two bundles.

"Rodrigo, do we have time?"

I didn't but my body was in control of my mind.

"Some—I have horses staked out..."

Reverently, she lit several candles and, as she did so, the painted walls came alive in a golden light. I took her in my arms and kissed her for a very long time.

She dropped her shift and stood before me in her magnificent perfection. She kissed me again as I laid her down and caressed her skin. My lips moved over her throat, her shoulders, her breasts..."

"What's wrong?" she whispered.

I closed my eyes and tried to concentrate on Francesca. Instead, I saw piles of stinking dead.

"Please, Rodrigo." She begged.

But I could do nothing. I saw little Amelia mounting the steps of *Coatepec.*

"Rodrigo, go slowly."

A boy was writhing on the end of my sword.

"*I love you, Rodrigo!*"

But there stood a starving Angela cradling a dead baby.

She bit my cheek. "*Now!*"

But I heard the groans of all the people who have ever died. I heard a faint laugh.

"*Man of the one-eyed God, you must bear the burden.*"

I got up from my woman. "I'm going outside."

"No, Rodrigo..." she started to weep.

●●●

Thus ended our noble conquest of Mexico. Francesca begged to come with me but I refused her. I left with the horses, joined Macitoc, and rode to the north—but that is another story.

Still, like a moth to a flame, I was drawn to the scene of our crimes. Collecting my horses, I rode to the shores of the Lake. Shoals of dead fish sloshed back-and-forth along with broken canoes, blackened timbers and the body of a child. The Lake itself was dying.

Silently, I peered into the darkness. In the direction of the ruined City there was a mass of glowing embers—a building collapsed sending a plume of sparks into the black night. I could hear the hiss and sizzle as burning walls toppled into a canal. I could smell the smoke, steam and aroma of charred flesh and the unburied dead. I tried to comprehend the whole thing and failed.

"The death of an empire," I whispered to myself, "and the taint of the future."

EPILOGUE

Mendoza looked to be near death but he was still capable of argument. "As pessimistic as usual, Your Grace. The world knows that Mexico is better off under our aegis. The nativos no longer have to fear a terrible and arbitrary power."

"They don't?"

"No. Their lives are immeasurably improved."

The old man's jaw jutted. "You are mistaken, Padre, but you *do* have a point. There is no denying that the Mexica regime was hideous but, at the same time, there can be no denying that our Castilian governance is brutal. I want you to consider this, Padre. The crimes of the Indios against the Indios were *their* crimes. Our crimes against the Indios add to *our* burden of sin."

Mendoza shook his head. "Yours is the philosophy of inaction."

The ancient man shrugged. "*We* have visited iniquity on Nueva España and it is *our* iniquity. We raped their women and forced a union between our peoples. We established governorships built—despite all of our fine words—not on Christianity, but on blood and greed. Ages may pass before these things pass away."

"Don't blame me, Excelencia, if the world is not perfect." Mendoza was weakening. "We only attempt to leave it a better place than we entered. Now if we could—please—discuss the conditions for my release and perhaps a good meal..."

The old Bishop, wrapped in his memories, wasn't listening. "The bones of my comrades litter the soils of México, Española, Cuba, Perú and the other lands we have corrupted." His voice dropped to a low whisper. "I am the only one left. All of my friends and enemies are long dead. The women I loved have withered and died. They are now only dust. Now, I alone carry the guilt."

ABOUT THE AUTHOR

Ron Braithwaite is the retired Chief of Pathology at Our Lady of Lourdes Hospital in Lafayette, Louisiana. He presently resides on a ranch in South Texas directly on the Rio Grande where he enjoys studying the Spanish Conquest of Mexico and making exploratory expeditions. This book marks the end of his first foray into fiction~the two-part novel consisting of *Skull Rack* and *Hummingbird God*.

To order copies of *Skull Rack* and *Hummingbird God* as well as
other titles from
Harbor House, visit our Web site:

www.harborhousebooks.com